The Stargazer

The Stargazer

MICHELE JAFFE

POCKET BOOKS

New York London Toronto Sydney Tokyo Singapore

POCKET BOOKS, a division of Simon & Schuster Inc.
1230 Avenue of the Americas, New York, NY 10020

Copyright © 1999 by Michele Jaffe

Library of Congress Cataloging-in-Publication Data

Jaffe, Michele.
    The stargazer / Michele Jaffe.
      p.   cm.
    ISBN: 0-671-02739-5
    I. Title.
    PS3560.A3136S72   1999
    813'.54—dc21   99-23454
                                     CIP

First Pocket Books hardcover printing July 1999

10 9 8 7 6 5 4 3 2 1

Designed by Laura Lindgren and Celia Fuller

Printed in the U.S.A.

*This book is dedicated to Daniel Goldner
and Holly Edmonds, without whom my dream of writing
romance would have ended in nothing.*

Chapter One

"My lord, I scarcely expected to see you here." Bianca looked up at the well-built man filling the doorframe and sneezed.

Ian Foscari, Conte d'Aosto, was uncharacteristically stunned.

"I should say not," he responded finally, focusing on the bloody dagger she had pointed toward him. Even as a trained observer, he was having trouble making sense of the scene that confronted him. The room was richly appointed; peach silk curtains embroidered with golden flowers flanked the tall windows, and Turkish carpets in luscious pastels covered the floors. The center of the room was taken up by an enormous bed, covered with the same silk that framed the window. Stretched out on the bed was the scantily clad figure of the courtesan Isabella Bellocchio, who would have appeared to be sleeping peacefully except for the large red gash in her chest. Above her, covered in blood and brandishing a dagger, stood the woman who had just addressed him.

Their gazes locked, and complete silence fell over the room as each contemplated the countenance of the other. The moment ended abruptly as she sneezed again, twice.

"What are you doing here?" she demanded, finally moving her gaze away from his face. Murderers, Bianca thought to herself, should really be harder on the eyes.

"I could ask the same of you."

"I should say it is obvious." Bianca sneezed, returning his glance with what she hoped was a scowl.

He scowled back at her, shocked by her forthrightness. "Yes, I suppose it is. But whatever possessed you to murder her?"

For the first time, Bianca realized how she must look. In her right hand she held the bloody dagger she had pulled from Isabella's heart, and her dress was covered with blood from her attempts to save the girl. The situation seemed almost comic, she thought, wiping her running nose with the corner of her sleeve, until abruptly, she remembered the insignia on the hilt of the dagger. Boldly she met Ian's eyes, holding the handle of the weapon up between them. "Should not I be asking you that, my honorable lord?"

It was undoubtedly his coat of arms emblazoned garishly on the hilt of the dagger in rubies and emeralds. He shrugged, moving his eyes from the gaudy re-creation of his heraldry back to Bianca's small oval face. "That certainly is not mine. Of course, it is my coat of arms, but I would never commission anything that ostentatious."

"I am afraid, my lord," Bianca sneezed, "that good taste is not an adequate defense," she sneezed again, "against a charge of murder." Bianca tried to keep her gaze level with his as she sneezed five times in quick succession. "Perhaps if you could tell me what you are doing here...?"

"It is certainly not any of your concern, signorina, but I received an urgent summons from Isabella."

Undaunted by Ian's frigid tone, designed to send her cowering into a corner, Bianca plunged ahead with questions. "What was it like? What exactly did it say?"

Ian was mad at himself. He had answered her first question without even thinking about it, instinctively responding to some sort of authority that oozed from her like vile jelly, and now he was doing it again. He knew it had to be another person who extracted the note from his tunic, unfolded it, and said to his unidentified interrogator, "Here, you can see it." The mutinous part of him extended the letter for Bianca's perusal.

Bianca's brow wrinkled as she sneezed again. The letter was written in a clear cursive hand on lightly perfumed parchment and signed by Isabella, begging the presence of the Conte d'Aosto immediately at her house. Bianca held the paper up to the light, studied it, and handed it back to the impossibly handsome blond man facing her.

"Was it delivered directly to you?" Ian nodded. Bianca scowled. And sneezed. "Then you are certainly not guilty." Her eyes moved from the note still dangling in his hand to the dagger she was holding. "And yet it really does appear that someone is trying to frame you. But who? Or is it me they are trying to frame?" She sneezed. "Perhaps if we tried..."

Ian put down the mutiny in his head and returned to his laconic, unhelpful self, striving to be even icier than usual in recompense for his earlier softness. "I cannot tell you how relieved I am to learn that I am not guilty," he rudely interrupted, "but I am curious about your reasoning and slightly alarmed by your use of the pronoun 'we.' I have no idea who you think you are, or even who you are, and I certainly have no use for some young signorina fresh from the schoolroom. I assure you, *we* will be doing nothing."

His words, designed to sting, hit their mark. Bianca cringed, not because his tone was as cold as the northern wind, but because of the patronizing way he had called her "signorina," as if daring her to disobey his impressive and sophisticated person. By the fingertips of Santa Barbara, he was arrogant! Bianca had no doubt that he used exactly the same tone when scaring available young women away from marriage. For herself, she had no interest in marriage, in being yoked to some idiotic lout who would waste her fortune betting on the ebb and flow of the tides and condemn her to childbed. But she resented that her desire to preserve her independence gave the high and mighty Conte d'Aosto the right to speak to her in that infuriating, condescending tone, reminding her with every word that she was only an inexperienced woman.

"Of course, you are right. I prefer to work alone anyway." Furious, Bianca had put down the knife and was cleaning her hands in a porcelain basin. Even worse than his arrogance was the rebellion going on in her head. How could she let herself be so easily convinced of the man's innocence and, what was worse, why was she so relieved? What difference could it possibly make to her if the glacially cruel Conte d'Aosto was innocent or guilty, or wealthy or extremely handsome, with those strong hands and long graceful fingers...

Her reverie was cut short by his voice. "You haven't told me exactly what convinced you of my innocence. The obvious answer would be that you yourself, whoever you may be, are the guilty party." He looked pointedly at her.

Bianca tried to sound incredulous as she sneezed. "My lord, you must be joking." She sneezed. "I, a murderess?"

Was that the hint of a smile he saw on her lips? Ian was damned if he would let her stand there looking so, well, innocent. "I never joke."

Even without the sharp tone in his voice, Bianca would have accepted this as true. She knew that Ian Foscari, Conte d'Aosto, was one of the wealthiest, most handsome, most aristocratic—and least sought after—bachelors in Venice. He was known as the man of stone, cold, distant, emotionless. Only his closest friends, the other Arboretti, knew of the vital being beneath the cold exterior, and even they could hardly remember what it was like. For the past two years, Ian had been a different person. He was as brilliant and efficient as ever, perhaps more so, but not previously prone to mirth, he now never laughed or smiled. Not even his brother, Crispin, could thaw the cold that gripped him, though he had tried for every day of the two years since the incident. Ian seemed to rejoice in keeping everyone at an emotional distance, routinely terrifying the young women whose mothers were vain enough to attempt a match with him.

But Bianca was no young signorina to be terrified, she assured herself, even when a stone block accused her of murder for no good reason. She squared her shoulders and summoned up all the courage of her twenty-four years to meet his eyes. "My lord," she said, "like so many other women today who are considered unworthy of education, Isabella was illiterate. She was no more capable of writing to you, than I am of using this knife to take someone's life—" she picked up the weapon again, sneezed twice, and pointed it at him "—or, for that matter, than you are of feeling anything through that thick, superior skin of yours." She sneezed three times like a rapid-firing cannon. "By Santa Lucia's eyes," Bianca demanded finally in exasperation, "what is the cause of this infernal sneezing?"

She dropped the knife and turned from him to face the window, sneezing ten times without stopping. As she wiped her runny nose and eyes on her sleeve, she studied the raindrops rolling off the glass panes, working to suppress the rising tide of her anger and frustration. Between the shock of discovering a corpse instead of her friend, the audacity of the semipetrified man to accuse her of murder, and the cruelty of her own traitorous tickling nose in making her appear a spectacle in front of him, Bianca felt her emotional control ebbing rapidly. She would not cry, she warned herself; she would not allow that golden-haired human stone the pleasure of seeing her cry, *no, no, no, she would not!*

Ian watched her face reflected in the glass of the window, watched her battle with her sneezing and her emotions, and felt nothing like superior. It had been so long since he had been impressed by anyone or anything that at first he could not identify the emotion, but he was soon able to label it: grudgingly he was forced to admit he felt admiration for her. Her deduction of his innocence had been so simple and so elegant, something obvious that he himself would have seen only after hours of thought. He realized that he did not even know the name of this woman who was as uncommonly intelligent as she was uncommonly beautiful, although she seemed to know him. Even as he was thinking that she might be a tremendous help in solving the mystery of Isabella's death, he caught himself appreciating the graceful curve of her body as she stood with her back to him, the way that a wisp of hair wound its way down around her neck and...

Was he going mad? This woman was probably a murderess. "*Probably*"—even his mind was in cahoots with her, injecting that seed of doubt into an otherwise obvious situation. For if a smart woman were planning a murder, wouldn't she think of everything, including those petty little details about writing and such that would never occur to a man? Women's minds were so utterly devious that they could be trusted to think of anything that would contribute to the illusion of their innocence, to remove the burden of culpability from their narrow shoulders. He had learned that lesson well and would not—*would not*—be duped again, not even by someone with shoulders as interesting as those of the woman before him.

First "Admiration"? Then "Probably"? And now "Interesting shoulders"? This could not continue. He was superior and thick-skinned, she had said so herself, and he would show it. "Now it is my turn to ask the questions, simple questions, which even a signorina like you should have no trouble answering. Let us start with, who are you?"

He had addressed her back, and she did not turn from the window as she answered. "My name," Bianca sneezed, haughtily she hoped, "is Bianca Salva, the daughter of..."

She sneezed again, and Ian seized the moment to interrupt. "Do not go on, I have heard of your family." If he was surprised to find a woman of noble birth covered in blood at the house of a courtesan in the middle of the day, he was true to his reputation as a stone and did not show it. His tone when he resumed his questioning was indifferent if slightly menacing. "Would you be so kind, Signorina Salva, as to tell me what you are doing here?"

He had used that word again, saying "signorina" as if it described the lowest of the Deity's creatures. Bianca knew then that she couldn't, or rather, wouldn't tell him the truth, which left her with only two choices: she could either refuse to answer him or tell a lie. She had never lied in her life, not even as a child when—against her father's strict orders—she had taken herbs from his workbox to mix a medicine for a poor girl her own age, or later when she had stolen anatomy textbooks from their lodger to learn the parts of the body. Those times and the hundreds of others like them that formed her education, Bianca had always admitted the crime and been forgiven by her saintly, understanding papa. But Papa was gone now, and the Conte d'Aosto seemed about as yielding as a stone pillar.

She turned away from the window, to face him. The sneezes were coming fast and furious now, and Bianca tried to speak quickly to avoid being interrupted. "I would prefer not to answer that question, my lord d'Aosto." She sneezed twice, as if she were allergic to his title, then went on. "I can't see that it has any bearing on the death of this poor girl," she sneezed, "for which I have already told you I am not," she sneezed, "responsible." Upon hearing this brilliant defense so airily punctuated by sneezes, Ian found himself closer to laughing than he had been for months. "Is something wrong, my lord? You appear to be in pain."

The urge to laugh left as abruptly as it had come. His eyes turned from crystal blue to gray, the only outward sign of his change in mood. "I am afraid, signorina—" Ian paused to watch the effect the word had on her; revenge was indeed sweet, "—that I cannot accept your failure to answer, despite your winning protestation of innocence. I ask you, why should I believe you?"

Bianca answered his question with one of her own. "What motive could I possibly have to murder this woman?"

"'Women need no motives, only means,'" Ian quoted the odious Venetian proverb. "You would do better to answer questions than to ask them."

Without realizing it, Ian had begun to count her sneezes. He was up to twelve when she resumed speaking.

"Then you," she sneezed, making it thirteen, "would do better," *fourteen*, "my most irreproachable and honorable Count," *fifteen*, "to ask questions worthy," *sixteen*, "of answers." Bianca sniffled, trying hard to make his title sound as despicable as possible. As she spoke, she began to gather up her belongings, using any excuse to keep her seditious eyes from straying to the contours of his face. "Indeed," *seventeen*, "your time would be better spent," *eighteen*, "as I intend," *nineteen*, "to spend mine—finding out who killed Isabella Bellocchio and why," *twenty*, "they," *twenty-one*, "wanted," *twenty-two*, "to frame you for the crime."

Ian shook himself from his calculations just enough to retort icily, "Besides questioning the prime suspect, the person found drenched in the victim's blood clutching the murder weapon over the body, what would you propose I do?"

"You might try looking for the actual murder weapon, which certainly was not this gaudy toy." Bianca concentrated on repressing a sneeze in order to resist the urge to see the effect this news had on him. "Or you could devise a plan to uncover," she sneezed, "the person willing to go to such expense," Bianca gestured with the gem-encrusted hilt of the dagger as she sneezed again, "to label you a murderer."

Ian, whose total was now up to twenty-five, refused to play into her hands by asking her to elaborate her wild claim about the weapon. He also had no doubt that she had a plan ready to implement if he seemed willing. She was cunning and clever, his little sneezing murderess. And even if she was not herself responsible for the murder, the odds were very good that she could lead him to whoever was. With his customary acumen, Ian assessed the situation and saw that Bianca could be very useful to him.

Very useful indeed. In a flash he realized that the murder was only part of it, even the smallest part. He completely lost track of enumerating Bianca's sneezes as the full force of his brilliant inspiration struck him. Staring at the defiant beauty in front of him, Ian saw the perfect way to put an end to Francesco's and Roberto's ceaseless urgings toward matrimony. Indeed, it was in order to escape another such a harangue from his uncles that he had so promptly replied to Isabella's—or the Salva girl's or whoever's—summons that very morning. And now, as if by destiny, he was being offered an opportunity to escape from them for all time. The plan he contrived in those few seconds was, he congratulated himself, gloriously simple and flawless. If he betrothed himself to the dangerous-looking Salva specimen and moved her into his house, he was sure that within three days—four at the most—Francesco and Roberto and the other Arboretti would be begging him to break the engagement and return to his bachelor ways forever. He was already savoring the taste of victory when he spoke.

"As it happens, signorina, I do have a plan." The corner of Ian's lip quivered, his version of a smile, as he watched Bianca struggle not to flinch at his intentionally condescending tone. He knew she would agree to his terms only if she were goaded into it, and he was surprised at how much he enjoyed the prospect of this goading. Plus, the madder she was, the worse she would behave and the faster his plan would come to fruition.

Bianca waited for him to continue, sneezing twice in the silence that followed his words. That twitching at the corner of his mouth told her she would find his plan distasteful, whatever it was, but she little expected exactly how bitter it would be. She had decided not to encourage him, yet after what felt like an eternity had passed she heard herself saying, "Ah, I see, my lord, you are indeed as clever as everyone says you are." She sneezed. "You plan to wait for the body to decompose, so that your problem will literally disappear."

Ian ignored her gibe. "My plan is to detain you until you explain exactly what you were doing here and tell me all you know about Isabella. You may do so here, now. Or I will find you quarters, as uncomfortable as possible you can be sure, in the basement prison at the Palace until you are ready to answer. Think of how quickly this sneezing illness of yours will worsen there. Not to mention how your family will react to hearing you have been incarcerated as a murderess."

Bianca blanched. With her brother gone on another of his last-minute journeys, there would be no one to protect her from the wrath of her aunt and uncle if she besmirched the family name yet again. But if they found out what she had actually been doing at Isabella's, it might be even worse than if she were accused of murder. She wondered if he could even guess the full force of what he was proposing.

The girl was genuinely conflicted, Ian noted with surprise. Perhaps, he mused, she really was innocent. What if he were persecuting an innocent woman? He hesitated for a moment, wondering if he should continue and then remembered that "innocence" and "woman" were fundamental opposites. Even if she were innocent of this crime, he decided, she had undoubtedly committed others, and besides, that mouth of hers had earned her some upset.

When he judged his last words had had enough time to make an impression on her, he continued. "There is, however, one other option, but I fear you will find it even less pleasant than the others." Ian then added, apparently as an afterthought, "It's too bad, because it would be very convenient for me. You see, my priority is to get as much information from you as possible. If you were to move into my house, I would be able to question you at my leisure—whenever or wherever I wanted and using whatever means of persuasion I preferred. I am rumored to have a rather fearsome staff."

There was something decidedly threatening in the way Ian spoke his last words, but Bianca refused to be scared off by him or his reference to the rumors that circulated around him. She was sure that his house contained nothing more terrifying than a morbid butler or a lecherous steward, and impertinent questioning in the home of a count was nothing compared to the horrors of the Venetian prisons. Of course, strictly speaking, it was not proper for a single woman to spend a few days under the same roof as an unmarried nobleman, but it would win her nothing like the infamy she would face having been imprisoned for murder. Her family might even thank her for the valuable social introduction.

Bianca sneezed and then prepared herself to savor the look of surprise on Ian's face when she agreed to his proposal. "Despite your best efforts to scare me away from it, my lord, I should say that this last option is decidedly the best. I accept it," she sneezed, heightening the dramatic effect of her final words, "with one condition."

Ian, disappointingly nonchalant, only managed to raise one eyebrow. "You can scarcely imagine how that surprises me."

Bianca ignored his sarcastic tone. "I would like to bring Isabella's body with me to study it for evidence of how she was killed," she sneezed, "and by whom."

Ian paused for a moment, thinking, and finally nodded. "Actually, that will work quite well. If I keep our possession of the body a secret, I can circulate a notice that Isabella is missing. This will make my inquiries easier and doubtless more fruitful." Ian, still lost in thought, was apparently speaking to himself. Bianca thought he might have forgotten about her until a violent fit of sneezing brought his eyes to where she stood.

"Fine," he said, facing her, "it is settled. I will send my man, Giorgio, with the gondola for you and the body. You will stay here until he arrives." Ian pulled a beautiful gold box out of his pocket, opened the lid, and glanced at the face. Beneath it, Bianca saw what appeared to be a very small version of the huge clock in Piazza San Marco. She was so absorbed by the intricate work and delicate mechanism that she missed the twitching at the corner of Ian's mouth as he resumed speaking.

He tried to keep his tone light, pretending the thought had just occurred to him. "Of course, it will be quite unseemly for you to reside under my roof." Ian leveled his eyes at her.

"My reputation does not concern me," Bianca retaliated haughtily, crushing his obvious ploy to make her shrink away, then sneezed four times.

"I don't doubt that at all, signorina, but mine concerns me. No, having you in my house like that won't do at all." She had walked right into his trap. Ian lowered his eyes to his watch again as if thinking, but actually to conceal the triumph on his face. He spent a moment reestablishing control of his expression, then moved to the threshold. When he turned to deliver his last horrible words, he already had his hand poised over the doorknob, ready for a clean escape.

"I see there is nothing else for it. I will have to announce our betrothal tonight at the meeting of the Senate." The sentence was punctuated by the click of the door shutting smoothly behind him.

As she stood staring at the space Ian had just occupied, too bewildered to protest or even sneeze, Bianca could have sworn she heard someone laughing.

Chapter Two

The young man followed the Moorish servant across the immense marble ballroom. Even the rich tapestries covering the walls could not keep out the chill of the rainy afternoon, and the visitor huddled deeper into his sable cape. The servant stopped before a massive mahogany door with a family crest emblazoned on it and waited to be admitted. As the door opened, the servant bowed his turbaned head and disappeared, leaving the man alone on the threshold.

The sight that greeted him as he entered went a long way toward warming his blood. The room was magnificently furnished, an enormous rich carpet covering the entire marble floor, and frescoes on every surface. But the main attraction was on the massive settee in the center of the room. There, each in a burgundy velvet dressing gown, sat two of the most breathtaking individuals he had ever seen. Every time he saw the sister and brother together, he was awed anew by their beauty.

As he entered, they beckoned him over. The woman shook aside her lush black hair and presented her cheek for a kiss as she suggestively ran her hand up his velvet hose.

She swept her half-open eyes over him. "How well my angel looks," she said, her lips curved into a half smile. "He must be bringing me good news."

Her brother smiled with her, happy that she was happy. As he gestured his visitor into the oversized seat nearby, he turned to his sister. "We are going to discuss business now, *cara*. Do you want to stay or would you like to have your bath? I'll send Diana in…"

"No, no, if he's to tell us about the whore, by all means, I will stay. I want to hear it all. I shall savor every detail." She closed her eyes and parted her crimson lips as if she had already begun to enjoy it. Then her eyes snapped open again, suddenly, and she pinned the visitor with a gaze that lacked even the slightest hint of seduction. "You have come to tell us that the whore is dead, haven't you?"

"Well, yes, I have. Or rather, that is what I should like to tell you." The young man tried to affect nonchalance as he shifted in the large chair. This gaze of hers was remarkably hard to meet.

"S'blood man, I didn't send for you so you could come and give me grammar demonstrations," her brother erupted. Since his birth, his only concern, his sole desire, had been to please his older sister. That his plan for the gift of all gifts might have failed, a plan months in the making, enraged him. "Is she or isn't she dead?" he demanded fiercely.

The young man again shifted position and began inspecting his fingernails with diligence. "Well, you see, Your Excellency, she was dead, only now…Well, my lord, can a corpse walk?"

"Will this catechism never cease? What do you mean by these evasions?"

The woman slid forward on the settee and put a calming hand on her brother's shoulder as she addressed the young man before her. Her voice was low now, serious, but strangely seductive. "Have I wasted all my time on you? Were you too selfish to do this one, small, thing for me after all I have done for you?"

As she had intended, the young man was mesmerized by the way her lips moved to form the words. "No, no, nothing like that," he hastened to reassure his mistress in a throaty voice. "She was dead, I saw to it down to that hideous dagger in the chest. A stroke of genius, madonna, that was, truly." The woman tipped her head gracefully to acknowledge his deserved flattery, but her brother began to growl with impatience. The young man hurried on. "Anyway, when we went back later, to close the trap you know, there was no one there. *No one*—not even the body."

It was too much to bear, the woman told herself. She was surrounded by incompetence. How could fate be so unkind to her? She deserved better, she knew, and needed someone on whom she could vent her anger at this grave injustice. It would not do to upset the young man, he could still be useful, and besides, she had spent too much time cultivating him and could not bear to think that her efforts would go to waste.

Instead, she exhaled sharply and turned toward her brother, tears of anger and betrayal quivering in her beautiful eyes. "How could you lie to me and say you loved me? How could you win my trust, my love, with your false promises?" Her brother's face was a mask of pain as the accusing tone in her voice escalated. "You said you would do anything for me, that you would punish him for what he did to me. But now it is clear; I see that like all men, you were not to be trusted." She paused to let her lip quiver, giving her audience the opportunity to admire the full extent of her distressed beauty, then went on to her finale. "I am all alone in the world; no one cares for me. I can trust no one, rely upon no one, am loved by no one."

"Of course we love you. Everyone who sees you must love you." Her brother mounted a protest as soon as he had regained the power of speech. "And it is not so bad as you say, *cara*, the girl is dead, the threat to us is gone. Think of the money we shall have, the beautiful clothes I shall buy you."

She waved his comment aside with a sneer as if he had insulted her by mentioning such mundane concerns. "The money is nothing. I don't want money. I want revenge." Her eyes were hooded, unreadable. "You don't care about my happiness any more than he did. You are nothing to me." She left the divan and approached the visitor, her manner changing, softening as she neared him. She took a hand and stroked his cheek, then let it move down over his torso.

She knew what this one liked, and how to control him. "You, my little angel, you are all my hope that is left. You will help me destroy that preening count, won't you, angelic one? You will find the body for me?" She filled her gaze with promises she knew he could not resist. The young man felt himself growing warm and had trouble finding his voice to respond to her.

When he did, he smiled up at her, a beautiful, beatific smile. "I think I already have."

"Come help me with my bath," she said, taking his hand and leading him out the door.

Chapter Three

"Lucia's eyes, will this pen not stay sharp?" Bianca glared down at the quill in her hand and then at the half-finished drawing in front of her. She never drew well when she was tired, and the forty-eight straight hours she had spent cloistered with Isabella's body had left her completely drained. But she was determined to finish before the hazy gray day was plunged again in darkness. Exhausted as she was, she was still excited by the wealth of material she had been able to gather. Not only had she learned much about the crime, but Isabella's body provided her with the first opportunity to draw the anatomy of a young woman. Her only female corpses before had been the poor old women of Padua who died without enough money for a proper burial. Isabella's healthy young corpse was a dream come true, from a scientific standpoint.

Her debts to Isabella seemed to mount even after the young courtesan's death, Bianca mused philosophically. A few more drawings and her book would finally be ready to go to press, revealing the female body accurately for the first time. She could almost sense her triumph as she proved to those stubborn men in Padua that women had their own perfect anatomy and were not just flawed versions of men. Wandering wombs, hah! she thought to herself. She remembered hearing of her father's debates on the subject with Andrea Vesalius when he was first starting his brilliant career, and she smiled as she imagined her book on a shelf somewhere as a companion to his. A vision of her future stretched invitingly before her—she would teach courses on female anatomy, study the female body and its cycles, do public demonstrations. It would be idyllic, truly. Except for this mockery of a betrothal.

She knew that once announced before the Senate, a betrothal bore the mark of law and was virtually impossible to revoke unless both the people agreed to end it, or one person was shown to be unfit. Had she realized what Ian had actually been proposing all those hours—was it really only hours?—ago, she would never have agreed. Or probably not. Maybe. The Conte d'Aosto had always had a strange effect on her. From her first night out in Venetian society nine months before, he was the only man she always noticed, or at least, she noticed his absence. But that was probably because he was also the only man who never paid any attention to her. He had not even known who she was when they met at Isabella's, she reminded herself. And now they were betrothed. It was positively idiotic.

As she thought, she worked to reform the nib of her pen. But when the full force of the betrothal hit her—no freedom, no lectures, no book of her own—she missed and cut the quill in half. "S'balls!" she declared, and then looked up to make sure no one overheard her speak such scandalous words. But she was alone. Since her father's death, it seemed as if she was always alone. But that was just how she liked it... wasn't it?

Clearly between her wandering mind, broken pen, and lack of rest, she could accomplish no more. With a sigh she stood up and removed her blood-soaked apron. She moved sleepily to open the door, but found it impossible to move. She tried again, twisting the cold knob with all her might, and again nothing happened. She was locked in. A mixture of desperation and indignation overcame her exhaustion, and she began pounding against the heavy door with all her force. Nothing. My God, she thought, he's left me up here to die with this corpse. Panicked, she went to the far end of the room and, with a running start, hurled herself at the door.

Ian heard her mad pounding from his laboratory. He had expected Bianca Salva to be difficult and even exasperating, but need she be so noisy? He pushed aside the rock-chip he had been looking at under his magnifying lenses and headed toward the other side of the palazzo, where he had given her space for her own laboratory. The noise seemed thankfully to subside as he approached the door and turned the handle.

He was never sure afterward just how he ended up pinned against the far wall of the hallway with Bianca in his arms, but he felt the bruises for more than a week. It had not been an unpleasant sensation, he mused, just unexpected. He vaguely remembered seeing something come flying at him as the door swung open, but how that something was Bianca Salva remained a bit mysterious. They stood entwined together for a few silent seconds before the body next to his began to pull away.

"My lord, how dare you?" Bianca gasped at last, stepping out of the circle of his embrace.

"I beg your pardon, signorina, but I believe it was you who leapt into my arms, not the other way around." Ian raised one eyebrow sarcastically.

She glared at him as fulsomely as possible. "That is not what I meant," she said with exasperation. "How dare you lock me in there with that body? I will not be your prisoner!"

"There you are mistaken, *carissima*. You are my prisoner—remember, we are betrothed. That gives me no end of power over you."

Bianca resisted the urge to slap him, barely. "This betrothal is a mockery, we both know that. What I do not understand is why you proposed it—you wouldn't possibly have suggested such a thing if you really believed I was guilty. Is it truly so hard to find someone willing to marry you, my lord, that you've had to turn to the criminal classes?"

"On the contrary." Ian matched her sarcastic tone with his own. "I have no more interest in marriage than you do. Hence a murderess is the perfect woman for me—I can dally with her at my leisure, destroy her mind and her reputation, and then turn her to the wolves when I am done. You will recall that a charge of murder is one of the honorable and legitimate reasons for ending a betrothal." Ian smiled smugly to himself as he waited for Bianca's next sally. But it did not come. Instead she sighed deeply and her shoulders began to sag. Oh no, he thought to himself, she is going to cry. Ian preferred anything to a crying woman, and was about to say so when Bianca opened her mouth.

"If I were you, my lord," she said, exhaustion shading every word, "I would try using kindness rather than cruelty on me in your interrogations. It is what I neither expect nor am accustomed to these many days, and it would surely be more effective to catch me off my guard. You might begin by telling me I don't have to sleep in there," she gestured wearily toward her laboratory, "with that corpse. Anywhere else, and I promise not to complain when you lock me in."

Ian warred within himself. Part of him was seized by a sudden urge to cross the rug that separated them and sweep Bianca back into his arms. The other part wanted to turn quickly around and flee from her. Incapable of moving, he stood riveted to the floor, staring at her. She stared back at him, looking deep into his eyes, searching. They faced each other like two statues, until a clock on the floor below began to strike the hour. Soon another in a different part of the palazzo began and before long there were ten, each making a different sound but each harmonizing with the others perfectly. Bianca studied Ian as he listened to the chiming of clocks, struck by his ethereal beauty. She smiled at him and, more remarkable than anything else that had happened to her in the previous three days, he smiled back at her.

"Beautiful," she whispered in awe.

"Yes they are, aren't they?" Ian sighed with contentment. "My cousin Miles makes them. He is the finest clockmaker in Italy, I would bet on it, but he only makes them for me."

She hesitated for a moment, wondering if she should tell him that it was his smile and not his clocks that made her heart beat so quickly. "You are very lucky. I should like to meet him."

Ian moved away from her, suddenly acutely conscious of their dangerous proximity. "Perhaps you will, but certainly not until after we have spoken further about the murder." His voice had regained its cold, formal edge. As he spoke, he closed the door on the corpse and locked it. He felt her eyes on his face, inquiring, scrutinizing, and led her quickly into the darker part of the corridor. Approaching the stairs down to the main living quarters, he saw that it would be more unnerving than he had anticipated to have this strange Salva woman under his roof. He would have to be as reserved as possible at all times. Reserved and cold. He would not let her manipulate him.

"Until you have told me what I want to know, you will see no one." He continued speaking as they walked. "Except your chaperons, of course. You may have as much commerce with them as you like, but be warned that they report directly to me."

"I can scarcely wait to meet these ogres. I suppose you will also have me sleeping in a dungeon?" Confused by Ian's abrupt change in behavior, Bianca tried to match his chilly formality.

"Of course. Where else would a murderer sleep?" Bianca thought she saw the corner of his mouth twitch again in that dangerous way and decided to stay quiet. They wound down a second staircase and through at least two ballrooms in silence before they stopped at a deep blue door. "This is the suite Francesco and Roberto instructed me to give you. It is not the richest one, but they selected it."

"Francesco and Roberto?" She looked the question at him.

"The ogres—your chaperons, my uncles. They have their apartments over there." Ian gestured across the vast central hall toward a set of doors along the other wall. He saw her puzzled expression and imagined what she must be thinking: two chaperons instead of one was unusual; that they were two men made it almost unseemly. He was about to explain how he had chosen them, but he remembered his earlier resolve.

"I couldn't ask one of my elderly aunts to share a house with a murderess, could I? Nor would I want some proper *gentildonna* with refined sensibilities interfering in my interrogations. No, one woman under my roof is enough." He spoke the last words with a shudder of distaste.

Bianca thought quietly for a moment. "Rather than protecting me from you, it seems they will be protecting you from me."

"You are, after all, the dangerous one, aren't you?" As he spoke the words aloud, a voice inside Ian's head whispered, *You have no idea how true that is.*

He scowled irritably and threw open the door of Bianca's dungeon. Finding herself not only not in a dungeon but instead on the threshold of the most magnificent apartment she had ever beheld, Bianca could not contain an exclamation of delight. The walls of the first room were frescoed with women of every age and every country, each in their native costume. There were female warriors in metal armor and Roman women in long gowns, and women naked but for the brightly colored designs painted on their bodies. With difficulty Ian ushered her from the sitting room into the main room of the suite. Surrounded by frescoes depicting ancient goddesses was a large bed hung with deep blue velvet. Bianca was so tired and overwhelmed by the beauty not only of the paintings and furnishings but also of the man beside her that she neglected to consider the impropriety of standing in a bedroom with him. She touched Ian's arm gently and whispered, "This is the most extraordinary room I have ever seen." She turned her gaze from the paintings to the man and, seized with a most indecorous urge, kissed him on the cheek.

Ian's mind reeled between past and present. A woman in his house. A kiss. This room. As Ian looked down at her, Bianca saw his eyes darken into a cold slate gray. She shrank away from him, conscious of having somehow offended.

"That was very improper, Signorina Salva. See that it never happens again." He turned on his heel and moved toward the door.

"It's a very bad habit, you know," Bianca said quietly.

Ian stopped abruptly and turned to face her from the safety of the threshold. "What did you say?"

"Running away like that. Making a grandiose pronouncement and then leaving the room without hearing what anyone else has to say. It's almost cowardly."

Bianca felt a surge of rage fill the room. Ian looked at her, anger legible in every contour of his face. When he spoke his voice was dangerously low and cold.

"If I were you, signorina, I would save my wit for tomorrow. You will need every particle of it to keep me from turning you in as a murderess."

Chapter Four

Ian finished reading the decoded letter aloud and passed it to Sebastian on his right.

"It arrived this morning, brought in by a fisherman. I'll never understand how our L. N. uncovers these things, but he's not been wrong yet."

The other four men around the table nodded in agreement. None of them had ever met their English cousin, Lucien North Howard, earl of Danford, but not for lack of trying. Miles and Crispin, who passed at least half the year on their estates in England, were by now accustomed to receiving polite denials to their invitations and being informed that their cousin was "sadly unavailable" by his genteel but slightly menacing butler in London.

The only indisputable sign of his existence was his frequent, copious correspondence. It arrived from all over the world and by means of the most fantastic conveyances. It might come on Arboretti ships or in the hands of a foreign messenger who disappeared as quickly as he came. The letters always mixed personal anecdotes and travel descriptions with business advice. Without this counsel even Ian's outstanding business acumen could not have made Arboretti one of the largest and wealthiest shipping conglomerates of its day. On L.N.'s advice they had expanded from their original cargo of lumber into every thinkable product from every place in the world. Arboretti ships carried fabrics, wines, spices, plants, animals, munitions, gold, silver, gems, anything that could be bought in one place and sold at a profit in another. In only eight years, they had grown from having the six ships left to them by their grandfather to having a fleet that rivaled those of most city-states on the peninsula.

As a member of the English ambassador to Venice's entourage, their grandfather Benton Walsingham had fallen in love with Laura Foscari-Dolfin, the only daughter of an ancient Venetian patrician family, and decided to settle in Venice. He immediately recognized a market for English lumber in Europe for the construction of everything from buildings to warships, and went to work setting up a company. He named it *Arboretti*—little trees— after this cargo, and left it at his death to his six grandsons.

Seventy years after its foundation, the name was more commonly thought of as a parody of the unusual height of the six men who oversaw the vastly successful venture. It was spoken with reverence among groups of merchants all over the world, and the tall young men who ran the company were routinely consulted by others more than twice their age. But it was with women that most of the Arboretti really found favor. Handsome and wealthy, they cut a wide swath through the female inhabitants of Europe, leaving expensive gifts and broken hearts in their wake.

From what the other Arboretti understood, L. N. was the worst of the lot. In every court in Christendom there was a beautiful woman still pining for her "beloved Lucien," "*carissimo* Luciano," or "*cher* Luc." The Arboretti followed the exploits of their enigmatic cousin avidly, jokingly keeping accounts of his conquests in love alongside accounts of the profits yielded by his information. How he had time to both conquer hearts and collect vital data remained a mystery to them, but they had learned to accept it without question. Indeed, they were forced to, for their grandfather's will had stipulated that in all things the earl of Danford, whom Walsingham had himself raised after the death of his youngest daughter, should have the final say.

So when L. N. instructed his cousins to halt a shipment of gunpowder and cannon shot to England and instead ship a cargo of ruined grain, they could only shake their heads and follow orders.

"But we've heard nothing of these pirates he says are threatening our cargo," Miles objected skeptically, pushing aside the lock of hair that perennially dangled in front of his eyes. "I promised that gunpowder to the lord chamberlain myself just two months ago for his battles in the Highlands, and I can't say he'll be pleased to get a bushel of rotten grain and rats instead."

"He could try feeding that to the northern rebels," Tristan offered from the end of the table. "Might kill them faster than fighting and would put less of a strain on the Royal Exchequer." He shook his dark head, his jade-green eyes light with mirth. "S'teeth, it's a fine idea..."

Tristan's raillery was interrupted by a long shriek from a distant part of the palazzo. Silence fell at the table and all heads turned toward Ian, who was rapidly leaving his chair.

"That sounds distinctly like my charming betrothed. If you will just excuse me for a moment..."

"After him!" Crispin exclaimed as Ian left the room. "It has been ages since anything exciting happened in this house and I, for one, don't want to miss it."

"AAAAAAAAAHHHHHHHHHHH," Bianca screamed hysterically. She had spent a restless night tossing and turning in the huge bed, pursued by the sensation of being watched. Opening her eyes, she was confronted by a grisly tusked monster leering over her. "Get away, get away! Help, help, help!"

The creature's hand covered her mouth. *"Sshhh.* Hush little one," said a soothing male voice in her ear. "Ian will have our heads if we set you to screaming like that."

Bianca twisted her neck around to face the voice and saw that it emanated not from the mouth of a hideous beast but from a normal-looking older man, with a round face and smiling eyes. Next to him stood another man of about the same age wearing a slightly more serious expression. From the hand of the lively one dangled a carnival mask painted to look like a wild boar. He held it up for her to look at, removing his hand from her mouth.

"Ian told us you were expecting ogres, so we decided we would oblige. And we thought your blood needed a little excitement. It has definitely been thinning these many hours." Nodding, he reached out to feel Bianca's wrist. "You see, you see, Roberto, I told you it would do the trick. Feel it now, pumping away like a blacksmith's apprentice!" Bianca's arm was pulled farther from the bed toward the other, more serious man.

"Yes, it does seem to have worked, Francesco, but I think a dose of Ian's fine brandy would have been less troublesome to the system. Look at her—he keeps complaining that she won't stay quiet, and yet here she hasn't even uttered a word. You've overdone it again, I am afraid."

Bianca turned from one to the other of them, trying to make sense of the scene. This had to be Francesco and Roberto the chaperons, but instead of ogres, Ian seemed to have left her in the hands of doctors. And not just any doctors but famous ones: her father had often spoken with admiration of Francesco di Rimini and Roberto Collona, and she recognized their faces from the portraits on the title page of their herbal which she had used when she was studying medicines. For a few moments, confusion at finding herself with these two renowned men made her overlook Ian's comment about her verbosity, but soon pride got the better of chaos. Before she had time to repudiate Ian's reported slander, however, she found herself shoved back into the bed, the covers pulled over her head.

She heard Ian's voice muffled through the blankets. "Is she up yet? I thought I heard her voice. Is it normal for her to sleep so long?" His questions toppled out one after the other in rapid succession.

"Just a nightmare, dear nephew, just a bad dream," Francesco assured him, letting the carnival mask fall discreetly to the floor by the bed. "Nothing to worry about. The sleep will do her good.

She'll be fine once she awakes, but we must let nature take its course. Don't you agree, Roberto? Best to let her keep sleeping?"

"Certainly, certainly, quite right, Francesco. We'll get you from your meeting at the first sign of wakefulness, of course, Ian."

"Ah yes, before she has all her wits about her, always the best time for an interrogation," Francesco added, eyeing his nephew keenly. "Just as a matter of curiosity, are you planning to use the dungeon for your work? Screws, nails, whips? Remember how well they worked on the last one. . . ."

"What the devil are you. . . ?" Ian's question was drowned out by Francesco's voice as Roberto leaned across the bed, trying to still the squirming Bianca.

"Quite right, not our business," Francesco continued, moving Ian toward the door. "Wouldn't want anyone to interfere with the interrogation, you said it yourself last night." Ian thought he detected a note of mockery in his uncle's voice. "Now get back to your job, which is to make enough money so we all continue living like princes, and let us do the work of ogres. Doesn't suit you at all." Aided by Francesco's insistent arm over his shoulders, Ian had almost stepped over the threshold when Roberto lost his hold on the wriggling lump of blankets.

Bianca exploded from under the covers, shouting. "Whips? You would use whips on me?"

The three men stared at her in astonishment. Her eyes were a mesmerizing deep brown and her lip trembled with fury. She threw her head back and raised her chin in challenge.

"Go ahead. Humiliate me. Torture me. Even whip me. But by the breast of Santa Agata I promise you, if you treat me like an animal, I will be silent like an animal. I would rather be left in a slimy dank dungeon somewhere to be eaten by rats with dull teeth than tell you what I know." She crossed her arms over her breasts and glared at Ian.

"You charming girl, you have solved the mystery!" a male voice rang out from behind Ian. Bianca looked up to see a contingent of tall men who she knew must be the other Arboretti enter her room.

One of them, a blond one who looked like a more boyish version of Ian, smilingly addressed her. "The mystery of how my brother spends all his time. Blunting the teeth of the rats in his dungeon. I've been such a dolt not to see it before now...." Crispin shook his head in mock contempt for his stupidity, while his companions struggled to contain their hysteria.

Now it was Ian's turn to glare. Turning his sternest expression on the intruders in the doorway, he ordered them out. "This is a lady's room. It is insulting to my betrothed to be beset by you barbarians in this way...."

"I don't mind. Really." Bianca smiled winningly at the four men on the threshold. "Come in, please. It is an immense honor to meet the famed Arboretti. I know women who would maim to have any one of you in her bedroom, let alone all five at once."

The Arboretti could no longer restrain their laughter, and Bianca joined them. She studied them through her laughter, never having had the opportunity to be so close to the noteworthy group. The one who had spoken she knew was Crispin, Ian's brother, whose reputation as a rakish bon vivant was marred only by his extreme good nature and immense kindness. Next to him, with a lock of hair spilling onto his forehead, she recognized the soulful features of Miles, Ian's clockmaker and a poet of high repute. His poetic skills were often ascribed to the ease with which he fell in love, once with as many as ten women in one day, but all to no avail, as he had been betrothed at the age of five. Behind the love-struck poet stood Sebastian, his dark coloring and skill with languages inherited from his Turkish mother, his deep blue eyes and mesmerizing smile the legacy of his Venetian father. Bianca had heard it rumored that he could seduce a woman across a crowded room, and while this seemed extraordinary, seeing him close up did nothing to diminish the probability of its being true. Alongside Sebastian was Tristan, whose days as the prince of Venetian thieves had left him with an amused attitude toward life and a sly smile that made everything he said believable. Bianca had heard that his contemporary art collection, housed in the palace he shared with Sebastian, was one of the finest in Europe and decided to ask him about it.

"Yes, Tristan is famed for collecting beautiful things." Miles rushed to speak before his cousin could reply. "But in you, Ian has outdone him."

The sincerity of Miles's compliment overrode Bianca's objection to being described as one of Ian's collectibles, and she laughingly thanked him. This easy camaraderie was not at all part of Ian's plan. The atmosphere was social, convivial, lighthearted, anything but the explosive tension he had been counting on. He felt completely outside the merry group. As if sensing his isolation, Bianca turned toward him, a welcoming invitation in her eyes. It was tempting, he could let go just a little, relax a little...Damn, he thought, pulling himself out of his seductive reverie, she was doing it again, bending him to her will, as if he were some untutored young lover.

Instead of relaxing, the muscles in Ian's jaw tightened. "Your meeting with my brother and my cousins is over as of right now," he announced to her sternly, watching the mirth die out of her face. He gestured all the men to the door with his arms. "Out, all of you, out. My betrothed and I have many matters to discuss and we prefer to do so in private." From the corner of his eye he saw Bianca open her mouth to say something and then close it. Good. She needed to remember who was in charge.

Several of the Arboretti hazarded a backward glance to smile or wink at Bianca sympathetically as they left the room. Francesco lingered on the threshold about to speak until Roberto persuaded him to come away. Finally alone, Ian felt Bianca's eyes on him, watching him expectantly. He felt strangely confused, unable to remember what he meant to be doing in this lush room with this lovely woman sitting tousled in bed. Moving closer to her, he wondered if the skin of her shoulders was as soft as the skin on her cheek. Or maybe softer. Were her nipples, barely visible through the thin damask nightdress she was wearing, more pink or more peach colored? What would her mouth feel like under his? Or her body?

With a shock he realized that he was growing aroused, here in the bedroom of this infuriating, manipulative, perilous woman. Ironically, he reflected, he could save quite a fortune by exercising his right to seduce his betrothed instead of visiting one of the expensive courtesans he frequented. But he had decided years ago never again to mingle emotions and sex, and this rule seemed especially important now, with the dangerous beauty before him. It would be better not even to approach her, he decided, simultaneously making a mental note to reserve the services of a favorite courtesan on a daily basis for the duration of Bianca's residence in his house. Maybe twice daily, he thought as her ankle strayed from beneath the covers.

Bianca's heart was racing. Ian had moved close enough to touch her, close enough for her to touch him. At last she was going to experience what she had been wondering about for so long. She wanted to reach out and take his hand, to lead it over all the places on her body she had fantasized about being touched. But his harsh reproof the night before stuck in her mind, and she hesitated, not wanting to send him rushing away. She felt herself growing warm in an unfamiliar but not unpleasant way under his gaze. Looking up at him, she willed him to touch her, willed him to bend over and cover her mouth with his lips. Her tongue moved slowly over her teeth, enticing him toward her.

Ian turned abruptly and walked to the door, pausing to issue commands over his shoulder. "I shall wait for you in the antechamber while you dress. We need to dispose of Isabella's corpse soon, so I should like to go over it with you this afternoon. Your clothing was delivered from your aunt's house this morning. You will find it in the armoire. Please be quick."

"Certainly, my lord. Of course, decomposition is a problem. I shall be out momentarily." Bianca strove to keep the hurt and confusion out of her voice. For a brief moment she had felt something, felt that perhaps he did not really hate her. But she had been wrong. He found her revolting, could not even bring himself to touch her. Their embrace the previous night had been a fantastical occurrence; he felt nothing but contempt for her. Besides, she assured herself, there were other men—gondoliers, butlers, servants, even the other Arboretti. A house this size must be filled with them. No, surely it did not require a count to teach her the lessons she had been longing to learn. When even this thought did not soothe her pain, she reminded herself that she was really there to find out who had murdered Isabella. Proving her innocence, she told herself, was more important than losing it, even to the Conte d'Aosto. Or at least it should be. Repeating this like an Ave Maria, she dressed quickly and went out to meet him.

Chapter Five

Bianca and Ian ascended the steps to the laboratories the same way they had descended them the previous day, in silence. Ian allowed Bianca to precede him into the cold room, following behind her with a handful of unlit tapers. The smell of decomposing flesh hit him as he entered, but he saw that Bianca did not even seem to notice it. He wondered if all murderers were so cold-blooded. Working together, they got the tapers lit and distributed in the wall sconces.

"I had Giorgio bring up more ice in the middle of the night." Ian gestured to the large blocks surrounding the corpse. "I thought it might slow the decomposition."

"*Umm*, yes, very good, my lord." Bianca was looking through her pile of drawings, trying to order her thoughts before she began her narration. After a few minutes of shuffling papers around, she raised her eyes to see Ian staring down wistfully at the dissected woman on the table.

The thought struck her like a boulder. Santa Apollonia's teeth, what an idiot she had been! Of course, he had been in love with Isabella and was deeply grieved. No wonder he hated her, the presumed murderer of his beloved. She remembered the locket she had found on the body, with hair exactly Ian's shade of blond carefully preserved inside. They had been lovers, Bianca thought to herself, suddenly jealous of the dead woman on the table. Damnation. What he needed now, she realized, was not a cold recounting of Isabella's anatomy but compassion.

She cleared her throat. "Would you like to talk about her, my lord?" Bianca had often spent hours consoling the relatives of ailing patients, helping them to express their grief. She knew from personal experience how hard it could be to lose someone you loved. When Ian did not respond, she began again. "How long had you, *um*, known her?"

Ian regarded her, surprised and a little confused. "'Known her'?" he repeated to himself, and then, "'How long'...?"

"No need to answer if it is too painful," Bianca cut in, embarrassed. She should never have asked; it was much too personal, and certainly no business of hers at all.

"'Painful'?" Ian looked blank again. Finally comprehension seemed to dawn on him and he spoke in clipped tones. "You appear to be under some misapprehension, Signorina Salva. I did not know Isabella Bellocchio. I set eyes on her for the first time four days ago when we recovered the body. She was not exactly in my social circle." Isabella was not the type of courtesan he sought out. Crispin had often spoken of her sweet innocence and childlike charm, but those were not qualities that appealed to Ian. He thought of explaining this to Bianca but decided it was none of her business. Let her think what she wanted.

Now Bianca was confused. Why was he lying to her? "But the locket..." she blurted out before she could stop herself. "She has your hair in her locket. Surely you were lovers."

"You would do well to refrain from assumptions about my love life, signorina, which can be no concern of yours." Ian was surprised by the asperity with which he spoke those last words. "And I know of no locket. My hair color, however, is that of at least half the patriciate of Venice. It is not so terribly distant from your own, for that matter." Ian scrutinized her. "How am I to know that the locket was not a gift from you? That you were not once friends but later became rivals for the attention of one of her clients, and jealous, you killed her?"

Bianca sneered at him and his absurd logic. "We did not have the same taste in lovers." It was not strictly untrue, she assured herself.

Aha! So she was not as innocent as she pretended to be. Ian felt triumphant—he had seen through her naïveté all along. "Isabella might have decided to broaden her palate. Is that why you went to Isabella's apartments, to get revenge on her for stealing your prize?" Ian watched her carefully, sure that he was getting close to something.

"Isabella was not killed on the spur of the moment in some fit of passionate revenge." Bianca sounded exasperated. "Whoever murdered her must have been planning it for months."

"How could you possibly know that unless you yourself had planned it?" Ian had her cornered. He saw her will giving way.

Bianca looked at him with surprise. "How would *you* explain the dagger and the note sent to you? Those surely are not details that one would think up at the last minute. But they are proofs of my innocence: although now that I know you better, it seems like a fine idea, what reason would I possibly have had to frame you for murder? And if I did, why would I linger at the crime scene until you arrived?"

It was a persuasive point, but Ian immediately saw a flaw. He shook his head. "Just like a woman to argue that looking manifestly guilty was proof of her innocence. I believe I was asking the questions and you were answering them. Do you have any other equally compelling proofs of your innocence?" Ian decided to make it easier for her. "I don't suppose you would care to explain, for example, what you were doing in Isabella's apartment, if not murdering her?"

Bianca glared at him for a moment. He was so peevish and stubborn, refusing to see reason. Her first inclination was to show him that she could be just as stubborn by refusing to open her mouth, but she thought better of it. Perhaps she could tell him enough to prove she wasn't a murderer without having to reveal everything.

"I was teaching Isabella to write. I went there every Monday at the same time to give her exercises. We had a standing appointment." She looked him in the eye, daring him to challenge her.

"Sounds very innocent. Why wouldn't you admit that before?"

"There was no reason to. I told you I had nothing to do with Isabella's death."

Ian was suspicious, she could sense it. She began moving around the room, cleaning up and preparing for the disposal of the body.

"Why did you do it?" Ian challenged suddenly.

Bianca spoke through clenched teeth. "I have just said, I didn't do it...."

"No, not the murder, that is not what I meant. Why did you agree to teach Isabella to write? What convinced you to potentially disgrace your family by cavorting with a courtesan? Surely there are other more adequate writing tutors in Venice that she could have hired than some chit who thinks she's going to be a famous doctor." Ian added the fruits of his research into her background that morning. "You have an immense fortune from your father, you certainly don't need money.... What possible motive could you have?"

"As you yourself pointed out, women don't need motives, only means." Bianca spit his words back at him. She could scarcely speak she was so enraged. He was hateful, she decided, completely odious. How could she ever have thought he was attractive? "Unlike the worthy, honorable, and exalted men of your social circle, women who desire education have a hard time finding it. At any rate, those of us deluded enough to think ourselves learned—although never nearly as gifted as you and your friends—are often approached by others less fortunate for help and instruction. Many women, like Isabella, are too vain to admit to a man that they are illiterate. Imagine, my lord, not being able to read history, natural science, a letter from a friend, even a love poem. Imagine not being able to keep your own accounts, not knowing how to do simple addition and subtraction. Without those skills, a woman is always at someone else's mercy. I suspect that you men prefer them that way. Wouldn't you agree, my lord?"

"It's an interesting theory, signorina, but like all your others it is missing one crucial element—proof. How did this arrangement with Isabella come about, for example? Did she pass you in Piazza San Marco and, overhearing you lecturing whatever poor fellow you happened to have gotten the ear of, ask you for writing lessons? Do you advertise your stenographic method? Or was it—"

Bianca interrupted his sarcastic litany. "Actually, it was after we became lovers. I wanted to receive letters from her when I was away and was disturbed by her inability to write."

Ian raised one eyebrow. "That, signorina, is the first sensible thing you've said all day."

"And also the first lie." Bianca sighed and looked at him, almost with pity. "My lord, while I am grateful that you think I have enough sexual appeal to woo a beauty like Isabella, I must insist that you put the notion of our having been lovers from your mind. I met her while working on my book. For my research it was necessary to see and speak to all types of women. I let it be known that I was available to give medicine and advice to any woman regardless of her ability to pay me for it. Isabella was one of my patients." It was all true, if not the whole truth. Why, then, did she continue to feel nervous as she waited to see if Ian had accepted it?

Ian could picture Bianca traveling all over the city visiting women, her gondola filled with medical potions and whatnot. No wonder her aunt and uncle had been so willing to move her to his house, despite the rather unconventional and improbable betrothal. He imagined they had urchins and messengers pounding on their doors at all hours of the day and night begging for the she-doctor. He shuddered, wondering when they would start the assault on his palazzo.

Bianca could stand his silent scrutiny no longer. "You see, my lord, I told you I was innocent. Now perhaps you will tell me what your researches have yielded."

"No." Ian shook his head, not apologetically. He had no doubt that she had told him the truth about her introduction to Isabella and even possibly their relationship, but there was still something she was holding back, of that he was sure. Her explanation was much too banal to have elicited so many denials at their first encounter. She was protecting someone, herself or someone she cared about deeply. And he needed to know who.

For a moment he toyed with telling her the steps he had taken to trap the murderer, circulating a call for information about Isabella's disappearance and trying to uncover the origin of that hideous dagger with his crest on it. Perhaps knowing how close he was would scare the truth out of her. But she was crafty, Bianca Salva, and could twist anything in her favor. Scaring this fierce little creature was probably an impossibility. "No, that would not do at all. What kind of fool do you think me, signorina," he asked finally, "that I would disclose my methods and findings to my only viable suspect? I may not be of your mental caliber," his lips twitched in that dangerous way, "but nor am I a brainless toddler fresh from his mother's teat."

Bianca was astonished. Her mouth opened and then closed twice before she was able to speak. "That is absurd. I told you what I was doing there. I've told you everything. I am innocent."

"Prove it." Ian assessed her through narrowed eyes. "If you did not do it, tell me who did."

"Santa Barbara's knuckles, you are the most pigheaded being alive. You still persist in branding me a liar and a criminal?" She drew close to him, pointing her finger into his chest to punctuate her words. "Do you think I am enjoying this sham betrothal?" She poked with her finger. "Suffering one humiliation after another," poke, "my reputation gone, my integrity constantly in question?" Poke, poke. Ian grasped her finger to avoid being turned into a pincushion and drew her close to him.

His proximity made Bianca feel woozy. She hated him now, she reminded herself, he was hateful. Hateful, she thought as she looked into his face. And not even handsome. Or maybe he was too handsome, yes, certainly that was his problem. Too handsome, in that exactly-just-the-right-amount-handsome way.

"I will give you one week, signorina. Seven days from today to prove your innocence." He consulted his beautiful pocket watch. "That gives you until midday next Thursday. One hundred and sixty-eight hours. You do know how to tell time, don't you?"

Hateful, she remembered. Hateful indeed. She pulled away from him and moved toward the door of the room. When she reached it, she turned to face him again.

"Very well, my lord—since you are clearly not up to it, I will find the murderer for you. But rest assured that you will pay and pay dearly, every day of our married life together." She tried to make her voice sound mean and menacing, to give her words a threatening undertone. "And through every long hour and every long week of every long year, you will have only yourself to blame." The door slammed shut behind her.

Ian stared into the space left empty by Bianca's departure. Yet again he did not doubt she spoke the truth, though he could not rid himself of the nagging feeling that she was hiding something. Ian rehearsed Bianca's arguments to himself. She certainly did seem to have an explanation for her presence at Isabella's. And even if he could devise a motive for her having killed the courtesan, she could scarcely have any reason to try to pin it on him, a stranger to her. He knew he had many enemies, but he took solace in the fact that he could at least identify all of them by name.

He realized he had not contemplated the possibility of her innocence, or her refusal to bow out of the betrothal. Not that it made much difference. He would have had to marry at some point and Bianca was as good a candidate as anyone. Her family was almost as old as his, even if her father had been a bit batty, and she appeared healthy enough for breeding. As long as they did not have to spend too much time together, it would work out fine, a typical patrician marriage.

There had been a time when he had looked forward to marriage, to having a family. He had pictured a relationship unlike his parents' cold partnership, a relationship of mutual trust and understanding, shared interests, even love. It wasn't that he now thought such relationships were impossible for everyone—Francesco and Roberto certainly lived that way—but they were impossible for him. He was unworthy of love, Mora had shown him that. Nor could he blame her. He alone had made himself hateful in her eyes. She had been right, he would disappoint anyone he got close to. Marriage to a woman who promised to hate him from the outset was what he deserved. Years of fighting, a house filled with anger, illegitimate heirs, those had been Mora's prophecy for him. She would be pleased to know how accurately it was going to be fulfilled.

Ian pushed those thoughts out of his mind as he had so many times before. He had business to attend to, he had neglected the other Arboretti for too long. And this room needed to be cleaned up, the body—or what was left of it—removed and respectfully buried. *Grazie a Dio* there was always work to do.

Bianca walked quickly away from the laboratory, color rising in her face as she went. Snatches of their exchange flashed through her mind, making her alternately angry and embarrassed. She was so caught up in the recollection that she walked right into Crispin's arms.

"Are you always this forward on the second meeting?" he asked as she looked at him with surprise.

"My lord, oh, oh my, I am sorry. I was not looking where I was going and…It's just that your brother…I am so sorry." Bianca blushed furiously and stepped away from him.

"*Niente*, my brother has this discomposing effect on everyone. He enjoys it, I'm afraid. You can run into my arms for comfort anytime you like. In a sisterly way, of course," he tacked on, noticing her alarm. "But there is no time for chatting now. I have been sent to tell you that your aunt and cousins have arrived to pay you a courtesy call."

"Would have been more courteous of them to leave me alone," Bianca muttered, and then, seeing that Crispin had heard her, she hastened to add, "I only meant that I am so tired today, of course. How charming."

Crispin, who had once spent twenty minutes with her aunt at a card table, eyed her skeptically. "Charming, *si certo*. Are you ready to see them or do you need some time to change?"

Bianca looked over the plain yellow dress she always wore to work in, saw that there were no egregious stains, and shook her head. "No, they are accustomed to seeing me in a whole array of shocking ensembles. They would probably be disappointed if I began to act more seemly once I was betrothed. But there is no reason for you to put yourself out. If you send me in the right direction, I am sure I can find the room myself."

Crispin laughed. "Not without a map and a lodestone, I warrant. But it is just down this way."

He took her arm and led her off. After winding through five corridors and down four staircases—"Does this house never end?" Bianca demanded—they arrived in a fair-sized room with enormous windows on two sides. In the middle, seated on couches, were her Aunt Anatra and her cousins Angelo and Analinda. Her aunt Anatra had once been the belle of the Venetian patriciate, or so Bianca had been told, but the only signs of her former beauty now were her children. Angelo, with his curling fair hair and large, innocent eyes, looked every bit the chivalric hero. His younger sister shared his features but in a softer, more feminine way; her recent entry into Venetian society had been very promising, at least if measured by the number of love sonnets she received as anonymous gifts. ("More than three dozen," she had confided to Bianca the previous week. "Even more than Catarina Nonte!") From Analinda's perspective, Bianca's betrothal to the wealthy and aristocratic count with all the handsome cousins was a gift from heaven. But she seemed to be the only member of her family who thought so.

The air in the room crackled with tension, despite Francesco and Roberto's best efforts to entertain Anatra. As Bianca and Crispin entered the room, her chaperons looked up with clear signs of relief. Crispin greeted the Grifalconi family, extending his hand to Angelo with whom he shared several clubs and many women, and casting an appreciative eye at Analinda before begging off, saying that business called. Bianca smiled warmly at her cousins and curtsied to her aunt.

"*Piacere*, Aunt Anatra. What a delightful surprise."

"Not nearly as surprising as your betrothal," her aunt replied in dry tones. "You do like to make trouble for a body, don't you."

"That is what you have always told me," Bianca replied in the same dry tones, standing straight before her aunt with all hint of a smile gone. Since the death of her father the previous year, Bianca had taken a house with her brother on Campo San Paolo. But social custom said it was unseemly for a single woman to live alone, so any time her brother went away on his secretive business, which of late seemed all the time, Bianca had been forced into residence with her aunt and uncle at their old palazzo in Cannaregio. Aunt Anatra had made no secret of her contempt for Bianca's father and would have liked to transfer the bulk of it onto his eccentric daughter. When she realized that in his frugal mode of life her brother had not only maintained but even augmented his fortune, however, she had tried to think better of him, or rather, of his heirs. Indeed, she had tried to think well enough of Bianca to marry her to her only son, the precious Angelo. But the spoiled chit had refused, again and again. And now she was betrothed to a count. All that money leaving the family. The thought made Anatra sick with rage.

"Strange that you never mentioned your attachment to d'Aosto before," Bianca's aunt mused aloud. "Stranger that he took you without a dowry."

Bianca was unsure what her aunt was alluding to, but felt confident it was not meant kindly. "I do have a vast personal fortune, remember," she coolly retaliated. "And being rich as Midas himself, it probably does not matter much to him at all."

Bianca watched gleefully as Aunt Anatra opened and closed her mouth, like a fish caught in a net. Angelo took his mother's hand to comfort her, at the same time flashing a beatific smile at Bianca. He had heard the news of his cousin's betrothal and removal from the house only that morning, upon returning from three days of debauched passion. He had sauntered into his family palazzo, the heady scent of his new lover's musk still in his nose and his cock limp from overwork, hoping to catch sight of his cousin Bianca. It was an experiment, actually, to see if she could still arouse him as she usually did, even in his satiated state. Years ago he had made unobtrusive holes along one wall of her room, facing a mirror, and he had spent hours watching her reflection bathe and dress. He knew every mark on her body, every perfect curve, every adorable dimple.

He had been infuriated to learn of her absence, even more so of her betrothal, but when he learned the identity of her betrothed, fury cooled to curiosity. Bianca and the Conte d'Aosto. There was something decidedly suspicious about this sudden betrothal, especially about its timing. Eager to know more, he had instantly corralled his mother and sister into making a call on the bride-to-be. But the results so far had been disappointing. None of the members of the household seemed the least put out by the betrothal, and Bianca was as nervy—and enticing—as ever. Whatever was going on, and there had to be something substantial to compel his stubborn cousin into marriage, was being very well concealed. He was wasting his time in polite social calls, he decided.

Suddenly impatient, he rose and bowed. "We shall be sorry to lose your company at Ca'Grifalconi." Angelo spoke politely, but his words somehow rang false. "And while I am green with envy, I am sure you will make d'Aosto a perfect wife." Bianca recalled the curse she had pronounced on Ian's head just minutes before and wasn't sure whether to laugh or groan.

Angelo took her hand and was about to put it to his lips when he noticed it was stained with ink.

"Have you spent these first days of your betrothal working? Cutting up dead cats and whatnot and committing their organs to paper?" He spoke with unconcealed disdain.

Bianca's heart started to pound. "One must stay busy, you know," she said in a voice she hoped did not tremble.

"You must admit, *cara* signorina, you have spent an unseemly amount of time in the laboratory upstairs since you got here. Why, just—" Bianca cut Francesco off with a look that might have killed a lesser man.

"Laboratory, *eh*?" Angelo's curiosity was finally being rewarded. "I would love to take a look at where a *dottoressa* works. Could I go there with you now, cousin?" As he spoke, he gripped her hand tighter and began to lead her to the door.

"I am afraid Signorina Salva does not have time to show you her work space today." Roberto's soft voice came from where he stood next to the fireplace. "We have so much planning to do for the party that her time is completely occupied."

Bianca tried to keep the question out of her eyes as she looked over at Roberto. "Yes, yes, thank you for reminding me, Dottore Collona, I am much too busy. Perhaps another time, cousin." She turned to smile at Angelo, pulling her hand from his grasp. Out of nowhere, a young servant appeared to usher the Grifalconi visitors out. Bianca curtsied as her aunt brushed by her, and stood to kiss Analinda on both cheeks. Angelo was the last to go, bowing deeply to her before taking his leave. As the door closed behind them, Analinda could be heard asking her mother who Midas was and if he had any unmarried sons.

Bianca, Roberto, and Francesco looked at each other and began to laugh.

"That was a lovely visit. Quite nice of them to come," Francesco said finally, slightly out of breath. Then, turning to Roberto, he asked, "But what's all this about a party? Why am I the last to know?"

"I only thought of it at that moment, but I am embarrassed we did not plan it earlier. No matter what strange circumstances have brought about this betrothal," here he turned a questioning eye on Bianca, "we should at least observe the proprieties. There must be a party to introduce the new couple."

"Indeed, of course, yes quite. And there hasn't been a party here since that witch Mor—" Francesco was cut off by a sharp look from Roberto. "For quite some time."

Roberto needn't have bothered, for Bianca was too busy making a list in her head to hear what passed between them. A clock on the far wall was striking the time. Only 167 hours left, Bianca reminded herself.

She turned to her chaperons abruptly, interrupting their discussion. "If I needed to borrow paper, ink, three thousand gold ducats, two gondolas, one set of men's clothes, and a nimble young boy, where in this huge house would you suggest I begin looking?"

Chapter Six

The massive dining chamber was lit with only a handful of candles, casting mysterious dancing shadows over its tapestried walls. The remains of a dinner for two lay scattered at the end of the long table. A few paces from the table a fire raged in a marble fireplace, fighting off the chill of the rainy winter evening. Before the fire, a cat finished the remains of a quail next to two lovers entwined in each other's arms under a fur rug.

"Tell me again about the girl," the woman said, pushing the man's head away from her erect nipple. "What does she look like? How does she seem? Will she make him happy?"

The man sighed and leaned away from her. "I've already told you." He felt her hand go to his organ, still sticky from being inside her. "She's plain." He began to grow hard under the stroking of her fingers. "She's dull." Her hand moved up and down the length of his solid member, lingering on the tip. She was teasing him, coaxing him on to the final point. "She will probably bore him to death." Her lips went down over his shaft, drinking him in. He had repeated the same untruths over and over during dinner and would do so a hundred more times for the same reward. Her gratitude was truly moving.

Her mouth was sliding up his throbbing organ when the door at the far end of the room opened. She drew away and the young man groaned.

"Where are you, *cara?* We must speak about..." It was her brother's voice.

"Down here with our little assistant." She pulled the fur over them and turned onto her stomach. "He has been telling me the most interesting story. The count is betrothed. Betrothed to be married. To a plain slut. I must meet her."

"You will find her just as described," her brother said earnestly. To him, as to most men, all women looked plain next to his sister. "But first we have a problem to discuss. I have just received word that at the last moment those ingrates changed their shipment from gunpowder to grain, and rotten grain at that." His voice quivered with indignation.

"That is rather inconvenient. How do you find these things out?" His sister sounded unconcerned.

He waved her question aside. "Without that gunpowder we are sunk. Everything will be ruined! We must speak about this. Now." He shifted his pointed gaze to the man beside her.

She sighed, realizing that her brother would not be easily appeased. Turning to her lover, she kissed him on the ear and then pushed him away. "It is time for you to go on your errand, my angel. Come back when you have something to interest me and I will reward you well. I know how you like to be thanked."

"Thank me first, then I will go," the young man said, brushing his erect shaft against her thigh. She shook her head and gestured him away again. He was a bit too pushy and needed to be taught discipline. She was willing to assuage his needs regularly, but she was not entirely at his disposal. With a petulant pout, he stood and walked over to his pile of clothes in the corner. Momentarily worried she had dampened the young man's ardor for the task before him by refusing him favors now, she sought for a way to rekindle his enthusiasm.

"Isn't he well shaped?" the woman asked her brother in a tone rich with admiration and loud enough to carry.

"You don't have to tell me, *cara*. I found him, remember. I am the one who trained him. I am glad you are pleased."

The object of their scrutiny smiled as they talked, his vanity flattered by their compliments. He was indebted to both brother and sister for more hours of pleasure than he could remember, not to mention a large number of the ducats he lost at the gaming tables.

When he was fully dressed, he went and stood before them. "Don't forget, *angelo mio*, the more you bring me, the more grateful I will be," the woman admonished, throwing her head back and parting her lips to accept his kiss.

"I will be back soon to collect my reward," he assured her huskily. Then he bowed to his patron and, pulling a black mask over his face, disappeared into the shadows.

Chapter Seven

Ian was running, his heart pounding. He was in a vast hall, the only light coming from a fire at the front of it. A woman lay on a gold fur rug, naked, beckoning to him. As he got closer, he could make out her oval face, wavy light brown hair, her brown eyes glowing gold with passion. He took in her full lips and her slim body, breasts like two of the small hard peaches that grew in Crispin's greenhouse. She reached out toward him and he tried to go to her, running as fast as he could, but she kept drawing back, just out of reach. His body painfully aroused, he leapt to grab her and heard a horrible familiar laugh in his ears. "Coward." The laughter turned into a voice. "Heartless coward. You will never have her. Never. Not even in your dreams."

Ian sat up in bed. He was drenched in sweat. His heart was racing. And his body was indeed painfully aroused. "Damn these women!" he said into the dark night. How could they have such an effect on him? He was familiar with nightmares that featured Mora's harsh words as their background, but this dream was unique. What made it so unsettling was Bianca. Dreaming about a potential murderer naked had to be a sign of some nervous disorder, he told himself. And not just dreaming about her either, but being aroused by her. Very aroused. This had to stop.

He stepped naked from his bed and left his room to wander through the house. As he traced the familiar path, the cool air of the rainy night calmed the arousal of his body. He went and stood at the windows facing onto the Grand Canal. The rain had stopped, for the first time that week, and the dark water below him was lit by the shimmering light of the full moon. How many times had he stood here like this, naked, with his head pressed against the cool glass panes of the window, watching the darkness recede into dawn? He had once stopped during the day to see if the floor was worn down in this one spot, to see if there was any external manifestation of the deep anguish that pained him within. But the stones yielded up no evidence of his secret midnight vigils. Taking his cue from them, he tried not to either.

He watched a gondola glide on the canal toward him, anonymously cloaked in black. In the palazzo facing his across the water, a window was still lit and he could see the French ambassador actively wooing his chambermaid. Ian tried to see if it was the same woman it had been last month, decided it was, and lost interest. The French ambassador had once confided to him that he behaved that way out of duty to his country, not out of shameless animal lust. He was convinced that the chambermaids were spies of other governments and that bedding them was the only way to ensure their loyalty. Ian admired the vigor with which he fulfilled his patriotic duty, thinking that his own performance as a member of the Senate and overseer of his *sestiere* was uninspired by comparison. Perhaps bedding a murder suspect...?

His disturbing train of thought was halted by a noise. Ian was familiar with the night noises of his house, and the squeak of a hinge was not one of them. He moved stealthily toward the staircase at the end of the room, glad he had not brought a candle with him. Unsure whether the noise had come from the courtyard below or one of the floors above, he stood stock-still and waited. Nothing. Then came another sound, like the scraping of wood on metal, which seemed to eminate from upstairs. He grabbed the first item he could lay his hands on, a silver spice holder Sebastian had found in Constantinople, and began to ascend the stairs. He had not gone more than ten steps before he saw a flickering light approaching from below. Figuring he had miscalculated the location of the sound—acoustics were notoriously tricky he knew—he turned to face the nearing light. As the intruder got close, it flashed through Ian's mind that this must be a pretty audacious criminal, completely unconcerned with concealing himself. Deducing he must therefore be dangerous, Ian decided to take him by surprise.

Ian sneaked up behind him. Holding his breath, he brought the silver spice container down against the back of the intruder's head. The criminal gasped, then collapsed onto the floor, unconscious. The candle fell from his hand and was retrieved by Ian. By its light he untied the black mask, but soon wished he had not. There, lying unconscious on the floor, was Bianca. As he stood over her, stunned and astonished, her eyes began to flutter. She groaned in pain as he tried to prop her up against the wall. Finally she opened her eyes.

And then she opened them even wider. She was completely distracted from the ache in her head by the vision that confronted her. Ian's naked body was more breathtaking than anything she had imagined in all her hours of imagining live male bodies. His limbs were taut with muscle, his arms and broad shoulders powerful, and his chest covered with golden hair that glimmered in the candlelight and descended past his slim waist into a triangle of darker curls at the junction of his legs. She was so rapt in admiration that she did not notice when he began speaking.

"Signorina Salva, Bianca, damn it, can you hear me?" he demanded finally, shaking her to get her attention.

She nodded slowly, dragging her eyes from his body to his face.

"What the devil do you think you are doing? I might have hurt you."

"I think you did," Bianca said, wincing as she felt the bump on the back of her head.

"You deserve that and more. Who suggested that you could go roaming around the house, dressed like a boy, at all hours?"

"Oh, no, my lord. You needn't worry about me roaming around the house. I have hardly been here. I just got back, actually."

Ian's anger was tempered by incredulity. "You went out? Dressed like that? Whatever for?"

"If you only had seven days to live, wouldn't you try to enjoy them to the utmost?"

"But if you were innocent, as you claim, you would have more than seven days to live. Is this a confession?"

"No. More like my assessment of life married to you." Bianca hoped to cool the triumph she heard in his voice.

It worked. She could have sworn she heard Ian growl. But then she realized the noise was coming not from the naked man before her, but from upstairs, in another part of the palazzo. Ian's head shot around to follow it, both their ears straining in the darkness. Motioning to her to be quiet, Ian turned to the staircase, taking the steps two at a time. Bianca followed behind slowly, hindered by the sharp pain that went through her body every time she moved her head. Nonetheless, she was grateful to be wearing tight breeches instead of layers of petticoats, which would have made following Ian nearly impossible.

At the top floor they stopped. Ian put the candle on a console along the wall and made a sign for her to stay there. Her head was aching, and she figured she had already antagonized him beyond endurance for one night, so she dutifully followed his orders. The noise seemed to be coming not from within his laboratory, directly in front of them, but farther along the hall, from hers. Of course, she realized with a flash, whoever had murdered Isabella had probably come in search of the body. What a fool she had been not to have foreseen it and locked herself up here to greet the malefactor when he arrived! Excitement got the better of her restraint, and she began to move more quickly toward Ian. When she reached him, he was turning the door handle slowly.

The door moved inward without a sound. Little by little Ian inched it open, reminding himself to give Giorgio a raise the next day for not having locked it. When the opening was wide enough for him to slip his head through, he silently peered into the room.

The laboratory was empty save for a figure, cloaked in black, with his back to Ian. The window on the far wall had been shattered by the prowler when he entered. Bianca's instruments had been thrown from their chests and cases and lay scattered around the floor of the room. The figure stood in the midst of them, attentively studying a pile of papers before him. Ian pushed the door open wider and stepped into the room, right onto something sharp. Cursing silently, he slipped closer to the intruder, ready to strike again with the silver spice container.

As he raised it over the intruder's head, it caught the light of the candle. A reflection flashed across the far wall. The intruder looked up from the papers for a moment, then looked back down apparently unconcerned. But he had been alerted. The man moved just as Ian brought the box down where his head should have been and was at the window before Ian realized what had happened.

Ian was on his heels as the prowler leapt from the window onto the roof of the adjoining house. Ian could see him in the moonlight, moving quickly over the rain-slicked terra-cotta tiles, gripping the pile of papers under one arm and using the other one to maneuver. Barefoot and empty-handed, Ian was able to make better time than his prey. The intruder jumped from one rooftop to the next, with Ian following closely. Ian lost his footing and began to slip, grabbing on to a nearby chimney pot for support. He righted himself and saw that his adversary had also fallen. Scrambling rapidly across the slick tiles, Ian finally caught up to him. He made a wild leap at the man's shoulders. For a moment the intruder lay pinned under Ian, his heart pounding rapidly.

It occurred to the intruder that if he got caught he would receive no thanks from anyone. Fired by the thought of his mistress's gratitude, he began to wriggle under the weight of the man on top of him. He ignored the cutting edges of the tile as he fought to break the clasp of his sable cape. All at once, the cape began to slide off, taking the man on top of it with him. Ian cursed and tried to get a handhold on a tile, but the fur cape only moved more quickly down the wet roof. He was going to die, he thought suddenly, naked, sliding on a fur cape down the steep slope of the Widow Falentini's old house. People would think he must have been mad. Indeed, he *must* be mad to find himself in this situation. Betrothal to a suspected murderess, a mad chase by moonlight— these could hardly be incidents in the well-ordered life of Ian Foscari. But they were, and he was...damn it, he was enjoying it. Suddenly he wanted to laugh. And he wanted to live. Then he saw the edge of the roof approaching rapidly as the cape continued its perilous descent. With all his strength, Ian reached out and grabbed at two broken tiles, praying they were not loose.

They weren't. He hung, suspended from two roof tiles, naked in the moonlight. It was only the second time in his life that Ian had felt close to death, but this time was different. The last time his survival had filled him with anguish. He had felt himself longing for death, for his death instead of Christian's. Now, instead, he felt exhilarated. "You always were good at self-preservation" he heard Mora's voice sneering, but it seemed unimportant. More important, he realized, feeling the ache in his arms, was pulling himself onto the roof. With a groan, Ian hauled himself up and stood.

He looked down into the dark streets, hoping for a sign of the intruder but knowing he would find none. The man was gone, leaving only his cape behind. Ian slung the garment over his shoulders as protection against the suddenly chilly air and began to move slowly over the roof tiles toward his house. Since he had made off with Bianca's drawings, the man had obviously been looking for evidence of Isabella's presence. But how could he have known the body had been there? Or even that there was a body? Ian had kept the news of Isabella's murder from the Arboretti, from everyone except those who had to know, Francesco, Roberto, and Giorgio. He had kept the laboratory locked the entire time the body was there so that none of his staff might stumble on it by accident. Only five people—himself, his uncles, Giorgio, and Bianca—knew about the body, so clearly one of them had told someone. He could vouch for the security of the first four, but Bianca was unguessable. Yet she had been under constant surveillance since she arrived. She could not have communicated anything to anyone from his house. Unless...

Unless this was her conspirator. Unless she had planned this from the beginning, planned to get into his house with the body. The dagger had been only the smallest element of the frame she had arranged for him. She had intended for him to find her with the body, to move her into his house, so she would have ample opportunity to fabricate even more evidence of his guilt. Of course! And tonight's escapade had been orchestrated well in advance. The two conspirators must have agreed on a time to enter the house, Bianca's clumsy approach drawing Ian's attention away from the intruder upstairs, who would be busy planting evidence. But Ian had foiled their scheme by breaking in on him, and the accomplice had been forced to flee. He must have taken Bianca's papers as a cover, or perhaps they contained some instructions for him. Anatomical drawings indeed! The devious, conniving, murderous slut. But the pair of them would not succeed, Ian swore to himself. They would not outsmart him.

He began to move more quickly, struck by the thought that Bianca might have tried to escape when she saw all her plans unraveling. His blood was boiling with anger and exertion by the time he approached his own rooftop. Fueled by the strength of his emotions, he leapt easily from his neighbor's roof, catching the windowsill of Bianca's laboratory with his hands. He hauled himself into the room, half-expecting to find it empty.

At first it appeared to be. A single candle sat on the table at the center, flickering unevenly as the night breezes entered the room. Bianca's tools were still littered around the floor, all the drawers and chests turned upside down. From the corner of the room Ian heard a sound, a small sound, something like a whimper. There, huddled in a ball and clutching something, was a creature. It took him a moment to identify the weeping mass as the wily criminal he had just been castigating in his thoughts. Bianca looked anything but devious as the tears rolled down her cheeks and over the object in her hands. Given the way he felt about crying women, Ian was tempted to step back out the window until she was done, but then he realized that this was the first time he had seen her shed a tear since she had been with him, and it certainly had not been an easy courtship up to this point. He was momentarily puzzled, wondering what had triggered it, when it occurred to him that it was probably just a ploy for sympathy, to mask her conspirator's flubbed attempt.

"Very tidy, Signorina Salva, trying to get me killed this way. I suppose after the first murder they get easier?" Ian's tone was harsh, his words cutting.

Bianca raised her eyes from the instrument held tightly in her hands, noting Ian's presence for the first time. She heard neither his words nor his tone, her attention riveted by the streams of blood trickling down his cut legs. She moved to stand, to find her bandages among the wreck of her instruments, but felt a firm hand on her shoulder.

"You will stay right there, *carissima*. I'll not have you attack me with this thing." Ian tried to remove the peculiar tool from her hands as he forced her back into the corner. It looked like some sort of strange cutting machine, with one long knife and one short blunt one joined together. But even the shorter blade looked dangerous enough, and Ian was taking no more risks.

Bianca refused to let it go. "No. It's all I have left of him," she said simply.

"This belonged to your accomplice, then? Is it, perhaps, the murder weapon?"

"My accomplice?" Bianca looked confused. "My father, you mean. It was his, a gift from King Henry of France for a special operation. My brother sold all the instruments when Papa died, without even telling me, but he couldn't sell this because Papa left it to me in his will. It is all I have of him. And now it is broken." Bianca shook her head miserably. Ian watched as the tears welled up in her eyes again. This was certainly a very good act, he thought, feeling a pang. Very pitiable. Very convincing.

As he looked down at her, crying and clutching the weird tool, he wondered again if perhaps she could be innocent. Then his gaze shifted to his leg. The blood drying in rivulets from his many cuts brought him to his senses, and his rational mind returned. Women were capable of anything, he reminded himself as warm goo trickled out of a particularly nasty gash on his knee, anything at all.

Bianca's eye followed his gaze to his bloody legs, bringing her back to her rational mind as well. "I am sorry, my lord," she said, shaking the tears from her eyes. "I should have attended to your cuts sooner. If you will just let me stand to find the bandages…"

Ian shook his head. "So you can stab me with that thing of your father's, if it really was his? You'll go nowhere until you give that over to me. Then, we will see."

Reluctantly, Bianca surrendered the instrument to Ian. "Please, my lord, do not give it away. It is the most precious thing I have and I should be very sorry to lose it."

Ian took it from her hand and examined it. It did seem to bear the shield of Henry III, but that was no guarantee that she spoke the truth. He set it down on the table and returned his glare to her.

"Perhaps now that you are done sobbing, you will tell me who your accomplice is? Or at least what he hoped to do here tonight?"

"My accomplice…?" Bianca murmured. "I take it, since you are asking me this question, you did not catch up with him?"

"So you admit that he was your accomplice?"

"No, my lord, I said no such thing. I fear your loss of blood is impairing your hearing. Perhaps if you let me bandage your legs…"

Ian ignored both her sarcasm and her proffered aid. "What is your relationship to him then?"

"I detest him," Bianca answered frankly.

"Aha! So you do know him?"

"That scarcely follows logically, my lord. Loss of blood does not usually affect the powers of reason, but—"

"Cease these lessons on anatomy! Tell me, *carissima*, how you know you despise him if you don't know who he is?" Ian's demand had the tone of a much worn syllogism.

"By Santa Olivia's ring finger, I should say it is obvious. He broke my father's scissors and he stole my drawings. Both are unique, irreplaceable, and infinitely valuable to me."

Ian's eyes raked her face, looking for signs of deception, but found none. It was all so plausible, it would be so easy to believe. But she might be a devious murderer, or at least know someone who was. Someone who, he reminded himself, had first tried to frame him and then had nearly gotten him killed. He forced his mind back to his earlier train of thought.

"If you will not admit this man was your accomplice—" Bianca tried to interject something but Ian continued over her. "If you persist in denying that, perhaps you will explain how you came to be sneaking into the house dressed like a boy." A very shapely boy, Ian now thought to himself, wondering how he had failed to notice it before.

Bianca paused, deciding how much to tell Ian. Her concern for his cuts and preoccupation with the loss of her treasures had made her momentarily forget that she hated him. That and the sight of his naked body in the candlelight earlier that night. But his repeated insistence on her "accomplice" and her evil intent—not to mention the ache in her head where he had bashed her—reminded her, and she decided he deserved to know very little. "I was investigating," she said finally.

"Investigating?" Ian snorted. "Where, some gambling hall? What sorts of investigations require murderesses," he used the word to be deliberately cruel, "to dress like men?"

Bianca ignored his attempt to rile her. "Though you are probably not aware of it, my lord, women's clothing is quite restrictive. It is impossible to row a gondola in female attire, or scale a wall, or even mount a—"

"Because," Ian interrupted, "women are not to do those things. I hardly think, Signorina Salva, that you are in a position to be giving lectures on appropriate dress and deportment."

"Nor are you in much of a position to comment on those subjects," Bianca retorted, looking pointedly at Ian's attire, or lack of it.

This was madness, Ian realized. He was completely nude, standing in a freezing room, surrounded by a pool of his own blood, arguing with a tricky female who used logical arguments to avoid giving him any information. It was so mad that it was funny, and for the third time in as many days the unthinkable happened: Ian laughed. It began as a small chuckle but grew and grew until it was reverberating off the walls of the small laboratory. Head thrown back and eyes closed, Ian let wave after long-repressed wave of laughter roll out of him.

Bianca was first startled, then alarmed, then very alarmed. This was not normal, not for anyone, and especially not for the notoriously mirthless Ian Foscari. Clearly his wounds were more serious than she had realized and he was temporarily out of his sane mind. Slowly she slid up the wall into a standing position, trying not to alarm the hysterical figure in front of her. She watched him in his mad merriment, waiting until he was calm enough to be spoken to.

"My lord," she began tentatively, reaching out a hand toward his arm. "My lord," she tried again, louder. "I really think I ought to tend to your cuts. This behavior is, well, most disturbing."

Ian opened his eyes and looked at her, a chuckle caught in his throat. Who was this creature who had turned his sober, well-ordered, content—not really content, he admitted to himself—but definitely rational life upside down? She truly was most exquisitely beautiful, he thought, remembering the comments of the other Arboretti. He reached out and caught one of the dark gold curls that had sneaked out of her black cap, watching the candlelight play over it. He wanted to bring it to his lips, to tickle them with its silky smoothness. Then he would move his mouth to her delightful ear, flicking lightly with his tongue, whispering words to make her ready for him. His hands would caress that body, the body with the small firm breasts and velvety thighs, the body he had dreamt about, the one he now ached to bury himself inside of.

Why not? Ian asked himself. It was, after all, his privilege as the betrothed. And it was probably the best way to stop having those disturbing dreams about her. He knew from experience that once he had lain with a woman he no longer found her as fascinating. At times this frustrated him, forcing him into a constant search for satisfaction that often took him far from Venice. But at other times, as with that succulent Spanish courtesan the previous year, or with the dangerous but irresistible woman in front of him, it could be handy. He remembered thinking that making love to her would be dangerous, but now it seemed more dangerous not to give in to the pull of her charms. Yes, that was the answer, he realized, surprised that he had not thought of it earlier, the way to restore order to his life and his dreams: he must make love to her. And, if his body had any say in the matter, the sooner the better.

"Come." Ian took Bianca by the arm and led her from the icy room, closing the door behind them.

Bianca was too puzzled to speak, so they walked the long hall-way and descended two flights of stairs in silence. She was sur-prised when, instead of stopping on the floor that contained her apartments, they turned to continue their descent. Could he be making good on his promise to take her to his dungeons? she thought with alarm. She had been a bit impetuous, she admitted to herself, and had sorely tried his patience. Perhaps if she apologized he would give her another chance.

"My lord," she began tentatively, but Ian cut her off, laying a finger on his lips in a sign of silence. Bianca closed her mouth and followed behind him docilely, hoping that by acquiescing now she would minimize whatever tortures awaited her. The black sable cape swung gracefully with every step Ian took, giv-ing her tantalizing glimpses of his sculpted anatomy. If she reached out to touch him, would his body feel more like stone or more like flesh? She felt her foreboding giving way to a growing sense of excitement as they walked down another set of stairs. At last they stopped before an ornately carved mahogany door twice as big as the door leading to her apartments, through which Ian preceded her.

Moonlight streamed in through four tall windows, illuminating a vast sleeping chamber with a russet-silk bed. Without speaking,

Ian gestured Bianca into the middle of the room and turned to light the fire. Although he was making love to this woman out of duty and necessity, there was no reason he had to be so cold he could not enjoy it, Ian reasoned to himself. Besides, he found the way that flames lit up her hair particularly appealing.

When the fire was well lit, Ian reclined on a velvet divan before it, carelessly letting the cape slip to the floor. The fire accentuated the planes of his face, his high cheekbones and strong, firm chin, turning him from a man to the very image of a golden-haired god. He stretched himself to his full length, concealing nothing of his meticulously carved body, and spoke for the first time

"Come here." His voice was husky with arousal and expectation. Bianca stood before him willing herself not to tremble. He motioned her closer, leaning forward only long enough to tug on her tight black jacket and command, "Take this off."

Bianca hesitated for a minute and then began to unlace the jacket with unsteady fingers. She slipped out of it slowly, all the time aware of the moist heat collecting between her legs and of Ian's hooded gray eyes on her. She had never undressed in front of a man before and she found the process surprisingly arousing. Despite the fire, her nipples were visibly erect, two taut nubs pressed against the fine white cambric of her blouse. It was all Ian could do to keep himself from reaching out and taking one between his thumb and forefinger and massaging it slowly through the thin fabric, but he forced himself to wait. He would do this slowly, making her body yield up all its secrets, so it would no longer hold anything to allure him. Instead, he contented himself with picking up the black jacket and throwing it on the fire.

"But, but, that is mine," Bianca spluttered in disbelief as she watched the flames crackle around the garment.

"It is inappropriate for you to wear such things and I suspect the only way to keep you from doing so is to make sure you do not have access to them." Ian tersely dispelled her complaint, much more interested in seeing her without her clothes on. "Now take off your hose."

"As inappropriate as it is for me to wear these clothes," Bianca said, assuming a defiant stance, "certainly it is less appropriate for me to be wandering around your house at night nude. Not to mention how indecorous it would be for me to present myself naked before you, my lord."

"Your concern for propriety is really quite touching, *carissima*," Ian said sarcastically in the impatience of his growing arousal, "but, as usual, sadly misplaced. That doorway," he said, gesturing over his shoulder, "leads to a staircase which links my apartments to yours, so you need not worry about running into anyone, no matter what your state of undress. And I scarcely see how it could be inappropriate for you to bare yourself to me, seeing as you are my betrothed."

For a few moments they were both silent, the only sound in the chamber coming from the fire as it consumed the last scraps of the black jacket. "Are you," Bianca asked finally, her voice quivering, her heart beating so hard she thought it might burst from her breast, "are you going to make love to me?"

The simplistic naïveté of her question, her tone of fear mingled with longing, stirred something unnameable within him. For the second time that night, Ian doubted her guilt. Could she indeed be innocent, not only of murder, but also of *this*? Was she really the mere slip of a girl that she appeared, young and alone in the world? Ian studied her form caressed by the firelight behind her, looking for answers in her lean curves and smooth skin, until his body, more aroused with each passing minute, demanded his attention and pushed such unsettling thoughts from his mind. "I believe I asked you to remove your hose," he reminded her finally in a low voice.

As she struggled with the elaborate laces of her leggings, Ian imagined cupping her behind, smooth and warm from its proximity to the fire, in his large hands as he pushed himself into her. He found his breathing almost as uneven as hers, his own heart beating almost as expectantly. Once free of the lacings, Bianca slipped the hose down over her thighs and stepped out of them. When Ian bent to push them into the fire, he caught the first delicious scent of her arousal and he knew his restraint was nearing the breaking point.

Ian's arm brushed her thigh as he sat back, sending a wave of the most delicious sensations through Bianca's body. The thin, almost transparent shirt she wore just covered the mass of golden-brown curls below her stomach. Without waiting for Ian's order, she pulled it over her head, threw it on the fire, and stood completely naked in front of him.

Ian found himself awed by the beauty of the woman before him, more alluring than anything he had dreamt of. He could never have thought up the small clover-shaped birthmark on her stomach, a hand's width above her left thigh, or the tender curve between her small breasts, just large enough to rest his head in. The light from the fire turned her hair to molten gold as it fell in waves over her breasts, making her glow with an inner radiance like some alchemist's healing elixir.

Bianca stood silently, not moving, as his eyes caressed her body, scarcely able to breathe much less to speak. Her dream was about to come true, the moment she had been waiting for was about to take place. She was about to be initiated into the mysteries of lovemaking. She had expected to feel scared and a little excited, but nothing could have prepared her for the entire loss of her senses that she seemed to be experiencing. The thought of pressing her cheek against the downy hair on his chest, of his muscled thighs wrapped around her, of those hands skimming her body, overwhelmed her. Her skin was tingling, her throat dry, her heart beating so hard she was sure Ian could hear it. But most surprising and wonderful of all was the novel heat that spiraled out from between her legs through every inch of her body.

Ian reached out, finally, and pulled her onto his lap. She caught her breath as her thigh brushed against his aroused shaft, and again when his hand gently rubbed the underside of her breast. She lifted her face to his, and their eyes met and locked. What she read there during that split second filled Bianca with the longing to take Ian not only into her body, but into her soul. Then he pulled her head down, covering his lips with hers.

As their mouths touched Ian felt a spark leap inside of him, and her kiss seared through him in a way he had never before experienced. This was something more than mere passion, this burning sensation that threatened to take over his body. In a flash he knew that this woman of molten gold emanated a heat that could melt every reserve, every barrier, every layer of self-protection he had spent the past two years creating. She had already begun to turn his world topsy-turvy, why not let her continue? All he had to do was to drink her in, open himself to her, let her work her medicinal magic on him. He would feel again, laugh again, love again...and hurt again.

In a single abrupt motion Ian pulled his mouth away from hers and pushed her off of him onto the floor. "Go! Now." He spoke with his head turned from her and his voice shaking with emotions he could not recognize. Stunned, less from the impact of her fall than from his horrible rejection of her, it took a moment for Bianca to react. "Go, leave me. *Get out!*" he repeated, more stridently this time, as he felt her reluctance to leave. He sensed she was about to speak, but he cut her off. "If you do not leave now, without a word, I shall have you arrested tomorrow."

Trembling with embarrassment and rage, Bianca ran toward the door Ian had pointed out earlier. She paused with her hand on the doorknob and looked back at the figure reclined before the fire, his eyes squeezed shut, his jaw squared. Caught in the web of her own tortured feelings, she was oblivious to the pain emanating from him as she glared in his direction. "I hate you," she said under her breath, just loud enough for Ian to hear, as she pulled the door closed.

He remained motionless for a moment after the lock clicked into place, then spoke aloud to the empty room. "You are not the only one."

Chapter Eight

Bianca lay on her back in the middle of the deep-blue-velvet bed, glaring at the ceiling above her. More accurately, she was glaring *through* the ceiling, aiming her anger at the degrading man who had so cruelly rejected her a short while before. The bump on her head was still tender and painful, but it was nothing compared to the ache inside of her. She hugged her knees close to her chest, trying to erase the feel of his body from her breast, her thigh, her lips. A wave of embarrassed nausea washed over her as she remembered the way she had exposed herself to him, asking him to make love to her. She had been a fool to think she was anything but repulsive to him, and he had made sure she realized it. Embarrassment gave way to anger as, recalling the obvious signs of his excitement, she reasoned that he was aroused by manipulating her. He had never had any intention of making love to her; he simply wanted to toy with her, to mock her in her inexperience.

Only the intermittent chiming of the clocks and the feeble rays of light filtering in through the heavy curtains of the chamber alerted her to the passage of time. She sighed and uncoiled her body, realizing she should probably rise and dress, but found herself completely without energy to do anything. Perhaps if she stayed in bed, hid herself all day or all month or all year, perhaps the horrible emptiness and loneliness that had wrapped itself around her emotions would recede. She could leave this place, run away and live on her own forever.

But there was no running away, she reminded herself. Her leaving, if she could leave, would only be taken as a sure sign of her guilt by Ian. She refused to give him the pleasure of thinking he was right. She had to stay and vindicate herself. Then, when it was all over and Isabella's killer had been punished, then she could run away. But for now she had a crime to solve.

She tried to focus her mind on the findings, or rather lack of findings, from her previous night's investigations. Isabella's apartment had been completely devoid of clues, curiously so, unless someone else had gone through it before her. She had been convinced that the murderer must have left some scrap of evidence behind, but she had found absolutely nothing. Even more than that, she had sensed that something was missing from the room, something that she half remembered from the day she found the body, but she could not recall what it was.

With her eyes closed, Bianca pictured the room as it had been when she first walked in. The far wall was taken up by a row of gothic windows, under which was a carved oak marriage chest. The bed with its elaborate hangings protruded from the right-hand wall, facing a bureau with a mirror over it. Bianca recalled that the mirror was curiously angled and wondered how anyone at the bureau could see into it, until it occurred to her that it was positioned to be seen from the bed. The thought made her blush and think of how wonderful it would be to both feel and see Ian's sleek body on top of her at the same time.

"Santa Flora's canine tooth, I have taken leave of my senses! This man is driving me mad."

"It is funny, my dear Signorina Salva, but it seems you have the same effect on him." The kindly voice from the doorway was unexpected but not unfamiliar. As Francesco and Roberto entered the room, Bianca sat up, glad that she had remembered to don a bedgown the night before.

"Ian is in one of his moods again this morning, storming around the house ordering that the staff be beheaded one minute, staring quietly at a mote of dust the next. I haven't seen him like this for years..." Francesco's voice trailed off.

"Two years," added Roberto quietly.

"Did he send you to make sure I hadn't escaped or did you need something from me?" As soon as the words were out of her mouth, she regretted them, especially their tone. Francesco and Roberto had been all kindness to her and certainly deserved better than her petulant whining. "I mean, is there some service I might perform for you?" she rephrased, hoping she sounded more genteel.

"Yes and no. We were trying to perform a service for you, but we found ourselves in disagreement about how to please you. Yesterday you asked for a 'nimble young boy'—those were the words, were they not, Roberto?" Francesco paused just long enough for Roberto, busy opening the window curtains, to turn and nod in agreement. "Roberto was convinced that you wanted this creature to run errands for you and the like, but Ian has teams of people on hand to do that, so I assumed you wanted someone for other, let us say, more companionable purposes. Certainly understandable, given the way Ian behaves."

Bianca's eyes grew wide as her confusion gave way to comprehension and she grasped the meaning of Francesco's words. Before she could offer an explanation, Roberto intervened.

"Not being in a position to decide, we brought you one of each." As he spoke he opened a small door at the far end of the room that Bianca had yet to notice. How many secrets did this massive house have? she asked herself, as two young men entered her room.

They were about as unlike as any two beings could be. One was probably near Bianca's age, tall, muscular, and very handsome. Bianca's eyes traveled up the length of his taut body, trying to decide whether his clothes would be a viable substitute for those she had lost the night before. His swagger as he strode toward her and the leering glance he shot in her direction when he bowed suggested that he had mistaken Bianca's appraisal of his clothes for interest in what lay beneath them. "Madam, I wait upon your pleasure," he said, laying extreme emphasis on the final word.

In the wake of his openly seductive invitation, there was no good way to ask him to shed his clothes, Bianca realized. It was a pity because she was quite intrigued by his hose, of a design she had never seen before, using small clasps rather than laces at the waist. She allowed her eye to linger wistfully on them for a few moments and was only brought back to herself when Francesco cleared his throat directly in her ear.

"You appear, *ahem*, well satisfied with this youth. Shall I send the other candidate away?"

Bianca suddenly realized how her sartorial examination must have appeared, and blushed furiously. "No, actually I have no interest in this fellow, he is too mature for my pleasure." Francesco's eyebrows rose, and Bianca blushed even more heatedly at her poor choice of words. "Lucia's eyes, what I mean to say is, I was in fact looking for an errand boy, not a..."

Her voice trailed off as she turned to focus on the second candidate. He could have been no more than thirteen, with a mop of curly brown hair hanging over two serious hazel eyes. While Francesco ushered the first young man from the room, the young boy stood apart studying Bianca intently. A flash of recognition crossed his face, and he moved swiftly toward the bed talking as quickly as he walked.

"I know who you are. You're the doctor lady who fixed my aunt Marina. She was sick and everyone said she would die and that it was God's judgment and then you came and made her better. 'By Santa Agata's breast,' you said when you first saw her."

It certainly sounded like something she would say, but beyond that his words stirred nothing in her memory. Bianca scowled at the child, trying to remember even the vaguest hint of the episode he described so vividly. Seeing her confusion, he added, "It was when Sebastiano Venier was still ruling Venice as the Doge. I would have recognized you sooner, but you were not so old then."

"Neither were you," Bianca retaliated warmly, before reminding herself that if she had to look older, she should also act it. She was trying again to place the boy, searching her memory for the dates of Venier's dogeship, when the thought struck her. "Sebastiano Venier has been dead for more than six years! How can you possibly remember that far back?"

"I remember everything," the boy said quietly. "I just need to see or hear something and then it is stuck in my head."

"Everything? Really every thing you see or hear?" Excitement mingled with incredulity in Bianca's tone.

The boy appeared almost hurt by her doubt. "We walked up exactly sixty-two steps to get here, plus one hundred forty paces that were not steps. There were thirty-two lamps lighting the way, and five dusty paintings, all of women. We passed through eight doors, six of them with locks, including the door to your room, which we had to open with a key. They key was brass and had four grooves, three on one side and one on the other. The first words I heard you say were: 'Santa Flora's canine tooth, I have taken leave of my senses! This man is driving me mad.' Then this man said," he paused to gesture toward Francesco, "'It is funny, my dear Signorina Salva, but it seems you have the same effect on him.' Should I keep going?"

Bianca, Roberto, and Francesco gaped at him, all momentarily at a loss for words. The child, accustomed to such reactions, was relaxed under their astonished gazes. Bianca was the first to recover.

"That was magnificent. What is his name?" She looked first at her chaperons and then again at the little wizard.

"May I present Master Nilo, Signorina Salva?" Roberto shed his reverie to make a proper introduction as the boy bowed solemnly. "He lives with his aunt at the arsenal, but she has agreed to put him at your service for a small fee. Hearing word of his remarkable talents, we thought he might be useful for your investigation."

"Yes, he will be quite an asset." Bianca was wondering how much Francesco and Roberto knew about her investigation when Roberto's words triggered something in her memory. Of course! Six years ago she had spent the bulk of her infrequent trips from Padua to Venice ministering to the needs of the poor prostitutes the city kept in dormitories for the shipbuilders at the arsenal. The idea was that if there were women easily available nearby, the shipbuilders would never need to skip work to have their libidinous needs met and Venice could continue to boast of producing an entire warship every day. An efficient system, Bianca thought wryly, and one clearly designed by men. She remembered how stunned she had been by the conditions in which the women and their families lived, and by the stories they told about lying with ten or fifteen men in one day. To her that seemed a feat comparable to the construction of a warship, but it was not one the city chose to brag about. Undoubtedly Nilo's aunt was one of these hardworking, miserable women. She looked at the boy and wondered whether his fine memory was a blessing or a curse for one who had grown up in such a place.

Before she could be too deeply occupied with such thoughts, a clock began to strike the hour, and then another, and then another. Their harmonious if noisy marking of the passage of time reminded Bianca of the immense task before her. One hundred and forty-six hours left, she calculated, rising from the bed.

"Thank you both very much for finding me such a treasure." Her smile moved from Roberto and Francesco to Nilo, who looked quite pleased at being described that way. "Indeed, I find I have a job ready for him right now. If you gentlemen will kindly excuse us...?"

Congratulating themselves on a job well done, Francesco and Roberto were in search of a celebratory libation when a uniformed servant rushed over to them with an urgent summons from Ian. Ordering the man to follow shortly with a bottle of prosecco, they made their way downstairs to Ian's library. One wall of the room was almost entirely glass, and overlooked the courtyard of the palazzo, while the remaining three walls were crowded with volumes in fine leather bindings, save for the space occupied by an immense marble fireplace. The ancient Persian rug given to Doge

Foscari a hundred years earlier still covered the floor, now supplemented by a thick sheepskin, removed from one of Crispin's English flock, placed in front of the fireplace. Unlike the libraries of many of Ian's wealthy contemporaries, both the room and the books it contained were often visited by its owner, who used it as an office and a sanctuary.

Roberto and Francesco found the stormy head of the household seated at his ivory-and-walnut desk, glowering at something near the windows.

"We were just about to toast... My heavens, whatever is that?" Francesco exclaimed, noticing the strangely twisted plants arrayed before the glass for the first time.

"Crispin's newest acquisition. An amazing find, some rare species of flowering plant brought from the Mongol Empire, or so he told me. To me they look like dead sticks from my villa at the lake, but we know how bad I am with living organisms." Ian's rancorous tone told his uncles that his mood had not lightened since the morning.

He turned his glower from the Mongolian rarities to his beaming uncles. "I have been searching the length and width of this whole bloody palace looking for you two this morning. Where have you been?"

"We had an errand to do for your charming betrothed."

Ian snorted. "Charming. Like one of Satan's minions. You think she is saintly like those women she always swears by, but I tell you that girl is most likely a murderess, or at least some kind of criminal."

"So you say," Roberto spoke quietly, "but we know how bad you are with living organisms."

Roberto's quiet and unexpected remonstrance earned him an extra glare from Ian.

"Your judgment about women is not exactly above reproach," Francesco added, coming to his partner's aid and sending Ian into a fit of muttering.

"Just wait, you will see my maligned judgment vindicated. You think you know her better than I do? What about this?? Look what she tried to use on me!" Ian pushed the strange instrument he had liberated from Bianca the previous night across the desk toward his uncles.

"Surely not." Roberto shook his head vehemently. "No, certainly, you must be mistaken. She would never use this as a weapon. For one thing, it is broken. For another, it must be her prize possession. It was given to her father by King Henry the Third when he passed through Venice, and it's all she has left of her father's tools. That's correct, isn't it, Francesco?"

"Oh yes, the rest were auctioned off by her brother. There's a bad one for you, that brother of hers. If you are looking for someone with the Salva surname to suspect of murder, I suggest you try him." Francesco picked up the scissors and eyed them wistfully. "I would say this is the only tool not accounted for in the inventory. It's a lovely piece, but it is a pity that it is broken. How did that happen?"

Ian goggled at his uncles. Surely they could not have been so quickly swayed to Bianca's side that she could persuade them to tell a lie of that complexity.

"So she told you that story too, and you believed it?" Seeing Roberto again shake his head, Ian challenged, "How else could you know all this?"

Roberto spoke slowly, hoping his measured tone would help penetrate Ian's thick skull. "We learned the story when we were lucky enough to be the highest bidders for her father's instruments, shortly after his death."

"And the scissors are quite famous. They were left to her in her father's will, so they could not be sold with the rest of the lot, although they would have fetched far more than all the other tools combined. Look at this workmanship." Francesco extended them for Ian's admiration but he just pushed them aside. "You didn't say how they got broken...?"

"Ask her." Ian stood and strutted toward the window, taking care not to knock over Crispin's precious specimens. He needed to be alone, to think about what he had just learned, not to mention the failure of his plan. That his betrothal was not having the desired effect was clear, and became even clearer when his uncle resumed speaking. Francesco's voice seemed to be coming to him from a thousand leagues away.

"About the betrothal party, Ian. We were hoping you would talk to the Council about having the sumptuary laws lifted for the occasion. It is only right that Bianca wear the Foscari topaz, and you know it is valued at far more than the measly thousand ducats prescribed by the laws as appropriate for a bride-to-be. Roberto has already seen about the fabric for her dress, and the jewels will be just marvelous, if only—"

"Yes, fine, I will see it is done. " Ian responded with his back to them, restraining himself to sound civil.

"Wonderful, wonderful." Francesco plowed ahead enthusiastically. "In that case, we were thinking that we could send to your place in the mountains for one of those delectable wild boar—"

"Don't forget about the special musical piece we were thinking of," Roberto reminded him.

"I was getting to that, but first the peacocks for the garden. We were planning to cover them in gold leaf, just the tails of course—"

Ian's patience had reached its limit. "Do whatever you want, spend whatever extravagant sum you need, invite whomever you please, I do not care. I doubt whether I will even be there." He hoped his tone was brusque enough to remind them there was a door available for their use. It appeared to do the trick, for instead of argument Ian's ears were greeted with the blissful sound of that apparatus shutting firmly behind them.

His first thought as he stared into the gray day was that Bianca had spoken the truth. Everything from her father's tools to the gift of old King Henry seemed to be corroborated. But that did not mean that everything she said was the truth. There were still too many unanswered questions and too many unresolved coincidences. Why had she been at the scene of the crime in the first place and why wouldn't she tell him? Where had she gone last evening? Who was the intruder?

He tried to make himself recall the events of the previous night, from hearing the intruder to his mad dash across the slick rooftops of the city, but his mind kept returning to what had happened after. Bianca's naked body, warmed by the heat of the fire, filled his memory. He could see her and feel her and smell her again. He heard her voice, her unnameable but alluring tone, as she asked him if he was going to make love to her. *Yes,* he hungered to tell her, *yes, yes, yes.* His senses began to tingle and his body to grow hard, and he found himself wondering if perhaps he shouldn't seek her out.

"Fool, idiot, madman!" he spoke aloud to himself, halting just in time, before he managed to open the door. What was happening to his mind? What had she done to him? Francesco had called her charming, and indeed she was, like some ancient sorceress bewitching men to their ruin. It wasn't that conniving, seductive Salva scamp he needed, he told himself, it was a woman. Any woman. The sooner the better. That day. That hour if possible. Moving with a new sense of resolve, Ian stomped out of the library and began barking orders for his gondola to be made ready.

Bianca was staring out the empty hole where the window of her laboratory used to be when she heard the noise. It was so faint she thought she had imagined it, but as it grew louder and more insistent she realized that it was coming from the wall to her right. Just as she was about to step toward it, the whole wall moved in her direction with enough grinding and squeaking of hinges to raise the dead.

A hand appeared around the side.

Then a foot.

And then a handsome blond head.

"Oh, good, I was hoping to catch you in here." Crispin greeted Bianca jovially, as if his entrance had been anything but extraordinary.

Bianca tried to match his nonchalance, shoving her trembling hands under her arms. "Do all the walls in the house do that?"

"Not *all* of them, no. But many of them do have trick doors and secret passages. This house has more secret compartments and hallways than the entire Doge's Palace. It seems that when the house was built our ancestors were involved in something shady that required quick escapes and inviolable hiding places. They must have been a more interesting bunch than the lot of us who lives here now." He crossed to the glassless window and looked out, then turned to regard her. "Of course, you've livened things up a bit with your presence."

"I'm sorry, Your Lordship. I realize that I have caused nothing but inconvenience for everyone since I arrived. I will, of course, pay for the new window and..."

Crispin cut her off mid-sentence. "On the contrary, it has been a pleasure to have you here. It does my heart good to see Ian so animated."

"Animated? I would describe him as raving. How do you stand it?"

"I would rather see him acting alive like a rabid dog than doing that walking-corpse imitation he has spent the past several years perfecting."

"Two years?" Bianca asked quietly.

The gaze he turned on her was questioning. "Yes, *ah*, something like that." He did not know how much his brother's betrothed knew about the incidents of 1583, but he was certain he did not want to be the one to disclose them. If Ian wanted to keep his secrets, who was he to intervene? And if he did not, it was his own responsibility to disclose them. Besides, Crispin admitted to himself, he wasn't sure he even knew what had happened all those years ago in that hot desert. His mind raced for another subject to introduce.

"It is not terribly warm in here." *The weather?* Even to his own ears it sounded pathetic and he wanted to cringe at his lack of wit.

Bianca recognized his feeble evasion for what it was and acquiesced, trying to suppress an untimely chuckle. "Yes, it follows that without the window..." She gestured toward the empty space, through which a light drizzle of rain was now entering. After a pause, she thought of her own conversational sally. If she was not going to unearth Ian's secrets, she could at least learn those of his house. "Tell me, where does that door go?"

This time Crispin answered with enthusiasm. "To my potting room. Would you like to see it? It's not much to look at, but I would be honored if you are interested. I know it's very rude, but I fear I must walk ahead of you."

She followed him around the back of the wall-door, through a short narrow passage that led to another, more door-sized door. The first thing to impress her when she stepped through it was not the room's large size or its tidy organization, but its overpowering stench. Indeed, standing in the dark as they were, the only senses available to her were smell and touch, and the odors assailing the first erased any urges she had to exercise the second.

"It takes a while to get used to," Crispin was fiddling with something as he spoke, "but within a few minutes you will hardly notice the smell."

A few minutes? The prospect made Bianca even more queasy than the odor alone. But before she could protest, Crispin had lit a lamp and was holding it above them to illuminate the room. Again, though it was both large and tidy, these were not the characteristics that most struck Bianca. She was fascinated by the expression she now saw on Crispin's face. His features, similar to Ian's but softer somehow, were suffused with a look of such pride in his odoriferous workshop that she was swept up in his enthusiasm.

"I am experimenting with different types of soil and nourishment for my plants," he explained, gesturing toward the large containers of sinister-looking goop that lined the walls. He launched into a detailed explanation of the merits of vegetal versus mineral matter and had just begun a defense of his latest mixture when a man covered in dirt entered through a side door. Without giving them another look, he began assiduously scooping something from a vat near where they stood,

"That is Luca," Crispin whispered to Bianca. "He pretends to be my employee, but I think I take more orders from him than he does from me. He hates it when I bring visitors up here, especially women, because he is afraid they will distract my attention from the plants." He turned to address the dirty man. "Luca, you need not worry. She is not interested in me in the slightest, *peccato*. This is Ian's new betrothed. You should meet her. You might like her."

Luca looked Bianca up and down pointedly. "Woman," he said, nodding, as if having had a nasty suspicion confirmed, and turned to leave.

"Don't take it personally. It is not you he is objecting to…"

Bianca waved his explanation aside. "I have noticed a decided lack of enthusiasm for women in this household." She had been grateful that, despite her fortune, she had grown up dressing and grooming herself when it became obvious that there were no lady's maids on the household staff. She wondered if there were any other women in the household at all. "Are all the employees male too?"

Crispin nodded. "It has not always been this way but, well, for the past several—"

"Two," volunteered Bianca generously.

"—years," Crispin continued with consternation, "there have been no women living under this roof."

There was an uncomfortable silence, until with wide-eyed innocence Bianca observed, "It is not terribly warm in here, my lord." Her lips bore the hint of a smile as she continued, "If it will not upset Master Luca too much, I would love to see your plants. Your collection is quite famous, you know."

Bianca's joking raillery and her polite flattery brought Crispin's good humor back in a flash. He took her arm and ushered her toward the side door through which the dirty figure had disappeared. They passed from the potting shed into a room flooded with light.

Bianca felt herself afloat in a sea of brilliant color. She was surrounded on all sides by benches filled with flowering plants of every hue and shape and size imaginable.

"Santa Helena's jaws, this is tremendous! There must be a thousand plants in here!"

Behind Bianca, Luca grunted to show what he thought of her estimate.

"Five thousand," Crispin corrected, shooting his employee a warning glance. "From all over the world. But this is only the first room. There is also the herb room, an orchard, and a room for seedlings and experiments."

Bianca considered the space she was standing in and realized she had never seen anything like it. The room was larger than her laboratory and, except where it attached to the wall of the palace, was made entirely of glass fastened together by wooden boards. Despite the gray day outside, it was warm and filled with light.

"It was Ian's idea to make a glass room," Crispin began when he noticed her interest in the design. "Something like this would not even be thinkable for my estate in England, because glass is so hard to get there. But since Venice has its own glass makers, it was easy here and it allows me to grow plants that otherwise could not exist in this climate."

Luca gave another grunt and Crispin added with good humor, "I mean, it allows Luca to grow plants. I am only a dilettante."

"Not but that you have a good touch, that I'll grant you, *ragazzo mio*." Luca's voice was gruff, but his tone was affectionate. He turned his dirt-smeared face to Bianca. "This boy could make flowers sprout from the hindquarters of a dead partridge, be damned if he can't."

Bianca's mind was so taken up with trying to picture this remarkable exercise that she completely overlooked the impropriety of the image. Crispin, on the other hand, blushed furiously.

He spoke quietly through clenched teeth. "Enough, Luca. I told you she is not interested in me. There is no reason to scare her off."

"Who is trying to scare the hussy off? Not but that I spoke the truth, be damned if I didn't."

The laughter that burst from Bianca startled the two men. "I am sure you did no more than justice to His Lordship's talents, Signore Luca."

"You've got reason, mistress, and I wouldn't have thought it, what with marrying His Other Lordship. That one's a crazy one, I tell you. I was giving the plants their last watering of the evening late last night, when I saw him skedaddling naked across the rooftops, be damned if he wasn't. Now, you ask me, is that how a sane man spends his time? and I tell you, no, s'blood, 'tisn't."

Crispin, clearly incredulous, was about to say something, but Bianca spoke first. "Did you see anyone else on the rooftops last night?"

"You mean that other bloke, with the cape. But he wasn't dashing about all naked for Widow Falentini to see, and Lord knows that woman's heart isn't any too good and doesn't need the sight of naked men to send her on over to the other side."

"I am sure you are right," Bianca's voice was strident, "but did you see the other fellow? Anything about him?"

"And I'm telling you, no, I did not, because he was wearing proper clothes. All I saw was black, black, black and then here comes Ian, naked like the day he was born. I remember that day too. He's a darned sight better looking now than he was as a babe, damned if he isn't. Now *ragazzo mio* here, he was a fine-looking child, sunny and cheerful from that first day—"

Luca's narrative would have been briskly interrupted by Crispin if he had not been preempted by a loud banging at the door at the far end of the room.

"Is Signorina Salva in there?" a voice shouted through the door as Crispin went to open it. "Ah, there you are, mistress; I have run over the entire house looking for you!" Nilo was impervious to the fantastic show of color and form around him as he nimbly navigated the rows of flowers. "You must leave word for me of where you are going! This house is so big, and should anything important come up, as it has, how will I know where to find you?"

Crispin and Luca contemplated the small, chastising figure with surprise, but Bianca was so eager to hear his message that she did not notice his importunate behavior. "What has happened? What is urgent? Was your trip successful then?"

"She says if you come at once, she thinks she has something that might interest you. But you must come at once. She is a very busy lady." Nilo took Bianca's hand to underscore the urgency of their departure.

"Thank you both for your courtesy," she managed to say over her shoulder as Nilo dragged her toward the exit of the glass house. "It was a pleasure to meet you, Signore Luca and to speak with you, Your Lordship. I hope one day to see the rest of your fine collection."

The door closed on her last words and the two men were left alone in the greenhouse.

"Women," Luca muttered, shaking his head. "Come around, asking questions, acting all interested-like, making nice. And then someone younger comes along and they leave you, just like that, worse than they found you, damned if they don't."

Chapter Nine

"Do you think the rouge on the nipples is too much?" Tullia cast an appraising eye over her voluptuous anatomy in the mirror and then lifted her gaze to meet Bianca's, standing behind her.

"You know well, Tullia, that I am the last person you should solicit for advice about how to please men. You had better ask Daphne." Bianca tried to make her tone light but Tullia did not miss the hint of melancholy in it. Tullia was the first courtesan Bianca had gone to for assistance with her research, and the two women had developed a strange sort of friendship. As the reigning queen of the Venetian courtesans, Tullia d'Aragona was generally regarded more with envy than with affection by others of her profession and was therefore hard pressed to call any of the women she knew friends. While other courtesans would pretend to a genuine interest in her affairs, she knew from experience that they were more likely to respond to her troubles with jubilation than compassion. In Bianca she had found, for the first time in many years, a true friend, and she was disturbed to see her looking so distraught.

"So you still have not succeeded in ridding yourself of your persistent virginity. I know plenty who would sacrifice their real teeth for the privilege of seducing you." She turned away from the mirror and toward Bianca, one of her famously captivating smiles on her lips. "I would. But you refuse to have me."

In typical fashion, Bianca laughed the offer off, knowing that anyone as magnificent as Tullia d'Aragona wanted no traffic with an unadorned virgin like herself. While Tullia's status at the top of her profession had been earned by hard work and her razor-sharp mind, her breathtaking beauty and sinfully voluptuous body had certainly helped. Bianca watched, fascinated, as Tullia's Greek maid, Daphne, prepared her mistress for her next client. Dressed in a gossamer-thin gown, Daphne was only a shade less beautiful and more clothed than her mistress. Bianca admired and envied the two stunning women, who loved and used their bodies, who knew how to give pleasure and how to take it. Watching them together was like being a privileged spectator at a sensual ballet.

Even as she prepared her mistress's toilette, it was obvious that Daphne's companionship with Tullia went far beyond that of a mere chambermaid. Daphne carefully teased Tullia's nipples to a point, gently rubbing each between her fingers so as not to disturb the rouge. She then used the tail of a wild rabbit to dust them with a powder of finely crushed diamonds, letting the puff caress the length of the courtesan's torso. The powder caught the light from the elaborate pink glass chandelier at the center of the ceiling, making Tullia's body glimmer alluringly as she reclined on a Chianti-colored chaise.

Although she always felt horribly ill-shaped there, Bianca loved the overwhelmingly luxurious and sensual environment of Tullia's house. Covered in rich silk, thick velvet, or the softest furs, every surface invited intimate exchange. The walls throughout were lightly gilded, each with a strategically placed mirror that diffused the soft light from the chandelier and gave the whole space a warm, sensual, ethereal glow. But Bianca's favorite part was the heady scent that emanated from the body of the courtesan to fill every corner of the well-appointed rooms. She watched with rapt attention as Daphne brought over four ornately wrought glass flasks, presenting them to Tullia for her selection.

"Gardenia today. It is his favorite, I think, though it has been such a long time I can hardly remember."

Daphne went to work, applying measured drops from the flask to the hollow of Tullia's neck, the deep curve between her breasts, the soft flesh along the inside of her thighs. She ended by tracing the outline of the triangle of red-gold curls at the apex of Tullia's thighs, pausing to carefully arrange them with a small mother-of-pearl comb.

"What would I do without you?" Tullia kissed the girl's fingertips appreciatively. "Now Bianca and I have serious matters to attend to. Bring me the lace dressing gown and the pearls Rono gave me, and off with you!"

When Daphne had assisted Tullia into a wrapper of the finest lace Bianca had ever seen, tucked a few stray hairs into her elaborate coif that would undoubtedly be tumbling down in one-eighth the time it had taken to erect, clasped a double strand of pearls around her throat and threaded two large pearl drops through her ears, she left them, closing the door softly.

Tullia resettled on the silk chaise and finally turned to the matter that had brought Bianca to her.

"Your boy said you were worried about Isabella's disappearance and you wondered if I knew anything about it. I won't ask you what has triggered your interest in Isabella," Tullia said, "but if you wanted to tell me, I must admit I am dying to know. Was it an *affaire de coeur?*"

"Why does everyone think that?" Bianca was exasperated.

"Everyone?" Tullia cocked her head to one side and studied Bianca closely.

Bianca brushed the second question aside. "No, I was neither having an affair nor was I in love with Isabella. I am just worried about her welfare."

"Good, then I need not be jealous. And you need not be worried. From what Isabella told me two weeks ago, her welfare is being well looked after. She is going to be married."

"Married?" That explained why Isabella had asked her to write out a love sonnet at their last meeting, Bianca mused, but it still seemed odd. "Are you sure? Married?"

"Yes. I, too, found the prospect sufficiently unlikely to express a doubt, but she was adamant. When I mentioned the alarming disproportion between the number of marriage proposals courtesans get and the number of married courtesans, she said something like, 'I've got a charm he just cannot free himself from.' You know how intolerably conceited she is about her charms." Tullia shrugged one polished shoulder. "I suppose she had a right to it, given how quickly she managed to snare a wealthy protector to set her up in her own house. Valdo Valdone has always had a soft spot for the charms of youth."

"Was," Bianca quickly corrected herself, "is he the man she is to marry?"

Tullia laughed aloud. "Decidedly not. Isabella's fiancé, if we are to take her at her word, is a young patrician from an old family with fine prospects. She fished a piece of his hair out of a locket she was wearing, and it was certainly not the gray, wiry substance that still covers a small part of Valdo's pate. Indeed, I suspect this is why she has gone away, to avoid a confrontation between her old paramour and her new. If Valdo were to find out that she was planning to marry, no doubt he would cut her off without a ducat or challenge the fiancé to a duel. Or quite possibly both. In either event, it would provide fodder for the gossip mills, not at all the way one would want to begin life as a patrician wife."

Bianca's mind was filled with questions, but she knew asking too many would arouse Tullia's suspicions. She finally selected one as the most important. "Did she happen to tell you the name of her bridegroom?"

"Surely, *bellissima*, you know Isabella better than that. The woman who was too vain and petty to have even a single female as a maid for fear her lovers' eyes would stray? No, she would rather have given up those glossy eyelashes of hers than reveal his name to the grasping likes of me."

Bianca could only laugh at Tullia's inapt description of herself, although the information that accompanied it did leave her in a bit of a tight spot. The identity of Isabella's fiancé could at least give Bianca a place to start her inquiry. She decided, at the risk of seeming overcurious, to pursue it one more time. "Have you any idea who it could be?"

"Given the color of the hair in the locket—blond bordering on a light brown—no more than one half of the patriciate, I would say. Eliminating those who are neither young nor promising, that leaves roughly three hundred possible candidates. That's assuming she spoke the truth about his prospects. Elsewise we shall have to include all those without promising prospects, and that at least doubles the total." Tullia saw the color die in Bianca's face and decided to be more serious. "But there are probably only ten or so who see Isabella regularly, not counting her protector. Off the top of my head I can think of Sergio Franceschino, Lodivico Terreno, Brunaldo Bartolini, Giulio Cresci, your cousin Angelo and your brother, Giovanni. Oh, and of course, the feathers in Isabella's cap, two of the Arboretti, Tristan del Moro and Crispin Foscari."

Without thinking, Bianca blurted, "What about Crispin's brother, Ian?"

Tullia laughed again and fluttered a hand. "It is funny you should ask about him. No, Isabella is not his type at all. She is too vivacious and, well, too insipid for the intellectual and brooding Conte d'Aosto. Her childlike naïveté and innocence, considered her chief assets by most of her lovers, would grate on his nerves like an out-of-tune viola. His tastes run to the more mature, like me. Indeed, I am expecting him any moment."

Bianca gaped at her friend, realized what she was doing, and tried to close her mouth. Swallowing deeply, she willed her heart to go back to its proper place instead of trying to crawl out her throat. She thought back to the pleasure with which she had watched Tullia's preparations for her client and felt the nausea of the morning return with reinforcements. Her sole desire was flight.

"I see. Oh, my, then I really must not keep you." She extended a hand, relieved to see it was not trembling. "Thank you for giving me so much of your time. You have been most helpful, Tullia, and it was a pleasure as always to see you."

Tullia, busy arranging the folds of her dressing gown so they seemed to reveal more than they concealed, did not notice Bianca's agitation. "If there is anything more I can do for you, *bellissima*, please rush over or send for me. You know I always wait on your pleasure." She took Bianca's extended hand and gave her a feathery kiss on the palm.

Bianca had not quite reached the door when it opened of its own accord to admit Daphne. "His Lordship is here, madam. Shall I send him up?"

Tullia nodded and then frowned at Bianca. "Your reputation will not benefit in the least from encountering a nobleman on the stairs of this house, my dear. No, that would be a travesty." Bianca, stunned into immobility, could not have agreed more.

"That armoire," Tullia spoke rapidly as she gestured toward a large, glass-fronted piece of furniture in a corner, "is the door to a passage that leads directly to the canal. But if you are not in a hurry, you may stay and watch, in secret, from behind its glass panels. I had them specially made for a client of mine with rather unusual tastes, and now I find that I work better when I know someone is watching. Especially someone as delicious as you are, *bellissima*."

Their conference was cut short by the sound of footsteps in the hall. Bianca quickly concealed herself in the armoire, closing its door at the precise moment the door to the room opened. She ordered herself to turn and leave, but could not bring herself to turn away from the scene being played out before her eyes. She watched as Ian approached Tullia, kissing her hand, and presented her with a small wooden box embossed with the initials of one of Venice's foremost goldsmiths. He looked superb, his hair slightly tousled from the wind outside, his doublet cut to accentuate the poetic lines of his body. Bianca could see only Tullia's back, but her exclamation of joyful surprise came clearly through the armoire. Taking the enormous emerald earrings from the box, Tullia moved toward the mirror and held them up to her face. Ian moved behind her and stood, watching impassively as she replaced the pearls with his gift. She reached around and pulled Ian's hand up to one of her breasts, slipping it inside the lace dressing gown as she leaned her body against his. Then she craned her neck around and gave him a deep kiss of gratitude.

Ian inhaled deeply as his hand strayed from her soft breast. He was pleased that she had remembered that he liked her in gardenia, and felt the exorbitant sum he had spent on the earrings was well justified. He gently nudged her back to the chaise, removing the dressing gown from her shoulders as she walked by him. He ran his hands along her body, kneading her soft buttocks, caressing her peach thighs, exploring each curve and every silky inch of flesh. Then he motioned her to sit before him and led her hand to his groin, at her eye level.

"It has been a long time, Tullia, but you are looking better than ever."

Tullia responded to his flattery by deftly unhooking the laces of his hose, to liberate his organ from the tight fabric encasing it. He smiled as she reached for his thick shaft, but leaned over to stop her before she took him in her mouth. Usually he enjoyed her intimate touches but today something was different, wrong. There was something missing.

Bianca could see only Tullia's back as she undressed Ian, but she had a clear view of her betrothed. She watched, unable to move or even to breathe, as his lips curled into a faint smile when Tullia ran her hands over his body, and although she could not hear the words they exchanged, she was sure she heard him sigh with pleasure. She had never witnessed anything of the kind before, and she felt a certain amount of awe, mingled with jealousy. But overlying all of these was the deepest sense of loneliness and self-doubt she had ever known. Why wasn't that her, why wasn't it her body Ian was embracing, her mouth he was kissing, her damp heat he was plundering? She had offered herself up to Ian, for free, and he had scoffed at her and pushed her aside. Was she so hateful, so unsightly that he had to toss her away like a sack of rubbish? Would she ever know the feel of his hands on her body, of his lips on hers? Or of any man's, ever? Hardly holding back the tears that threatened to pour out, she turned and made her way down to the canal.

As Bianca left, the couple in the room was moving toward the elaborately hung bed. Perhaps he just was not in the mood for fore-play, Ian reasoned with himself, desperate to understand what was happening to him. For the price of two large emeralds, Ian knew he had bought at least four hours of sensual attention, still an out-landish cost but hopefully worth it. It was medicinal, he told him-self, he was taking a cure for the unnerving fantasies that had begun to plague his waking and sleeping moments.

But even in Tullia's enchanting presence, in her most seductive boudoir, he found he was still, unstoppably, thinking about Bianca. He reached out to caress Tullia's hair and wondered why it was not blond. Her body, once her main attraction to him, seemed too voluptuous, too perfumed, too artificial. When he took her breast in his hand, he was disappointed to find it was not small and hard like the small, firm breasts he had seen the previous night. He was even about to fault her for not having a clover birthmark above her left thigh. But he still had three and a half hours, and there was no telling what kind of magic Tullia could work in that time. Ian stretched out to his full length, pulled her on top of his body, and decided to let her try.

It was a disillusioned Ian who departed for home some hours later. Tullia had outdone herself, employing her body with all the exper-tise of her ten years as a courtesan, but nothing had been able to free Ian from the chimera that had taken hold of his senses. She later had occasion to tell a companion that no one had ever treated her with such a divine mixture of hunger and delicacy as Ian did that day. He had not even made love to her, Tullia recounted, but only wanted to hold her like a lover would his beloved. Once, she admitted blushing, he even called her *carissima*.

But Ian's psyche refused to be deceived by childish games of pre-tend, and he felt his desire for Bianca deepening rather than ebbing as the afternoon wore on. His body, which had been alarmingly unresponsive to the exertions of the queen of courtesans, responded promptly to the slightest thought of Bianca. He would simply have to bed her, he finally rationalized, half with excitement and half with dread. For while he could not exorcise her image from his mind, he also could not forget the way her kiss had scorched him. He suspected her of trying to manipulate him, of trying to use her physical attractions to blur his judgment and convince him of her innocence. It was a trick all women used on men, using sex to accustom them to their feminine guile and bend them to their wills. But having recognized it, he reasoned soberly, he could protect himself from it and refuse to be torqued around like a pulley rope.

S'blood, he could go her one better, he could turn it back on her: he could use intimacy to manipulate her, to keep the reins on her behavior, even to probe her innocence...or her guilt. He found himself beaming as he thought of it. Of course, there was a downside. He had no doubt that, after their first night together, he would be tired of her charms, yet he would have to continue to seduce her if he wanted to continue to control her, and especially if he wanted to get to the bottom of this murder. But it was his duty, as a man and as a citizen of Venice. Yes, he would even court boredom for the cause of justice and his beloved homeland. He began to think that his neighbor, the French ambassador, had a very good idea. He would go to his club first, have dinner, lose some money at the tables, really think the thing through, and then return home to undertake his mission. Congratulating himself on his selflessness, Ian sighed deeply, a long, content, and very patriotic sigh.

Chapter Ten

Scented steam curled around the two figures in the bath. The woman tossed her head back, eyes closed, as her maid dexterously sponged her voluptuous contours. Lost in their ablutions, neither woman saw the door facing them open, nor the visitor enter.

The young man crossed to the tub and looked down at the two women. Too preoccupied with pleasing her mistress, the maid had not heard his footsteps, but the other woman languidly raised her eyes to take in their guest. As usual, he was impeccably dressed, his coat cut to emphasize his broad shoulders and slim waist, his leggings sculpted on his strong thighs, his massive codpiece alluding favorably to the burden it concealed. He smiled down at her as she reluctantly pushed her maid away.

"I came as soon as I got your note." He tried to keep the agitation out of his voice. "I passed Ian Foscari on the way. Was he coming from here?"

The woman laughed, not merrily. "Is my angel jealous? Worried that after his pathetic performance last night I am looking for a replacement? Someone who loves me enough to bring me real proof, not tattered scraps of paper with obscene drawings on them? Someone who does not place their comfort and happiness above mine? Someone who cares about pleasing me?" The woman's eyes moved from the young man's face to her maid's, then back again.

Color rose in the young man's face. He had risked his life, almost been killed by that madman, Ian Foscari, and she spoke of not caring enough about her. S'balls, it wasn't his fault that the place had been gone over from the roof to the floorboards, leaving not even as much as a trace of blood. The body had been there, he was sure of it, but no one would ever be able to prove it. He thought the gory drawings might help, but all they had done was earn him the wrath of his impetuous mistress. And worse, he had been banished from her bed. He felt hollow inside when he thought of the pleasure he had missed, and determined to do everything necessary to re-ingratiate himself.

"I know that I cannot apologize enough, madonna. I admit that I failed miserably to bring back the proof you were looking for. I beg you to allow me some way to regain your good graces."

He was rather handsome when he groveled like that, the woman thought to herself. Also, uniquely suited for the plan she and her brother had concocted in the early hours of the morning. Their last attempt had been too subtle; this time there would be no way for those Arboretti worms to squeeze their way out of it. The woman sighed at the magnitude of the task before her and rose from the bath. The maid was about to rise too but her mistress motioned her down.

"My angel will attend me. You deserve a rest after all your hard work." She gave the girl a significant half-smile and the young man regarded the foreign maid with envy, not for the first time.

The woman let herself be wrapped in her silk dressing gown, then led the young man through to her bedroom. He was already undoing the clasps of his jacket when the woman reached out to stop him.

"There will be time for that after, but not now." She pitched her voice low, knowing exactly the tone that would most arouse him. "First, I have a very important task for you, but you must concentrate as I describe it, for every detail matters."

It took her almost an hour to explain his errand, but it would take him ten times that to carry it out. Watching him with veiled eyes, she noted his growing reluctance and began to punctuate her speech with fluttery kisses on his wrist, his thigh, his chest, the places she knew would arouse him most with the least effort on her part. "When you have done this successfully, sometime early tomorrow morning, come back." She slowly ran a finger up the inseam of his hose and let it linger under his codpiece, gauging his reaction with a practiced eye. When she knew she had him at her mercy, she brought her red lips to his ear and whispered breathlessly, "Nothing you could do could make me more grateful. I will spend the time you are gone thinking up an appropriate reward."

The young man shuddered in anticipation. This time, he promised his overwrought body, he would not fail.

Chapter Eleven

Ian felt as though there should be heroic fanfare to mark his homecoming that night, but instead he heard nothing save for the pounding of the fierce rain against the windowpanes. The clocks had only struck nine but his house was as quiet as it would be in the early hours of the morning. It seemed as if a pall had come over it, and Ian wondered briefly if someone had died. Hearing the sound of voices above his head, he took to the stairs and stopped before Roberto and Francesco's apartments.

His uncles looked dire. They were seated before the fireplace, each in his favorite chair, with a decanter of grappa between them. When Ian entered, Francesco paused mid-sentence.

"Hello, d'Aosto," he said coldly, and Ian stopped abruptly. Since he was a young child, Francesco and Roberto had addressed him by his title only when they had something very serious or very dreadful to tell him. He waited, reminding himself to breathe, while the silence stretched to a minute.

"Has someone died?" he asked finally, unable to contain his curiosity any longer. "It's so damn quiet here it feels like we are in mourning. But if we were, you wouldn't be drinking my best grappa. What is going on?"

Roberto and Francesco exchanged glances, each willing the other to speak. "Ian," Roberto began finally, "you know that I am not really your uncle and therefore am not actually in a position to chastise you as a member of your family." Roberto and Francesco had been together for so long that few people, including Ian, remembered that he was not in fact a relative. He only brought it up when he was so distraught by someone's behavior that he desired to stand apart from the family. Ian was now well and truly worried.

"Instead," Roberto continued, "I berate you as a man. You cannot take a living person and lock them up and accuse them of murder and toy with their emotions and not expect to be held accountable. I do not know what you did to our charge today but she is a different woman. You have broken her spirit, a spirit which not only survived the death of a beloved father but has been indomitable enough to pursue a career in medicine, unthinkable to most men, let alone women. It is quite an achievement. Her misery is so palpable that the entire house has responded to it. You will find few of your staff well disposed to you, and fewer still of your relatives."

Ian, aghast, stared at him. "The little witch. The little manipulating, lying, saint-swearing, innocence-touting siren has told you all some false tale of my cruelty and you believed it! This is a betrayal—"

"Silence!" Francesco was livid, his cheeks flushed with anger. "You dare to accuse us of betrayal? We who have stayed with you, protected you, supported you, loved you through the last two years when you gave us nothing back? You, young man, are not fit to speak of betrayal. Nor of that fine creature you have so cruelly betrothed and immured. No tales of cruelty passed her lips, not a single word about you was said."

"You don't need to go on, Dottore di Rimini. I can tell him myself. But thank you for your kind support." All three men swiveled to look in the direction of the small voice coming from the doorway. Bianca walked further into the room and curtsied deeply to Ian. "A word with you, my lord?"

She did seem somehow broken, smaller and frailer than the last time Ian had seen her, but no less beautiful. If anything, her beauty was only intensified by the deep air of misery emanating from her. Looking at her, he understood how she might have captivated the imagination of his household, her unusual eyes appearing even larger and more striking against the pallor of her skin, her cheekbones more pronounced, her hair falling in tendrils around her face. But her beauty alone did not give them the right to brand him a villain, he thought indignantly. Nor to make havoc with the patriotic plan he had been so carefully laying out since he left Tullia's, especially with his body growing aroused just looking at her there.

"Come," he said, sweeping past her through the door. Francesco and Roberto began to protest, but Bianca made a sign to silence them and followed Ian down a flight of stairs and into his library. Under any other circumstances, this first glimpse of such a room would have filled her with indescribable joy, but as it was she hardly noticed the thousands of volumes crowding the walls. She went and stood in front of the fire, wondering if it was any match for the chilly look Ian was aiming at her from his perch at the end of his desk. She rehearsed the opening line of the speech she had composed one last time, gathered as much courage as was left in her, and turned to face him.

"I want to tell you something, and then I want to ask you a question. If you believe I speak the truth about the first thing, will you promise to answer the question truthfully?"

"That depends entirely on the question. I will consider it."

Unsatisfied but without an alternative, Bianca went on. "I want to tell you the other reason I was at Isabella's house. I really did have a standing appointment to teach her to write, and she really was helping me with my book, but there was also something else."

Ian and Bianca's hearts were both beating hard, Ian's with the bittersweet expectation of a confession of murder, Bianca's with embarrassment. She swallowed twice and continued.

"In exchange for teaching her to write, Isabella was teaching me something." She paused, searching her memory for the words she had prepared, wondering if it was really necessary to admit everything. "She was teaching me, describing to me really, what it was like to be with a man. To be intimate with a man." Bianca stopped talking. Unable to meet Ian's eyes, she stared at a spot in the vicinity of his chin.

"That's all? That's what you did not want to tell me?"

Bianca earnestly addressed his chin. "My lord, you must understand how difficult and embarrassing this is for me. To tell you, whose only interest is in women of experience, and whom I would have liked more than anything to make love to me, to tell you—"

"What?" Ian sat up, paying very close attention. Not only did it look as if his plan might work, but it might work even better than expected. He had thought he would have to spend a good half hour making her want him so he could withhold his favors until she agreed to his demands. But if she wanted to be seduced, it would be even easier to use her desire as a means of manipulation. Ian was so busy contemplating his luck and his growing arousal that he hardly heard her question.

"Which brings me to my question. What is wrong with me, my lord?"

In an unparalleled act of courage, Bianca shifted her gaze from his chin to his eyes. She noticed with alarm the dangerous twitching at the side of his mouth that always augured badly for her and wondered if he was going to laugh at her or bite her. She let Ian contemplate her for a few moments, giving him time to inventory her imperfections, before asking her question again.

Ian brushed it aside. "I was just thinking about whether it would be better to make love to you first on the carpet in front of the fire or in a bed. Which would you prefer?"

Bianca's mouth went dry. "I don't know...ah...um...the fire is awfully nice...?"

Ian nodded but did not leave his position at the end of his desk. "Take off your dress," he commanded softly.

"You are not going to undress me just so you can repudiate me again, are you, my lord?" Bianca's hands hovered over the bodice, awaiting his answer before proceeding.

"It depends on how well you answer my questions and comply with my demands."

Something about the way he spoke made Bianca shudder. Her hands fell to her sides. "I will not be humiliated again, my lord. I did not ask you to make love to me, only to tell me what was wrong with me. I know I am not beautiful and sensual like Tullia—"

"Whom?"

"Santa Catarina's head, you know well who I mean, you spent the afternoon with her!"

Ian was momentarily stunned. "Are you having me followed?" He stood and drew close to her, making his voice dangerously low. "You wouldn't dare, would you?"

Bianca scowled at him to show him what she thought of his idiotic suggestion and then deeper to remind both him and herself that she hated him. "Oh yes, I have a small battery of men at my disposal for exactly that purpose. I figure it is worth expending the better part of my fortune to trace your movements as you traipse from one boudoir to another, until you come home and decide to humiliate me." She turned to go, but Ian caught her arm and swung her around to face him.

"Humiliate you? How do I know you do not want to humiliate me? Last time we talked, you told me you hated me. Now you are begging me to bed you." He regarded her through narrowed eyes and tightened his grip on her arm. "If you are not having me followed, what makes you think I went to Tullia's, which I am not admitting? I told no one of my destination."

Bianca rolled her eyes. "I applaud your discretion, my lord, though not your powers of logic. I actually *preceded* you to Tullia's. It was an accident that we were there at the same time. I was just leaving when you arrived. Now, if you would kindly peel your fingers from my arm, I might possibly avoid having bruises to match the bump on my head you gave me last night. I begin to understand why you selected doctors as my chaperons. Another few days under your solicitous care, however, and it's an embalmer, not a doctor, I will be in need of."

Ian ignored her gibe, but loosened his fingers on her arm. "If you were at Tullia's when I—theoretically—arrived, why didn't I see you leaving?"

Bianca regarded him slyly. "What makes you think I left?"

"You were there, at Tullia's, when I was there?"

"Don't you mean, *if* you were there?" Bianca's efforts to be helpful met with glaring ingratitude from Ian.

"What were you doing? With whom?"

"You might say I was alone. Or you could say I was with you. Since I could see you the whole time."

"You watched? You were watching me?" Though he would admit it only later, Ian found the thought arousing. Indeed, it made him want to know more. Now, however, he took his growing arousal as a fine sign of his patriotism and exultation at the revival of his carefully laid plan. His tone was different, no longer challenging, when he asked, "What did you see?"

The atmosphere in the room changed instantaneously. Ian's grip on Bianca's arm was transformed from one of restraint to one of invitation. The pain that she had complained about turned into an intriguing warmth emanating from that single point of contact. His eyes no longer looked suspicion and malice on her, but something different and infinitely more appealing. Bianca did not want to pass up this opportunity, possibly her only opportunity ever, to experience the delights of the flesh. But it was more than her unbounded interest in experimentation that drew her closer to him.

She started to answer his question, hesitated, then began again. "I left before you moved to the bed." She paused. "I don't think I could tell you what I saw. But I could show you?" She sent a questioning gaze toward Ian's face and reached with a none-too-steady hand for his hose. Before she could begin on the laces, Ian stopped her hand.

He had a decision to make. He could tell her the truth, that nothing had happened between himself and Tullia that afternoon, but he decided against it. Ian had spent the entire expensive afternoon lying alongside Venice's most famous courtesan, consumed with fantasies about Bianca. Now, miraculously, he was being given the opportunity to enact them exactly as he had imagined them. He saw no reason to spoil his immense good fortune. Besides, he could not let her think she had any power over his thoughts.

When Ian spoke, he found he had trouble controlling his voice. "If we are to do this properly, you must undress. Tullia was nude, if I remember correctly."

This time he removed Bianca's clothes himself, taking care with each detail. He untied the laces of her cream bodice and pushed the garment off her shoulders onto the floor. He unhooked her modest petticoat, taking advantage of the opportunity to run his hands down her silk-stockinged thighs. Bianca heard him make a noise, something between a low moan and a chuckle, but she was concentrating too hard on not letting her knees turn to polenta to be able to accurately identify it. The feel of his hands on her body, sliding over it, undressing her, triggered the same spirally sensation of heat as it had the previous day. It grew more intense when, asking her to raise her arms, he lifted her light underdress off over her head, pausing to caress each of her lovely breasts. Finally her stockings came off and she stood before him, again, completely nude.

As Ian stood back and assessed her from a distance, smitten by the beauty he saw before him but trying his hardest to feign cold detachment, an irresistibly arousing image entered his mind. "As I recall, Tullia was wearing jewels. Pearls, I believe."

"And emeralds," Bianca added incautiously, wondering where this was going.

Ian cleared his throat, surprised by the wave of guilt that washed over him when she mentioned his extravagant payment. "Yes, well. If you will promise to stay here for a few moments, I think I know where there is a bauble you can wear."

Before Bianca could protest, Ian was out the door. Her first thought was that she had never before spent so much time alone and naked as she had with this strange man to whom she was betrothed. That turned her mind to the previous night, and she wondered if he was actually going to come back or if this was simply a more subtle form of abandonment. She pushed that unpleasant possibility aside by concentrating on what she had seen in Tullia's apartment that day. She was nervous about knowing what to do or doing something wrong or looking foolish or...but mostly she was excited.

She laid herself on the thick sheepskin by the fire and closed her eyes, picturing Ian's stunning physique as it had been revealed to her through Tullia's armoire. She recalled how sleek he had looked as Tullia undressed him, the intimate smile he had smiled when Tullia touched him, and she grew aroused at the prospect of inspiring similar responses in him. Momentarily she cursed herself for leaving so early, for not watching so she would learn what came after, but she found the idea of discovering the unknown excited her even more. This was, she told herself hastily, a completely academic inquiry. It had nothing whatsoever to do with Ian Foscari.

Having reassured herself on that point, she remembered something she had been curious about that day, and reached down to touch herself between her legs. Many of the women she helped had told her about a "special place," but she had never been able to find it on her body. At first she felt nothing, but then sliding her hand toward her belly, she found a point of such exquisite tenderness she couldn't decide if she was feeling pleasure or pain when she touched it. She stroked it again and decided for pleasure. She was so engrossed in this research that she did not hear it when the door opened and Ian reentered the room.

Nothing could have prepared him for the jolt of arousal that he felt as he walked in and saw her lying before the fire, touching herself. Her eyes were closed, her lips slightly parted, her back arched very slightly. He approached as silently as possible, not wanting to disturb her, and kneeled beside her.

"May I?" he asked, moving her hand aside and replacing it with his own. He had intended to come back and proceed to enact his fantasies of the afternoon, but the prospect of touching her like that was unforgoable. He was looking down at her when her eyes fluttered open. Their gazes met as he continued to caress her delicate nub, making gentle circles while rubbing it between his forefinger and thumb. He was still watching her when her eyes grew large with surprise and, as she emitted a long, low sigh in which he flattered himself that he heard, "Oh, Ian," he brought her to a climax. Then he stretched out alongside her and pulled her close to him.

Bianca was suffused with a joy she had never dreamt of. Her body still trembling from her first climax, she was being held tightly in the arms of the man who had given it to her. She felt warm and free and very very relaxed. She wasn't even sure if she could move.

"My lord?" she ventured plaintively.

"Yes, *carissima?*" For the first time he spoke the term of endearment without sarcasm.

"Is it always like that?"

Ian was nonplussed. She could not possibly be that innocent.

"Isn't it always like that for you?"

There was a moment's hesitation while she decided whether to answer truthfully or to pretend to more experience than she had. "I don't know, I have nothing to compare it to." She tried to sit up but he held her close to his chest. Instead, her eyes sought his. "Will you teach me about making love?"

Ian regarded her for some time. Her question went well with his plan, but for some reason he was reluctant to say yes on those grounds alone. Having watched her come to her first climax and being the likely recipient of her virginity, he felt suddenly protective of her. Not that he did not want to bed her, that was still high on his list, but somehow the bit about patriotic honor and duty had less and less appeal. Some part of him questioned his other part's motives, and it began to look as if the two sides would be embroiled in a lengthy battle, so he decided to ignore them.

"Yes," Ian answered finally, standing and pulling her up with him, "as long as you promise to be a good pupil. You can start by donning this."

At first Bianca did not believe her eyes, but what he was holding out to her could be nothing other than the famous Foscari topaz. It was an immense stone, surrounded by twenty-four diamonds, which dangled from a simple wrought-gold chain. When Bianca moved closer to protest, Ian clasped it around her neck. The stone hung perfectly in the valley between her two breasts, like an irresistibly inviting beacon. Ian pulled away and cast a discerning eye on her, deciding that the stone became her even better than he had imagined. Perhaps even too well, he thought, as he felt his self-discipline becoming eclipsed by his arousal. Not entirely cognizant of his actions, Ian reached out and took her nipple between his fingers, as he had wanted to do the previous night and as he had fantasized about all day. He bent his mouth toward her breast and suckled at it, delighting as much in its feel in his mouth as in the small noises emanating from Bianca. Her sheer pleasure at their physical contact brought his arousal near the breaking point.

He moved his head back and began to undress. She stood before him, not wanting to blink for fear of missing something, as he peeled off first his linen shirt, then his deerskin hose. When he was completely unclad, she bent down on her knees, nervous yet eager to resume what she thought was their reenactment, but he gently pushed her down onto the rug.

"The best part comes after that," he explained, recollecting his fantasy and stretching out beside her. They were each lying on their sides, facing each other, his aroused shaft rubbing provocatively along her thigh. He was trying to decide whether to take her on the bottom or on the top, when he was assailed, again, with a pang of guilt. He stopped and tilted her head up to meet his eyes.

"Are you sure you want to do this?" he asked her, serious.

By way of an answer, she reached out to hold his aroused shaft. At the first touch of her timid fingers, Ian realized that he was closer to the breaking point than he had imagined. Then she grew more daring, moving her hand along the length of his smooth organ, running her fingers along every curve and indent, delighting in the feel of it. Ian groaned and gritted his teeth, not wanting to stop her delicate exploration but also not wanting to forgo what was still to come. But then she spoke, quiet words, looking right into his eyes, and he knew he could wait no longer.

"Please, Ian. Please make love to me."

He slid his hand back between her thighs and found her, if anything, hotter and wetter than before. He let one finger linger on her delicate pearl of flesh while he slid another inside of her. She was tight, impossibly tight, and he prayed for reserves of willpower to hold himself in check so he would not hurt her. He pushed her onto her back and moved astride her. Bianca felt his divine touch again, and then more profoundly when he slipped something inside her. That wasn't so bad, she thought to herself, making a mental note to include the new information in her book, when suddenly the something was replaced by a bigger something, pressing against and into her. She looked up at Ian, to make sure everything was okay, but his face was constricted with the effort of his restraint. Instinctively, she pushed her hips up to meet his and felt the tightness ease, her body open, and a thrilling feeling of jointure. She had never been this close to another person before. Ian's eyes were open now, looking down at her as their bodies moved together. Just before he reached his release, he leaned over her and covered her lips with his. He felt the burning and searing of her kiss as he buried himself in her, his climax rolling over him in successively intense waves. It went on and on, longer and more intense than anything he had ever experienced before. Finally, he lay panting and spent on her breast, filled with awe and wonder.

A voice from somewhere inside him commended him on his patriotism and his fine duty to his country. It sounded sarcastic. A voice from somewhere outside him, without a trace of sarcasm, commended him on his performance as a teacher.

"That was, it was—"

"Too short," Ian interrupted.

"I'm sorry, next time I will try to do better."

"If you do better next time it will be even shorter. It is something we will have to practice." Ian slowly withdrew himself, despite Bianca's complaints, and raised himself on one elbow to study her. He was testing to see whether his immunity to her charms had developed yet. He forced himself to study her magical, keen eyes, her perfect nose, the arc of her eyebrows, her long glossy lashes, her lips parted for another kiss, the way the stone snuggled perfectly between her two breasts. He found he could not satiate his longing to simply look at her, to wonder at her. Her hand had again strayed between his thighs and was easily teasing his spent organ into readiness. No, his immunity was decidedly not yet in place.

"What are you doing?" Ian demanded finally, trying to reassert his authority as the authority.

"I thought we were going to practice." Her eyes were innocent, but the smile playing on her lips told Ian she had already learned several of the finer lessons of intimacy between men and women. "Besides, that time I did not get the feeling of tingling, spiraling heat in my stomach, so I want to try it again. Certainly there is more for you to teach me. I want to learn all about your body. What happens if I do this?" She trailed her fingers up his inner thighs to the small soft sac below his organ.

Ian moaned with distraught pleasure and moved her hand from his beleaguered shaft. If he was to have time to recover, he would have to distract her. Always clear-headed under pressure, he dragged his eyes from her face and went to work. He began by kissing her, first on the nape of the neck, then trailing down her breasts, some kisses harder, some softer, along her ribs, across her stomach, lingering on her adorable birthmark, and coming to rest at the sensitive point between her thighs.

"What are you...*ohhhhhh*," was all she managed to say as Ian began flicking her tender nub with his tongue. She arched herself toward him, willing him to engulf her, but he responded only with the lightest and most tender of touches until she sang out, "Oh, please, please, Ian." He raked his teeth over her, ever so gently, and then drank her in, sucking her completely into his mouth. He sucked first softly and then harder, constantly moving his tongue over her. Its bumpy surface skated lightly over her slick little nub, rubbing more aggressively against it as she kept arching higher toward him, demanding that he take her more, harder, deeper. This was a totally different sensation from the other she had experienced, intoxicating and breathtaking, shaking Bianca to her very toes. She wantonly pushed herself into his mouth, reveling in the warm wetness, the texture of his tongue resting on her sensitive place, the feel of his teeth grazing over her, the sensation of his lips on her, the softness of his hair against her thigh, the vision of his golden head between her legs, his warm hands on her backside drawing her deeper into him, until she could stand it no more and her pleasure exploded in a glittering, overwhelming, trembling climax.

This time there could be no doubt about the words she spoke. "Oh, Ian," she said, and repeated it, over and over, until he hugged her tight to his chest.

The clock was striking four when Ian carried Bianca, naked, to her room. She had finally fallen asleep a half hour earlier, after demanding feats of sensual prowess he would not have thought himself capable of the day before and which he was sure he accomplished only through his deep sense of patriotic duty. But what could explain his need to watch her as she slept, as fascinated by her beauty as by the way she instinctively adjusted her body to coil around his when he moved.

She had not been alone in her maiden voyage, for the lovemaking they had shared was as unfamiliar to Ian as it was to her. She was definitely the most curious, adventurous lover he had ever entertained, but it was something more than that. The way she gave herself to him, with generosity and blind trust, made Ian feel he had been made the custodian of a rare and precious treasure. He looked down at the burden in his arms, at the large gem still dangling between her breasts, and felt a curious sense of pride, well-being, and satisfaction. He ignored the voice inside his head telling him what a fool he was, reminding him of the duplicity of women, especially this woman, and of his own shortcomings. He wanted to savor this strangely pleasurable moment, to preserve it, safe and untainted by doubt.

He nudged the covers of her bed away and gently set Bianca down on the soft mattress. He tried to unentwine her fingers from his arm but was distracted in his work by the vision of her there, her hair spread over the deep blue pillow, her chest rising and falling with her even breathing, the Foscari topaz still framed by her breasts. If she did not want to let go of his arm, he thought to himself, who was he to argue? Besides, he reasoned, intent on staying cool-headed, the more she came to depend on him, the closer she got to him, the more easily he could manipulate her. Feeling that he was going above and beyond the call of duty to the last, he climbed into the bed beside her. Her body was curled snugly around him as soon as he was settled, and before he could think any more patriotic or even unpatriotic thoughts, he had fallen into a deep and well-earned sleep.

Bianca's first notion was that Ian's voice had changed overnight and his hands had gotten smaller. Her second thought was that the callused little palm shaking her shoulder certainly was not the same hand that had given her hours of pleasure earlier. Her third thought was that she had made the whole thing up. With that, her eyes sprung open, only to be confronted with the welcome sight of Ian's muscled chest in front of her. Before she could close them again with relief, the small voice spoke again, from behind her. Turning, she saw the less welcome sight of Nilo standing tensely by her bed.

She was momentarily embarrassed to be found naked, in bed, with a man, but remembering where Nilo grew up and the occupation of his guardian, she felt sure he had seen many worse things. Embarrassment gave way to concern when she noted the expression on his face.

"Mistress, mistress, you must come with me at once!" he whispered without waiting for her to speak. "It's my aunt Marina, she is bleeding again, like the last time you saved her but worse, and the baby won't come. Oh, mistress, please, you must help me."

Bianca did not waste time on questions. "Run up to my laboratory and get the black case," she ordered. "I will dress and meet you at the gondola."

As soon as the boy had left the room, Bianca rose and pulled on the simple dress she always wore when she made her professional calls. She turned to see if Nilo's disturbance had roused Ian, but he was still plunged deep in sleep, his face peaceful and beautiful in the dawn light. She became aware of the Foscari topaz dangling between her breasts under her dress, and toyed with the idea of keeping it near her until she remembered the rather large danger of robbery in the arsenal. Leaving it and a hastily penned note of explanation on her dressing table, she kissed Ian on the cheek, whispered, "*grazie,*" in his ear, donned her warmest cloak, and went in search of Nilo.

She found him anxiously awaiting her arrival at the water gate of the palace, having already roused Ian's night gondoliers. As soon as Bianca was installed inside the covered cabin of the gondola, they set out, Nilo barking at the gondoliers to go as fast as possible, the boatmen muttering to each other about bossy squirts and what they had coming to them.

They were ready to come to blows by the time the boat passed through the imposing portal of the arsenal. Bianca, filled with a sense of elation completely out of place for the task ahead of her, had spent the journey trying to clear her brain of thoughts of Ian. She needed to exorcise from her mind the scent of his hair, the friction of his early morning growth of beard against her breast, the feeling of his strong thighs wrapped around her, the security of being held tight in his arms, if she was going to be able to concentrate. But it was the sight and the smell of the arsenal, its sinister fires leaping into the sky at all hours and in all weather, that really brought her back to her senses.

Nilo made a sign to the guard on duty who lifted the heavy gate just enough for the gondola to slide through. Bianca remembered thinking on her first visit there that Dante had been completely accurate to use Venice's arsenal as the basis for a description of hell, an observation that seemed even more true this rainy dawn. There were men moving all around, some carrying heavy rolls of newly worked cordage, others stirring the large stinking cauldrons of pitch, still others high on scaffoldings, putting the finishing touches on a hull or mast. The arsenal was the key to Venice's imperial power, its production of a warship a day the linchpin that guaranteed Venice's merchants free passage in the waters of the globe. Bianca's father had once described a banquet thrown at the arsenal for a visiting dignitary that opened with the laying of a ship's keel and, after the three thousand guests had satiated their appetites, concluded with the then finished galleon being launched. In the intervening years, the arsenal's production capabilities had been even more streamlined, Bianca knew, with an expanded workforce and the permanent implementation of day-and-night operations. Like some sort of fiery monster, it never slept and would suffer no check to its ceaseless machinations.

While the arsenal itself seemed only to grow and thrive, the dormitories that housed the prostitutes at the center of the complex were even more squalid and horrible than Bianca remembered. She allowed herself be led by Nilo through a doorway whose door had rotted away, down an airless corridor covered in places by water a finger deep. As they ascended the damp, rickety stairs at the far end, a pathetic wailing assailed her ears, growing louder with each step toward their goal. Pushing aside a door crudely fashioned out of shipyard scraps, Nilo let Bianca precede him into the minute, dank room he shared with his aunt.

The only light came from a small window on the wall closest to Bianca, but unfiltered by glass or even grease-paper, it was adequate to show her a pregnant woman only slightly older than herself, gasping in pain on a rickety couch. Nilo ran to her, dragging Bianca by the hand.

"I brought her, Aunt Marina, look, I told you she would come."

Bianca knelt beside her, placing one hand on the girl's forehead and the other on the girl's wrist.

"Can you hear me, *cara?*" Bianca intoned softly, and the girl nodded. Her face was streaked where tears of pain had rolled across her dirty cheeks, and her nails digging into Bianca's hand were no more than encrusted stubs. She was covered by a coarse sheet that might once have been white but could now aspire only to gray.

"When did the pains start?" Bianca directed the question at Nilo but kept her eyes on Marina.

"Yesterday," the girl answered first, her voice strained. "Then, today, the bleeding."

"I came home from your palace," Nilo was speaking quickly, "and I found her here, like this, with Donna Rosa." Nilo gestured behind him, and for the first time Bianca noticed the cluster of older women along the far wall. "I wanted to get you earlier, but they stopped me."

"Didn't want you losing your job for nothing, little one." Donna Rosa's voice was hoarse, but her tone was not unkind. The midwife turned to Bianca and lowered her voice. "There's nobody can do nothing for that girl now. That babe's wedged in there so tight, it ain't never coming out. I seen more pregnancies than you have lived days and I know when it's a lost cause. Only one way this thing can end, the sooner the better, God willing."

The old woman crossed herself fervently as Bianca struggled to comprehend the import of her words. If the baby could not be removed, it would be impossible to stem Marina's loss of blood and impossible to prevent mother and child from perishing. Knowing the vast experience of the arsenal midwives, Bianca did not doubt Donna Rosa's diagnosis—as far as it went. There was no way for the busy midwives, most of them unlettered and unschooled, to be versed in the latest medical developments. Bianca trained her mind back to the month before her father died, when she had clandestinely attended an anatomy lecture in Padua. A famous Spanish doctor demonstrated the technique he thought had been used during difficult pregnancies by the ancient Romans, most notably on Caesar's mother. To avoid detection, Bianca had hidden herself in a far corner of the auditorium where the sound was good but her vision of the operating table obscured. She had heard his general description of the operation, but had been able to see none of the specific demonstration. Even if she had seen it clearly it would have been only marginally helpful, since the procedure was performed on a dead corpse, not a live woman.

Despite her rather unsteady understanding of the procedure, Bianca knew she had no choice but to attempt it. With the operation, Marina and the child stood a minimal chance of survival; without it, they had none.

"Nilo, I will need clean water, lots of it. And some grappa." She tossed him the purse at her waist and motioned him to hurry. As soon as the boy was out the door, Bianca hoisted her skirt and untied her garters. The thin linen bandages in her bag were designed to bind superficial wounds, not stop a hemorrhage. Under the surprised gazes of the women along the wall, Bianca removed her thick woolen stockings and then cut a wide swath from the heavy fabric of her dress. When Nilo returned, Bianca administered a large dose of grappa to the beleaguered girl, holding her head up so she would not choke on the strong liquor. She then moved to the foot of the bed, lifted the sheet, said a fervent prayer to Santa Lucinda, and set to work.

Slightly more than an hour later, a spent Bianca was considering whether a marble monument with a pregnant woman on it or one featuring a baby would be the more appropriate sign of gratitude to the patron saints of childbirth. Marina was already holding her large, healthy baby son to her breast when Bianca tied off the last of her stitches. For years afterward, Marina would proudly display the scar on her abdomen and explain that it was no wonder her son was such a success, born as he was like Julius Caesar. But those first moments, between the hours of pain she had suffered and the intermittent doses of grappa Nilo had fed her, she was too groggy to do anything other than hold her baby tightly and repeat, "*grazie,* Madonna, *grazie.*"

As the end of the operation had grown near, an idea had occurred to Bianca, and its appeal had increased as she had worked.

It was only proper for a noblewoman to have a lady's maid, she told herself. Surely Ian would not object to her wanting someone to help her with her toilette, to attend to her clothes, and do the myriad of other vital things that Bianca was sure a lady's maid did but—never having had one—could not actually list. Of course, Marina would need a long spell to recover, but undoubtedly her recuperation would be faster at the Foscari palace than in the unwholesome atmosphere of the arsenal dormitories. That way Bianca could monitor her progress and make sure that both mother and baby remained healthy. Not to mention the bonus of having Nilo nearby at all times. The only problem, as she saw it, was moving the woman so soon after her operation.

The last thing Bianca had expected was for the girl to balk at the proposal.

"I couldn't, ma'am. There's only one trade I know, and it's not being a lady's maid. I don't know the first thing about that."

"And I don't know the first thing about having a lady's maid, so it will be perfect. We can learn together."

It took Bianca nearly another hour to convince Marina that her offer was good and her motives pure. Among Marina's concerns were that she would have to curtsy—"I've never been a very steady one on my feet"—and that she would have to eat cinnamon, which she used to like but was strictly against ever since a sailor had told her it was the Sultan's favorite spice. Fortified with Bianca's assurances that neither curtsies nor cinnamon eating formed regular parts of a maid's duties, Marina allowed herself to be carried by the two gondoliers into the comfortable covered boat waiting below. Donna Rosa followed after, rasping out a steady stream of advice and admonishment. Nilo, who had been silent throughout the women's exchange, stopped Bianca before she could leave the room.

He took her hand to his lips and bowed deeply with all the solemnity of his thirteen years. "Thank you, mistress," he said in a trembling voice, and turned his face away so Bianca could not see his tears. Not knowing what he did, he accepted the sleeve she proffered to wipe his face on and then drew back in embarrassment.

"Come on." Bianca smiled down at him. "We don't want to miss our boat."

The weather had worsened into a proper storm while they were inside, the rain now coming in sheets rather than drops. Bianca paused to search the heavy gray sky for any sign that the tempest might subside. As she stood looking to the west for a break in the clouds, the ground began to tremble. Then the whole sky lit up as if Jove's entire stock of lightning bolts had been let loose. She heard a massive, deafening boom, saw a bright flash, and everything suddenly went black.

Chapter Twelve

So accustomed was Ian to the nightmares in his head, that it took him a moment to realize that the shouts and rapid footfalls he heard were coming from somewhere outside the room. Seeing the unfamiliar bedhangings, he became even more disoriented, but the events of the previous night came flowing back to him and he felt a marvelous sense of satisfaction. He reached out to give Bianca one last caress before investigating the source of the uproar outside the door, but her place in the bed was vacant.

"Bianca?" he demanded of the empty room, and again, more stridently, "Bianca?"

Undoubtedly she had some hand in the din, which was growing louder by the moment. Probably part of her plan to drive him mad, lull him into a deep sleep, then rouse him hours later with mayhem. Before Ian had time to contrive a way to stop her, there was a loud pounding on the door, and then Giorgio burst in.

Though Giorgio was five years Ian's senior, they had grown up together, albeit in different parts of the palace, giving their relationship a deeper and more relaxed quality than that of most masters and servants. Giorgio was the only person who could tease Ian without risking life or limb, and he took advantage of that privilege that morning as he shook his head at his master in amusement.

"You'll be wanting these, I reckon. Strangest thing ever, but I found them in the library."

Ian snatched his clothes of the night before from Giorgio's hand and started dressing. "What the devil is going on out there?"

Giorgio's amusement gave way to seriousness. "Your warehouse at the arsenal blew around six this morning, fire and debris everywhere. It's not quite as bad as 1563, but only because half the place was already flooded by the rain. Tristan sent a messenger over a quarter of an hour ago, and your brother is already on his way. Would have woken you sooner if I could have found you, instead of just your clothes." Giorgio's mock reproach earned him Ian's most cutting glare, which he brushed aside. "Your uncles are waiting for you in the gondola."

"And Bianca? Where is she?"

"Seems to me you would know more about that than I would. All I can tell you is that one of the boats is missing, and the two night men with it."

Ian's jaw tightened, then relaxed. If she had been trying to escape, surely she would not have taken his servants with her. Unless it was another of her elaborate plots. That woman was capable of anything, he reminded himself grimly, but only half believed it. Could he have been duped by feigned innocence? Was she that accomplished? His unpleasant reveries were interrupted by a loud exclamation from Giorgio.

"Hi-ho, look here. Might be the key to your mystery."

The Foscari topaz slipped into his hand as Ian took the note from the table. At least whatever else she was, she was not a jewel thief. Ian was surprised that his fingers were not more steady as he moved into the doorway for light to read by, that her absence affected him so deeply. In the space of a minute Ian's face showed first relief, then rage, then fear. How dare she leave, he demanded silently; how dare she do anything to endanger herself.

"Damnation," he shouted, angry at himself for his treacherous thoughts, and stormed out the door past Giorgio.

· · ·

Francesco, Roberto, and Ian spent the first half of the trip to the arsenal in silence. No trace of the rancor of the previous evening remained, but each was too preoccupied with his own thoughts to attempt a conversation. When Giorgio had woken Francesco and Roberto, he had brought with him news not only of the explosion but also of the two sets of clothes carelessly discarded on the library floor. Although they were bursting with the desire to congratulate Ian on his fine about-face, they knew he had other, weightier matters on his mind. This explosion meant not only a loss of merchandise, but also possibly a tremendous loss of business. The Arboretti were one of only two trading enterprises granted the privilege of selling and storing munitions in Venice. A large-scale investigation would have to be undertaken to determine whether their privilege should be continued and especially whether foul play was involved in the explosion. All their current and future business transactions would come under intense official scrutiny. While the Arboretti themselves had nothing to fear from such an investigation, some of those with whom they dealt would welcome nothing less than the inquisitive eyes of the law on their books and would even withdraw from a profitable deal rather than submit to an audit. At this moment his uncles would have sworn that Ian, ever the efficient man of business, was calculating ways to minimize the potential losses brought on by the explosion, until he began to mutter aloud.

"I hope she is alive so I can wring her neck," was the clearest sample they received of his train of thought.

"Very sound, very practical," Roberto concurred, nodding vigorously.

"You are, no doubt, speaking of Bianca." Francesco tried to keep the amusement from his voice. "What devilish deeds can we fault her for now? Did she set her league of demons upon you last night?"

Ian suddenly saw a possibility and pounced on it. "How long does it take to deliver a baby?"

This unexpected line of inquiry rendered them speechless, but only momentarily. "Anywhere from two hours to two days. It would depend on the circumstances. Why the sudden interest in child-birth?" Roberto regarded him quizzically.

The grim expression on Ian's face was augmented by his dire tone. "Three hours ago your precious Bianca left the palazzo to deliver a baby. At the arsenal. Chances are that she is still there. Although what her chances are of still being alive, I cannot say."

The patter of rain against the cabin of the gondola had stopped, and nothing interrupted the dark silence that fell over the boat until they neared the arsenal. When they were still out of visual range, they began to hear the loud cacophony that always accompanied a crisis, a mixture of men shouting orders, babies wailing, people running, machinery being moved or dismantled, buildings collapsing.

The gondoliers expertly wove their way through the crush of boats at the entrance of the arsenal, pulling up before the Church of Santa Maria, attached to the arsenal gates, where a makeshift hospital had been set up in the loggia. Roberto and Francesco disembarked from the gondola there, having decided that they could be of the greatest help in a medical capacity, while Ian surveyed the scene. A portion of the nuns who lived there were frantically trying to accommodate the swarms of wounded arriving by foot, wagon, cart, and even on the backs of others. The rest of the Sisters of Santa Maria were reporting to a small figure in the midst of the fray who was quickly issuing orders. Ian was shaking his head wondering how this little barefoot person had come to assume so much power, when he did a double take. Nothing about the bare feet, tattered dress, soot-darkened hair, and bandaged head looked like Bianca, but in a flash Ian knew it had to be her. His intuition was confirmed when, seeing Francesco and Roberto approaching from the boat, she left her post and ran toward them.

"Thank God you are here!" Bianca was tempted to throw her arms around their necks and kiss them, but time was too precious. "The official arsenal doctor and staff were the first of my patients, and only one nurse had minor enough injuries to do any work. Most of the people coming in now have burns, but there are some broken bones. So far, we have had no casualties."

Roberto touched the bandage on her head, and Bianca winced visibly. "Are you sure you should not be lying down?"

"Yes." Bianca began to nod her head, winced again, and went on. "It's not very serious. I was just temporarily knocked unconscious when, *um*, something fell off a building onto me."

"What exactly?"

"The facade." She rushed on. "But Nilo revived me after only a few minutes, and as you can see I am fine, and we really have no time to talk."

The three of them hurriedly made their way back to the temporary hospital while she was speaking, and Bianca introduced them to the others who were assisting her. As Ian watched, Francesco and Roberto disappeared from view into the chaotic press of people on the church porch, but he could still make out Bianca.

His unexpected relief at seeing her alive had been quickly followed by the return of his angry indignation at the fact she had endangered herself at all. What was she thinking, coming to the most notorious part of Venice by herself at night, without even asking his permission to leave his house? Did she not understand that she was essentially a prisoner? He was on the point of marching up to berate her, but realized there was much work to be done and, assuming she did not manage to get herself killed in the meantime, his complaints could wait. Instead, he turned and entered the arsenal proper.

He had to pull his shirt over his mouth and nose to avoid inhaling the thick black smoke billowing from fires all around him. Ian's first thought had been to assess the damage at the Arboretti warehouse, but the mayhem around him suggested that there were other, more crucial needs to be addressed. Buildings that had not yet caught fire were being doused with huge barrels of water to try to save them. To his left, he saw a group of men trying to stifle a fire on the unfinished hull of a ship. On his right, another group of men were forming a long line to hand water into a building burning far from the canal. A boy, probably a shipbuilder's apprentice, staggered under the weight of one of the large pails of water. Ian ran to assist him, hoisting the pail onto his own shoulders, and was immediately absorbed into the file. Working like a machine, they put out first one fire, then another and another. Long rows of similarly inspired men had formed all around, their concentrated efforts finally succeeding in beating back the fire from the bulk of the arsenal.

What seemed like hours later, the groups of men began to break apart, some heading toward the hospital to attend to minor injuries, others rushing out to search for lost loved ones and friends, still others dropping from exhaustion exactly where they stood. Ian had just begun to make his way toward the Arboretti warehouse when he heard a small voice crying plaintively behind him. Turning, he saw what was once a dormitory, but which now looked more like the cross section from an architectural drawing. One half of the building was completely gone, and on the top floor of the remaining half Ian could make out the figure of a small girl. A quick survey showed Ian that when the other half of the building fell, it had taken the stairs with it, leaving the little girl stranded.

He raised his face and shouted up to her. "Jump, little one, I will catch you. Don't be afraid. I'm right here." At first the girl was too preoccupied with her desperate cries to realize they had produced a savior for her. When his words did finally penetrate, she just shook her head.

Ian tried twice more to coax her down, muttering under his breath about the contrariness of females. Realizing that there was nothing for it, he moved closer to make an inspection of the remains of the building, looking for anything he could use to ascend toward her. In the normal Venetian manner the boards for walls had been laid horizontally and those exposed when the building split could be used, Ian decided under duress, as footholds and handholds. With only two, or six, missteps, Ian managed to scale the building, growing more and more apprehensive about its structural soundness with every move he made. The unsupported floorboards groaned under his weight as he approached the little girl on the top floor.

Her wailing had ceased as she watched his ascent and approach, her eyes open wide, but as soon as Ian was near enough to reach her, she ran to him and began to bawl.

"No, no, you mustn't do that." Ian was desperate. Try to save a woman's life and she dissolves into a mass of tears, he thought to himself bitterly, ignoring the fact that the woman in question could be no more than six years old. He was looking around, wretchedly, for someone to relieve him of his soggy burden when he saw Crispin approaching below out of a cloud of smoke.

"Up here," Ian called, waving his arms to catch the attention of his brother. "You are good with women. Make her stop crying." Crispin looked around and finally craned his neck up to take in the scene at the top of the building.

Ian rendered impotent by a crying six-year-old girl was one of the most entertaining sights Crispin had ever seen, but the miserable expression on his brother's face made him take pity. He spread his arms wide and spoke in his most reassuring voice. "Jump, *cara*, I will catch you. Don't be afraid, I never miss."

It was as if Crispin had spoken some magic formula. Without even a moment's hesitation, the girl stopped crying and leapt from the roof into his arms. She looked at him for a second, then wriggled free and took to her heels, running headlong into the throng of people crowding toward the exit of the arsenal. Ian shook his head in disbelief, first at the powers of his brother, then at the perfidy of women. But his musings were brought to an abrupt end when the boards under his feet gave way and he fell, bottom first, onto the level below, and then through that level and the next, until he reached the ground.

Crispin heard Ian muttering something about never assisting a woman again, as he rushed over to help him up. When they were both righted and Ian had ascertained that all the parts of his body worked, though not painlessly, Crispin began walking in the direction of the Arboretti warehouse.

"Giorgio told me Bianca is missing." Crispin did not disguise the concern in his voice.

"Another woman," Ian grumbled, as if proving a long-contested point, and then sneered at his brother. "So, she got to you too? You need not waste your energy worrying about her; she is very much in her element, surrounded by blood and gore on the porch of Santa Maria's. Women like that sort of thing."

Crispin was puzzled about how his soon-to-be sister-in-law had ended up in this inferno, but decided to hold his questions for a time when Ian's mood had not been worsened by contact with a crying female. The continuing tumult around Crispin reminded him that he had a much more timely errand to perform. "I had actually gone in search of you just now. There is something wrong at the site of the explosion. For one thing, the damage to the warehouse is less than we would have expected. Anyway, we need your expert opinion."

At one point during his adolescence, Ian had developed a fascination with artillery and in particular with gunpowder. He had passed one summer enclosed in his laboratory, emerging finally with what he promised would be the most volatile explosive ever. The first demonstration was less than spectacular, managing only to scare a few rabbits from their holes, but with a little tinkering he finally succeeded in blowing up a large and notably horrible stone monument erected by one of his ancient forebears at his house in the mountains. Even more than for its strength, the gunpowder was remarkable for the fact that it was impervious to water, making it ideal for sea battles. It was in gratitude for the secret of this new and massively potent form of gunpowder, the key to the Venetian naval victory at Lepanto, that the Arboretti had earned the right to sell and store explosive merchandise in Venice. And it was that same gunpowder that had caused the destruction that surrounded the two brothers as they drew up to the remains of the warehouse.

Surveying the wreck of their storage space, Ian had to agree with Crispin. Because of the postponement of the munitions shipment to England, the Arboretti warehouse had been full to capacity of highly combustible ammunition. That quantity of incendiary matter should have caused an explosion powerful enough to level the entire arsenal, not to mention knock down the walls of the warehouse. But the front wall of the building was intact, and the adjoining wall was still partially standing.

Ian moved to inspect the two remaining walls from the inside, where he was joined by Tristan and Miles. He bent to study the black patterns left by the heat of the explosion, looking for clues to its cause and, even more, its partial failure. There were only two possible explanations for the latter. Either, the ammunition had somehow lost its potency, by exposure to some disabling agent; or there had been less of it in the warehouse than they had thought. While Ian had his professional pride and would not like to think that his product was less than perfect, he preferred the first solution to the second because the implications were not as troubling. The Arboretti were meticulous in their bookkeeping, especially when dealing with particularly precious or particularly dangerous commodities. Gunpowder being both of those, Ian oversaw the accounting for it himself. If the supply in the warehouse had been smaller than his records indicated, there could only be one explanation, judging from the explosion's results: someone had stolen more than half of it, about seven hundred tons.

This was the unfortunate conclusion he had formed by the time he stood up again. When, jaw set, he announced it to the other Arboretti, there was a battery of questions. The most obvious, who was responsible? was followed by the most perplexing: why steal only part of the supply and leave the rest to explode? Why not make off with all of it? Because it was located on official Venetian property, the Arboretti were not allowed to employ their own guard for the warehouse and had to rely instead on the protection of the army. Tristan and Miles related their unsuccessful attempts to locate anyone who had seen anything strange around the building earlier that day, and Sebastian concurred. Even with an army of men, there was only the slimmest chance that the Arboretti would be able to find anyone who had seen anything and had not been paid off to keep his mouth shut.

"We do have one clue." Miles cocked his head to one side and pushed his hair out of his face. "The fact that they did not take all the gunpowder. Perhaps they only had a market for a small quantity of it and had no place to store it, so only took what they could sell."

"Or maybe they got interrupted," Sebastian offered, his blue eyes glowing with anger at the insult to the Arboretti.

"Or maybe they only had a small boat." Tristan's comment, as usual, brought unwilling smiles to at least four of the cousin's lips.

Ian's forehead was wrinkled with concentration. "There is another explanation which does not require a stoop toward the comic. What if someone intended there to be an explosion? That would explain why some of the gunpowder was left behind, and also suggests a direction of inquiry. If we assume the explosion was premeditated, then we must assume that whoever did it bears some grudge toward the Arboretti."

Tristan, unfazed by Ian's dismissal of his earlier sally, looked skeptical and became uncharacteristically serious. "Under those circumstances, why take any of the gunpowder at all? Surely the larger the explosion, the more harm done to our operations."

"While a larger explosion might have caused more buildings to tumble, I for one am not sure it could damage our reputation any worse than this one will." Crispin's limpid blue eyes looked melancholy. "But what if whoever did this knew that, and therefore saw no harm in selling off a little of the gunpowder on the underground market, as Miles suggested. That way, in a single stroke, they could ruin us and make a profit."

"Let us hope so," Ian spoke solemnly, "because the only other possibility is that they have plans for another explosion. And I would hazard that we are the likely targets."

Had it not been for the people still milling about the smoldering remains of the buildings near them, the Arboretti would now have been standing in absolute silence. The prospect of someone harboring the desire to destroy them was chilling, especially while they stood surrounded by a demonstration of the lengths to which that person would go. When they turned as a body and made toward the exit of the arsenal, even Tristan would have been hard-pressed to conjure a smile out of any of them. Sebastian, whose keen investigative instincts and ability to extract information from anyone or anything made him the natural choice to head the investigation, looked grimmest of all.

It felt as though they had been inside for days, but consulting his pocket watch, Ian saw it had been only four hours. There were no visible fires anywhere, and two crews had resumed their work on partially finished ships. Passing through the brick pillars of the entry, the exhausted Arboretti scattered, each in search of his gondola and, eventually, a midmorning nap. All except Ian. Refusing Crispin's offer of a ride home, he directed his steps toward the Church of Santa Maria. The time had come, Ian decided, to wring Bianca's neck.

It looked as if all the chaos previously taking place around the arsenal had been transplanted onto the porch of the church. The scene revealed to him as his eyes adjusted was horrible, blood all over, bodies littered everywhere. Ian wove his way through the maze of patients, narrowly avoiding a run-in with a ferocious-looking nun carrying a large tray of linen bandages. It was not until he had entered the church proper that he could identify the lithe figure with the large bandage on her head. The sight of her there, injured and barefoot, diminished the relish he had been feeling at the prospect of wringing her neck, but only slightly.

He walked up behind her and waited while she finished changing a dressing on the arm of a burly sailor. As she stood, he swung her around toward him. Her look of melting softness was met by his hard gray eyes, and she began to tremble in fear. At least, that was how Ian had concocted the scenario in his mind. But instead of melting softness, or even relief, the expression in her eyes was one of fury.

"Unhand me, d'Aosto." Ian was even more startled by her use of his title than by the failure of his scheme. He let his hand fall, wondering if that was the cause of her strange response, and waited for her to explain herself.

But she didn't. As he watched, she turned and walked away. It was too much to bear, even for the rational, controlled man Ian knew himself to be. This time, he not only grabbed her but, crushing her against his body, lifted her off the ground. Patients, nuns, and his uncles watched in disbelief as he carried the kicking, screaming, squirming figure out of the church. He did not stop until he had found one of his gondolas and stuffed Bianca inside the enclosed cabin. As he hastily gave orders for them to make off, foiling Bianca's attempts to leap ashore through the door by firmly grasping her ankles, he saw his uncles rush out onto the porch of the church in concern.

"Do you know how to swim?" Ian asked her when they were under way. He refused to loosen his grip on her legs until she admitted that she couldn't, but was tempted to tighten it again when she added that she would rather drown in the Grand Canal trying than share a gondola with a marauding kidnapper like him.

"At least," Ian's voice was cold as he spitefully hurled the word at her, "I am not a murderer."

"Really, my lord?" Her voice was even colder. "No one died in that explosion? My most recent tally was twenty-five. That is about four people for every one of you Arboretti."

The last word was spoken with such contempt that Ian's insides curdled. Then he remembered the theory he had himself espoused less than an hour before and regarded her quizzically. She *had* stealthily left his house at the crack of dawn, but if she had been planning the explosion, it was unlikely that she would have either left a note saying where she had gone or remained at the scene of the crime. And yet, those two elements provided her with a perfect cover. Before he could stop himself, suspicion had again overtaken his powers of reason. "You hate us, don't you? You started that explosion yourself to ruin us."

Ian finally got the satisfaction of seeing Bianca tremble, but not with fear. Rage swept through her, a rage stronger than any she had ever felt, and the only thing that kept her from assaulting the man in front of her was that her hands were shaking so much she wasn't sure she could hit him. She took three quick breaths and gave him the most glacial look she was capable of.

"I never would have guessed you could be so vile. You would worm your way out of your responsibility for this horrific disaster by blaming me? If I am the miscreant you seem so eager to cast me as, why would ruining the Arboretti have to be my goal? Why not the sheer pleasure of mending bashed skulls and listening to the agonized screams of burned children for hours on end?"

Ian ignored her sarcasm, already sorry that he had given vent to his anger, but damned if he was going to admit it. Instead, he turned her questions around. "What do you mean my 'responsibility'? Surely even you don't think I would set fire to my own warehouse?"

"No, my lord, I am not daft. But you, who know so well the dangerous potential of the gunpowder you manufacture, decided to store it in the center of the most densely populated part of the city. How could you be so negligent, so careless about the lives of other people? Don't tell me that with your vaunted intellect, you never thought about it. Don't tell me that the convenience of having your stores so close by blinded you to the murderous danger you created. Even a woman could see that a disaster like this was inevitable."

When Ian did not respond, she railed on. "Would you store this volatile substance in your own house? Would you?"

"No, of course not. The city would not allow it. You know that explosives of all kinds are prohibited in our quarter of Venice."

"Why are the lives of some of Venice's inhabitants more valuable than the lives of others? Why does wealthy Widow Falentini deserve protection, while the widows of the men who build and fight for the Republic deserve nothing?"

Ian was at a loss how to respond. She was absolutely right, he was culpable because of his sheer lack of consideration. His culpability, however, was not the issue he had planned to discuss, he remembered with relief. Leaning back into the gold velvet cushions that lined the enclosed cabin of the gondola, he strove to assume an attitude of aloofness as he moved to change the topic. "I fear that when you became party to a murder, you forfeited your right to judge the behavior of others. Neither my conduct nor the conduct of the city of Venice are subject to your censure, *carissima.*" The sarcasm was back with added force, an effective diversion. "Your behavior, however, that is a worthy topic of discussion. What made you think you could just caper off this morning, without asking for permission, without taking an appropriate guard? Surely you can't pretend there was no one on hand, as you had so coyly coerced me into sharing your bed with you. Or perhaps you thought that after last night you could bend me to your will?"

The throbbing pain in her head, the scratchiness in her throat, the exhaustion in every corner of her body, were nothing compared to the complete despair that then took hold of Bianca. Ian's accusations about their previous night's intimacy stung her far more than all of his other allegations about her character. She harbored no illusions that it had been as special to Ian as it had been to her, but to hear it reduced to the level of petty manipulation was too much. She had been honest with him, she had given herself to him, willingly and entirely. And he had taken her, without any sign of restraint, whispering hot words, compliments, endearments, at the height of his pleasure. How could he pursue his delusions about her, even after that?

When she spoke, her voice was calm and measured, betraying none of her inner torment. "In the space of ten hours, my lord, I have lost my virginity, miraculously delivered a baby, been buried under a collapsed building, set up a hospital, bandaged two hundred burns, set fifty broken bones, removed a burst appendix, and sewed a leg back on a young girl's doll. While I am flattered at your conception of my capacities, I'm afraid I cannot also take credit for having maliciously seduced you. Not only do I not know how, I simply did not have time."

She sighed and went on. "As for leaving your house without permission or a guard, I was not aware either were needed. And even if I had known, I probably would have neglected it because I departed in such a rush. Had I been delayed even another five minutes, a woman and her baby would have died. Would you really put your rules before their lives? Really?"

There was neither challenge nor malice in her voice when Bianca asked the question, just curiosity. Nor did her gaze, leveled squarely and openly at Ian, contain anything to make him defensive. In the absence of her hostility, he admitted to himself that he had overstepped a boundary, accusing her of orchestrating a seduction he had himself spent hours planning. What he would have called anger only minutes before, he now recognized as a messy mixture of emotions, remorse, uncertainty, despair, confusion, pain. There was of course also some anger, but the emotion most prominently filling his breast at that moment was relief, relief that she was safe, relief that she had not abandoned him. Or rather, he corrected himself hastily, that she had not escaped.

"You will not leave that way again." Ian stated it, but Bianca chose to interpret it as a question.

"I cannot make that promise, my lord. Perhaps if you could explain what right you have to ask me for an accounting of my movements?"

"Even if I did not have the right of the law on my side—which, as your betrothed, I do—it would be obvious to the greenest observer that you are not fit to take care of yourself." Ian swept his pointed look from her bare feet and legs, to her missing hemline, and finally brought it to rest on her bandaged head.

"That is uncalled for, my lord. Certainly this is an extraordinary occurrence. It's not every day that wealthy libertines undertake to explode the arsenal."

Ian continued as if she had not spoken. "You will check all of your outings with me. And you will always take one of the staff with you as a guard. A grown member of the staff, not that little hellion you found for yourself."

"Your uncles found him for me. I cannot believe you would quibble with their judgment after setting them up as my wise chaperons."

"I don't care where he came from, he is not adequate protection."

"Be reasonable, my lord. I am conducting a murder investigation which requires discretion and wit. I cannot tromp around with an army of men behind me and you rushing up at inopportune times to ruin everything. If I had a mind like yours, I would suspect that you were purposely trying to hinder my work, intentionally attempting to make it impossible for me to prove my innocence."

"You will do as I say."

"Maybe."

In the strained silence that followed her ambiguous statement, Ian studied her.

She was filthy and unkempt.

She looked beautiful.

In a flash, he had a brilliant inspiration. He had had the perfect means of persuasion at his fingertips the whole time. How had he neglected it so long? It was precisely for situations like this one that he had concocted his clever scheme the day before. Clearly appealing to her reason he would get nowhere, so he would appeal instead to her body. Ian poked his head out of the cabin to murmur something to his gondoliers, then closed the curtains on the windows, reached for her at the other side of the cabin, and pulled her to his chest.

At first she resisted, using her minimal remaining strength to keep herself firmly planted on her seat. Soon, her strength ran out, and she had to give in. She fought as hard as she could, she consoled herself, but she was simply too tired. And the feel of Ian's hands on her, the warmth of his body, the smell of his skin after hours of exertion, were not entirely without attraction. But she would just lie there, she told herself, doing nothing, so he could not accuse her of trying to seduce him. Yes, that would be fine, she just would not move, would not make a sound.

Ian was surprised but not displeased by her passivity. He pulled her head onto his chest and gingerly brushed her hair aside. He began lightly rubbing her neck, his strong fingers kneading away the knots of tension and strain that had formed there, then moved his hands to her back. It felt heavenly.

His hands moved expertly down her thighs and calves, stopping at her feet. It had never occurred to Bianca that so many pleasurable sensations could emanate from her feet, but that day she learned her error. He ran his thumb up her arch and let it rest on the ball of her foot, kneading it in delicious circles. His hands worked magic from her smallest toe to her heel, melting away her stress, and with it, her reserve. When his hands moved back up to her thighs, pulling the hem of her dress with them, she barely resisted the urge to moan. As his fingers worked to open her to him, she had to clench her jaw to stop from calling out. And when he began to stroke her, gently insinuating the fingers of one hand into the waiting, wet lips between her legs, slowly stroking her sensitive spot with the fingers of the other, she bit her tongue to keep it in her mouth. But that could work for only so long, and before she knew it she heard a voice, presumably hers, begging him to touch her harder.

"Do you like this?" Ian's voice came to her, low and seductive, his fingers rhythmically probing her moist heat.

"Yes, yes. Don't stop, please. Whatever you do, don't stop."

Ian smiled into her hair, biding his time. Just as he heard her breathing quicken, he lifted his hand.

"No, no, don't stop," she pleaded, turning her eyes, bright with arousal, to meet his.

Ian lifted one hand from her tender bud and brought it to his lips. Under her unwavering scrutiny, he sucked his index finger into his mouth and then pulled it out again. "Delicious," he said huskily, and the hand he still had between her legs felt her contract with renewed arousal. How could he excite her without even touching her, Bianca wondered to herself, but not for long because Ian was whispering in her ear.

She sat, unable to move, as he described all the things he wanted to do to her, how he wanted to stroke her hard until right before she climaxed and then have her mount him and take him, grinding her hips around him, her breasts hanging over him so he could cup them with his hands or suck them into his mouth, flicking her nipples with his tongue until he felt her tighten around him in climax.

"Would you like that?" he whispered finally, tracing the outer contour of her ear with his tongue, trailing it down her neck, to her shoulder.

Unable to speak, she could only nod.

"Do you promise not to leave the house without my permission anymore?" He asked, his voice husky.

Bianca would have agreed to anything at that moment to experience the pleasure he had described. "This is blackmail. Or a bribe." Her voice sounded small and wistful.

"Think of it as a contract," Ian volunteered. "You get something you want, and I get something I want."

It sounded perfectly reasonable to Bianca, whose powers of reason had fled the minute Ian put a hand on her body. But on principle, she knew, she should not give in without a fight. She played with the gold hair peeking out from the neckline of his shirt for a moment, considering, then made a counter offer. "Can I have a climax first, and then another one when you are inside me?"

Ian knew he had won. His surge of victory felt strangely like arousal. "Greedy, aren't we?" he asked rhetorically as he passed his hand back down between her legs.

Ian was glad that Bianca came almost instantly, because he could hold himself back only a short while longer. He loved the way her eyes grew wide like saucers and filled with surprise when she found her release. He strained his ears to hear the little gurgling noises that began in her throat and bubbled up out of her mouth as joyful exclamations of pleasure.

As Bianca was fumbling with the laces on his pants, he allowed himself momentarily to dwell on the fact that his repeated interactions with her were not diminishing her attractions in his eyes, but he decided that the more time he spent buried within her tight little body, the quicker he would build up his resistance. It was therefore with great vigor that Ian, his hard shaft freed from the constraint of his tight breeches, plunged himself into her.

He was partially reclining against the velvet seat of the gondola with Bianca astride him. When she had taken him entirely into herself, she threw back her head, her eyes closed, and began to make wide circles with her hips. Ian thrust himself into her, and she had to reach around and grab his thighs to stay atop him. She steadied herself with one hand against the roof of the gondola, leaning forward to take him in deeper. He reached out to stroke where their bodies met, but she caught his hand and moved it to her lips. As they moved together, around and around, she delicately kissed each of his fingertips, then ran her tongue in circles on his palm, relishing the salty taste of his skin. Suddenly hungry for the feel of her pressed against his chest, for her nearness, Ian pulled her down to him and drove himself inside her with all the strength he was capable of. She pushed herself into him, letting their bodies melt together and almost cried with joy when, at the height of his shuddering climax, she heard him speak her name for the first time.

After two tours around the island of Venice, during the second of which the rain had resumed, Ian's gondoliers were relieved to get the signal to head for home. One of them was already picturing his warm, dry bed in the servants' quarters of the Foscari palace, but the other had an errand to do before he could sleep. He wondered how much he would get for his rendition of how Ian had spent his time on the journey home. In the past the sums had been adequate, but he anticipated that his description of the activities of his master and mistress during this gondola ride would have an especially high value. He did not know how many of the other servants had taken that strange man up on his offer to pay for information about the goings-on at the great house, but he had augmented his already generous salary quite a bit with his harmless eavesdropping and snooping. He thought of that pretty little number he had deposited at the Foscari place earlier that day, to be his mistress's new maid, and wondered how much more spying he would have to do to afford her favors on a regular basis.

The growling of a tiger or the braying of a donkey would have been less unexpected to Ian than the sound that met his ears as he disembarked from his gondola. At first it was so unfamiliar that he could not make it out.

Ian was cringing. "What is that infernal noise?"

"Oh, I forgot to tell you. I hired a maid," Bianca responded brightly.

Ian identified the sound and the cringe deepened. "Are you raising her up from an infant?"

"No, that is Marina's baby. The baby I delivered today. You should see him, a handsome boy. They named him Caesar, but Ian is his middle name, in honor of you, my lord," Bianca lied, hoping to soften him.

"You hired a maid who has just given birth? That's idiotic. She won't be any good to you for at least two months."

"No matter, I don't really need a maid anyway. I just wanted to give her a better place to live. Or," Bianca continued snidely, "since her house was destroyed in the explosion, a place to live at all."

"Why stop at her? Why not move an entire body of displaced females into my house and pay them to sit around doing nothing?"

"That's a wonderful idea, my lord. Let's! I can have it all arranged by tomorrow."

It was too much for Ian. The Arboretti were under direct attack, he was betrothed to the prime suspect in a murder investigation, and someone had introduced a baby into his house. Between Bianca's feigned misunderstanding of his sarcasm and the continued wails coming from Colpo or Caruso or whatever the damn thing's name was, Ian was completely undone. He cast a last baleful look on the beautiful woman whose obvious goal was to destroy his life and headed for the stairs as the clocks on the floor above struck twelve.

Chapter Thirteen

Ian had barricaded himself in his laboratory. He was trying to figure out how many adjustments would be necessary to make it a permanent living space. His meals could easily be brought up, but because every available surface was covered with some substance—animal, vegetable, or mineral—it was hard to find a place adequate for sitting, let alone sleeping. Since these days he rarely had time to sleep, he consoled himself morosely, it probably wouldn't matter much anyway.

This fit of house moving had been brought on by the shrieks and gurgles that had accompanied his bath and grown louder while he dressed. He had stormed out of his room to silence the unholy racket, only to discover the largest part of his household gathered around a hideously ugly bundle in a white blanket in the middle of his reception hall. Each scream issuing from the bundle seemed to elicit broader smiles from Bianca, Francesco, Roberto, Crispin, and most incredibly, Giorgio. When he spoke to demand order in his house, he was brusquely shushed by all of them and told to keep his voice low so as to avoid waking the sleeping mother. It was then that, muttering threats and blasphemies, he had fled, taking the stairs without stopping, until he was safely locked in his laboratory.

That had been over two hours ago, and Ian found he was not

only peevish and hungry, but also in need of several items from his room. He cautiously opened the door of his laboratory and stood, waiting. He heard a door close. He heard footsteps. He heard a man's voice. More doors. More voices. The normal sounds of his house. That meant no wails, no slurps, no baby noises at all. Maybe they had found a cage for it, he mused, or better yet, sold it. Bravely, he ventured forth onto the landing and, after a brief pause to be sure, descended like a man who has just tasted victory.

Halfway down the second staircase, he was met by Giorgio.

Ian regarded his most trusted servant bitterly. "I saw you with that infant. Good god, man, I thought I could count on you, and now I see that you, too, are a party to this travesty. I and that boy, Cholera or whatever his name is—"

"Caesar," Giorgio supplied.

"—Cretin," Ian continued, "he and I will be the innocent victims of it. Both doomed to lives made unbearable by the machinations of women."

"*Mmmm,*" Giorgio murmured sympathetically.

"Did you come here to mumble at me?" Ian demanded fiercely. "Have you lost your powers of adult speech? I suppose that before the day is out we will all be prancing around, gurgling and burping."

"And spluttering. You are doing a fine job of it now, my lord."

Giorgio came close to getting the neck wringing Ian had previously earmarked for Bianca, but the servant knew his master well and quickly dodged out of the way.

"Actually, I came to tell you that you have a caller and to find out where you will see him. Il Signore Valdone. He assures me it's not about the arsenal fire."

"Damned nuisance," Ian gurgled, scratching his chin. "I suppose that Clotin creature has been put away for the afternoon? Is it safe to descend? Or could you send Valdone up here?"

"I would suggest the library. Caesar is sleeping down behind the kitchens, and I give you my personal assurance that you will hear no more from him today. Additionally, your caller does not look quite up to the ascent to the laboratories. He is rather over the normal size."

That Giorgio had not done Valdo Valdone justice with his description was revealed to Ian upon his first step into the library. The man was squeezed uncomfortably into a chair that, though ample for a person of normal dimensions, only accommodated him with difficulty. He tried to rise, but Ian, concerned about the effect of that operation on his furniture, motioned the man back down.

Though they had never met, Ian knew of him by reputation. As he crossed to the chair behind his desk, Ian hastily reviewed what he had been told of the man. Originally a farmer from the small town of Thiene, he had developed a fortune turning his plants and herbs into perfumes and unguents for women. Instead of cultivating a courtly clientele, creating unique perfumes for every duchess and countess, Valdo Valdone had decided to make his products in large quantities. This meant that they could be sold at prices accessible even to the wives and daughters of small shopkeepers. From a makeshift stall in the middle of one of the shoddier squares of his hometown, Valdo had moved his enterprise to Venice, where he had met with such success that he now did business down the entire length of the Italian peninsula. With each success, it was said, his body grew a little more, so that the size of his corporation was directly proportional to the size of his corpus.

At least, Ian thought, taking in the immense figure before him, he is to scale. It was not just his body that was large, but also his head, eyes, nose, and mouth.

And his voice, Ian soon learned. "I would never have presumed upon you, my lord, nor especially on a day like today, had I not thought it rather urgent."

Ian nodded to him to continue, wondering if such loud noises could have a damaging effect on the structure of his house.

Valdo cleared his throat, a sound akin to the roar of a cannon. "I heard through several channels that you are making inquiries about Isabella Bellocchio. You know, looking for personal information."

The large man leaned forward in his chair and gave Ian an unfriendly look. "I demand to know why."

Ian eyed him for a moment to give his inner ear time to stop vibrating, then turned up a palm. "I might tell you, but only if you first explain why you are so eager to know."

Valdo turned his head around, scouring the room. "What I will tell you is very private. Is this a safe place to speak?"

"I vouch for the security of my home and staff," Ian answered haughtily, pretending to feel insulted. Mainly what he was feeling was hungry, and the prospect of inviting his large guest to dine was so unappealing that he decided instead to hurry the interview to its conclusion by employing his famed coolness. It had no effect.

"Of course. I didn't doubt it, you know, really it's just that," Valdo paused to clear his throat again, "well, where that girl is involved I just can't think. I ask you plainly, my lord, are you courting her affections?"

Ian was surprised. When he did not respond, Valdo continued.

"You asked me to explain my interest. I love Isabella. More than I have ever loved anything, or anyone, even more than my poor departed mother." He paused to cross himself. "I bought her a house, I give her clothes and presents. I had a perfume specially made for her. I won't say that she loves me back, that would be too much to ask, but I will say that she has, you know, a certain affection for me." He spoke with pride, and Ian wondered for the millionth time how men could be such fools where women were concerned.

"If you know she has affection for you, why worry about me?" Ian's stomach rumbled impatiently.

"*Ah*, so you are courting her! Are you planning to marry her, take her out of my reach?"

Ian noticed for the first time that Valdo's ears were disproportionally smaller than the rest of his body. "I said nothing of the sort."

"But you implied... You suggested..."

Ian decided that he needed to hasten his lunch. There would be no real harm, Ian's stomach rationalized, in speeding Valdo's departure by telling him what he wanted to know. If Valdo Valdone was the murderer fishing for information, Ian's stomach pointed out logically, he would get nothing from Ian's explanation of his interest in Isabella. And if he was not the murderer, Ian might learn something important from him. While still getting to eat lunch.

"I have never met Signorina Bellocchio and feel no amorous desires toward her. My inquiries were initiated only to please my betrothed, who is, let us say, a *demanding* woman. It seems that she and Isabella had become friends or correspondents, and—"

"Why, that's impossible! Isa can't write a word."

Ian brushed aside the objection, but made a mental note that Valdo knew of Isabella's illiteracy. "Somehow, at any rate, they developed a certain degree of intimacy and, not hearing from Isabella for some time, my betrothed grew concerned. On her request, I spread the notice that I was collecting information about Isabella Bellocchio, presumably the notice you heard."

"Then you were not going to marry her?"

"S'blood, do I need to repeat myself like a parrot?"

"No, no, I am sorry, my lord. I just wanted to get it straight. I told you, where Isa is concerned, I can't think."

Ian's stomach told him that Valdo had no information nearly as important as that contained in the serving dishes on the floor below, and he decided to bring the meeting to a close.

Ian was rising from his seat. "I hope that sets your mind at rest. If—"

"Anything but," Valdo boomed, propelling Ian back down by his sheer volume. "How can my mind rest when she has disappeared? I haven't slept these five nights. And there is no one I could tell about it, no one I can trust. If my wife found out…" The large man shuddered. "Then I heard about you, and I was so relieved, but first I had to be sure. You know, sure that you were not trying to take Isa away from me. It's not like Isa to go away without leaving word. Usually she will send a messenger or tell someone at my club or have Enzo tell me where she is going and for how long. But not this time, I have looked all over and asked everyone. I am beside myself with worry. I can't even eat."

On hearing that, Ian reconsidered inviting him to lunch, but decided against it. Instead he made a noise that he hoped sounded sympathetic and followed it up with, "Is there something I can do for you?"

"Of course!" Valdo looked puzzled, as if it were obvious. "You can find her. I can't do it myself, you know, can't let my wife find out, but you are already making inquiries for your betrothed, so why can't you also make them for me? Do you know where she is?"

"To be frank," Ian lied, "I have no idea where she is. My inquires have gotten nowhere. I was hoping you could help me. Do you have any idea?"

"I've been thinking and thinking but have come up with nothing. She sometimes goes to a little cottage I have near Lake Maggiore. In fact, it has quite a nice view of your lovely villa, my lord." Valdo paused for Ian to thank him for the gratuitous compliment, realized it had been ignored, and rushed on. "But I sent my man there to look around, and it is deserted, no sign of anyone."

"Does she have any relatives that might have taken ill? Any friends that might have required her assistance?"

"Not that she ever spoke of." Valdo's eyes lit up. "But here's something! She told me once that if her father, a poor but religious cobbler, ever found out what she had done with her life, he would be less than pleased. Maybe he came and found her and took her away with him."

In Ian's experience, even the most religious of men had been known to adjust their morals where money was concerned. If Isabella had been in a position to make her father's life comfortable, it seemed unlikely that he would do anything to disturb that. Ian said as much to Valdo and had the satisfaction of seeing that the large man's enthusiasm was visibly dampened, but by no means extinguished. After a moment of quiet thought, Valdo boomed his next suggestion. "She might have gone off with one of her other clients for a brief span, mightn't she? You know, to one of their houses or something?"

"Has she done that before?"

"No, never." Valdo shook his massive head slowly. "But what if someone forced her to go away? What if her father or one of her lovers coerced her into departing and would not let her leave word? You know, someone jealous or deranged. Someone who wanted her all for himself." He paused and then added in a different voice, "Or someone who wanted her away from me."

Ian had been about to say something, but stopped before the words left his mouth and adjusted them. "How do you think your wife found out about your arrangement with Isabella?"

"W-w-w-w," Valdo stuttered, then got control of himself. "I did not say anything about my wife. Did I?"

"This is patently ridiculous." Ian slapped the top of his desk with his palm, a gesture he knew to be particularly awful, and for the second time rose to leave. "You cannot enter my house, uninvited, ask me to do you a favor, and then lie to me. Do you take me for a fool, man?"

"Wait, wait, don't go," the large man pleaded piteously. "I just need a moment to collect myself." Valdo lowered his head and put his hands over his eyes. After a few minutes, he righted himself and began nodding vigorously.

"You are right, my lord. I do suspect my wife. Our marriage is not an unusual one. You know, we married very young, when we still lived in Thiene. She was the most desirable girl in the town, easy on the eyes, nice to hold. But the years passed; we moved to Venice.... You know, the eye wanders, the appetite craves younger morsels."

Ian nodded for the sake of doing something, wondering why, if Ian already "knew" all this, Valdo was taking up his lunchtime retelling it.

"It would never have occurred to me to suspect Lucretia, that is, my wife, except that two weeks ago she began acting strangely. Very strangely. I can't explain it, but something changed. She became very aloof and distant. Sometimes when I came upon her, she would be smiling to herself, as if she knew a secret, a secret about me and she was plotting ways to use it. She is a very crafty woman, my lord, much more clever than I am. It was her idea to make the perfumes in the first place, you know, the ones I have made my fortune off of. If she put her mind to it, she could do anything."

"Anything? Do you think her capable of violence?"

Valdo looked shocked. "No, certainly! She would not harm Isa. She would just, you know, put her out of my reach. Send her somewhere I could not find her."

"Why? What could that achieve?"

"I don't know." Despair again filled Valdo's baritone. "That is what I want you to find out. And where. You know, where she sent Isabella."

The task was infinitely distasteful to Ian. Given his certainty—well, partial certainty—of Bianca's guilt, he wagered that time spent talking to this Lucretia would be time wasted unpleasantly for nothing. On the other hand, she might be able to tell him something that would help him force a confession out of Bianca. And, he reasoned finally, the means of meeting her were easily at hand.

"Very well, I will speak with your wife. You have heard, no doubt, about the betrothal ball we are throwing here in two days' time."

Valdo nodded. Everyone had heard about the special lifting of the sumptuary laws and the elaborate preparations hastily under way. There had not been a gala event like that at the Foscari palace in years, and the excitement it caused was feverish. The whole city had been turned upside down upon news of it, goldsmiths, glassblowers, cooks, and bakers working day and night to be ready on such short notice. His own wife had been forced to send for five different dressmakers before she found one not already too busy with other orders for extravagant gowns to be worn that Monday night.

"I thought perhaps, on account of the fire, it would be canceled."

"Nonsense." Ian sounded positive, although he had just made the decision that moment. "The fire was a tragedy, especially to those who live in the arsenal, but it has scarcely damaged me or my interests. Besides, it has nothing to do with my betrothal. Your wife will attend you, I presume?" When Valdo nodded his large head, Ian continued. "Very well. I shall speak to her then."

He was rising for the third time, hoping at last to be on the way to his lunch, when Valdo spoke again.

"I have another idea."

Ian gave up hope and collapsed back into his chair. By now all the caramelized fennel and wine-braised beef stew would be gone. He would hazard his fortune that Bianca had gleefully fed his portion to that baby, that Caesar or whatever he was called.

"I was thinking that maybe it would be easier to get information, you know, to get people talking, if you offered some kind of reward. A thousand ducats or something. Of course, I would put forward the money, but you would have to be in charge of distributing it. I could not have it known that I had any part in it."

As Ian, picturing the trail of indigents lining up before his door when word of such a reward got out, was figuring out how to refuse the commission, there was a knock on the door of the library.

Bianca entered and strode up to Ian's desk, pretending not to see the enormous man in the chair before it.

"My lord, we have been waiting lunch this eternity, and I for one am quite near death. Do you intend to eat, ever?"

It was a ridiculously flimsy pretext, and Ian saw through it in a flash. Not only was it impossible that she had not seen the immense being in front of his desk, but calling the master of the house to table was the type of errand for which Ian employed any one of thirty servingmen. No doubt, he guessed correctly, she had heard of the arrival of Valdo Valdone and wanted to know what was being said. He wondered briefly how she knew Valdo, discarded the possibility that he might be her accomplice because the vision of him skating over the rooftops of Venice was too ludicrous, and decided that out of gratitude for her timely intrusion he would give her a little satisfaction.

"*Ah*, my charming betrothed. This, *carissima*, is Signore Valdo Valdone."

Bianca turned and feigned surprise to see another person in the room. Then she curtsied gracefully and held out her hand to be kissed.

"*Piacere.*" She smiled politely, quickly taking in every detail of Isabella's beloved. He was not a horrible-looking man, she tried to make herself believe; it was just that his ears were too small. "I am so sorry to have disturbed your conference. If I had known, I never would have burst in like this."

"No doubt." Ian spoke wryly, since she made no move to leave. He was sorry that he had not been able to watch Bianca's face as she curtsied, to look for signs of recognition, but Valdo seemed appropriately overwhelmed by her beauty, despite the small bandage over her right temple, which suggested he had never met her before. Ian was curious, however, about the effect of his next piece of information on her. "Signore Valdone has just offered to put forward a reward of one thousand ducats for information about the whereabouts of your friend Signorina Bellocchio."

Valdo's mouth opened and closed a few times. "B-b-but, no one is to know that. You said you would keep it private."

"My dear sir, my betrothed is to be trusted in all things. Man and wife are one, no?"

Bianca made a small choking sound as Valdo uneasily nodded in agreement. "I suppose, yes, well, if you trust her."

"Implicitly." Ian spoke emphatically, but the irony in his voice was not lost on Bianca.

Finally having stifled her laughter, she spoke. "That is a fine idea, Signore Valdone, and one I have already implemented myself. I let it be known Thursday that I had three thousand gold ducats for anyone with information about our dear Isabella, and already I have had appreciable results." Or at least, she hoped to have by the end of the afternoon. "Why don't you withhold your reward money until mine has been exhausted? That way we will not be unnecessarily doubling our efforts."

Both Valdo and Ian were surprised by her revelation, but Valdo recovered first. He was all gratitude as he rose, with difficulty, from the small chair.

"Madam, only your goodness can match your beauty. I am glad to know that Isa, *ah*, Signorina Bellocchio, has a friend such as you." Valdo turned to Ian, still standing rigid by his desk. "You are a fortunate man, d'Aosto, and I envy you. Thank you for your assistance. I look forward to seeing you on Monday." Bowing deeply, he walked toward the door of the library and was escorted out by one of Ian's servants.

"Do you think he learned that from a book?" Bianca asked to cut through the uncomfortable silence that had descended on the room.

"What?"

"'Only your goodness can match your beauty.' I feel that I've read it somewhere. Unless it is familiar because it is one of the lovely sentiments that drips like honey from your lips."

It was not he, it was she that was mad, Ian realized all at once, mad as the south wind from the Africs. But if he wasn't careful, he would soon share the malady. Escape was the safest policy, he decided, and made for his lunch.

"My lord," Bianca called after him, following in his wake. "I did not really come to call you to lunch, you know. We were waiting, yes, but I actually came because I needed to tell, *ah*, ask you something."

Ian eyed her narrowly as they descended the steps. "Where did you meet Valdo Valdone?"

"Santa Barbara's fingers, my lord, you were there. Is your memory that flimsy that you can't remember two minutes ago in your library?" What about last night, Bianca wondered to herself. Can you remember that, as I do?

"Damn your impertinence! You mean to tell me you've never met him before? Why did you then rush in like that with your fabricated errand?"

"I was about to tell you!" Bianca huffed. "I had never met Valdo Valdone, but I had heard of him, as Isabella's patron, and I was curious to see him. He seems to me a very likely suspect, although he wouldn't to you, since you already know who the murderer is."

"If he killed her, why offer a reward for information about her whereabouts, which could eventually lead me straight to him?" Ian countered.

"*Bravo,* my lord! Shall we use the same logic on me? Why, if I killed her, would I likewise offer a reward?"

Ian was only momentarily stymied. "He asked me to administer the reward, whereas you are administering yours yourself. Any information you get will be tidily dealt with by you alone, using the reward money to bribe others into silence. Nor have I any proof that you really have offered a reward. It would not be the first time you lied about your actions. " He regarded her with triumph.

"How is it that with your broad forehead and ample skull there is only enough room in your brain for a single thought?"

"Is that the best defense you can invent? Insulting my cognitive powers?"

"You do that yourself, my lord, when you fail to employ them." Bianca returned Ian's glare.

Then she chastised herself. Why must she completely lose control of her tongue when she was around him? She had no time for sallies of wit and games of words. She should be using every minute of every day she had left to prove her innocence to Ian, not to antagonize him beyond endurance.

On the threshold of the dining room, Bianca touched Ian's arm to stop him. "I apologize for my remarks, my lord. They were uncalled for."

Ian spun to face her. Never had he ever dreamt of hearing anything like this pass her lips. He knew it had to be a stratagem and was eager to see it unfold. But he refused to be softened. Instead of speaking, he bowed his head slightly to indicate he had heard her apology.

Bianca opened her lips to proceed, saw the dangerous twitch at the side of his mouth, paused to bolster her courage, and finally spoke. "As I told you, I went to your library to ask you something. This morning you wrangled a promise out of me that I would leave the house neither unreported nor unescorted. I am therefore asking your leave to go out on an errand this afternoon, after lunch. I will take whomever you recommend with me."

"Where are you going?"

"I would rather not say, my lord."

"Then I would rather you did not go." Who knew how many babies and stray women she might come back with?

"Damn you, Ian," she spoke his name without realizing it. "How am I to prove myself innocent of anything if I cannot leave the confines of this palace?"

Ian considered for a moment. "Is it necessary for you to go out? What kind of errand is it? Another visit to a whorehouse?"

"No, my lord, that is your pastime," was on the tip of Bianca's tongue, but did not make it out of her mouth because a thought occurred to her.

Instead, brows drawn together pensively, she said, "You have a point, my lord. Perhaps the errand could be performed here. Tell me, if you were present during an interview with one of my informers and you yourself handed over the money, would you still feel that I was trying to use my reward as a bribe?"

"Would the interview interfere with my lunch?" asked Ian wearily.

"No, of course not. I will schedule it for four o'clock this afternoon. But since you mentioned lunch, why have you kept me lingering here outside the dining room? Don't you ever intend to eat? I for one am positively famished."

Chapter Fourteen

The conversation at lunch had moved quickly from the fire, about which nothing new was known, to the newest inmates of the household, Marina and Caesar. More precisely, the assembled diners had wanted to hear all the details about Bianca's miraculous delivery of the child. Ian, stout of heart and sturdy of appetite, found his food sitting less and less well as the gory details were described with unsettling precision. When he begged for mercy, the conversation was postponed until dinner, a meal that Ian promised himself he would not attend. Although the food at his table was among the best to be found in Venice, he would willingly forgo even his favorite dishes if they were to be accompanied by an anatomical lecture.

He was just explaining this delicate point to Bianca for the fourth or perhaps fourteenth time, when their awaited guest was announced. Bianca was so relieved to have the discussion of her table etiquette postponed that she rose and opened the door of the library herself to admit him, almost knocking over Giorgio, who had intended the same office from the other side of the door.

Enzo looked more suited to a life of patrician leisure than to his job as Isabella's butler and housekeeper. He was dressed in the height of fashion, or perhaps even beyond it, gold medals dangling from his carefully cut jacket, his hose closed with a complex series of knots that Bianca avoided focusing on only with difficulty, his long hair free around his shoulders, his beard carefully shaved into a goatee. When he spoke to greet them it was half in French with a hint of a French accent, an affectation carefully copied from an army sergeant he had once met, in an attempt to pass himself off as a member of a forgotten branch of the royal Valois line. The whole effect was, as Bianca described it later, stunning.

Indeed, neither she nor Ian managed to say anything until after the man had made them each an elaborate bow and meticulously seated himself in the chair earlier occupied by Valdo Valdone. While his two hosts were openly staring at him, he took in the elegant and expensive furnishings of the room. There was money to be made here, he told himself and indiscreetly licked his lips.

As part of her ongoing effort to convince Ian of her innocence, Bianca had agreed to let him do the bulk of the questioning, but it began to look as if she was going to have to step in. The frown that had crossed Ian's face when Enzo entered had only deepened as he studied the man. Finally, he spoke in disbelief. "You are Isabella's houseboy?"

Enzo smiled, more cunning than attractive. "I prefer, *monsieur,* the label *capitaine.* So much more expressive, *non?*"

"Was there something in particular you wanted to tell us?" Ian hoped the interview would be brief because he was not sure that he would not rather hear little Cronos's screams than this man's hideous accent.

"No, *mon comte,* nothing particular, but I felt, perhaps, I could be of help to you. I know the lovely *Mademoiselle* Isabella very well, and I hear you are interested in information about her, so I come and offer to you my services. Perhaps there are the questions I can answer?"

"How long have you worked for Isabella? How did you get the job?"

"I have been Isabella's *capitaine* since she has lived in the charming house she now occupies. But we knew each other before that, from when the days were not so rosy, *vous comprennez?*"

"Did you grow up with her? I mean, it is obvious that you have spent much time in France," Ian said, trying not to falter on his lie, "but where were you born?"

Enzo was visibly pleased by what he took as a compliment. "You are clearly a man of discernment, *mon comte,* so I will tell you. It is a sad tale. My family was—"

Ian was getting more than he bargained for. "I would not dream of prying into your difficult family matters. Just tell me, did you know Isabella when she was growing up?"

"We had occasion to meet, *oui.*" Enzo, disappointed by the interruption in his narrative, settled sullenly back into the chair.

"Do you know her father? Have you met him? Have you seen him recently?"

"*Son père?* He is dead these ten years!"

Ian sighed. At least he had learned one, minute, piece of information from this man. He felt Bianca's curious gaze on him but refused to meet her eyes. Instead, he resumed his questioning.

"Do you know where Isabella has gone or with whom?"

"*Non.* I have heard *rien,* nothing, from her. But that is not so unusual. She is a woman." Enzo spoke as if that settled it.

"Has she gone off like this before, without leaving word? Without telling you anything or even asking for your assistance as she packed?"

"*Mais oui.* She is a very private person. There is much about her that no one knows, not even her dear *ami* Enzo. You know, she would not have a maid or a staff really, because she wanted to preserve her privacy. She attended to most things herself."

"Wouldn't you have seen her when she left?"

"*Non,* not necessarily. You know, that *charment* house used to be two separate houses, so it has many entrances. There are two that enter on the ground floor, one from the canal, and one, which we call the side door and almost never use, from the street. From them you can use the stairs to reach the floors above. But there is also another door from the street, the front door, that goes directly to the second floor, directly to Isabella's apartments."

"Has anyone come to see her since she left?" Ian watched him.

"You, *mon comte*, for one." Enzo smiled again, that same strange smile. "And her protector and those with standing appointments." Enzo chuckled to himself at his raunchy pun, since few of Isabella's regular clientele spent their time in her house standing.

"Can you supply the names of her regular clients?"

Enzo shook his head as if he were truly sorry. "That would be to break my code of *honneur*."

Ian snorted at him, wondering exactly what a pimp's code of ethics might include. "Have any women been to see her?" he asked finally.

This time Enzo directed his disturbing smile at Bianca. "The lovely *Mademoiselle* Salva of course."

"And others? What about Signora Valdone? Have you ever seen her at the house?"

Enzo hesitated for a moment, deciding whether to feign ignorance or tell the truth. "I have never seen Madame Valdone around our house, no. But I have encountered her elsewhere. You know, the places that wealthy women like that go."

"I don't. Where do they go?" Bianca chimed in, her curiosity aroused.

Enzo looked hopelessly at her. "There are women with, let us say for the sake of the lady, unusual needs. They go places to have them met."

Ian was repulsed but Bianca was enthralled. Without thinking she asked, "Could you be more specific?"

"Also this has a bearing on Isabella?" Enzo asked doubtfully. "Isabella is not one who enjoys being with animals or feeling the sting of whips or hearing harsh words. You know," Enzo looked at Ian, "she is pure."

If one more person that day told Ian what he "knew," he thought he might bite them. As it was, he was having trouble controlling his rising frustration. His questions were getting him nowhere, and looking at the preening figure in front of him was giving him a headache. Not to mention Bianca, who seemed more interested in sexual perversion than in gathering information.

She had remained standing near the edge of the desk throughout Ian's questions, and she now wore a little frown. When Ian asked if she wanted to make any inquiries of their guest, "any legitimate inquiries," he had intoned coldly, it took a moment for her to come out of her reverie.

"Yes, yes, of course." Making a mental note to ask Ian what one did with whips, she refocused her mind on the task before her. She turned from her betrothed to face Enzo. "Is it possible for someone to enter the house without your knowledge?"

"Why, certainly! I have said about the three doors. All of Isabella's regular clientele have their own keys. Isabella does not want me to be bothered all the time, opening and shutting doors." Enzo shuddered, thinking of a life confined to those mundane tasks.

"Of course, I am sure you have many more important things to do." Bianca nodded at him sympathetically and began to pace the floor between his chair and Ian's desk. Ian, growing dizzy, was about to command her to cease her promenade when she suddenly stopped and faced Enzo. "When people come to the house, do they usually use the front door that leads directly to Isabella's apartment or the side door?"

Enzo looked thoughtful for a moment. "Those coming to see *her* usually use the front door."

Bianca leapt on his words. "Are there some people who come not to see her?"

"*Oui.*" Enzo smiled again, and Bianca had the uncomfortable sensation that *he* had led *her* to this point, rather than the other way around. "Recently, a group of men, always the same, have been meeting in the parlor, the room underneath Isabella's room. But what I am saying, what I tell you now, this is all very secret, yes?" He looked first at Bianca and then at Ian, waiting until each of them had nodded. "I tell you plainly, from the first, I do not like them. They make me suspicious, you see, because they always use the side door to enter. And always, Isabella, wearing a veil, must be there to admit them. But then they go straight to the parlor and they close the door and they will not admit my mistress. In her house, they are meeting, and they will not admit her. Not only am I suspicious, but I am hurt for her, you understand."

Bianca gave him another sympathetic look. "Did you ever ask Isabella about it? Share your suspicions with her?"

Before she had finished speaking he was nodding violently. "*Bien sûr!* I asked her why they always sneaked in, like insects and not like men, and she told me they do it for her, because she does not want old Val—I mean, her protector, to know about their coming."

"Does that answer satisfy you?" Bianca sounded incredulous.

"It did not originally, no. But then... This is very private, yes? You have given me already your words? I will share the joyful news with you. Three weeks ago, Isabella, my dear mistress, she tells me she is to be married! To a great lord, and we shall live in a palace. At the same time she tells me this, the meetings stop. So I think to myself, these meetings, they were to make her lord rich enough to marry her, and of course, she would not want her protector to know. Now, all we are doing is waiting to be happy."

"You are certain they were meetings, not, say, men gathering to gamble stakes higher than those allowed at the legal casinos?" Bianca wanted to be sure.

"*Mademoiselle,* I know the sound of cards being played and I know the sound of a meeting. They are not indistinguishable to one such as myself." Enzo sounded almost insulted. "I assure you, these were meetings."

"Do you have any idea what was discussed at those meetings?" Ian reasserted his right to ask questions, watching Enzo closely.

Enzo tilted his head to one side. "I tell you they will not admit my mistress, and you think perhaps they have admitted me? No," he said with a genteel snort, "I have no knowledge of their affairs. And I do not care to. It is enough for me that the husband of my mistress shall benefit."

"Will you name the men who attended the meetings?" Ian demanded.

Enzo said nothing, just sat and smiled at Ian.

"I suppose," Ian said after the silence had lengthened to almost a minute, "you could at least tell me when the meetings were held? Or even when they stopped?"

"You say it is information about my mistress you want, yet all you ever ask is about these men, these meetings. I do not think this is right, this prying into the affairs of other people. I do not think I was right to trust you." Enzo swept a sorrowful gaze from one to the other of his questioners and stood. "I come to help you, but I see I was wrong. I shall now collect my money and leave."

Ian was getting ready to argue with him, but Bianca spoke first. "Without names, without dates, your information is only barely helpful to us. We will pay you five hundred gold ducats now. If you change your mind, we can pay you more, much more. As long as someone else does not bring us the information first."

For a moment Enzo could not make up his mind. He could be comfortable for a while on five hundred ducats, even more comfortable and independent with three thousand. Or with six thousand. But something mentioned in the interview had made him think of another equally moneyed buyer for his information, and he wanted to approach him before he made an exclusive contract. Since he alone possessed the knowledge he wanted to sell, he knew he was in no danger of losing out by waiting another day.

"I shall keep that in mind." He bowed stiffly and took the money Ian tossed across the desk at him. Summoned by Bianca, Nilo appeared and escorted Enzo out. Then Bianca slid into the chair Enzo had just left and regarded Ian.

"So?" was the best opening line she could manage.

"So?" he echoed.

"So, did I bribe him? Did I conceal any information?"

"There was nothing worth concealing." Ian spoke contemptuously. "Certainly nothing worth five hundred gold ducats."

"I disagree completely, my lord. I think we learned the motive for the murder. Or at least, we learned of a potential motive."

Ian refused to be led along by her. "You mean Enzo did it because his pants were chafing him?"

"How can you make light of this, my lord, when you are holding my life in the balance?" Bianca's tone was more serious than Ian had ever heard it. "I know you regard me as more of a nuisance than a pleasure, but surely you cannot be so callous as to joke about the fate you have arranged for me. I know I can't."

Bianca stood and began to pace as the clock struck five. "You have decreed that nothing short of naming the murderer will convince you of my innocence. Even the ancient barbarians had a more equitable system of justice than that! But that is beyond the matter. I have accepted your challenge—I had no other choice—and now I have less than five days left to satisfy it."

Here was the difficult part. "I know if I asked you what passed between you and Signore Valdone in this room earlier, you would scoff at me. Likewise, if I asked you to reveal any of the other information which I am sure you have gathered. But what if I were to ask you specific questions, based on my own surmises? Questions to which you need answer only 'yes' or 'no.' Would you reply?"

Ian was touched by her assessment of his information-gathering abilities and certainly wanted to do nothing to impair it. "It would depend on the question."

Their eyes met when he spoke those words, the same words he had spoken to her the night before in that room under very different circumstances. For a second, memories of the previous night, and that morning, threatened to flood Bianca's mind and wash away her rationally ordered thoughts. Santa Felicia's ears, how did he do this to her? She closed her eyes for a moment to gather herself together, exhaled sharply, and began again.

"I have a theory, but before I set it forth I would like to know if you have learned anything to discredit it."

"Please continue," Ian said generously, finding he quite enjoyed hearing how Bianca's mind worked. Perhaps at the end of all this he would write a book on female dementia.

Bianca stopped pacing and sat. "Do you have reason to suspect that Isabella's father is not actually dead and has had some hand in this business?"

Puzzled, Ian answered, "No."

"Do you know something that makes you think Signora Valdone is involved in this?"

This time Ian took a moment to answer. "Yes and no. From what I heard just now, I would have to say no."

"Do you suspect anyone else?" Seeing that Ian had sat forward and his face was twitching that dangerous way, Bianca rushed on. "Besides me, of course."

He sat back and looked disappointed. "No."

"Very well, that leaves the conferences that Enzo mentioned. You need not take my word alone for the fact that Isabella was petty, jealous, and nosy. Half Venice could back me up, including, if pressed, Enzo. I have heard him say it myself, on other occasions." Bianca put up a hand to stop Ian's interruption. "Given those predominant personality characteristics, how likely does it seem to you that Isabella would allow people to meet in her house without observing or at least eavesdropping on their conversations?"

"That is not a 'yes' or 'no' question."

"Of course, I would not want you to go out on a limb for me. All right, I will tell you. It seems unlikely. Very unlikely. It seems equally unlikely that Enzo did not listen. In fact, he said as much."

"Was this in the same conversation when he told you how petty Isabella was?" Ian's tone showed he clearly thought she was fabricating the entire thing.

Bianca stayed patient. "No. It was here, just now, you heard it too. 'I know ze sound of cards being played and I know ze sound of a meeting.'" Bianca's imitation was even more grating than the original. "But if you think about it, my lord, there really is no difference between the sound of cards being played—men's voices, coins, paper being passed—and the sound of business being transacted, unless you can hear the content of the conversation."

Why was he still astonished by her intelligence? Ian asked himself. To all appearances, or at least when viewed in a certain narrow light, she had probably managed to commit a murder without leaving any traceable evidence, without making a single revealing slip to him, despite the, *ah*, close proximity in which he had kept her. She had even eluded his best efforts to trap her for five days while living right under his roof, and Ian's powers of reason had never had as strong a workout as they had during that period. It was too bad she was touched in the head, otherwise it would be a pleasure to match wits with her. Her deductions constantly dazzled him. They were elegantly simple, logically obvious, and yet, always a surprise to him. He found himself awed again, but determined not to admit it.

"Sounds specious to me. Are you suggesting that Isabella or Enzo or both actually participated in the conferences?"

"Nothing of the kind. I see no reason to doubt what Enzo said about Isabella being excluded. In fact, it is the basis of the second half of my deduction."

"Then how do you propose they heard the conferences? I did not know that courtesans possessed omniscience."

Bianca felt sorry for him. His wit was definitely slipping, taking his mind with it. She wondered if it was age or only exhaustion, and hoped for the latter. "Why couldn't Isabella and Enzo have listened clandestinely, through a hidden door or a peephole?"

"Do you know of one?"

"No, not for certain, but it would not surprise me at all to find one. Your house is not alone in having secret passages and concealed alcoves. Every old house in Venice probably has its share of those things."

"That is not a sound argument," Ian bluffed. "I can scarcely wait to hear the second premise you have based upon it."

"Your confidence has so heartened me that I have changed my mind. I see no reason to tell you anything at all, ever." Bianca, her eyes glowing with anger, stood to leave.

Ian was disappointed. He had been enjoying her fanciful narration; he enjoyed the way her nose scrunched up when she thought, and he was vaguely interested in what she had to say. He had to think quickly, had to come up with some artifice to force her into staying. "If you tell me the rest of your theory, I will tell you if I know anything to contradict it."

She was unsure how to proceed. Ian's brusque dismissal of her conclusions was infinitely depressing, and she did not think her psyche could bear much more. On the other hand, it might be the only way available to her to learn what information he had gathered.

"My theory depends on the fact that Isabella, excluded from the meetings, eavesdropped on them. If you are unwilling to accept that, I may as well stop right now."

"I will accept it, for the sake of argument." Ian was very polite.

"Whatever they were discussing was sensitive enough to exclude their hostess and require them to meet in an untraceable location. I would wager that Isabella decided to put the news she overheard to work. I think she used it to blackmail one of the participants at the meeting. But not in the conventional way, not for money. If it had just been that, she probably would not have been killed."

"What other form of blackmail is there? Gems, furnishings, luxuries, they all reduce to the same thing. And they were probably not much more than what he was paying her for her services anyway."

"Not all a courtesan's clients are as generous as you are, my lord," Bianca shot back at him, displeased by his interruption, and had the satisfaction of seeing him recoil. "Nor is your definition of blackmail entirely inclusive. Enzo told us that the meetings stopped at the same time that his mistress announced her plans to wed. To marry a nobleman. As you know, men of your class never marry courtesans. It seems likely, nay, almost certain, that Isabella used the information she learned to force one of the men who met at her house into marrying her." When Bianca had reached the end of her explanation, her face wore an expression of exaltation. Ian, still stinging from her earlier retort, decided she looked much too pleased with herself.

He shook his head in mock sympathy, like someone older and wiser addressing a promising but misguided student. "It sounds to me like you are drawing conclusions from coincidences."

While not entirely substantiated, not yet anyway, her theory was not completely groundless and certainly did not deserve Ian's blithe dismissal. Worse even than what Ian said, though, was the way he delivered it. Bianca felt as if she had been slapped in the face. So she decided to get even.

"I suppose I should have been prepared for you to protect Crispin that way."

"Crispin? My brother?"

"Of course. He perfectly fits the description of Isabella's fiancé that Enzo gave us. He is a great lord and he does live in a large house. It would be like Crispin to be considerate enough to provide you with a *capitaine* on his marriage too, since you don't have one."

Ian did not like a single word she spoke. Even though he knew for certain, or at least almost certain, that Crispin was not mixed up in this, the idea of the cringing Enzo moving into his house had completely and uncomfortably entered his imagination. "Crispin has nothing to do with Isabella's murder." He spoke firmly, as much to convince Bianca as to reassure himself that Enzo would not soon be living under his roof.

"Are you sure, my lord? Really sure that Crispin has not engaged himself to Isabella?" Bianca was all wide-eyed innocence.

"Of course. He would have told me." Ian hoped he sounded more sure of that than he felt.

Bianca's innocence turned to incredulity. "That he was engaged to a courtesan? How would you have reacted?"

"This is simply not open to discussion. Crispin is not engaged to Isabella or any other woman."

"Maybe not now, now that Isabella is dead. But was he? Can you prove it?"

"Signorina, you go to far." Polar bears could have lived happily in the atmosphere created by Ian's voice.

"Only as far as you go, my lord." Bianca matched his glacial tone. "It seems only fair that if you may require proof of me, I can ask the same of you. Call him and put the question to him. Unless you are too unsure of the answer."

He should have wrung her neck when he had the chance in the gondola. She had him trapped now, and he was miserable. He had no desire to do her bidding, but his sense of fair play told him that he should acquiesce. He pulled the bell rope near his desk and asked the prompt servingman to show his brother into the library.

Bianca and Ian sat in frigid silence as they awaited Crispin's arrival, glaring at each other, two tigers waiting to pounce. The tense atmosphere of the room hit Crispin like a boulder as he entered, tempting him to turn and run. Instead, he bowed politely, smiled at Bianca, nodded at Ian, and offered his services to them.

"Are you engaged to be married?" Ian did not give him time to finish his greeting.

Crispin was well and truly baffled. "Not that I know of. Do you know something I don't know? Did Mother rig one of those horrible betrothals for me when I was in the cradle, like Aunty Renata did for Miles?"

"Satisfied?" Ian spoke not to Crispin but to Bianca, who shook her head.

Bianca kept her eyes at Ian. "What your brother meant to ask was, were you ever affianced to Isabella Bellocchio?"

"She's a courtesan! I couldn't marry her even if I wanted to. She is charming and entertaining, to a point, but marry her..." Crispin shook his head in disbelief. "That would be condemning a man to a miserable life indeed."

"Now I am satisfied." Bianca sat back in her chair smugly. Ian did likewise. They were regarding each other this way, each trying to look more smug than the other, when Crispin interrupted them.

"Would one of you please explain what is going on?"

Ian answered brusquely. "No. And please do not repeat this conversation to anyone."

"What conversation? What could I possibly repeat? That the two of you occasionally hissed the word 'satisfied' at each other?" Crispin started to laugh, noticed the unfriendly expressions on both their faces, and stopped. "Is it safe to leave you two alone together?"

Ian growled at him, and Crispin made for the door. Before he reached a hand for the knob, it opened to admit Francesco and Roberto.

"I wouldn't go in there if I were you." Crispin stopped them on the threshold. "Not unless you have your gladiator armor on."

Francesco and Roberto looked puzzled.

"I think those two are allergic to each other," Crispin confided in a whisper. "On second thought, perhaps you should go in. You are doctors, maybe you can cure them. Personally, I am leaving. I don't know when I'll be back. I will probably send for my things in a few days. Moving the plant rooms will be hard, but..."

"I'm sure we can arrange something." Ian finally turned his head to glare at his brother. "Leave your new address with Giorgio."

"That is easy, I can tell you that right now." Crispin was grinning. "Have them sent to the house of Isabella Bellocchio. That is B-E-L-L-O-C-C—"

"Out!" Ian rumbled in a voice he might have borrowed from Valdo Valdone. Laughing, Crispin bid adieu to his uncles and left.

Ian was regarding the space left absent by his brother with such rabid malice that Bianca had to work hard to conceal a smile. When she had her face under control, she greeted Roberto and Francesco.

"We did not mean to interrupt anything important," Francesco began, the look of puzzlement still on his face.

"My conference with Signorina Salva should have ended an hour ago," was Ian's chilly reply.

"Good, then you will not mind if we steal her away from you."

Ian snorted. "Mind? Heavens no. If your aim is to please me, don't stop at stealing her. Sell her off. And don't be too concerned about getting a good price."

Bianca now had no problem restraining her smile. "If selling me into bondage will free me from his harassment, I am ready." She stood and held her arms out in anticipation of being led to the auction block. "Only promise me you will use the proceeds of my body wisely and not give them to the honorable Conte d'Aosto. He will just use the money to bribe some expensive courtesan for her favors."

Ian's face was as white with rage as Roberto's and Francesco's were red with embarrassment.

"Actually, we just wanted Bianca to meet with the seamstress and try on her ball gown for size. Unless you have changed your mind in the last hour and decided to cancel the party?" Roberto let the question hang.

"Ha, and miss the opportunity to celebrate this happy betrothal? Never!" Pushing his chair away from the desk, Ian rose. It was too hard to glare at Bianca when he was seated.

She turned her back to him and addressed Roberto and Francesco. "I have plenty of dresses. I can wear one of the gowns I already own. I am sure I do not need a new one. It would be a pity to waste all that money on clothes for a slave."

Roberto and Francesco exchanged looks. How could they tell her that her plain, coarse dresses, while fine for her medical house calls, were not appropriate either for the ball or for her impending position as a countess. Francesco hit on the perfect tactic first. "You must have a new gown. It is traditional that the chaperons give the new bride a gown as a betrothal present." He hoped that Bianca knew little enough about proper betrothal practice to keep her from spotting the lie.

"Indeed," Roberto continued, "These days it is common for the chaperons to provide the new bride with an entire wardrobe. We hope you will not mind if we have taken that liberty."

"A new wardrobe?" Bianca had never been concerned with how she looked, and since her mother had died while she was still in swaddling clothes, no one had ever bothered to tell her she should be. Her aunt Anatra had graciously helped her have several gowns made for her debut in Venice, picking out colors and styles whose most recent heyday had been in the last century. Because she could not entirely lock Bianca and her fortune away, Anatra's intention had been to render the girl so homely that her son would have no competition for her hand, but the unfashionable attire had done nothing to reduce her niece's appeal to the suitors that flocked around her.

"I admit I need a new work dress, since my favorite one was destroyed in the fire, but an entirely new wardrobe?"

Ian had always been too busy fuming at her or picturing her naked to pay much attention to Bianca's clothing, but he now found himself intrigued. He imagined her in a plush blue-and-gold brocade, the dress's low neckline framing a rich sapphire choker. Then he imagined her out of it, wearing just the sapphire choker, and his earlier anger fused into intense arousal. To conceal it, he reseated himself behind his desk.

"Francesco and Roberto are just being polite. Your wardrobe is a travesty." Ian spoke to his uncles. "Order the gowns from Rinaldo Stucchi. And remind him that I like blue-and-gold brocade. I will of course pay for everything."

Bianca gasped when she heard the name of Venice's foremost gown maker, and again when Ian said he was paying. It was one thing to accept a traditional gift from her chaperons, though she did not remember ever having heard of such a practice, but it was another to have to be beholden to the maddening man who couldn't even bother to remain standing through an entire discussion. She was about to express this, and several other sentiments, but Francesco cut her off.

"Indeed, we are keeping Signore Stucchi waiting right now. He has arrived with ten dresses for a fitting." Francesco paused to catch his breath, saw that Bianca was again going to attempt to speak, and rushed on. "Your offer is very generous, Ian, but of course we mustn't take you up on it. It is our duty, and our privilege, to supply your betrothed with her wardrobe. You know the customs." Francesco looked pointedly at his nephew and then at Bianca, who had finally stopped trying to interrupt.

Ian decided to let his uncles get away with their subterfuge. He knew that they had made up the renowned custom of wardrobe provisioning on the spot, just as he knew that any money they spent would inevitably come from him. But the thought of Bianca dressed properly, or actually, the thought of undressing a properly dressed Bianca, was too delicious to interfere with, and it seemed clear she would accept nothing from him.

Bianca attempted several more arguments about why she did not need new clothes, but stood no chance against the combined front of Roberto, Francesco, and Ian. As the clock struck six, she finally gave in and allowed herself to be led from the library, looking only slightly less unhappy at the prospect of spending hours with a dressmaker than she had when she offered herself up as a slave.

Eight hours later Bianca was sound asleep in her bed. Three of the proceeding hours had been spent, not disagreeably, with the dressmaker, and she had to admit that the beautiful new gowns they had ordered thrilled her with a sensual pleasure she had not expected. But after the long session with fabrics, pattern books, measuring instruments, and detailed discussions about the difference between appliqué and embroidery, she had been exhausted. During dinner with Roberto and Francesco, she had been incapable of reciting the narrative of Caesar's miraculous birth she had promised them, and spoke nary a word until the topic of flowers for the ball arose. Then, to the surprise of them all, she blurted out, "Gardenias are Ian's favorite flower," hastily excused herself, locked herself in her apartment, and burst into tears. Instead of worrying about the desperate state of her life and her emotions, she acted on the instructions of her physician—herself—and went straight to bed.

It was there, therefore, that Ian found her when he soundlessly entered her room late that night, or rather, early the next morning. Returning from his evening out, he had convinced himself that another test of her attractive powers was in order before he slept. He began by objectively studying her face on the pillow in the candlelight of the taper he carried with him. With her eyes closed, her long lashes made graceful arcs on her cheeks, he noticed, and he had the sudden urge to see if they would feel like butterfly wings against his hand. She was lying on her side along one half of the large bed, facing the other half. One of her arms, its thin sleeve pushed up past her elbow, had strayed to the empty half of the bed and lay there outstretched, like an invitation. As he watched her sleep, the blankets going up and down with her even breathing, Ian felt an emotion he could not describe, but he was sure it was not arousal. He congratulated himself on the effectiveness of his cure, and decided that since he was no longer in any danger of being seduced by her, he should accept the offer made by her arm and join her in bed.

But once he had stripped off his clothes and climbed in next to her, once she had pressed her warm, tender body against his, he realized he had been duped. Whatever his earlier emotion had been, it easily gave way to a powerful rush of desire. The thin, soft fabric of Bianca's nightgown brushing his thighs sent a shiver of excitement through him. And when she burrowed deeper against his chest, her small hand straying first to his cheek, then to his neck, he thought he might begin to rave. It was lunacy, he told himself, to be so excited by the least erotic of touches. The brush of a piece of fabric! Clearly, his cure needed more time to work, and the only possible treatment was lovemaking. Resigned, he reached down and caressed her face, willing her to open her eyes and ask him to enter her.

In Bianca's dream, Ian made love to her. His hand was on her cheek, then her neck, then her breast. She gave a little sigh and trailed her fingers from his neck down his chest, over to his side, and then up his back. Ian began slowly, very slowly, to push the material of her nightgown up until it was above her waist. She could feel the delicious warmth of his hands through the fabric as they moved up and over her body. When the lower half of her was naked, Ian moved his body closer to hers and began to rub his hard shaft along her thigh.

Her hands now moved down his back, luxuriating in the feeling of his warm, muscular flesh, his smooth skin, and finally his wonderfully graspable backside. She left her hands there, using them strategically to push him toward her as she shifted slightly so that his shaft was rubbing hard against her sensitive place. She let her legs part slightly, not enough for Ian to slide into her, but enough for him to move up and down between her thighs, to be caressed by the wet, waiting lips of her sex.

In Bianca's dream, she was wanton. She pushed Ian onto his back and climbed atop him so she could more easily rub herself over his shaft, pressing against it, until she felt her climax nearing, and then she took her hand and guided him into her. She heard him moan softly as she kept her hand between their bodies, rubbing his wet organ with it as he plunged into her body. She whispered to him, told him of the sliver of pleasure that she was feeling, described it as it grew larger with each of his thrusts, told him how she would close around him when she climaxed, her passage becoming snug around his tense shaft. She felt it coming and moved her hand away, commanding him to grind himself into her, ordering him to take her, to touch her, to bite her, her words barely distinguishable from her loud cries of pleasure that began soon after and went on and on until Ian mingled them with his own.

In Bianca's dream, she told Ian she loved him.

Chapter Fifteen

The room was pitch black and stank. At the center of the room, the man bound to the chair began to regain consciousness. His entire body ached from his beating, and when he licked his lips, he tasted blood. When he tried to move his right arm, the pain was so intense that he almost passed out again. He took several deep breaths to rouse himself and gagged on the foul-smelling air. He was not sure that being unconscious was not somehow preferable.

Voices penetrated from someplace outside the room. He strained his ears to make them out, but the words were muffled by the thick walls. Even faintly, however, he could be certain he heard her voice.

He had recognized her instantly when they had arrived, the young man acting as his escort. She had arranged herself on a couch, her shapely legs revealed between the folds of her diaphanous dressing gown, her maid languorously combing out the thick plaits of her hair. It fell in glossy tendrils over her breasts, skimmed her shoulders, curved under her chin. The woman knew the power of the performance she was orchestrating, the sensuality of even the simplest acts when seen voyeuristically, and pretended to be unaware of her audience.

It was exciting to watch, and both he and his escort had found themselves filled with longing by the time the spectacle was through. The woman took notice of them, finally, and beckoned them over, sending her maid away.

His escort had introduced him and stated the purpose of his visit. The woman regarded her guest sharply with a half smile that was both inviting and quizzical. He felt as though she were reading him, trying to learn his pleasures, and his weaknesses. He told himself to be wary, so when she asked him several questions, he had refused to answer unless an amount was agreed upon.

Praising his carefulness, she had gestured him onto the divan alongside her, dismissing his escort and saying she was sure they could help each other. For an hour, she listened intently as he spoke about his background, his family. She sighed sympathetically when he told of their misfortunes, colored with anger when he described the lies that had been told about them. Her eyes filled with melting tears as he described the wrongs perpetrated upon them by their enemies. At that point she reached out her hand to show her support and let it rest casually on his thigh, her eyes locked on his.

He knew as he spoke that she was falling in love with him. He could feel it, there was no mistaking her responses. No woman had ever warmed to him the same way, had ever given him such completely rapt attention. When she asked him if he would help her, if he would be her champion, he could only say yes. She leaned over and kissed him, her taste and scent filling his head dizzyingly. She would be his, she told him, and his heart thrilled at the prospect. He had only to tell her what had passed in his meeting earlier that day.

It was such a small thing, such an easy thing, she told him. She did not want there to be any secrets between them, any hesitation, any unknowns, and he agreed. He told her everything, described the meeting in detail. He had given them no names, had told them nothing, he swore it.

But she did not believe him. She turned her eyes from his and summoned back the young man to be his escort.

"He is unkind to me," she told his escort. "I have been candid with him, have opened my heart to him, and what do I get in return? Ungrateful of my attentions, he lies to me. He is no friend of mine. He has betrayed me."

Her guest, the subject of her charge, moved to speak, but the woman interrupted. "Do not speak. Your lies, your treachery to me, cause me too much pain. You are my enemy." She cast a final injured glance on her guest, then turned to his escort. "Take him away, take him to your place and quiz him. I cannot bear to look upon him, to hear his web of lies, any longer." The pout of her lips changed slightly, suggestively, as she continued. "You know how pleased I will be with my angel if you find out what I want to know. I will come to you soon, I promise."

In the hours that followed, he had been beaten mercilessly. His escort had discovered that interrogation was not only tiring but also arousing. There was something about watching the well-dressed figure grovel and writhe before him that the young man really enjoyed. He had pursued his information-gathering task with a vigilance that he knew would well please his mistress. By the time the woman had arrived, he was in a frenzy of anticipation for his reward.

After she had accommodated and satiated his bodily desires on one of the benches lining the dark room, the young man had delivered a report on the results of his inquisition.

"He swore, even under my most creative tortures, that he gave them no names. He said they asked for them but he refused to supply any."

"And yet," the woman paused to run her fingers down his stomach, "he claims they, or rather, she, paid him five hundred gold ducats. Is she fool enough to throw away money like that?"

The young man looked thoughtful for a moment, then spoke with more certainty than he felt. "Yes, I would say she is."

The woman raised herself on her elbows, struck by an idea. "Are you certain that they paid him at all? Did he have the money on him?"

"When I came upon him, he had already been at the tables for some time, and he appeared to be losing badly. But he still had over three hundred ducats in his pocket. Even if they did not pay him the full five hundred he claims, they paid him a large amount."

She drew circles in his golden chest hair, rewarding him for his thorough inquiry. "I still do not understand it, but I suppose if she is as half-witted as you say she is, it may be true. Do you think we can learn anything else from him?"

When the young man shook his head she resumed, speaking in a low voice near his ear. "You will give him his payment then? Just the way I said?" The young man groaned in agreement and pushed her head down toward his rising shaft.

On the other side of the door, Enzo listened to his cries of pleasure with envy.

Chapter Sixteen

Her heart beating rapidly, Bianca sat straight up in bed and saw there was no sign of Ian. She sniffed the air and did not smell him. It had only been a dream. She had dreamt it. None of it was real. Especially not the last part. She sighed deeply with relief and stood.

Her relief was momentarily dampened by the stickiness between her legs, but she concluded that had to be a natural result of the dream. Still, she was not completely at her ease as she dressed, and she would rather have encountered a herd of wild boar than Ian that morning. She mentally reviewed the list of tasks she had decided on the night before, making a face when she remembered her dress fitting at six, and set out for the servants' quarters.

She descended the two and a half flights to Marina and Caesar's new room. Both mother and son were doing well, but the clock was striking twelve by the time Bianca had finished her visit. Concerned that she might run into Ian on his way to the dining room, she climbed the four and a half flights to the laboratories on the back stairs.

Her goal was not her own laboratory but Crispin's glass rooms, or more precisely, Crispin himself. Bianca told herself she was just going to ask Crispin a few questions about the Arboretti and about

Isabella, just to get to know him better, but if he wanted to give her any insights about his mysterious, maddening brother, that would be fine as well. She knocked on the door of the glass room, got no answer, found it was unlocked, and entered.

She had unwittingly used a different door than the one she had entered by before, and she now found herself in a magical but unfamiliar room filled with benches and benches of fruit trees. There were oranges, peaches, plums, apples, and tens of other plants whose identities were a mystery to her. She was looking around in awe when someone spoke behind her.

"Thought I heard someone who ought to not be up here being up here, be damned if I didn't," was Luca's welcome to her when she spotted him behind a furry brown fruit tree.

"Good day, Signore Luca." Bianca curtsied politely as she spoke, hoping to soften the man, but instead increased his ire as her skirt nearly toppled a tub of lemons.

"Thems women's things, always making a nuisance for everyone." He began muttering to himself and passed through another door before Bianca could apologize or tell him how much she would rather be wearing men's leggings.

Cursing her inconvenient petticoat, she followed him into the room she had seen two days earlier. It looked as if there were even more flowers than before, with dozens of them sitting in pots of water against the far wall. Luca was parading up and down the aisles with a huge knife, pausing every now and then to cleanly slice a flower from its stalk. Bianca watched this operation for almost a minute, enough time for Luca to assemble a large bouquet, and then tried to get his attention again.

"I am sorry to disturb you," she began, "but I was looking for Crispin.'"

"What for? Isn't one of them Foscari brothers enough for you?"

Bianca was confused. "I only wanted to," she sneezed, "ask him some questions."

"That's how it starts, be damned if it don't. What's this, what's that, where's your affections, do you like this gown? Before you know it, you'll be fluttering those eyelashes at him and then where's your questions? Nope, I won't let that happen to *ragazzo mio*. You can have Ian, but I am keeping Crispin away from the likes of you, yes, I am. And anyway, you missed him by hours and hours. He was here last night but he's not up here now, so you needn't be either."

Three quick sneezes were Bianca's only reply.

When the sneezing first began, she had thought nothing of it, but now an idea blazed across her mind. She began moving quickly up and down the benches of flowers, ignoring the rain of curses that the antagonized Luca was sending down upon her. She was just starting up the fifth and last row when she spotted it.

Two red flowers were growing from a single bulb, buried deep within a very ornate flowerpot. As far as she could see, neither the plant nor the pot had a twin anywhere in the glass rooms. She stopped in front of the pot, her eyes watering, and wondered how she could have forgotten about it. Of course! That was what had been missing from Isabella's room when she went there to investigate. She raised her hand to pick up the pot, but Luca was there before she could reach for it.

"It's bad enough you come in here, bumping around letting those women's things run riot across my plants, but don't now be setting yourself to touching them. These plants don't like the female touch, specially not this one I would say from the way you're sneezing at it."

Bianca had to concede that she and the plant did not get along. She moved away, but only slightly, and tried to control her nose enough to speak.

"Has that plant," she sneezed, "been here for a long time?"

Luca scowled at her, then transferred the scowl to the plant. "That plant has something fierce against you, be damned if it doesn't. I'm not sure it would like me telling you its biography, the way it feels."

Bianca saw she would have to beg. She interrupted a series of sneezes to plaintively choke out, "Please, Luca," before sneezing again. "It is very important."

Luca took a closer look at the plant, sniffed it, and sneezed once himself. That settled it.

"For all that, not a very nice kind of a plant to send as a present, if you want my opinion. It arrived this morning, all wrapped up fancy in paper, and I think to myself, here is something good, damned if I didn't." He sent a disappointed glance at the plant and shook his head. "Now, I've never seen its like before, of that I am sure, and neither had my Crispin, but that don't make it worth looking at or coming a-badgering people with questions, especially not people as have a job to do."

Bianca was deeply miserable. Not only were her eyes and nose watering, but she noticed small itchy red bumps coming up on her hands. She had to leave the plant rooms, but first she had one more question to put to the unfriendly plant man.

"Do you know," she sneezed, and sneezed again, "who sent it this morning? Where it came from? Anything about it?"

Luca was regarding her with pity, almost. "Did I not say you ought not be in here, be damned if I didn't. And now look at you, worse than horrible, even for a woman. I don't know where the plant came from, and I don't see why you care to either, not as if you'll be wanting to write them a thank-you card." He put a hand on her shoulder to usher her out, almost managing to conceal his distaste at having to touch a woman. "You'll need to be leaving now, take my word for it."

Bianca had no choice but to agree with him. Once in the hall her sneezing slowed and her eyes began to water less. She still felt strange and a little logy, but she pushed those feelings aside and went in search of Crispin. Her desire to find out about the plant overrode even her discomfort at encountering Ian, and she marched bravely into the dining room. Only Roberto and Francesco, deep in conversation, were still seated at the table. They looked up briefly when she walked in, then did a double take and stared.

"Heavens, my child, what has happened to you?" Roberto moved toward her as he spoke, putting his hand on her forehead.

Francesco was there too and would have opened her mouth to peer in if she had not first sneezed and then begun to speak.

"Nothing." She sneezed. Bianca acted nonchalant. "I had a slight," she sneezed, "reaction," she sneezed, "to one of Crispin's plants." She took a deep breath and tried to speak without sneezing, knowing her argument would be more persuasive. "But I am fine now and was looking for Crispin."

Francesco led her to a large mirror at the far end of the room. "Look at yourself. You are not fine."

Bianca now understood why they had been staring at her. The red dots on her hands were also visible on her face and neck, nicely complementing her red-rimmed eyes and pink nose.

"But I feel," she sneezed, then sneezed again, "fine." She turned away from the mirror to emphasize the disparity between her looks and her health.

Roberto and Francesco, however, would have none of it. They conferred between themselves, shushing Bianca's attempts to distract them, and finally agreed on both an elixir and a treatment. They would give her a large glass of wine and send her to bed.

Bianca balked, saying that she had errands to do, and finally, in desperation, reminding them about her dress fitting.

"Do you expect to attend the ball looking like that?" Francesco asked cruelly, swinging Bianca around again to face the mirror. She was forced to admit defeat and allowed herself to be ushered upstairs and put to bed. It was little consolation to her that the Chianti she gulped down was probably the best in Ian's cellar, but Francesco and Roberto found it very soothing to their nerves when they split the remainder of the bottle later.

The gossip reached Palazzo Foscari at about the same time that Ian returned from his meeting at Sebastian's. Sorting through all the possible enemies of the Arboretti and figuring out the best mode of inquiry into the explosion had been grueling. The wretched possibility that one of the Arboretti themselves was the traitor had to be owned up to and resolved, which created an atmosphere of such unpleasantness that, although it was decided that one of their number had not planned the explosion, Ian and Crispin were barely on speaking terms by the time the meeting concluded. Ian was so relieved to be at home, with the prospect of uninterrupted hours in his library, that he did not even notice Caesar's wails as he entered the house.

But his relief was short-lived. Less than half an hour after he had cloistered himself in the library, Giorgio entered, looking grim.

"You told me you'd want to know right away if I had any success tracing the source of this," Giorgio laid the jeweled dagger on Ian's desk as he spoke, "but I think you might want to reconsider."

Ian knew that Giorgio, while prone to joking and mockery, would never deliberately toy with him, especially not in his present mood. "What are you suggesting?"

"Merely that maybe the information is not worth having anyway."

"S'bones, Giorgio, cease your evasions. Who made the dagger?"

"That question is easy, Federigo Rossi made it. I told you none of the goldsmiths in the city would own up to it the first time I asked, but when I tried the strategy you suggested, pretending it had been a betrothal present and we did not know who to thank, they opened right up. And no wonder, because your idea was even more plausible than you imagined." Giorgio paused, deciding whether to continue or try to change the subject. "You see, the dagger was commissioned by Giovanni Salva."

"Bianca's brother!" Ian echoed loudly, and then sat glaring at the weapon on his desk. Damn that woman, damn her with her protestations of innocence, her sensual words, her promises. Damn her for toying with him. Her brother! How could she be such a fool? Or how could he be? He found he had gotten so used to the idea of her probable innocence that he could scarcely believe her guilt, did not want to believe it. But what else could explain *this?* His incredulity turned to icy rage. He would confront her with it and she would have to crumble. There would be no more fancy lies and excuses from her now.

"Send Bianca to me." Ian's lips were pressed together so tightly that they were barely visible.

Giorgio hesitated. "Before I do that, I think I should tell you one more thing, something you are not going to like any better. It may not be true, I heard it myself only a short time ago in the kitchens, but I think you had better know. That man, Enzo, that I brought up here yesterday to meet with you and Bianca?" Ian nodded for Giorgio to continue. "His body has been found floating in a canal not far from here."

Master and servant regarded each other morbidly, each with the same unpleasant thought.

"I asked around a little, but the answers are inconclusive." Giorgio preempted Ian's question. "Marina, that is, her new maid, says she was with her from about half ten until the clock struck twelve, but none of the staff saw her after that. Your uncles claim that she came to the dining room as they were finishing luncheon, sneezing and covered with bumps, and they sent her to bed. She is there now, I just looked, but no one checked on her between, say, two o'clock and five. And even if she really was ill then, there is still the period from about noon until one when no one saw her. One of the serving men said he thought he saw her heading for the back stairs and puzzled over it at the time, but he did not stop her. I have not yet confronted her with any of this, figuring you would want to do that yourself."

Ian nodded. "Bring her."

When Bianca entered the library, all the stoniness that Ian had shed in the course of the previous week had returned and even redoubled. He sat more like a mountain than a man, contemplating her silently. All that remained of her horticultural reaction were the red rims of her eyes and a slight pink tinge on her nose. She did not look sick, Ian told himself, and another part of him whispered, nor does she look like a murderer. It was not enough that she had infiltrated his household, but she seemed also to have taken hold of some part of his mind. He heard her dreamy words from the previous night in his head, and a tremor went through him. She had tried to manipulate him, tried using the most familiar of tricks, and it had almost worked. The idea that a woman could do that to him augmented Ian's fury and deepened his steely glare. He was determined not to let the moments they had shared together blind him to the truth. His earlier softness and the strange emotions he had begun to feel galvanized instead into a steely determination to make Bianca confess her guilt. When he spoke, his voice came from the deepest, coldest, stoniest part of him.

"It is time for you to tell me the truth. All of it."

This again? They were back to this? Bianca, too tired to argue, was filled with despair. "I have already told you the truth. The whole truth. You know everything."

Ian pounded his fist on his desk and looked at her with fury. "Lies, all lies!"

"Why? Why must they be lies? There is nothing to contradict them. Nothing." Bianca, as if infected by Ian's anger, felt her rage returning and with it her strength.

Ian held up the dagger. "There is this. And I know who ordered it."

"Who?"

Ian would have sworn that Bianca was genuinely interested. Damn, but she was sly.

"Your curiosity is so persuasive," he sneered, "that I think I shall gratify it. It was commissioned by Giovanni. Giovanni Salva. Your brother."

Ian had to compliment her again on her performance. Her look of surprise was very real, and her gasp added a nice touch. The hands flying to her face might have been too much, but he supposed she was stalling for time, trying to compose her next elaborate lie.

Apparently she could not think of anything adequate. Looking bewildered, she asked only, "Are you sure?"

"You mean, is there any way for you to wriggle out of this? No, there is not. I am sure. You had your brother commission this dagger, and you planted it on the body. I am still not certain whether you or your brother committed the actual murder, but I *am* certain you will soon tell me. Is that who you have been protecting all this time?"

The idea of Giovanni as a murderer rendered Bianca dumb. She and her brother were not particularly close, but she knew him well enough to know that he was not evil. At least she thought she did.

"I'm afraid I don't know what to say. I wish I had some way to explain Giovanni's actions, but I really don't. We are not that intimate."

"*Ha-ha!* Just like a woman to worm out of it by letting the blame rest somewhere else. I tell you, the theory I favor is that you did the whole thing yourself, just using your brother for this one little chore. And I'll tell you why I prefer it. Because I know about your other murder."

This would have been the appropriate moment for the flinging-of-hands-to-face maneuver, Ian thought, completely unimpressed by Bianca's blank, puzzled look. He should have known she was too slick to confess, so he went on. "Enzo's body has already been found. I am surprised you did not work harder to conceal it. Surely a few well placed rocks could have done the trick. We know you have no discomfort pawing the bodies of the dead."

"Enzo? Isabella's Enzo?"

"Very unoriginal to feign ignorance. Yes, Enzo, the man whom you pretended not to be bribing so generously yesterday. Now I understand why you were so willing to let him walk out of here with my money."

"It was my money," Bianca interjected.

"Yes, well, it probably is now, as I am sure you liberated it from him when you killed him."

"The body was found naked." Giorgio spoke from behind Bianca. Not caring to leave his master alone with a murderess, he had decided to linger through the conference.

"Easier than going through his pockets." Ian nodded to himself. "I bet you are saving his clothes for the next time you decide to go gallivanting around dressed like a man. And I am sure you had no trouble enticing him out of them, probably inviting him to enact one of your perverted fantasies. What was it, whips? Animals? Oh, I know. You like to watch."

Bianca let out a yelp. Until then she had been in a state of shock, but when Ian spoke his last words, she felt as if she had been punched in the stomach. Trembling and on the verge of tears, she tried to speak, but no words would come out.

"Don't bother to speak unless you are planning to confess. I will not tolerate any more of your lies."

"How dare you? How dare you, how dare you, how dare you?" Bianca was on her feet, moving to the desk where Ian sat, her hands balled into tight little fists. Before she got close enough to make him her next victim, Giorgio grabbed her from behind and held her, squirming, in his arms. It was then, with Bianca suspended in midair, that the door opened to admit Francesco and Roberto, who, finding her absent from her bed against doctor's orders, had gone in search of their ward.

"Bravo, fine performance," Ian was saying caustically when they entered the room. "Your 'outrage' is much better than your 'surprise.' I almost found myself believing it."

As they regarded the sputtering figure still clasped in Giorgio's arms, Francesco and Roberto were completely persuaded.

"Set her down at once!" Roberto commanded Giorgio, who reluctantly acceded but remained standing behind Bianca's elbow, just in case.

"What under heaven is going on here?" Francesco demanded, deeply flushed.

"I was trying to kill him." Bianca gestured at Ian.

"I see." Francesco was nodding. "Certainly you are not the first to want to do that, he is very provoking. What exactly did he do to you?"

"I caught her in a web of lies too sticky to escape from." Ian spoke before she could, sounding satisfied. "I now have proof of her guilt."

"You have no such thing!" Bianca worked to control the rising tide of her anger. "You have a dagger that someone close to me ordered, and you have a dead body that someone in this neighborhood discarded. Neither of those point to me in any way."

"Bosh! I know you and I know your cunning ways. Your signature on these crimes could not be clearer."

Bianca was shaking her head in disbelief. This, this was the man she had bared her soul to. This was the man to whom, she feared, she had revealed the deepest secret of her heart. And he had misunderstood everything. Willfully. What had happened to him to make him so blind and so unyielding? And why did she have to be its innocent victim?

Half of her wanted to jump into a canal and keep company with Enzo's corpse, but the other half of her told her to persevere—if only for the pleasure of vindicating herself and proving that horrible, hateful, stern, stony, implacable, unlovable, irresistible man wrong. Using cold, hard, reason she saw that the first option precluded the second, but the second did not preclude the first, therefore the most advisable course was to pursue the second until it was proven unfeasible and then implement the first. Thus, she decided to continue her search for the murderer and jump into the canal only when all hope was lost. Relieved to have found such a sound solution, she faced Ian with renewed vigor.

Francesco and Roberto were remonstrating with him when she broke in. "You gave me, my lord, one hundred and sixty-eight hours to prove my innocence. I still have ninety-one hours left. Have you so lost your sense of honor that you would break our agreement?"

Ian glared at her. "Given that I now have proof of your guilt beyond any shadow of a doubt, I see no reason to let you continue your investigations." Bianca tried to interrupt, but Ian would not let her. "However, as long as you do not leave this house, I see no reason not to let you continue to try. It might be amusing to watch. I warn you, however, I am going to arm the staff. And don't imagine you can seduce them into compliance like you did poor Enzo. My men will not be ruled by the dictates of their bodies."

Bianca spoke reassuringly. "Don't worry. If I have learned only one thing from you, it is that seduction is far more tedious than it is worth." With that she turned on her heel and marched out under the astonished gazes of four sets of eyes.

Chapter Seventeen

Ian spent the rest of the evening very out of sorts. He felt as if his world were somehow crumbling, the Arboretti suspicious of one another, his household in an uproar. At the first opportunity, he sought Crispin in the plant rooms and apologized to him, an occurrence so rare that Crispin almost fainted. While Ian was there, Luca mentioned Bianca's morning visit, which accounted for at least part of the gaps in her day. Ian was surprised at himself. He felt glad to hear that she had an alibi for the morning, probably because, he reasoned, it narrowed his field of inquiry and thus made his investigation easier. Certainly, that was it.

Still restless, he decided a walk in the rain would be good for him, and he set out without any particular direction. He was surprised, or at least tried to be, when he found himself confronting the two street doors of Isabella's house. He was shocked when he noticed that he was tinkering with the lock on the side door, and astonished when he felt himself entering.

Once inside he moved quietly and quickly, not wanting to disturb his conscience or anyone who might be there. Deciding that Isabella's room was the likeliest place, he went there first, relying on the light from a small window. Miraculously, he had thought to bring candles and flint with him on his walk, you know, for eventualities, but he did not yet want to use them. He paused at the landing to listen, heard nothing but the beating of his heart, and proceeded to Isabella's door. It opened soundlessly and he walked in.

Then someone broke his back. At least that seemed to be the goal of the man pinning Ian against the floor, where he had been thrown during the initial assault. That the rug needed to be shaken out was Ian's first thought after he gratefully realized that his back was only severely contorted, not actually broken. Nonetheless he kept still, his mouth pressed into the dirty rug, as his adversary replaced the knee he had been using to hold Ian down with the barrel of a gun.

"What are you doing here?" the adversary demanded. Ian had an antagonizing comment ready on the tip of his tongue, it being his noted practice to provoke anyone and everyone, but he swallowed it when he recognized the unmistakable voice.

"Valdone! Damn it, man, you nearly killed me."

The aggressor thought he also recognized a voice but was not sure. He scrambled to his feet, as quickly as his large size would allow, and held a lighted candle up to Ian's face.

"D'Aosto! What are you doing here?"

"Investigating, at your request." Ian's tone was dry. He moved his head from side to side, testing to ensure that it was both still attached to his body and fully functional. "Were you waiting for me, or did something else bring you here?"

Valdo shook his head and dropped onto the bed, setting the candle next to him. He ran the fingers of one hand over the peach silk bedspread.

"She loves this color. It is her favorite. I had it specially dyed for her in England, and when she saw it the first time..." It looked as though the large man was going to cry, and less than a crying woman or a crying baby could Ian tolerate a crying mountain.

"It is very nice. But you still haven't said what you are doing here."

"I am waiting. Sunday night is the night she and I always spend together. We have dinner, then, you know. I thought maybe she would come back for it." His voice suddenly lost its wistful edge. "You heard about Enzo?"

"Yes, most disturbing. That is part of why I am here. I want to check a theory which, *ah*, I am developing. You could give me a hand. It would help to pass the time." Ian hated himself for perpetuating Valdo's hope.

"I may as well." Valdo shrugged and dismally lifted himself off the bed. "What are we looking for?"

"Peepholes."

Working by the light of two candles, the two men covered every inch of the floor and found nothing. No loose boards, no prying holes, not a single sign of a secret place for listening or watching the dealings of those below. Then they moved to the next room, and the next. Ian's back ached doubly, from Valdo's attack and from leaning over to scour the floor, and his outlook was bleak. He stood to stretch, cursing himself for acting on the harebrained idea of a woman, when an idea of his own developed. Women were such petty creatures that their tolerance for discomfort was very low, and listening to hours of conversation bent over with your ear pressed to the floor would be very uncomfortable. Clearly they had been looking in the wrong place. The peephole or listening device would have to be located somewhere more commodious.

Almost tripping on Valdo, who was sprawled in the middle of a floor testing the floorboards for looseness, Ian rushed back to Isabella's room. He stood in the middle and took it in, slowly. He went first to the bed and lay down, using his hands to search the wall behind him. Though he did not know exactly what he was looking for, he was sure he would recognize it when he found it.

Whatever it was, though, it was not behind the bed. Not ready to give up, he went and sat at Isabella's vanity table. He opened all the drawers, one by one, then the cabinets. Nothing. He uncorked all the perfumes, unscrewed all the unguents. Still nothing. The mirror was hinged so that it could be angled in a variety of ways, so Ian began adjusting it, folding each piece along its hinge. That was how he saw it.

Behind the third and fourth sections of the mirror was a wide tube with a cork in it. Ian removed the cork and looked into it. All he saw was darkness, but a tingling in his body told him he was right.

"Valdone!" he called, and waited for the large man to lumber over. "You sit here while I go to the parlor. Keep your eyes on the tube, and if you hear or see anything, shout."

Ian had taken his candle and was rushing down the stairs before Valdo could question him. Based on the position of Isabella's room, Ian guessed which of the three doors went to the parlor, found it unlocked, and entered. He put the candle in the middle of the large table and began to recite poetry.

"*Nel mezzo del camin' della nostra vita...*" Before he reached the end of the first line, he heard Valdo shouting.

"I hear you. I see you. Perfectly, clearly. This is amazing."

Ian concurred when he had his turn at the tube. He studied the ingenious system, making mental notes so he could duplicate it at home.

"What I don't understand is how you knew about it. You know, I spent all my free time here and never had any suspicion of such a thing." Valdo was speaking from the parlor to Ian in the bedroom.

"It is long story, and I would rather not explain it until I have everything figured out."

The large man was now too in awe of Ian's cognitive powers to press him, willingly abiding by the adage that geniuses must be given space to work. Though he did not understand what it had to do with restoring his Isa to him, Valdo was sure that the listening tube was an important clue. He was still congratulating the count on the find when the two men left together a little later. He had given up on Isabella for the night, but his adventure with Ian had left him slightly less dejected than usual.

Ian declined Valdo's offer to ferry him home, hoping the slight drizzle and the walk would ease the pain in his back and help clear his head. The existence of the listening tube validated, at least partially, Bianca's theory about the murder. That was hardly surprising if she herself was the murderer, though it was not clear why she would willingly spell out her motive. Perhaps she figured that if she suggested it, Ian would never believe her, since he always assumed she was lying. That had to be it, she was counting on him taking it as a lie. Obviously Enzo had to die because he could have confirmed it as true.

And yet he could not rid himself of a nagging feeling of doubt. Unwilling though he was to admit it, part of him, a large part, could still not believe Bianca capable of such horrible deeds. He cursed himself again, this time for his softness, for being taken in by her feminine wiles, for letting his heart beat faster when she spoke his name, and even faster when she said...when she said she loved him. Even if it was not part of a plot to weaken him, he knew that words said in the heat of passion carried little weight. So he was a fool to be thinking about it, about her at all. Reason told him it was more likely now than ever that she was a cunning murderer. She had even admitted today, before witnesses, that she wanted to kill him.

Come now, the voice in his head said, she did not really mean it and she was roundly provoked. Ian shook his head like a lion shooing off a bothersome fly, trying to dislodge the annoying voice that was growing increasingly familiar. He noted for the first time that this new voice seemed to have replaced Mora's abusive critiques, and he wondered if he was not happier, or at least less confused, before the switch. Mora had never instructed him to trust a murderer. Only *maybe* a murderer, the voice said. Ian growled at it.

By the time he got home, the voice had convinced him that he owed Bianca an apology. Not for his repeated accusations of murder, those would stand, but for some of his more personal attacks. His sense of honor told him he had been needlessly provocative to her. Besides, it would be easier for her to reveal herself to him if they were on speaking terms. Most minor of all was his ongoing curiosity about whether her attractions had yet abated. That day in the library he had not felt anything in her presence, which he took as an auspicious development.

To lose no time in commencing his test, or his apology, Ian went directly to Bianca's room. He anticipated seeing her there as she had been the night before, peacefully stretched out and inviting. He would apologize quickly, she would accept, then he would climb into bed for the test. He sighed a manly sigh, admitting that he would have to force himself to perform if he wanted to regain her trust, and reminded himself of his patriotic duties.

But his efforts were wasted, because Bianca was not there. Nor was she in the adjacent sitting room. Nor the library. Nor even the dining room, small dining room, blue reception room, green reception room, gold reception room, wood reception room, meeting room, sewing room, Ian's room, Roberto and Francesco's rooms, Crispin's rooms, any of the ballrooms, servants' rooms, storage rooms, or kitchens. Ian was desperate, terrified that she had left him. Or, rather, escaped. If she was going to escape, he surmised, she would do it by boat because it would be too easy to trace her traversing the deserted streets of Venice on foot. Before sounding a general alarm or rousing the household, he counted the gondolas. They were all there.

Finding her was suddenly the most important thing, indeed the only thing, that mattered. He took the stairs four at a time and then thundered down the hall toward her laboratory. Ian flung the door open with so much force that he ripped it off its hinges. He would gladly have had a hundred hinges replaced for the sight that greeted him when he stepped into the room.

She was there on a stool before the gaping space that had once been a window. She had taken one of the large woolen rugs that covered the floor and draped it around herself for warmth. When Ian burst in, she turned, though not with surprise, since nothing could surprise her anymore.

The rain had stopped and the sky was beginning to clear. In the silvery moonlight her face looked ethereal, like that of a mountain nymph or a particularly sensual Madonna. Ian tried to suppress these romantic thoughts by sternly reminding himself of his two-pronged mission, and approached her.

Bianca had turned back to her contemplation of the sky. She had nothing to say to Ian, or nothing she should say. Seated on that stool for nearly two hours, she had been trying to sort through the complicated emotions that were coursing through her. She had begun by trying to focus on her ineffectual investigation, running her mind over everything she knew, hoping for a crack, but her brain had other plans and had returned again and again to Ian.

"I came to apologize." His voice at her ear broke through her thoughts, and Bianca found that she did still possess the capacity to be surprised. "I said some things today that were not strictly necessary."

Bianca did not want to face him because she did not want him to see the tears gathering at the corners of her eyes. "Thank you, my lord." Her voice sounded small, then got stronger as her mouth asked of its own accord, "Why did you say them, then?"

Ian, shook his head and responded to her profile. "I don't know. When I am with you, sometimes, I find I get," he cleared his throat, stalling as he sought the right phrase, "carried away."

Bianca suddenly had the urge to laugh but stifled it. She turned to face him. "I think it is because someone hurt you once, and now you want to hurt someone."

Ian's eyes grew hard. "An interesting theory, *carissima.*"

"I think it was a woman."

Ian's whole body stiffened. The right thing to do was to storm out of the room in anger, slamming the door and punishing her for bringing it up. But the door was broken. And curiously, Ian did not want to leave.

Instead, he changed the subject. "What are you doing up here? It is freezing."

Bianca was still studying him. "Looking at the stars. Or actually, looking for my father's star."

Ian was skeptical. "What do you mean? Is it different from other stars?"

"It is indistinguishable, except when he gives me the sign. He will notice me watching for him and something will happen, it will flicker or get bigger or something."

"Have you observed this phenomenon before?"

"No. That is just it. I have been looking since he died and I have never found it." Ian noticed that there was a slight tremor in her voice. "I know he would not forget about me, would not abandon me, but still, it would be nice to see it. It would make it easier to keep believing in him. And not to feel alone."

Ian considered sweeping her into his arms and telling her she was not alone. He thought about kissing her gently and filling her with his warmth. He contemplated promising to protect her and care for her. The idea of explaining to her how utterly unforgettable she was crossed his mind.

He opened his mouth to speak. "From everything I have read about them, it seems unlikely that stars are actually the souls of the dead."

With alarm Ian saw that Bianca's lower lip had begun to quiver, and he knew what that meant. He racked his brain, trying to decide what Crispin would do in this situation, realized that Crispin would never be in this situation, and then rushed on, saying the first things that occurred to him. "What I mean is, perhaps you are looking in the wrong place. Perhaps your father has been giving you signs every day, many of them, but because they were unexpected, you did not notice them."

Her lip had almost completely stopped quivering, and she was regarding him with an expression he did not recognize. It made him ecstatic. And nervous.

"But of course, I could be wrong. If you really are interested in stars, I have a machine in my laboratory that makes them look closer. Maybe that would help you see your father."

Bianca's mind was dizzy from trying to follow Ian's twisted reasoning, but the invitation to see his laboratory required no thought at all. She had been itchy with curiosity about it since her first day in the house, but had been too respectful of its sanctity to enter without an invitation. Plus, she had heard stories about unfortunate servingmen who, lost in the sinewy corridors of the house, had accidentally found themselves in Ian's laboratory confronted by anything from a machine pitching rocks at them to a poisonous snake. One man's eyebrows had never grown back after a brief encounter with a new type of oil that initially appeared too harmless to wash off but later, when he was lighting the kitchen fire, turned out to be highly flammable.

She nodded her acceptance of his invitation. Still wrapped in the rug, she followed Ian to the big door at the end of the hall. He used a key to open it, a precaution undertaken after the eyebrow incident, and proudly ushered her into the largest room she had ever been in. At least that was the illusion put forward by the mirrors that covered all four walls. Turning around she saw a staggering number of Biancas reflected on every wall from every angle. She was so disoriented that she bumped into the two big workbenches filling the middle of the room. One of them was heaped with books and on the other, there were several strange-looking machines, or rather, one strange-looking machine in several sizes. As Bianca was taking all of this in, wide-eyed, Ian lit and distributed a handful of tapers.

"What do these do?" She pointed at the machines on the worktable.

"Those make things seem bigger than they are. If you put a rock under one of them, for example, you would see not only its surface texture, but almost the particles that make up the texture."

"That could be immensely useful in my work." Bianca's eyes were bright with excitement and Ian was reluctant to dull it.

"These are just prototypes, and not very good ones. It is all still in the experimental stages. In time, though, I hope to develop one that will allow me to see through things and know what is beneath the surface of everything."

Bianca looked closely at Ian. What would she not give to be able to turn such a machine on him, to see under his surface and probe his secrets.

She was regarding him in the way that made him both delighted and nervous again, so Ian tried to distract her. "But we did not come to talk about those machines. We came to look through this one." Ian extended his arm and pointed to a large device that looked disappointingly like a tube.

"This is the machine that makes the stars look closer?" Bianca was incredulous as she studied it. "How does it see the stars? There are no windows on any of these walls."

Ian began pulling on a heavy cord against one wall. At first Bianca noticed nothing, but gradually the light in the room changed. She was puzzled until she looked up and saw that where the ceiling should have been there were now thousands and thousands of stars. Her first thought was that Ian had somehow made the roof disappear, but then she understood what had really happened. The rope Ian had been tugging on controlled a very large cover that had masked the true ceiling, which was made entirely of glass. The effect was marvelous and Bianca could not keep herself from gaping.

They exchanged no words while Ian worked in deep concentration to set up the telescope. He fastened the long tube into an elaborate stand, which held it steady while directing it up toward the sky. Using a pole, Ian pushed open one of the panels of the roof as if it were a window, so that the view through the machine would be clear and uninterrupted by the glass. Then he looked through the eyepiece, jiggled some knobs, twisted some screws, moved a stool into place to give her added height, and beckoned Bianca over.

It took her a moment to understand what she was seeing, but when she did, she cried out in delight.

"This is a magical machine! I can see everything, so close I feel like I could touch it! Did you make it? How does it work?"

She could not see it, but Ian was beaming. "I will explain it to you one day, but not tonight, it would take too long. It works on the same principle as the tube at Isabella's house."

Bianca turned her face sharply toward his, and he quickly erased his smile. "What? What at Isabella's house?"

"The listening tube you sent me there to find. The one she eavesdropped on conversations with."

"There was one? It was there? And you found it?" Bianca was

thrilled to have her hypothesis confirmed, even more thrilled that Ian had taken it seriously despite his professed skepticism.

"Oh, yes, I was there tonight. It was just as you said it would be."

"Then certainly you must see that I am innocent! And that is why you apologized!"

"I apologized because I had overspoken. The tube does nothing to prove your innocence. If anything, your knowledge of it could be taken as strong proof of your guilt." Ian's voice was neutral but he was berating himself for having introduced the subject.

"But I did not know about it. I merely suggested it as a possibility. How was I to know if there was a listening device in the floor boards or behind the vanity?"

"*Ha!* You did know. You just named exactly where it was."

"By Santa Regina's knuckles, I just named the obvious places. I am sure they were the first places you looked too. Besides, why would I tell you about it if I were the murderer? Why would I spell out a potential motive to you?"

Ian nodded and expounded his reasoning more as if he were talking to a collaborator than his chief suspect. "I thought of that too, but then I saw a possible reason. You were counting on me to take what you said as a lie, because I almost always do. But this time I was too clever for you."

"Too clever for yourself actually," there was no malice in her voice but something more like disappointment, "for that is the most absurd idea I have ever heard. What could have inspired me to do that? Why would I have mentioned it at all? It seems like an awfully large risk to take for no reason."

"The reason is clear: to force me to broaden my list of suspects. It might have worked if Enzo had not been killed too, but that made it obvi—"

Ian stopped talking because Bianca's lips were on his. It had been an impulse, and she acted on it, and was delighted by the results. For one thing, it had made him cease his insufferable accusations.

"Can't we save that for the morning?" she whispered up to him when their lips parted. "I was so enjoying being with you, can't we forget about all of that until tomorrow?" Seated on the tall stool, her head even with Ian's, she was looking directly into his eyes.

Ian was not sure when he had lost control of the situation, but it was extremely obvious that he would not need a battery of tests to find out if he was still attracted to her. It felt as if every particle of his body was responding to her unexpected touch. Some part of him said it was unwise to let their conversation be sidetracked that way, but he realized that Bianca had a point, there would be plenty of time the next day for confrontation, and right then it was more important to make love to her. His body happily concurred.

Their heads moved together for another kiss, this one slow, deep, sensual. Bianca was touching his cheek, running her hand through his hair, making soft little designs with her fingers on his neck. For a long time they stayed that way, touching gently and just kissing, but Ian's growing arousal soon overtook his willpower. He lifted her from the stool and carried her in his arms to the emptier worktable, carefully setting her down atop the rug she had been wearing for warmth. He undid the lacings at the neck of her night-gown and pushed the garment down over her shoulders.

For a moment the sight of her, naked, waiting, excited, in the middle of his laboratory rendered him unable to move. But her impatient fingers working hard on his leggings soon brought him back to himself, and he assisted her by shedding his shirt. She watched in the mirror behind them as her hands moved over his back, fascinated by the view she now had, by being able to touch and see at the same time. She shuddered with a new kind of arousal as she watched Ian take her nipple in his mouth, watched his tongue moving lightly along it. Abruptly, she drew away from him, suddenly self-conscious.

When she spoke, it was in a voice full of self-doubt. "Today, in the library, you said I was perverted. Am I?"

Ian now realized that his apology had been wildly inadequate. "No, *carissima*, you are not. You are simply very open." The unsure, pained expression that lingered on Bianca's face was like a dagger to him. How could he have been so nasty earlier that day? he asked himself. What cruel impulse had made him want to throw her wonderful, infectious sensuality in her face? Although he would scarcely admit it consciously, he had been afraid that afternoon, afraid that she really was guilty, afraid he would have to give her up, and he had hurled his fear at her like a weapon, lashing out at her and punishing her for making him feel again. Was there anything he could do to remedy the effect of his words? The prospect of having ruined the most exciting partner he had ever encountered, even if she was possibly some sort of dangerous criminal, was dismal, especially given his increasing arousal. Quick action was needed.

Bianca was confused as he tugged her off the table, seated himself on a stool closer to one of the walls, and positioned her between his legs, facing away from him but toward the mirror.

"I want to give you a gift. I want you to see how beautiful you are when you climax, *carissima*," he whispered in her ear in a voice that went far toward banishing her doubts.

With one hand he gently teased the nipple of her left breast, while the other slipped lower and lower to the moist curls below her stomach. To begin with he just combed through them with his fingers, untangling them, twisting them, gently letting his palm rest atop them. Then his index finger slid lower, in search of the small pearl of flesh that he knew would bring her pleasure. She watched his finger as it found its place and began gently tracing circles over it. Ian's other hand came down to join the first, delicately pulling her open so she could watch his long sensual movements as he rubbed first his fingers, then his palm, up the length of her hot, wet lips. He was now rubbing her sensitive place with both hands, pressing and pulling it with all ten fingers in a sensual display that took her breath away. It was obvious that she was getting near to her climax, but Ian was not ready to let her go.

He wanted her to see herself at her most excited, wanted to be sure she knew how indescribably lovely she looked when she peaked on the highest of sensual waves. Keeping his hands in place he slid off the stool and stood behind her for a moment. She was just leaning into his warmth, enjoying the feel of his hard shaft on her backside, when he bent at the knees and appeared to disappear. When she saw him again, he was edging her legs apart, making room for himself between them.

He drew his hands away for a moment as he kneeled in front of her, then used them to open her again. In the mirror Bianca could see only the back of Ian's fair head, but she could feel his tongue and lips on her. She had thought she was close to climaxing before, but the sensations she now felt were so much more intense, she had to pray for the strength to stand. Looking at herself with a man's golden head between her legs, licking, sucking, and nibbling her as he slid a finger in and out of her waiting passage, was thrilling. She felt experienced, desired, wanted, beautiful, assured. She watched her hand take Ian's head and push it harder between her legs, newly confident in her desire. She moaned louder as he slid his fingers in and out of her faster, his tongue continuing its sensual dance over her, around her, across her. Finally, he sucked her in with all his strength, sucked her through his teeth and wrapped his tongue around her, and she climaxed again and again in his mouth.

When she clawed his head with her hands and called his name, completely lost to reason and concern, Ian knew his gift had been accepted. He drew himself up to her and kissed her, his lips still wet with her dew. She pushed herself toward him, wanting to be close to him, wanting to feel his arms around her, to smell the scent of his skin mingled with the scent of her arousal. She looked at them in the mirror, Ian's chin resting on her head, his muscular arms pulling her toward him, her breasts pressed against his chest, and she never ever wanted the moment to end.

She began to notice Ian's shaft pushing harder and harder against her thigh and remembered that she was not the only one who deserved to feel wave after wave of shattering pleasure. She caught Ian's eye in the mirror and let her hand stray to his organ.

His jaw clenched as her fingers caressed him, and he knew he needed to be inside her soon. He wondered if he dared test their new, delicate truce with the fantasy that he had been having.

Remembering her willingness and openness and unable to ignore the dictates of his hard member, he pulled away from her slightly, turned her around so her back was to him, and moved her toward the stool.

As if reading his mind, she bent over it, its surface cool and smooth on her stomach, and reached behind her to pull him closer. She watched in the mirror as he moved toward her, his shaft long and hard, and placed himself behind her. His entry felt so delicious that she shuddered, bringing him dangerously near a climax. He bent over her and cupped his hands around her breasts, massaging them as he pushed himself into her, relishing the feeling of her against his thighs, the tightness of her passage, the ripple of her muscles as she pushed herself up to meet him. He let go of her breasts and stood up straight, pressing into her as hard as he could, reveling in the feeling of her eyes on him in the mirror as he brought her hips toward him and ground himself into her.

When Ian reached his climax, he felt her contracting around him, matching her release with his, prolonging it, intensifying it, amplifying it. Their cries of pleasure mingled together, leaving the laboratory through the roof and flying up into the heavens.

Too spent to return to their rooms, they lay together later on the table in the middle of the laboratory. Bianca had dozed off, but Ian, overfull of a feeling that, though unfamiliar, he could only describe as joy, was unable to sleep. For a while he had watched the sleeping figure next to him, struck by how familiar and comfortable it was to have her there, but then his eyes had strayed toward the sky. He was looking up, wondering what was happening to him and what was going to happen to the two of them, when something incredible occurred.

Ian was too stunned to move, but his cry of astonishment woke Bianca. She followed his eyes up toward the ceiling, and then gave her own cry. It was as if the heavens had opened up in celebration. Star after star after star was taking flight, trailing across the sky with long white tails of light.

Chapter Eighteen

Bianca ran to a window, looking for the source of the shrieking that had roused her from her sleep. Pushing aside the heavy draperies, she found herself face-to-face with a peacock—a large, mean-looking peacock with a shriek that could have driven the most peaceful matron to acts of violence. As she stood there, the door to her room flew open and Nilo came running in, followed by Francesco at a slightly less vigorous pace.

"Don't touch it, don't touch it," Nilo was shouting as he bounded for the window.

"It is just scared. It will be fine," Francesco huffed, stopping to get his breath where Bianca stood. "It was quite a shock. We did not know they could fly."

Bianca nodded solemnly. "Will there be other animals? Tigers? Can we use the second ballroom as a zoo?"

"Signorina Salva," Francesco spoke formally, puffing himself up as if offended, "you do not know the first thing about throwing a gala party. There must always be peacocks."

He marched away from her and approached the distraught and still shrieking bird on her balcony. When Bianca left her apartment a short while later, he and Nilo were deep in serious consultation about how to return the animal to the floors below and keep him there.

The shrieking was less audible outside her bedroom, but the house was by no means tranquil. The staff appeared to have been tripled in size, and there were serving men draping every banister, dusting every corner, spreading new rugs over every floor. Bianca had to dodge an armoire that seemed to have grown legs, a tray of newly blown glasses, and a large orange tree that appeared intent on filling the entire staircase, to make her way to the dining room.

When she arrived, relief washed over her for two reasons. First, none of the furniture in the room seemed inclined to move of its own accord, nor was there anything even remotely out of place. Second, seated at the table, alone, was Crispin. He was the person she most wanted to see, but she had been worried that she would have to risk antagonizing Luca and the new plant by going up to the plant rooms to seek him.

He greeted her warmly as she plopped herself down on a chair.

"Tell me, my lord, is it always necessary to have peacocks at a gala party?"

Crispin's expression was grave. "Why, certainly. The more birds, the more gala. Typically, Ian won't attend anything with under ten peacocks, but I am less stuffy than he is." He leaned forward to confide in her. "I once went to a two-peacock ball, but I admit it only under duress."

"I promise to keep this information like a sacred trust in my bosom." Bianca bowed her head slightly.

"Of course, I would expect nothing less. Tell me, is that the question you came to the plant rooms to ask me yesterday, or was it something more trivial?"

"I am sorry. I must have annoyed Luca beyond bearing."

Crispin smiled and waved her apology aside. "Think nothing of it. It's good for him."

Bianca had taken a large bite of the pastry in front of her and chewed it slowly to give herself time to think. When she had swallowed it, she addressed Crispin.

"I guess you also heard about my encounter with your new plant. I asked Luca where it came from, but he did not know."

"It was very strange." Crispin looked thoughtful as he spoke. "It arrived yesterday, beautifully wrapped and addressed to me, but there was no signature. It puts me in a bit of a spot because I don't know to whom I am beholden, nor where the plant came from."

"Does that happen often?"

Crispin laughed. "Usually when people give you expensive things, they want to make sure you know exactly where it came from so you will know exactly where to direct your gratitude."

Bianca wanted to work around to her next question as subtly as possible. "Has anyone ever sent you anything dangerous?"

"Me? A dangerous plant? Why would someone do that?"

She feigned nonchalance. "Maybe if someone were envious of your plant rooms? Or if they did not like the Arboretti."

Crispin was suddenly paying more attention. Had Ian, still suspicious, put her up to interviewing him after their heated discussion the day before? He had suspected Ian's apology had concealed some dark motivation. "We Arboretti certainly have our share of enemies, but I—"

"Like whom?" Bianca threw caution to the wind.

Crispin did likewise. If Ian was going to send her to interrogate him, he wanted to make sure she got an earful. "Anyone whose prices we have undercut or whose shipments we have beaten, people such as the Bartolini family, who will never forgive us for cornering the market on cardamom. Envy is a powerful motive too, and there are dozens of people, like Oswaldo Cresci or Fillipo Nonte, with whom we've never had dealings but who envy our size and success and would probably go out of their way to damage our prestige if they could. That is speaking only of the company in general. There are also more personal animosities, like Morgana da Gigio's grudge against Ian or L.N.'s ongoing feud with the prince of Navarre."

Crispin sat back, satisfied by the effect of his words on Bianca. Her surprise had quickly given way and he saw the dawning of her comprehension.

"Santa Dorotea's throat, *she* is the woman! The woman from two years ago!" Bianca was almost stuttering. If Ian and the young, rich widow had been lovers, it was no wonder Bianca had seemed unappealing to him. When Morgana da Gigio was in a room, no other woman existed. Not only on account of her magnificent beauty; it was more than that. She seemed to emanate something that put people under her spell. Bianca had only seen her from a distance, at other balls and gatherings, but she had always been fascinated by her.

"Mora lived here in the palace for several years. She and Ian were very good friends. Yes, she had definitely bewitched Ian." Crispin was nodding his head to keep from licking his lips in anticipation of the beautiful fit his brother would throw when Bianca reported back to him.

"What happened? Why does she harbor a grudge against Ian?" Bianca's voice was almost steady.

Crispin shrugged and pushed his chair back from the table. "You will have to ask Ian about that, when you report to him later. Be sure to tell him that I refrained from mentioning the putative Foscari heir."

As Crispin walked from the room, Bianca's world fell apart. She was too stunned to ask what he meant about reporting to Ian, too shaken by the news that Ian and Morgana da Gigio had been lovers. And perhaps also parents. In her mind she imagined herself next to Morgana da Gigio, plain, hideously unsophisticated, horribly boring. She cringed at the comparison, and again at the thought of the effort it must have been costing Ian to lie with someone as untutored as she was after the raptures he had experienced with Morgana. For it was obvious just from looking at her that a night with the wealthy widow was a night one would not soon forget.

If he had known the effect of his words, Crispin would never have spoken them. Bianca would certainly not be repeating them to Ian, in large part because she knew she could never face him again. What did she have to offer him that could compare to the delights he had already sampled with others? She should have known better, should have seen it from the start, or at least that day at Tullia's. She cursed herself and the desire for knowledge—or even just the plain desire—that had propelled her headlong into this mire of questions and emotions.

The clocks in the house chimed ten, a brutal reminder of the depth of that mire and the hard work in front of her if she was to stand a chance of proving her innocence. She had only seventy-four hours left to catch a murderer, and she still did not have the faintest idea how to begin.

Guests began arriving as the clocks struck eight, first in a trickle, soon in a flood, with a line of gondolas that clogged the Grand Canal. Invitations had been issued to every prominent family, and it appeared that they had all decided to accept. Some arrived out of friendship or loyalty, but most came out of curiosity, to see Ian betrothed at long last. Of as great interest as the stony count, however, was his betrothed. Bianca had turned enough heads at the few balls she had attended to earn her the disapproval of the bulk of the patrician mamas, not only because she was young, beautiful, rich competition for their daughters, but more because she was, as one matron described her, "so heedless of what is proper." As the guests congregated throughout the palace, sipping prosecco and admiring the elaborate decorations, most of the talk was speculation about the nature of Bianca's inevitable social gaffs that night.

Custom dictated that the betrothal couple remain out of sight until all the guests had gathered, but the other Arboretti were in plain view, gallantly entertaining the available females, while Francesco and Roberto ensured the older members of the patriciate were not neglected. Jugglers and acrobats moved through the crowd, stealing sips of drinks, telling jokes, and making gold ducats appear from ears. The peacocks were also there, milling about in gilded splendor, the light of the candles on the ground floor making them look like beasts from a fairy story.

Women's gowns in all colors of the rainbow—this one woven with gold, that one edged with pearls—presented a riot of color almost as impressive as that in Crispin's glass room. Their wearers eyed one another expertly, gathering in groups to comment on the neglected modesty of necklines ("She looks like a wet nurse, ready to suckle"), the overpadding of shoulders ("I suppose when you have been bedding your gondolier for years, you lose perspective"), the role of hemlines ("If I had wanted to see the ankles of a donkey, I would have gone to my place in the country"), and whether Signora Ricco had managed to buy back her diamonds after her gambling losses or if she was still wearing paste. Even before the feasting and the dancing had commenced, everyone was ready to agree that the party was a smash.

When the clock struck nine, an expectant hush fell over the collected guests. People crowded into the central ballrooms on all three floors in the hope of catching a glimpse of the couple as they made their ritual descent into the crowd. A quartet began to play a slow but lighthearted melody, specially designed to last the duration of their entrance.

Then they played it again.

They were about to commence for the third time, masking the repetition with improvised solos, when a servant arrived with the message to stop. There would be no descent. The bride-to-be was nowhere to be found. Guests nodded knowingly to one another, not even bothering to lower their voices as they commented on this newest example of Bianca's indecorous morality.

Ian was far less complacent. He was pacing the floor of Crispin's apartment, from which they were to set out, as though he wanted to test the overstated promises of exceptional wearability given by the merchant who had sold him the rugs. His mind raced ahead of his feet, running through an alphabetical list he had begun two days earlier of ways to torment Bianca. He had only reached *D*, for "dangling over boiling oil," when Giorgio entered, pushing the woman in question ahead of him.

"I found her in the servants' quarters with her maid, Marina." Giorgio had a way of preempting Ian's questions.

All thoughts of boiling oil, sarcastic retorts, snide remarks, and biting criticisms vanished when Ian saw her.

Her dress was of velvet the same color as the topaz that hung from her slender neck, lined and edged with pure white silk. It was cut to highlight her small, perfect décolleté, in the middle of which the topaz was nestled. Both the dress and the lining were embroidered in gold with flowers of every conceivable size and form, painstakingly copied from originals supplied by Luca. Her hair hung loose around her bared shoulders as was customary for unmarried women, held off her face by an elegant headdress of gold and diamonds. Her remarkable eyes looked even bigger, her lips even more tempting, than usual. Ian felt a lump form in his throat at the possibility that such beauty might one day be his.

"You look marvelous," Ian meant to say, though what came out was, "Did you plan to escape through the kitchens when no one was looking?" The thought of her leaving him made the words ring out more harshly than he had intended.

Bianca looked grieved. It had not been her intention to displease or upset him, just the opposite. "I needed help with my hair." Her voice was small. "I did not want to embarrass you."

The lump in Ian's throat grew bigger.

"You could never embarrass me," was on the tip of Ian's tongue, but what he said was, "As if this delay were not embarrassing enough. Come, we don't have time to hear any more of your silly excuses." He took her hand and roughly pulled her toward the door. "Tell them we are finally ready, Giorgio, that my charming betrothed has seen fit to return from the scullery."

Ian tried to turn a cold eye on her, to let her feel the full force of his wrath, but as soon as he looked in her direction, his anger evaporated. Instead of a cold glare, somehow, he found himself kissing her, crushing her to him with all the strength in his body, holding her as close as he could.

"Bianca," he breathed when they separated, his tone different from the one he had just been using. "Bianca," he repeated, softly, almost with reverence. But any words Ian might have spoken were abruptly interrupted. As if on cue, the opening strains of the processional were heard, bringing an end to the betrothal couple's interview and forcing them out into public to greet their guests.

Giorgio was smiling to himself as he descended the stairs, but his smile did not last long. Just as the quartet struck up their now familiar refrain again, the rumble of voices from below drowned them out. The cause of the disturbance was only briefly a mystery, for Morgana da Gigio in person could be seen ascending the staircase, magnificent in crimson silk. She had timed her arrival to coincide with the descent of the betrothal couple, hoping to embarrass Ian and highlight as much as possible the discrepancy between herself and whatever boring patrician chit he was marrying. She wanted to make it plain to Ian what he had lost through his selfishness. Ideally the girl would burst into tears and require Ian's unwilling attention, but that was not strictly necessary for Mora to feel her plan had been a success.

It worked admirably at the beginning, her arrival causing a pleasing stir, her admirers flocking around her in support. But when she encountered Ian and the chit on the stairs, something was awry. The girl did not look like one of the plain, dull women who predominated in her class. She simply was not ugly enough. And Ian looked nearer tears than she did. Mora curtsied low, low enough to reveal her nipples over the lace of her bodice to several happily placed young men, and greeted the betrothed pair.

Bianca held out her hand as Ian made them acquainted under the eyes of a thousand of Venice's leading citizens. "*Carissima,* this is Morgana da Gigio, my former mistress."

Nothing Mora could have done would have caused as tremendous a stir as Ian's introduction. For weeks afterward people talked about the endearing way he had addressed Bianca and its contrast with his clinical description of Mora. While the act earned him the hatred of some of her admirers, it also worked to replace his chilly, stonelike reputation with a new image of him as a romantic hero. By the night's end, Ian had decided with despair that he preferred his old reputation, which had never subjected him to the adulation of the teams of young women who suddenly found him unbearably gallant. Bianca wanted to lean over and kiss him but knew that would be stoutly frowned upon.

Ian had won the battle of wits, and Mora knew it. Conceding defeat, she stepped aside, but not without first giving Ian one of her famous, dazzling smiles, more for its effect on the chit than for its effect on him.

It worked. No meeting could have underlined the difference between Bianca's plain, dull self and Ian's fascinating former mistress better. The strength that had suffused Bianca after Ian's kiss left her all at once. Indeed, with her mud-colored eyes and curveless body, Bianca felt herself growing smaller and uglier each time she breathed. But the assembled guests pretended not to notice, treating her not only civilly but with affection as she and Ian continued their descent. She knew it was only pity that motivated their kindness, but she was grateful nonetheless. By the time they had reached the ground floor and had successfully led off the first dance without anyone commenting audibly on the likeness between her and an ungainly monster, she was feeling almost human, and certainly strong enough to begin the first of the tasks she had set herself.

Since Ian had confined her to the house, Bianca had decided to seize the opportunity the ball presented to interview all the men identified by Tullia as possible candidates for the role of Isabella's fiancé. She spotted Brunaldo Bartolini standing by a fountain with his twin sister and considered approaching the gloriously good-looking pair but was reluctant when she noticed how intimately they were talking. There were rumors that they were closer than a brother and sister should be, scarcely surprising since not many people were as handsome as they were, and though Bianca did not believe the talk, she was nevertheless wary of interrupting anything too personal. Continuing her survey, she caught sight of Lodivico Terreno and was about to approach him when a hand on her shoulder made her turn.

With his small deep-set black eyes, slicked-back hair, and whiny voice, Giulio Cresci knew he was irresistible to women and therefore did not waste any charm convincing them. "Dance with me, signorina," he ordered rather than asked, and Bianca found herself being shuffled gracelessly about the dance floor. Under any other circumstance she would have marched away with her head high, but as he was one of the men on her list to interview, she valiantly persevered. Weaving in and out of the other dancers, they exchanged scattered words, but Bianca soon saw that she would need to organize a tête-à-tête with him to get her questions answered.

Feigning exhaustion, she allowed him to drag her toward a bench. She regretted it almost instantly, for he seemed to have a misguided idea of her intentions. She was able to put her questions to him, but his responses were something less than helpful. He addressed her only in mildly raunchy puns, which were bad enough without his curious habit of repeating the punch lines to himself and thus making it impossible for Bianca to feign polite misunderstanding.

When she asked him if he had houses in the country, he smiled knowingly at her and retorted, "Planning to wiggle your way out from under Ian? Wiggle out from under? Wiggle under?"

When she asked him how he felt about the Arboretti, he raised his eyebrows saying he was more interested in his own little tree, and offered her the opportunity to help make it grow, make the tree grow, make it grow big.

When she asked him if he had any interest in flowers, he asked her if she wanted him to press her petals and make her bloom, press and bloom, press and bloom. It was when he offered to demonstrate that last technique that Bianca, ungraciously, fled.

Though none of her other interviews were as taxing, they were equally inconclusive. She learned that the Franceschinos had sold their estates on Lake Como, that Lodivico Terreno had an interesting collection of medicinal plants, that Brunaldo Bartolini kept bees, and that they all professed to admire and like the Arboretti. Something about the way Brunaldo spoke Ian's name made her suspect that there was a bit of animosity between the two men, but he rebutted all her attempts to make him admit it. At the end, she had learned nothing but that it was exhausting to interview people in the middle of a ball.

Ian's attempts with Signora Valdone were no more informative but far more suggestive. Lucretia, as she insisted he call her, was not quite as large as her husband, nor quite as proportional. She had responded to Ian's invitation to dance with such a profusion of lash fluttering and loud exclamations that Ian thought she might be collapsing in a fit, but it soon became clear that for her such behavior was normal. It became equally clear that she had no interest in her husband's amorous exploits because she was much too busy carrying out her own. When she propositioned Ian the first time, he was slightly surprised, but by her third unsubtle hint, this time accompanied by gestures, he was inured to it. He was able to untangle himself only when one of his serving youths succeeded him in her attentions, and he made a mental note to give the young man a bonus, should he ever see him alive again.

The night slid festively on, the guests and the peacocks eating, drinking, and dancing to satiety. Making a wrong turn, Bianca had stumbled over Ian's cousin Sebastian giving Cecilia Priuli an extended lesson about palm reading in a secluded alcove. Bianca's retreat was checked by her cousin Analinda, who, having received two compliments from Crispin, hugged Bianca close at the assured prospect of their soon living under the same roof again. Tristan seemed to be making equally good progress with Catarina Nonte, even under the sulky eyes of her overprotective brother, Aemilio. It was while watching them that Bianca's mind wandered to her own brother, and she began to wonder where he was, what he was doing, and if he was a murderer.

The last thought brought with it a wave of emotions that, in her exhausted state, she had difficulty controlling. Excusing herself from the group of young women who had gathered around to congratulate her on her happy match, she stealthily sneaked off to her apartment for a moment of solitary relaxation. She was just passing through from the sitting room into the bedroom when she heard the door behind her open and shut, and a female voice call her name.

"I thought I would find you in here, *carissima*." On Mora's lips the word had a foreign sound that both attracted and repelled

Bianca, who suddenly felt a tinge of fear. Telling herself she was being foolish, she turned and curtsied to the other woman.

Mora drew up to her and regarded her. "You look exhausted. Come, sit, let us relax together." She led Bianca toward a divan against the side wall and sat down close to her. "You know this was my suite. Ian had Paolo Veronese paint it for me."

Bianca nodded, not because she had known but because it made sense. It was a glorious suite of rooms, well worthy of a glorious occupant. What did not make sense, what she did not understand, was Mora's seeking her out in this manner.

As if reading her mind, Mora smiled at her. "You are wondering why I am here. Why I am passing my time with you rather than in a crowd of my admirers. It's obvious, actually." She reached out and took Bianca's hand in hers, meeting her eyes openly, candidly. "Ian asked me to find you and to instruct you in what he likes. He says he has been trying to teach you his preferences but that you are, well, a little willful."

Bianca was too shocked to pull away. It sounded false, completely improbable, but Mora was meeting her eyes with complete candor, and no one could lie that convincingly. Having admitted her shortcomings to herself that afternoon, she had already surmised she was routinely disappointing Ian, and it should come as no surprise that he had arranged for an expert tutorial. It was actually kind of him, to give her this chance to learn, before discarding her altogether.

At least that was how Mora put it. She had spent the hours since her first glimpse of Bianca in moody meditation, trying to contrive some way of making the chit hers. Her hatred for Ian was only part of her motivation, for she found as she watched the girl move about the room, talking or dancing or laughing, that she started to desire her. Mora was not sure that an interlude between her experienced arms would completely erase the girl's desire for Ian, but she knew her powers and that she could realistically count on them to at least dampen it. Almost by magic, the moment she hit upon the right approach the girl withdrew from her band of insipid companions and made haste for her room. Mora's room. It was too perfect to be true.

She brought Bianca's hand to her lips and kissed the fingers gently, all the time keeping her eyes locked on Bianca's. Her shoulder dipped as if by accident and one of her coral nipples peeked out of her deep red gown. She smiled apologetically and slipped Bianca's hand down to touch it, pushing Bianca's unwitting fingers over it until it formed a hard little peak. Then she slid the hand around so Bianca was holding the whole of her large breast. "This is what Ian likes," Mora purred, moving Bianca's hand over her voluptuous anatomy. "Don't you?"

Bianca felt as if she were caught in some sort of spell, unable to move or breathe, to acquiesce or to protest, somehow outside her body. Her fingertips tingled where they were touching Mora's impossibly soft skin, and she imagined how much Ian must miss resting his head on the smooth, ample globe. She thought sadly of her own meager anatomy and how little it had to offer to him. It was clearly a disappointment to Mora, who was regarding her with a look of deep pity.

Mora had to exercise intense restraint not to reach down and cup the girl's deliciously fresh breasts. She allowed herself only to caress Bianca's wavy hair where it spilled onto her milky skin, to brush her fingertips over the girl's silky soft décolleté. She considered starting there, planting a kiss first at the nape of the girl's neck, then one lower, then lower still, until the bodice of her gown was dispensed with, but realized she did not have the luxury of time because they could be interrupted at any moment. Instead, she pulled her closer and brought Bianca's lips to hers.

The kiss—warm, yielding, sensual, and very real—had begun before Bianca realized what was happening. In a flash, her powers of reason flooded back. It was impossible that Ian had sent Mora to her, completely inconceivable, and if she allowed herself to be seduced by the remarkable woman, she would become simply another part of the pain that Ian carried around with him, another pawn in a game of revenge that she did not understand

and which had gone on too long. Abruptly, she pulled away from Mora's lips.

"I am afraid I must return to my guests. Thank you for the lesson." Bianca turned and left the room.

All the girl's gratitude could not counter the fact that Bianca had repudiated Mora's advances. She, Morgana da Gigio, had sacrificed time with her admirers to offer herself as a tutor to the selfish, inexperienced chit and had gotten nothing but paltry thanks in return. Bianca had taken advantage of her, Mora realized with outrage, had let her feel her little hands on her body, let her imagine the suppleness of her touch, and then, ungrateful of the honor of Mora's affections, had walked away from her. Mora's only consolation was the surprise and horror that would cross Ian's face when he learned what she had done. Perhaps it would even be enough to make him repudiate the girl. No one abused Morgana da Gigio without repercussions. The girl would get what was coming to her.

For the time being, Mora needed something to remove Bianca's taste from her lips, the ungrateful and selfish girl's image from her mind. She considered calling one of her admirers in to make love to her there, imaging that it would be almost as disrespectful as the seduction she had attempted earlier. The impulse was tempting, and yet somehow unappealingly crass in the room Ian had built for her. No such objections existed to her next idea, however, and she made haste to execute it.

It was not quite dawn when Bianca, Tristan, and Miles saw the last guests to their gondolas. Sebastian had left earlier with a mysterious excuse about having a meeting to go to, and no one had seen Crispin or Ian for hours. Miles, who was well embarked upon a crush on Bianca, was warmly praising her for her performance that evening and running over the litany of flattering comments people had made about her. But she was too preoccupied to hear what he said, or even to smile as Tristan rallied her on her conquest of Miles. What she needed was to find Ian, to hear from him that she had not embarrassed him at the ball. When Roberto and Francesco approached to exchange further pleasantries, Bianca made an excuse and bade them all good night.

She went straight to her room, or the room she had once considered hers, but only for the sake of appearances. Without even pausing to change out of her elaborate gown, she made for the hidden passage at the far end that led directly to Ian's bedroom and descended. She had the doorknob in her hand and was just about to burst in when she heard the voices.

They were not voices, really, so much as moans, which grew faster and louder as Bianca stood, stunned, on the threshold. Unable to move, she heard the sounds build in intensity until, suddenly, she could clearly make out words.

"Yes, yes, Morgana; oh, yes, Mora, Mora, Mora," a deep male voice was shouting over and over in a fever pitch of ecstasy.

Chapter Nineteen

The time had at last come to throw herself into the canal, that was clear to Bianca. The only decision still to be made was whether to throw herself off her own, or rather, Mora's, balcony, which might not be high enough, or off the roof of the palace. While the roof would be slightly harder to get to, it had the advantage of guaranteed success. Running back up the stairs of the secret passage, she opted for the roof. She passed through her beautiful room, not even pausing to admire the fine frescoes one last time, and made for the main staircase, moving as quickly as her legs would carry her. She had traversed the first set of stairs and was halfway up the second when she ran directly into the wall.

Like all the walls in the palace, this was no ordinary wall. As Bianca stood, trying to regain her equilibrium after the impact, the wall grew first arms, then a voice, then a second voice.

It was the second voice that spoke. "Is it always like this for you, d'Aosto, as soon as you speak a woman's name, she comes flying into your arms?"

"One of nature's few gifts to me." Ian tried to keep his voice light to match the tone of his interlocutor, but one look at Bianca's face told him that something was desperately wrong. He wrapped his arms tighter around her stiff figure as he introduced his companion. "*Carissima,* I believe you know the Duca d'Aquila. He was just asking me about your anatomical work."

Bianca had met Alessandro Cornaro, Duca d'Aquila, at one of her first balls and had found him more than typically diverting, but just at the moment she was too perplexed to take advantage of his conversational skills. Her body told her that she was standing in the safe circle of Ian's arms, but her mind knew that was impossible. How could Ian be here with her when he was three stories below in bed with his no-longer-former mistress?

"Thank you for the tour of your laboratory, d'Aosto," Alessandro was saying when Bianca came out of her reverie. "It is a splendid space. When I return from my next voyage, you will have to come out to my estate with me to look at the ruins of the Roman observatory. I would love to hear your opinion of them. And of course, yours too, signorina."

"You have been in the laboratories?" was Bianca's none too genteel interjection.

"Yes, d'Aquila shares my, or rather, *our* interest in stargazing." Ian felt her body relax against him as he spoke. He looked down at her, trying to read the confused emotions in her eyes, and she returned his look with what he supposed was supposed to be a smile. It wasn't.

Alessandro felt a pang of envy as he watched the intimate exchange of glances between the couple. They looked as if they shared a world apart, a magical space all their own, and were eager to get back to it. He was too much of a gentleman to linger when it was painfully obvious that they wanted to be alone, so he politely took his leave, telling them not to bother escorting him out. While descending, he berated himself for not having pursued Bianca with more vigor during her first months in Venice, then reminded himself he would never have had a chance against the Conte d'Aosto.

Only when they were finally alone did Ian loosen his grip on Bianca.

"You were in the laboratories with the Duca d'Aquila?" Bianca repeated.

"Why do you keep asking me that?" Ian's confusion sounded like annoyance, and Bianca pulled away from him. She wanted to be able to see his face clearly when she asked the next question.

"You were not with Mora? In your room? In your bed?"

Now Ian really was angry. "Did she tell you that?"

He had not denied it. Bianca struggled to keep her voice even. "No. I heard you. Through the door."

As soon as the words were out of her mouth, Ian was moving with grim determination, descending the stairs at a rapid pace. Bianca was torn between continuing on her way to the laboratories to throw herself into the canal, as planned, or following Ian. Her feet made the decision for her, and she was already tripping down the stairs behind him when her mind hit upon the rationalization that the canal would still be there in another hour.

The smell struck him even before the sight, the seductive, singular scent of Mora. He could feel her there, feel her suffusing the room with her presence. A black silk stocking lay abandoned on the velvet divan, the silk coverings of the bed had been carelessly thrown aside, and the sheets still showed the impression of two bodies caught in a passionate tussle. But the room was empty, the bodies gone. She had defiled his room, purposely, blatantly, filling it with the smells and signs of her body, and then left. Ian was seized with a deadly rage.

The signs were unmistakable, but Bianca felt suddenly clear-headed. "You do not need to explain, my lord, nor deny it. I understand why you would be drawn to her. I felt her attractions myself. I am just going to go up to the roof—"

Bianca stopped speaking because Ian had grabbed her and was looking at her with eyes filled with dark emotion. "Stop it!" he commanded in a voice that left no room for disobedience. "It was not me, not with her, not ever again. You must believe that."

Bianca had never wanted to believe anything so much in her entire life. "I do, my lord," she assured him, hoping to banish the hunted look from his face. When Ian relaxed his hold on her arms, she swallowed deeply and then asked the question whose answer she was afraid to know. "Did you send her to me to tutor me? To teach me to make love the way you like?"

Ian was aghast. The idea that Bianca had anything to learn from anyone about lovemaking was so ludicrous he almost wanted to laugh. But the way she seemed to be holding her breath for the answer told him this was no joke to her. "Of course not! Who told you that? Actually, there is no need—undoubtedly it was Mora herself." Ian looked away so she would not see the deep anger in his eyes and misunderstand its object, but a noise brought his attention back to her. "What are you doing?" Bianca had burst into tears.

"Oh, *madonna*. She hurt you, didn't she? I will kill her. What did she do to you? Tell me, Bianca, damn it, what did she do?" Ian's voice was rapier sharp with rage.

Bianca shook her head and tried to stop her tears of relief. When she spoke, it was between little gasps of air. "No—no—nothing. She didn't do anything except kiss me. But I was so worried, I was so worried that you had sent her like she said, that I displeased you, that you were dis-dis-disgusted with me—"

Bianca was again silenced by Ian grabbing her, but this time it was to hug her close to his chest. He would protect her, he vowed, he would show her how completely undisgusting he found her. He gathered her against him and held her there with all his strength. She thought she felt him shaking, but it could merely have been the trembling of her own body.

Without speaking, they moved to the bed. Ian helped Bianca undress but refused to let her remove the massive stone that still hung between her breasts. When they were both nude, they climbed into the russet bed and reclaimed it as their own, making slow, deep love. Afterward, they spoke of their experiences at the ball, cuddling close together like a blissful couple long accustomed to intense intimacy. The mood was spoiled only when Bianca described her conversation with Giulio Cresci and Ian stood to challenge the man to a duel, but with a few well-placed kisses Bianca persuaded him to lavish his heated attention on her instead.

As the embers in the fireplace died out, they fell asleep entwined tightly together, listening to the light rain on the windowpanes.

Something heavy fell on Bianca's nose, waking her, but if it hadn't, she would have awoken a moment later when the shouting started. It was indistinct, more noise than words, but it was unquestionably coming from the man next to her, the man whose arm was presently hindering her breathing.

"Ian," she said, first softly, then again more insistently, but not loud enough to be heard over the shouting. She wriggled out from under his arm and moved to shake him, but as soon as she touched him, he pushed her away and off the bed.

"*Ian!*" she shouted, righting herself, gripping his shoulders and shaking him as hard as she could. "Santa Beatrice's scars, Ian, wake up!"

Ian sat up, panting, and looked around him disorientedly. He looked down at the hands still holding his shoulders, then up at the woman standing over him before he remembered where he was and understood what had happened. The nightmare had been different this time, more realistic and more intense than ever before. It was all Mora's fault, suffusing his room with her smell and her presence, bringing back the memories and the pain of that time with unmatched clarity. He shuddered as Bianca climbed back into the bed next to him, putting her arms around him and resting his head on her chest.

It felt nice lying with her like that, and Ian relaxed enough to catch his breath. She stroked his hair soothingly with one hand, her fingers lightly massaging his scalp. When his breathing had slowed to normal, she spoke.

"Why don't you tell me about the nightmare?"

He went rigid again and tried to pull away from her, but she held fast. She wanted so desperately to understand him, to know what had made him so impossibly hard, to see into his secrets, and to help him heal his wounds. After the torturous moments of self-doubt she had experienced that night, she was not going to let him pull away from her again. "You have to tell someone. If you keep them to yourself, they will never go away."

Rain streaked the windows and the silence stretched. Bianca's arms stayed around Ian, protective and warm, and his head stayed on her breast. Its softness was wonderfully alluring, and as he moved his cheek back and forth against it, he felt himself becoming aroused. He would make love to her, he decided, and then they would sleep and then she would stop pestering him with questions. He was vaguely aware that he was doing something wrong, but decided to ignore the feeling, to lose himself in the delicious woman next to him. He took her hand from his shoulders and moved it down his torso toward his already growing shaft. At the same time he rotated his body so he was on top of her.

"Make love to me, *carissima*. Take me into you," he whispered in a voice that promised pleasure, a voice he knew she could not resist.

"No." She shook her head and met his hooded eyes. "Not until after you have told me about your nightmare. I want to know what pains you so much. I want to help you stop it."

She was unprepared for Ian's demonic laugh when it came. Still over her, he pulled himself up on his elbows to laugh at her. The laugh was anything but mirthful, and the expression on his face sent a chill through Bianca's body. Ian laughed and laughed. She wouldn't make love to him until he told her his nightmare, she claimed, but he knew she wouldn't make love to him afterward. Afterward she would not want to touch him; she would leave him, as fast as she could. And that was what made Ian laugh the hardest, because, of course, she was trapped, she was his prisoner, a criminal or his betrothed, either way she could not leave. She would have to stay, and he would make love to her, watch her cringe away from him, feel her pull back from his odious touch, know that she found him hideous, horrible, disgusting. All of Mora's predictions would come true. Bianca had once said she hated him, but that was nothing compared to the complete revulsion she would soon feel.

Ian continued to laugh, even when Bianca called his name, even when she tried to push him away. He would give her a reason to hate him, and then he would not have to explain. She wanted to know him better, be closer to him. Fine, then he would help her to see him as he saw himself.

"You will make love to me. Now." It was a command, issued in a voice she did not recognize. "It will be better this way, easier for you to hate me. Believe me, *carissima*, it is better this way."

As he spoke, Ian reached down and tried to pull her legs, clamped shut, apart. Her effort to push him away seemed to work, but only long enough for him to get his arms up over hers, to pin her hands above her head. This time he shoved his knee between her legs, managing to spread them as she writhed under him. He held both her hands in one of his and used the other first to roughly fondle her breasts, then to guide himself into her. He saw her face fill with fear but closed his eyes before he saw the loathing that he knew would follow it. She kicked against him, screaming, fighting, as the full horror of his sudden madness swept over her.

"No! No, Ian, no!" He kept his eyes closed as he struggled to subdue her and enter her. "It won't work, Ian, it will not work. You cannot make me despise you!"

Her words brought a grim smile to his lips, and he opened his eyes. "Make you? I thought you already did. You told me so yourself, in this room only days ago."

"I was wrong. My feelings had been hurt and I spoke rashly," Bianca apologized.

Ian, or the man who was once Ian, grunted. "I will hurt more than your feelings this time, *carissima*."

Now feverish to be inside her, he redoubled his efforts to rip through her defenses and plow himself into her. But she fought back just as hard, kicking with the full force of her strength.

"Call me a bastard," Ian whispered in her ear, squeezing her wrists tighter and tighter as she refused to speak. "Tell me that I am a coward. Call me a rapist."

"No," she repeated over and over, "no, no, no," her last defense against the pain in her wrists.

"Tell me you hate me." Ian's face was only a hair's breadth from hers. "Say it, damn you, say it!"

Bianca shook her head and spoke in a new voice, a voice that was calm and quiet. "It is no good, my lord. I won't. This is not the right way, to run and hide, pushing away the people who try to care about you. You may hurt me, my lord, you may violate my body, you may pollute my womb, though I don't believe you will. But you cannot make me defile my mind or my mouth with statements which are untrue. I will not be stopped so easily."

It was her voice as much as her words that broke through Ian's dementia. His face contorted with pain, and he collapsed on top of her, suddenly without strength. Bianca, too, felt spent but at the same time euphoric. She had saved both of them from a violation that would have scarred them each forever. She had penetrated Ian's defenses, fought her way inside the stony fortress he had erected around his emotions. Nothing could be the same between them again, but she dared to hope it might be better.

As soon as his hand slipped from her wrists, Bianca brought her arms around Ian and held him as he lay on top of her. There was no question this time that he was trembling. He was mortified and horrified, shattered by the violence he had almost perpetrated on Bianca's body. He did not know what had happened to him, what demon had taken over his mind. Or rather, he knew too well. He felt as if he had made the nightmare true, acting out each of the hateful labels that Mora had assigned him. Reflecting on his loss of control and the horrible cruelty he had almost committed against Bianca brought with it a wave of nausea and self-disgust so acute that he could scarcely bear to be in his body.

But then he felt Bianca's arms around him, holding him close with no malice. If she could forgive him, after what he had just done to her, certainly he could forgive himself. He owed her an apology. And an explanation. He would have to tell her, tell her the history behind the nightmare, the history for which there could be no forgiveness. But he wanted to put it off as long as possible, to relish one last time the quiet splendor of her body before it was forever out of his reach.

"I am sorry," he finally mumbled where he lay, into her breast.

"Now tell the other one." She spoke quietly and seriously.

He turned his head and spoke clearly to the other breast. "I am sorry."

She raised his face to hers, her eyes a smoldering gold. "Now kiss me."

"Are you sure?" Ian suddenly felt boyish and insecure, but looking into her eyes, those deep, unusual eyes, his compunctions vanished. He brushed his lips over hers, gently, then spoke into her ear. "I am sorry, Bianca. I am so very sorry."

She nuzzled against him, using her arms to pull him closer. "I know you are. I do not want it to happen again. You scared me."

The simple honesty with which she spoke penetrated deep within Ian. He owed her honesty in return. But he, too, was scared, scared that once she knew the truth about him, she would despise him as he knew he deserved, and as he despised himself. Even a suspected murderess had a right to feel superior to a coward.

He did not allow himself to wonder what it might mean that he was so worried she would repudiate him. Nor to ask himself why he suddenly wanted her to know all of it. He just started talking.

"I have told only one person this story before, and I hope never to tell it again. No one else, not Crispin, not the other Arboretti, know this. It would bring great dishonor upon all of them. I ask you, please, not in my interest but in theirs, never to repeat it." Ian paused long enough for Bianca to nod, then turned and settled himself so he would not have to look at her face. When his back was against her chest and her arms were wrapped around him, he resumed in a businesslike voice.

"Christian's birthday was only two days after mine, and we grew up together, like twins. Indeed, everyone joked that we looked and acted more like each other than like any of our siblings. Our families were close, so we had the same tutors, practiced the same sports, accompanied one another on vacations, attended the same university, and then later, often traveled together. Our friendship was deep and unlimited. He would do anything for me, and I would do anything for him. Or so I thought. But I am getting ahead of myself.

"I had to go to Sicily for business, and at the last minute Christian decided to accompany me. He had just broken off an engagement with an heiress from Florence and wanted to get away from the gossip it had caused. I was thrilled to have the company and the opportunity to talk to him. He had spent much of the past year in Florence orchestrating his betrothal, and we had not had time to spend together. Also, I had been...busy. Needless to say, I was excited by the prospect of a journey together with him.

"We sailed to Messina, then proceeded by horseback to Syracuse. My negotiations there were brief but tremendously successful, and I was eager to get back to share the news with the other Arboretti." Ian stopped, shuddered once, and went on.

"It was summer, so the days were long, and I insisted that we travel with as much haste as possible. But into the second day of our return trip, Christian developed some sort of illness. He told me to go ahead, that he would catch up with me along the way, or at least at Messina, where we had left Giorgio with our ship. We were traveling with only a minimum of servants, and in any event, I was reluctant to leave him behind. The trip would be more pleasurable with him than alone, and I did not want to abandon him while he was ill. Despite his urging, I remained with him at our camp, hoping that he would improve. He did, and as dusk fell we rode out, planning to travel at least a few leagues before it got completely dark."

Ian shook his head. "I should not have been in such a rush. I should have known better. By day Sicily is safe, but at night merchant caravans are ripe prey for bandits. Foolishly I rationalized that since we had no actual merchandise, only papers, and since we were relatively small, no one would be interested in us. But the sun had only just dipped into the sea when we were set upon. There were five of them and eight of us until our servants, whom we had only hired for the trip in Messina, fled, leaving Christian and me to protect ourselves with only our swords. The bandits got between us, surrounding each of us separately, their horses sidling into ours." Ian's voice changed and sounded tighter, as if there were a huge weight on his chest.

"Three of them were around me, and I remember thinking that they were not very skillful as I slashed through first one, then another of them. Knowing that Christian was an even more adept swordsman than myself, I felt we would be fine. I was wrong. At the moment I was preparing to deal with my third attacker, I heard Christian shout out.

"I turned just in time to see them pull him off his horse and slice his throat. I watched as the knife went in, as they cut his head off. I must have watched and done nothing, just stood there. When I was found, four days later in an alleyway in Messina, I had only a few bruises. No sword wounds, no broken bones, no evidence that I had tried to defend him at all. I stood and watched as a man was killed, my best friend." Ian's voice faltered, and Bianca could feel his chest rise and fall as he gulped air. When he resumed, his voice was tight, emotionless, under control. "They killed the one person in the world I was really close to, and apparently I did not put up a fight."

Bianca's arms stayed around him, but he could not bear to see her face. He stiffened, anticipating her harsh words. "How did you get back to Messina?"

Ian exhaled sharply. She had asked a logistical question. She had been listening and had asked a question, not offered a rebuke. "I do not remember. I don't remember anything after slaying my second attacker. I suppose I blocked it out. But you know what they say about cowards, that we always have an explanation ready. At any rate, when I opened my eyes, Giorgio was standing over me and we were already at sea. He told me only that my body had been found in a small street behind an inn. He had made inquiries, but no one knew how it got there."

"What about Morgana?" Ian did not know the effort it cost Bianca to speak of her. "You said Christian was the only person you were close to, but you were close to her then too. She was living here."

Ian drew a deep breath. "When I came home, she had already heard the news, that is, she already knew that Christian was dead. She stayed with me and asked me to tell her what had happened, everything, every detail. I told her the story as I told you, and then she left." *As you will,* Ian added to himself.

He turned finally to face Bianca. "But not without first telling me what she thought of me. She said I was a coward, impossible to love. She told me she had suspected it but this proved it, that I would stand by and watch as bandits took the life of someone I claimed to care about. She pointed out that no one I said I loved could expect anything from me. She showed me that I did not know the first thing about love, about emotions, or about making her happy. She informed me the baby she was carrying was not mine, that I had not satisfied her for some time, that I was a selfish pitiful lover, more like a child than a man. At last she explained that I was a hateful, self-serving coward. I report this to you so that you will not feel you need to repeat it."

Ian turned his head away and willed her not to speak, but of course she could not resist. "Don't worry, my lord. I would never call you a coward. Irritating perhaps, stubborn, even thick-skulled, but never a coward."

She was making fun of him. He had bared his soul to her, and she was mocking him. Angry, he turned to berate her. But the words stuck in his throat when he looked into her eyes. They had tears in them.

"Provoking, certainly, that would be a good label for you. And antagonizing." She continued speaking as first one tear, then another rolled slowly down her cheek. "But also, fascinating, gifted, wonderful, and admirable. Shall I go on?"

Ian did not trust his voice, so he just shook his head. Then he changed his mind. "Are there more?"

Bianca looked deep into his eyes and laughed. "One or two. Smart. Brave. Very brave. And...likable." It was not the word she had intended to use, but it was safer.

"Likable?" Ian's forehead wrinkled. "That is not very exciting.

Couldn't it be 'ardent' or 'fiery' or 'scintillating'?" Or *lovable?* The voice in his head seemed to be back, intent on dismantling Ian's sanity. It reminded him of the words he had heard her speak two nights before, but which he dared not hope to hear again.

"Whose list is this?" Bianca demanded with mock annoyance. "Besides, I don't want it to go to your head."

Ian contemplated her in silence for a moment, tracing the path of one tear down her cheek with his finger. Then he bent, kissed her where it had landed on her collarbone, and rested his head once more against her breast. "Do you really think I am fascinating?"

"Santa Aemilia's middle toe! It was unpleasant enough having to produce all those nice adjectives for you, you may not now quiz me about each and every one."

"I am not kidding, Bianca." She saw his hand curl into a tight fist and realized that indeed he was not.

"Yes, my lord, I really do think you are fascinating."

"And attractive?"

"I don't believe I mentioned 'attractive' in my list." Bianca's voice was playful now.

"Then you don't." Ian sounded petulant.

"My lord, I doubt there is a woman in all Europe who does not find you attractive. There, are you satisfied?"

Ian nodded, though not completely satisfied with her answer. What did he care about the other women of Europe? He wanted to hear her say it, to know she found him attractive. But he did not want to seem too insistent, so he went on. "You did say 'brave.' Do you really think brave?"

"How many men do you know who would betroth themselves to a murderess, my lord?"

She had a point, Ian conceded, although right now she did not seem terribly dangerous. Except, perhaps, to his future happiness, the voice said. Damn voice. He ignored it, bracing himself to ask the final question, the one to which all the others had been leading.

"And...likable?" The word still sounded disappointingly generic, but he was afraid to use any of the substitutes.

"Yes, and...likable." With his head on her breast he could hear her heart beat faster as she spoke the last word, and he wondered what that meant.

"Still, after I told you about Christian?" He plunged ahead, steeling himself for her response.

"To be honest, my lord, I find you even more likable since then."

Ian needed to think about that for a moment. "You are not like other women," he said finally.

Bianca exhaled sharply. "I have been wondering when you would realize that, my lord."

"Ian," he invited.

"Ian," she repeated.

"Kiss me," he suggested.

"Kiss me," she echoed.

He did.

Chapter Twenty

They tiptoed toward the door, following Giorgio's signal for silence. First one, then another of the Arboretti put his eye to the keyhole.

"I don't believe it." Tristan was shaking his head. "He isn't really whistling to himself, is he?"

"Yes." Crispin shuddered. "And given his sense of music, it would be better if he didn't."

"*Dio mio,* I think I just heard a chuckle!" Sebastian was horrified.

Giorgio cut in, nodding. "He's been doing it all morning. I thought you should see it. It is very worrisome."

"Very," they all concurred.

"It could just be *her,* couldn't it?" asked Miles, whose developing crush on Bianca was obvious to his cousins.

"No, not a chance." Sebastian was emphatic. "Ian has had thousands of women, and none of them have had this effect on him."

"She is unusual," Miles, her champion, pointed out.

"So was Morgana, and she never got him singing like this. At least, not when he was alone." Tristan's pun got only a tepid reception from the others, all too preoccupied with the transformation in Ian.

"He seemed perfectly normal last night, didn't he?" Giorgio queried the cousins.

Crispin was nodding. "If you mean gruff, chilly, formal, and frightening to women and small animals, yes, he was in fine form."

"It is more serious than we think. Take a look." His blue eyes flashing with bewildered mirth, Sebastian redirected their attention to the keyhole.

Ian, no longer whistling, was seated at his desk in a pose that he had assumed a thousand times before, but with a single difference: he was smiling. "And not one of those typical Ian smiles that looks more like an affliction. This is, you know, well, *um*, a real smile." Miles, who was the poet of the group, struggled to find the right words.

"You must do something," Giorgio said sternly to the cousins in an undertone. "This is neither normal nor healthy. The last time he looked that way was right before he blew up Lord Roche-Bernard's place, and I am sure you have not forgotten what a mess that was."

None of the Arboretti could forget their rapid flight across the French border when Ian, taking offense at a comment made by Roche-Bernard about a woman at court, had decided to get even by testing his newest explosive on the man's country estate. Much to the dismay of the other Arboretti, the test had been a smashing success, and it had been years before they could return to France.

On the other side of the library door, Ian was feeling anything but abnormal or unhealthy. Indeed, he was feeling quite pleased with himself. His early trip to the Rialto had been a great success, and he had found exactly what he was looking for. Although he was reluctant to admit it, his sense of well-being came from more than just his shopping trip. It came from the hundred times that that morning that he had made Bianca repeat to him that he was likable. Even knowing what she knew about him, she still said it every time he asked. He was likable.

But he must not let it change his outward behavior, because she might have been lying, in which case he would look like a fool. She *was* a sly potential murderess—well, she was sly at any rate. Therefore, when the knock came at the door he made sure he used his normal, caustic voice to invite the knocker to enter. By the time the door opened, he had composed his face into its customarily determined look. At least he hoped he had. It was hard not to greet Giorgio and the Arboretti warmly as they entered, to confide his secret to them—he wondered if they remembered or had ever even known that he was likable—but he reminded himself that it was best to act as though nothing had changed.

He did such a good job acting his old, stern self that the Arboretti and Giorgio felt the keyhole must have been enchanted. His face bore no trace of a smile, and his lips were so tightly drawn together that it was impossible to imagine them capable of whistling. Could the typically grim man sitting behind the desk really have been chuckling to himself moments before? Crispin even went so far as to run his fingers over the lock, looking for evidence of fairy dust or some potion that might have distorted their vision. While he was busy with this, Sebastian started speaking.

"We did not know if you wanted to meet downstairs, as we normally do, or up here. I fear that your betrothed will draw quite a crowd for luncheon, and it might be more pleasant if we avoid it. While I wouldn't mind another glimpse of Cecilia Priuli, I could easily live without the dull witticisms and less than flattering comments about my mixed ancestry in which her mother seems to delight."

Ian had forgotten all about the traditional *pranzo* the day after the betrothal party, and he was sure Bianca had done likewise. He wondered which saints she had sworn by when she found out about it. Imagining the look that must have appeared on her face when Roberto and Francesco came to escort her down made him want to laugh out loud. Fortunately, he managed to contain the urge, reminding himself just in time that laughing was forbidden. Instead he nodded solemnly in agreement with Sebastian and asked Giorgio to bring more chairs to the library.

As servingmen filed in with chairs and refreshments, the other Arboretti continued to eye Ian curiously, but once they were seated, they redirected their attention to Sebastian.

"I asked you all here instead of waiting to tell you this at our normal meeting tomorrow, because I think time might be a factor, and besides, I need advice. As you know, I left the ball early last night because I had an appointment." Sebastian put up a hand before Tristan could interject. "And no, not with Cecilia Priuli on her *terrazza. Magari!* If only! No, with someone decidedly less attractive. My cousin Saliym."

Sebastian's father, the only male offspring of Benton Walsingham and his Venetian wife, inherited his mother's illustrious family name and his father's wanderlust. As the scion of the illustrious Dolfin family, Sebastian's father had served Venice for many years as an ambassador and emissary to the Ottoman Empire. While there in his official capacity, he had fallen in love and married a Turkish woman. And not just any woman, but one of the daughters of the current sultan. Sebastian was born in the imperial palace and spent his early life there, but the death of the sultan, Sebastian's grandfather, precipitated a power struggle within Turkey and allowed for the rise of a strong anti-Venetian faction. When relations between the Venetians and the Turks grew hostile, the family had relocated to Venice. In recent years an uneasy peace had been restored under the newly instituted sultanship of Sebastian's uncle. Saliym, the youngest of the sultan's sons, had been an occasional guest at Palazzo Foscari and was well liked by all the Arboretti.

"Saliym is here? Why didn't you invite him last night, instead of dashing off in that romantic way?" Crispin's tone made it clear that he was sure Sebastian was perpetrating a hoax.

"That's just it. He is not here. Not officially anyway, or I should say, not officially as far as the Venetians are concerned. You should have seen him last night—he is traveling as one of the sultan's high holy men."

Tristan, Miles, Crispin, and Ian asked in unison, "Saliym? A holy man?" It seemed somehow inconsistent with their memories of him on his previous visit to Venice. Tristan had a clear image of him sanguinely enjoying the ministrations of four young prostitutes at the same time, and Miles's breathing still quickened when he thought about the interactive dessert course Saliym had provided at a banquet in the Arboretti's honor.

Sebastian nodded, eyes alight with merriment. "No wine, no women, no socializing. He spent half the night describing his privations to me in as pitiful a tone as he could muster. Indeed, he risked ruining his disguise by contacting me only to find out if I knew of any extremely discreet courtesans. But in passing he mentioned something that I thought might be important to us."

He waved aside the interesting question of which women he had recommended and returned to his serious narrative. "Apparently, keeping the Ottoman Empire together has been more work than my uncle anticipated, and he is sorely in need of munitions. As you know, the English and the Portuguese are the only powers that will even consider selling gunpowder to the Turks, since they are the only powers the Turks have never directly threatened. Taking advantage of their monopoly, they have raised their asking prices a thousandfold. Saliym claims that careful calculations made by the sultan's accountants show it to be less expensive to move the whole of Constantinople to the New World than to buy a cargo of munitions from Queen Elizabeth. Indeed, it turns out it is cheaper to buy the stuff on the black market, and that is what the sultan has decided to do. The ship that Saliym and his fellow countrymen arrived on was supposed to rendezvous with a ship from a Venetian trading conglomerate—who had promised to supply them with twelve hundred tons of gunpowder."

Sebastian paused to let his words take effect. Even under the current unsteady peace, the Venetians remained wary of the Turks, their historical enemies. It was therefore not simply an offense but a traitorous act to sell any type of weaponry whatsoever to the Ottoman Empire. Well placed, a thousand tons of gunpowder alone could easily blow the whole of Venice out of the water, and still leave the extra two hundred to take care of anyone who might have survived. The deal Saliym had disclosed to Sebastian was treason on the most massive scale.

"You said 'was supposed to rendezvous.' Did they?" Even now Ian had to work to keep his tone appropriately grim. He wondered how he normally managed it.

"No. The boat never came, but an emissary from the group did, promising them delivery of a reduced shipment yesterday, but refusing to reduce the price."

"Let me guess. They said they could deliver seven hundred tons?" Tristan's customary smile was nowhere to be seen as he named the amount of gunpowder that had been removed from Arboretti warehouse just before the explosion.

Sebastian shook his head. "No, only five hundred. But the Turks refused to pay for merchandise they were not getting, and the Venetians refused to budge on their price, complaining about the difficulties they had endured to get the stuff in the first place."

Ian snorted. "'Difficulties.' Breaking into our unguarded warehouse and paying some people to keep their mouths shut. 'Difficulties.'"

"How do you know it was our gunpowder?" Miles queried, pushing the hair off his forehead. "As Sebastian just said, it does not correspond to the amount they took."

Ian turned up his palm. "The timing is too neat for it not to be. There is also the original quantity. Remember, the boat we were prepared to send off, the one L.N. warned us about, was supposed to have exactly twelve hundred tons of gunpowder on it."

"But there is nothing special about that number." Miles looked toward Ian when he spoke, but it was Tristan who answered.

"Exactly. That is why the coincidence is so strange. Why not an even number like a thousand tons, which is how things are usually sold?"

Crispin was skeptical. "Why did they sell only part of what they captured, if that is the case? What were they saving that extra two hundred tons for? To blow up someone's hunting lodge?"

"No, that requires only half a ton," Ian quipped before he remembered that he did not make jokes. He sobered himself quickly, hoping no one had noticed. "I suggested on Saturday, and I still believe, that we, the Arboretti, are under some threat. I would hazard that they have reserved two hundred tons of explosives to make that threat good."

"I am not sure I agree." Sebastian was shaking his head again, slowly. "It does seem that these Venetians had intended to use our gunpowder for their deal. But the information from Saliym makes it look unlikely that their interest in us goes beyond that. I suspect anyone with a munitions contract would have been choice prey for them, it did not have to be us."

Miles, Tristan, and Crispin all concurred, but Ian could not rid himself of the instinctual feeling that someone was attacking the Arboretti. Perhaps, he realized, his instincts went that way because he himself had felt under attack for so long, besieged by the voices of self-doubt and disgust that ruled his consciousness. The new likable Ian would not be governed by those doubts, he decided, nor would he cling to unsupported persecution theories.

"Very well." Ian's tone was conciliatory. "But we are still left with the fact that our gunpowder is being illegally pedaled by traitors. Even without a particular grudge against us, they could do us a world of harm if, for example, an enemy boat were to be captured and found loaded with gunpowder in barrels bearing the Arboretti seal. Not to mention that, beyond redeeming our property, it is our duty to see that their treason is punished. We must find out who they are."

"I have Saliym looking into that. He doesn't think it will be too hard to convince the crew to identify the Venetians, since they acted in such bad faith." Sebastian moved his gaze around the circle of his cousins and stopped at Tristan. "I was also hoping you might make some inquiries among your, *ah*, old friends."

Although Tristan's less-than-perfect past was a matter of record, it could often be a touchy subject for him, and his cousins were always reluctant to raise it. But they were aware that there were moments, such as those spent in the company of adventure-minded young ladies or times like this one, when his years in the underworld promised to be of assistance rather than an embarrassment, and at those times he did not mind having it spoken of at all. "I had already thought of that," Tristan said brightly, adding, "I should be able to find out something by tomorrow morning."

As their talk turned to more general subjects, particularly the party of the night before, they began to hear voices emanating from the floor below. Crispin crept down yet another secret staircase, accidentally running into a flustered footman, to survey the scene in the gold reception hall. If the throngs of women who were arriving for lunch had anything to do with it, Bianca was certainly going to be a big success.

"I would say one hundred and fifty, but that counts Widow Falentini as two, because she eats for two." Crispin returned and gave his estimate. "Even better than the turnout is the look on Bianca's face. It's not just that she looks in her element. It is something else. I can't describe it."

Tristan and Miles, their curiosity piqued, went down to look, and then reported back.

"I think it looks like she knows a joke which she is not ready to share with anyone. Something that might set her to whistling and laughing to herself when she was alone," Tristan offered, looking pointedly at Ian.

Miles was shaking his head, causing his hair to slip back into his eyes. "I can see what would make you say that, but that's not quite it." He stopped to search for a word and found it. "Expectancy. It is a look of sanguine expectation. I think she is eagerly waiting for something to happen."

"Or to make something happen." Ian knew her too well. He shook his head and jokingly muttered a prayer under his breath. "Sante Agata, Lucia, and Felicia, with all your assorted limbs and bits, please, I beg you, save us from the conceptions and connivings of my lovely betrothed." Forty-eight hours later he would not have used the same light tone.

"I did not know green was at all the thing this season." Bianca's aunt Anatra did not lower her voice or disguise the direction of her gaze as she critiqued Bianca's gown. She sighed and fanned herself with feigned resignation. "But I suppose I am just déclassé, of the old school."

"No, Ana darling, it is we who must maintain the standards. I can't recall the last time I saw anyone wearing green." Serafina Terreno was seated next to her bosom friend Anatra along the far wall of the full reception hall. The women's friendship, which had miraculously endured since girlhood, consisted primarily in their knowledge that they had once been more beautiful than all the other women in the patriciate, and that this (former) beauty granted them the privilege of acting as arbiters of taste and fashion.

"For all that, it does not look ill on her." Anatra and Serafina scowled jointly at the speaker seated alongside them. Carlotta Nonte had also grown up with them, or as they said privately, grown out. They had humored her as a pudgy girl because of the attractive contrast she provided to their own slim figures, but as a rounded-out matron she was harder to bear. It wasn't just that she had made the best match of the three, nor that her daughter Catarina was a celebrated beauty, but that she was always so good-natured. At times it was really more than a body could stand.

Anatra sighed heavily again and patted her on the arm. "Now you know, Lotte, how bad you are with colors. I meant to take you aside last night and tell you how much better your Catarina would look in browns than in blues. The way the blue brings out the blue of her eyes," another deep sigh, "well, it is really a bit much."

"Even vulgar," Serafina added, as if reluctantly. "I think loam might be good for her."

Carlotta regarded her friends with gratitude. Despite what her daughter said, they were always so thoughtful to her. "I don't think I know Loam. Is he a new dressmaker?"

Serafina and Anatra exchanged pitying glances, each nominating the other for the task of enlightening their unfortunate friend. Finally Serafina shouldered the burden. "No, Lotte, it is a color. Loam. A sort of greenish brown."

"Like mud. Loam is the color of mud." All three woman lifted their eyes to regard the new speaker, Anatra shuddering genteelly as her eyes were assaulted by the green of Bianca's dress. Their hostess spoke again. "I can't think of anything uglier than a loam gown."

"Indeed, we were just discussing your unique relationship with color," Anatra said in a tone that made it clear that what Bianca knew about color might conceivably fill a grappa glass, or perhaps a sewing thimble.

Bianca's mind was so focused on executing the plan she had contrived that morning that she was not even tempted to retort. Or rather, she was mildly tempted, since she had picked the fabric for her gown herself and was very pleased with it, but she stopped herself. Instead, with her heart beating with excitement almost as fast as it did when Ian was near her, she smiled widely at the three childhood friends. She could not have asked for a better audience on whom to launch her undertaking.

"Thank your for your compliment, Aunt Anatra, but I did not rush over here to talk about gowns. I have just heard the most fascinating gossip." Bianca spoke louder than usual while trying to keep her voice natural, as if she originated bits of gossip every day. "Some patrician is planning to marry Isabella Bellocchio, the courtesan. Just think, we shall have a real courtesan at our gatherings and balls. Isn't that exciting?"

" 'Horrifying' would have been a better word," Serafina said, giving Bianca a much needed lesson in morality. That accomplished, she probed for information. "Have you any idea who the wretch is? Some old bachelor, no doubt, who has long since forgotten his duty to his class."

"No, it's not like that at all." Bianca kept her eyes wide, hoping to look trustworthy and innocent. "It seems it is a young man, someone so smitten by her charms that he has even put the agreement in writing. Someone I know saw it, but they won't disclose the name. They will only tell me that he is blond. How diverting!"

The looks on the faces of the women before her were anything but amused. All three of them had sons who, in addition to being unmarried and the seat of all their future hopes, were also blond.

Indeed, more than half the faces in the room suddenly assumed a dire aspect as the news traveled between and among the clusters of women.

Bianca's plan was working like a charm; the news spread like fire on kindling, with the added benefit of bringing the onerous luncheon to a hasty conclusion. Before long, the women were politely begging off, mentioning other commitments and social obligations that they simply could not forgo. The bulk of them went rushing home to assure themselves that their children's affections were unengaged and that they would not soon be closely allied with some hussy. The rest, those with dark-haired sons, hurried off to order their wardrobes made over in green.

When she had seen the last of the distracted women to their gondolas, refusing to disclose either the nonexistent source of her gossip or the long forgotten name of her dressmaker, Bianca gave orders to have the remains of the recently dismantled luncheon taken away. Then, finding that she rather liked making and spreading gossip, she took to the stairs in search of available ears. The five Arboretti still gathered in the library would be perfect subjects for the news she had to share. Or so she thought, until she saw their solemn faces.

Ian's greeting was anything but warm. "What are you doing up here? Don't you have luncheon guests to attend to?"

Bianca shook her head morosely. "They abandoned me. They rose in a body and left."

"What did you do to them? Did you act in an untoward manner?" Remembering Miles's description of her expression, Ian had an ill sense of foreboding.

"No no, certainly not, my lord. In fact, I modeled my behavior on yours."

The other Arboretti tried unsuccessfully to stifle their chuckles. Ian glared at them, and then at his betrothed.

Bianca just smiled at him and turned to others. "I did not mean to interrupt anything. I just came up to tell you that it was safe to descend, now that the assortment of females has left. But you all look so glum. Don't tell me another of you has gotten yourself betrothed?"

Sebastian flashed his famous smile at her. "No, nothing nearly that grave. We were only speaking of treason,"

"Which does not concern you," Ian interrupted sourly.

"We were also," Crispin cut in, "speculating about which one of us garnered more admirers last night."

Bianca wrinkled her brow, as if exerting herself on a complicated computation. "I hate to have to say this, both for your sakes and mine, but I think it was my lord d'Aosto who won the most hearts last night."

Tristan nodded, not surprised. "You might consider taking up swordsmanship to keep your home free of nubile young women. I could offer myself as a tutor."

"Come, Tristan, surely you have not forgotten that I am the superior swordsman," Miles interjected, referring to a contest between the two of them when they were four.

"No matter." Ian entered the fray, trying not to look too pleased by this newest evidence of his likability. "With her razor-sharp tongue my betrothed has no need for a sword."

Bianca looked straight at him, a mischievous smile playing on her lips. "That will be fine for the girls, but how am I to discipline you, my lord?"

"With your winning manner, it will hardly be difficult to make me do your bidding," Ian retorted.

Sebastian spoke up. "I don't mean to be a sore loser, but I am curious to know if anyone said anything about the rest of us."

Bianca's expression communicated that she hated to disappoint them, but the opportunity was too good to forgo. "Unfortunately, most of the talk was not about men, but about women, or one woman, really. Isabella Bellocchio, the courtesan. It seems that she is betrothed to a nobleman. I think it is wonderfully exciting, but some of the other women had less favorable opinions of the news."

Crispin had opened his mouth to speak, but a look from Ian shut it. Miles spoke instead. "Who is it? Which of us has freed himself from the constraint of marrying a bloodless patrician woman?"

Bianca's brows rose. "My goodness. Bloodless? What an interesting idea. Then the substance in our veins must be bile. Miles, that is the most compelling explanation of female behavior I have ever heard!"

Miles was shaking his head violently. "I did not mean you, certainly. Not you at all. You are not proper and mannered the way they are, always stiff and polite and too beautiful to touch." Realizing that he had done more harm than good, he felt the color rise in his cheeks and began to stammer as he pushed his hair off his forehead. "What I meant, what I mean, what I should have said—"

Tristan, his jade-green eyes showing amusement, came to his aid. "You must excuse Miles. He is not quite himself around you, and he is always a bit animated on the topic of patrician marriage because he was betrothed at the age of seven. But his question is a good one. Who is the lovely Isabella going to marry?"

Bianca, still intrigued by the idea that women might not actually have blood in their veins, pushed the apology aside. "Actually, I was hoping you might know the answer to that question. The only hint I have gotten is that the husband-to-be is one of her regular clients." She paused and then added offhandedly, "Oh, and that he is blond."

Bianca had turned her back to Ian when she first announced her gossip and now unwillingly faced him when he called her name.

He waited until he had both her eyes locked with his before he began speaking. "From whom did you hear this information?"

Bianca kept her gaze steady. He must not suspect that she had started the rumor herself. "From one of the women at the luncheon. Maybe Carlotta Nonte?"

Ian scanned her face for a sign that she was lying. "And she did not say who the lucky man is?"

"No." Bianca's head moved from side to side slowly. "She said exactly what I reported. Not just to me, everyone heard it."

"I can think of one person who fits that description admirably." Tristan was grinning. "Crispin, why didn't you tell us you were going to be married?"

"Ask anyone—I am not the marrying type. Besides, you see Isabella more than I do," Crispin retorted. "In the right light, your hair could be blond."

Sebastian turned his keen investigative gaze on Tristan's deep brown hair. "Which light would that be, starlight?"

"Perhaps the light emanating from the eyes of his beloved?" Miles, ever the poet, suggested.

"Doesn't Isabella have any blond clients besides you two?" Bianca asked, fishing for even the slightest scrap of information.

"Probably, but one does not like to think oneself a member of a crowd where women are concerned," Tristan joked.

"What Tristan means," Sebastian did the interpreting this time, "is that when a man pays a courtesan, he does not like to think too much about her other lovers."

Bianca gave what she hoped was a knowing nod.

"Although at Isabella's it is sometimes hard to ignore the others. She schedules her appointments so close together you often pass on the stairs." Crispin was shaking his head. "I remember once I was almost knocked over by Aemilio Nonte sprinting up the staircase."

"It could be him," Miles pointed out eagerly. "He is blond. And it was his mother who told you about it in the first place. Maybe she was testing to see how people would react."

"I wonder," Bianca mused, adding Aemilio's name to the list of possible suspects.

Tristan, who had been sitting pensively, spoke to Bianca. "I just remembered. The last time I went to see Isabella I ran into your brother. He's blond."

"Indeed he is." Ian sounded mildly amused, in a way that Bianca knew was designed to displease her. "You have no idea whether or not your brother is her fiancé?"

"My brother does not see fit to share his personal life with me, my lord." She kept her voice steady, despite what Ian was implying. "I think it would be exciting to be allied with a courtesan. I rather hope it is him."

"I, on the other hand," Ian proceeded, "do not find the prospect of being nearly related to a courtesan at all appealing."

Bianca looked at him with pity. "You have no imagination, my lord."

"She's right, Ian." Crispin spoke. "If you thought last night was a good party, imagine how popular we will become if our galas begin to include members of the demimonde. I think it might even improve our bank rates."

The conversation was saved from further degeneration by the entrance of Giorgio, out of breath. Seeing the Arboretti still gathered together, he looked relieved, and even more relieved when his eye fell on Sebastian.

"My lord," he addressed Sebastian formally, "I have a most unusual question for you. Do you know if your uncle has a particular partiality for cinnamon?"

"My uncle the sultan? Cinnamon?" Sebastian repeated. The baffled tone in his voice was reflected in the faces of the other Arboretti. "Not that I know of. Why, are you sending him a present?"

"No, no, I was just wondering. I mean, someone I know was wondering." Much to Ian's surprise and horror, Giorgio began to blush. "Someone at the tavern," he lied hastily, but not before Bianca let out an ill-concealed giggle.

Ian scowled at her, then at his personal servant. Blushing. He was again seized with the uneasy feeling, with which he was growing familiar, that he had somehow lost control of his household and its doings. He would have to ask Bianca about it that night when they dined together. He felt sure she would be compliant when she saw the surprise he had prepared for her. He could almost imagine the look on her face....

"That reminds me," Crispin was saying to her when Ian emerged from his reverie, "I have news for you. We have resolved the mysterious origin of that plant you were asking about yesterday, though I am afraid the answer is not very exciting." She was listening to him intently. "According to Sebastian, it grows all over Constantinople like a weed. It is commonly given as a 'good faith' present between business associates at the conclusion of a deal, a sort of token of friendship and alliance. We have a ship just back from the spice markets of Turkey, and I am sure one of our men must have picked it up for me there."

"I see." The crease in Bianca's forehead and the far-off look in her eyes belied her easy acceptance of the mystery's solution. It was the look she got when she was at her most cunning, Ian knew, and it made him nervous to see it in connection with something as benign as a plant. His nervousness was compounded by suspicion when, soon after, she made an excuse to leave.

"Where are you going?" Ian demanded roughly.

Bianca cocked her head to one side. The far-off look was replaced by one Ian could only describe as playful. "I thought I would take a bit of air in one of your gondolas, then perhaps go to one of the places where women like me have their special needs met. You know, animals, whips, those sorts of things."

The Arboretti, including Ian, just gawked.

"Santa Barbara's hands, I am kidding, my lord. I fear that if I tell you my actual schedule, you might die of boredom, and then where would I be? A homely aged spinster once more without a husband." Bianca rolled her eyes at the thought.

Observing that Ian was on the point of regaining use, if not control, of his mouth, she rushed on. "If you must know the truth, I am going to check on Marina and her baby. Then I thought I would spend the day taking care of some *last-minute* correspondence." She paused to see whether her allusion to the short time left her had attracted his attention. "Really, my lord, the best way to be sure of my whereabouts would be to station yourself constantly at my side."

Ian was now back in full command of his faculties. "What if someone mistook me for a fawning suitor? Surely that would damage my burgeoning popularity with other women. Not to mention how it would eat into the time I would have available to them."

"Quite right," Bianca said, suddenly feeling anything but jovial. "I should never want to be a hindrance to *your* enjoyment of life."

"Don't worry," Crispin chimed in merrily. "Ian has not enjoyed life in years."

To Crispin's stupefaction, Ian concurred. "True, so true." Then, struggling to keep his voice morose and free from any hint of the excitement he was feeling, he addressed Bianca. "And to ensure I continue to be miserable, I request your company tonight for dinner when the clock strikes nine. It seems we have many things to discuss that are better handled in private." He added, as if an afterthought, "And don't forget to dress appropriately. Green is not at all the thing this season."

The room shook with the impact of the door slamming behind Bianca, but nowhere near as much as it did later when, recalling the expression on her face, Ian's laughter reverberated off the walls.

Chapter Twenty-One

When Nilo came back with the message, Bianca was in the servants' wing having Marina arrange her hair. She had passed the three hours since the boy's departure in an agony of expectation, for the success or failure of her plan hinged entirely on the answer he would bring her. Had she been able to, she would have climbed the walls of her room, but instead had to content herself with pacing its length, width, and diagonals. When she had exhausted the entertainment value of that activity, about five minutes after commencing it, she had picked up a book, read a page, put it down, unwittingly picked up a different book, read a different page, put that one down, over and over again with five books. That used up four minutes. She then consumed ten minutes checking over the lists she had made and the messages she had written should she decide to go ahead with her plan, five minutes assuring herself of the eventual success of the plan, thirteen minutes telling herself of its certain failure, nine minutes wondering what Ian wanted to talk to her about, fourteen minutes imaging what she would rather do with him than talk, twelve minutes trying to properly identify all the women pictured on her walls, eleven minutes making up new names for them, fifteen minutes staring into space, eight minutes trying to decide which of her four gowns to wear, another eight minutes changing her mind, and ten minutes maneuvering her body into the one she finally selected.

At that point, two hours later, it had been clear that neither her mind nor her room could offer her any further amusement unless she began moving the furniture around. Just as she was reflecting that she liked the arrangement of the furniture, it occurred to her that she should pay Marina a visit. Pleased at the prospect of having someone else to pass the interminably long minutes with, she grabbed two strings of pearls from her dressing table and flew down the stairs to the servant's room.

In her excitement, she forgot to knock and therefore was confronted with a scene not intended for her observation. Marina was propped up in bed, holding Caesar against one breast, while Giorgio gently massaged her feet. The baby was the only one not to bat an eye when Bianca came bursting in. Giorgio jumped up and away from the seat he had been occupying as if it had suddenly turned into a bed of snapping serpents, while Marina hid herself and the baby completely under the covers. Bianca, who had stopped dead in her tracks, began to laugh.

She was still gasping for breath when she spoke. "I- I- I apologize for bursting in that way. I did not mean to interrupt anything. I will just go."

Giorgio caught her arm before she could leave. "You won't tell His Lordship, will you?" His expression was so earnest that Bianca nearly began to laugh again.

"What? That you were performing an act of kindness for a fellow creature?"

"No, an act of kindness, when you put it that way, that is okay." Giorgio's voice dropped to a whisper. "But you won't tell him it was for a woman, will you?"

Bianca considered challenging him, but decided that was a prejudice best worked out between master and servant. "Very well. I won't tell him you were being thoughtful to a woman. I can imagine how that would ruin your reputation."

Giorgio shook her hand in gratitude, deciding she was the nicest suspected murderess he had ever met. Seeing that she was turning to leave, he stopped her. "I was about to depart, I have dinner to attend to, but you should stay. I am sure Marina wouldn't mind your company."

Bianca waited until the door closed behind him to address the bedcovers. "I was wondering if you would help me with my hair?"

"You will still have me?" Marina peeked out from a corner. "You're not going to toss me out?"

"Why? Because you seem to have captivated Giorgio's heart?"

Marina emerged farther from the covers, beaming. "Do you really think I have?" She giggled to herself. "I tell you, ma'am, never has a man been as nice to me as that Giorgio. Or for as little."

"I hope you are not exerting yourself too much on his behalf." Bianca's tone was arch. "You still need time to heal."

"Ma'am! I haven't exerted myself, as you put it, with him at all, that's just the thing. And yet he keeps on coming back here, all politelike, with a sweet or some wine or some little thing for the baby. Not like that other one, that gondolier. He just comes in flashing his toothy grin and the gold in his pockets. Time was he would have been the man for me, but I think my ways are changing."

Marina kept up a steady stream of conversation as she arranged Bianca's hair, pulling the top part back from her temples in two small braids interwoven with pearls and letting the rest hang in waves down her back. She had just handed Bianca a mirror to admire it by when Nilo burst in as his mistress had an hour earlier.

"Damnation," he cried when he spotted Bianca, rendering the two women dumb.

Bianca recovered first. "Nilo, that word is completely inappropriate."

"His Lordship uses it all the time," Nilo pointed out empirically.

"Yes, but His Lordship is taller than you are," Bianca offered, almost as empirically, hoping simultaneously that Nilo would neither question her logic nor undergo a growth spurt anytime soon.

The boy looked thoughtful for a moment, then nodded. "You are right. I won't use it again until I am as tall as he is."

"Very good. Now that we have settled that, what did she say?" Bianca's tone did little to mask her excitement.

"Nothing," Nilo replied, all innocence. "Oh, that is not strictly true. She said, 'Wait here, little one.'" The boy looked intently at his mistress, watching for the moment when he had frustrated her past endurance.

"And?" Bianca demanded.

"I waited," he replied simply. His stomach rumbled.

"And?" Bianca's tone made it clear that if he did not manage an answer of more than two words this time, he might have to bid farewell to his dinner, and perhaps to food in general, forever.

"And she came back and gave me this." Nilo pulled a letter from inside his tunic.

Bianca grabbed it, hastily broke the wax seal, and struggled to hold it steady enough to read. There were only two lines, written on scented paper and in a voluptuous script that instantly brought to mind the woman who had sent it. "*Cara*, All I have is at your disposal. It will be a pleasure to help you in any way I can."

She had agreed. The plan would go ahead. Bianca did not know if she was happy or terrified, and she did not have time to decide. The clock was striking eight when she had recovered enough from her excitement to stand. She quickly took her leave of Marina and Caesar, told Nilo to go to the kitchen for something to eat and to dry off a bit, and then to meet her in her room.

While waiting for him, she took the six cream-colored packages from her writing desk and inspected them one last time. Once they were sent out, she was committed, there would be no going back, no chance to change course. The plan was risky, very risky, but it was her only option. The messages would go out. The trap would be set.

Her greatest concern was for the boy. He arrived shortly, rosy-cheeked and smiling from his dinner in front of the kitchen fire, but the smile died when he saw the expression on his mistress's face.

As soon as Nilo had made his bow, Bianca handed him the six packages.

Her voice was unfamiliar when she spoke, cool and distant. "You must deliver each of these tonight. That, of course, will be no challenge for you. The challenge is that you must do it in such a way that you cannot be followed, caught, or recognized, either tonight or at any point in the future. You must be at your most nimble. All of the men to whom you deliver these will be upset, but one of them will be more than merely upset. He will be dangerous."

Nilo nodded seriously, all trace of his earlier playfulness erased, examining the packages with care. On one side they were closed with a heavy wax seal bearing an unfamiliar coat of arms, and on the other they were addressed in a hand Bianca had tried to make as different from her own as possible. He was studying the addresses when one of them caught his eye. Looking up abruptly, he held it out to Bianca. "Mistress, are you sure you have made this one out correctly? It says—"

"Yes, I know," she cut him off. "That one will be the hardest to deliver. It is also the most important. You must be sure it gets to him, and even more sure that you are not recognized."

Nilo carefully tucked the packages in his tunic to protect them from the rain, then made a deep and solemn bow to her.

"Be careful, little one," she said, her voice now familiar. "I do not want any harm to come to you."

"Nor I, to you," he said in a tone chivalric enough for a man three times his age.

Their solicitude for each other's well-being made them momentarily unaware that they had been joined by another person. Ian stood at the other end of the apartment and watched as Bianca spoke with strident gestures to her little servant. Finally tired of being ignored, he cleared his throat and approached them.

"I hope, sir, that you are not also making a bid for my lady's hand," he said seriously to Nilo.

The young boy blushed and kept his eyes on the ground. "No, my lord. Not until I am tall enough to say 'damnation.'"

Ian was unfazed by this new evidence of his betrothed's unusual ability to surround herself with lunacy. "Luckily for me, that will not be for some time. Until then, I hope you will not mind if I take her in to dinner."

Nilo, eyes still on the ground, shook his head back and forth, as Ian offered his arm to Bianca.

She was studying him, trying to recall why she had been angry with him that afternoon, wondering how she could ever be displeased with him. He was magnificent. The cuffs and collar of his silver-blue silk shirt, which was the exact color of his eyes, peeked out from under his tapered black velvet jacket. The jacket was fastened with two diamond clasps and ended just below his waist to give an unobstructed view of his sinewy thighs encased in leggings of silver-and-black velvet. Bianca found her breathing quickening as she took his arm and allowed herself to be led from the room.

They descended the first staircase but instead of continuing down the second to the dining room, or turning left to enter his apartments, Ian steered her toward a small door on the right that she had never before noticed. It gave onto a staircase wide enough for them to ascend arm in arm, brightly lit by candles. The staircase was decorated in the style of antique Rome which had been popular earlier that century, the walls a deep porphyry red and bordered by a frieze of frolicking satyrs and maidens painted to look as if they were carved statues. Bianca was so fascinated by the embellishments that Ian almost had to drag her up to the door at the top of the stairs with promises that the best was yet to come.

When Ian opened it and motioned her through, she saw he had spoken the truth. Her mind assured her that it was still a rainy night in November and she was still inside Palazzo Foscari, but her eyes told her that it was a beautiful spring day in a Roman garden. Each of the four walls of the room dissolved into a garden pavilion so skillfully rendered that Bianca was sure she smelled the fragrance of fresh jasmine and heard the rustling of a light breeze through the treetops.

"Where are we?" she asked finally, her voice filled with wonder.

"This was my grandparent's private dining room." Ian spread his arms wide, proudly. "My grandmother hated winter, so my grandfather brought Raphael up from Rome to paint her a room where it would always be spring."

"But are we still in your house?" Bianca was still stunned.

Without realizing that he had let his guard down, Ian laughed. "Yes, we are between the floor you occupy and the one I occupy, somewhere under Roberto and Francesco's rooms."

"What is that?" Bianca spun around, looking for the source of the music that had begun to fill the room.

"Magic," Ian said, but not in answer to her question. He was entranced by the figure spinning before him, her loose hair flying out behind her to catch the light of the candles. The dress was perfection on her, the dark gold of the brocade matching the gold of her eyes, the blue a sensational contrast with her creamy skin. He knew at that instant that the moment he had been waiting for, the moment when he would stop wanting her, stop feeling drawn to her, would never come. And he knew equally that he could never feel that way about a murderess. Ian had begun to believe, had wanted to believe in her innocence days before, but it was only then, at that moment, that it became an indisputable certainty to him.

He could have told her of his realization that night, but he was unwilling to risk spoiling their evening together by speaking of murder. There would be time for his confessions and his apologies later, he told himself, for they would have many years together. The thought suffused him with a delicious warmth, tempting him to skip dinner entirely and move into the adjacent bedchamber. His willful body was unable to override his mind, however, which was cogently advising him to savor and prolong every moment of the evening he had painstakingly planned.

Bianca noticed the dining table for the first time when Ian took her hand and led her to it. It was on a raised platform in a corner of the room, framed by an arbor that was covered with white jasmine blossoms. They looked so real that Bianca was tempted to reach for them, but she pulled her hand back just in time to avoid making a fool of herself.

"Go ahead," Ian said, reaching toward them. "These are real. My grandmother loved jasmine, and I keep these plants here in her memory."

Two weeks earlier she would never have guessed that granite-cold Ian Foscari, the Conte d'Aosto, was capable of such a romantic act, but now it seemed an integral part of his complex personality. She watched intently as he snapped a branch of the fragrant plant from a nearby stalk and tucked it neatly into the bodice of her gown. Her skin felt warm where he had touched her, and she wondered if he was too hungry to skip dinner. Before she could proposition him, however, he was directing her to a bench at one side of the elaborately set table.

The finest Foscari silver glittered atop the white damask table-cloth in the light of almost fifty candles hidden in niches through-out the room. As if in response to some telepathic command, three servants entered, one carrying a gold carafe of wine, and two bearing steaming silver tureens. Wordlessly they set their burdens down and were gone, as silently and quickly as they had come. Ian poured the sparkling, golden prosecco into two goblets, then took something from a pedestal next to him and set it on the table before Bianca.

It was a wooden box, with the initials of Venice's foremost gold-smith inlayed in the top. She had seen its mate, though not its twin, for this one was quite large, the day she had watched Ian present Tullia with the immense emerald earrings as payment for her services. Disgust warred with anger and then sadness as she looked at the box. Finally, she pushed it away and said in a bitter voice, "I cannot accept that, my lord."

Ian felt as though someone had knocked the life out of him. She was repudiating his surprise, and worse, she seemed to detest it. "What do you mean you cannot accept it? Why not?"

"Did I say 'cannot'? I meant will not. I will not accept it. Damn you, Ian, I fall in love with you, and in return you treat me like one of your whores."

Ian looked as if he suspected someone of tampering with his hearing. He knew he had misunderstood the first part of her statement—he was likable, not lovable—and the second part made only a touch more sense. "Giving you a present is treating you like a whore?"

"Yes." Bianca nodded vigorously. "You are giving me this so you won't have to give me something else, something infinitely more valuable and more difficult. You are giving me this," she moved to sweep the box off the table but Ian caught it, "so you don't have to give me your trust, your affection, or your love."

It would have been the perfect time to tell her that he thought she was innocent, to tell her that he trusted her implicitly, and that he suspected he felt some affection for her, some strong affection, but he was too rattled by the failure of his surprise. Plus, she was leaving.

Ian gripped her by the arm, hard, and brought her back to the bench. He put the box back in front of her. "Open it," he commanded.

Bianca sat and stared straight in front of her.

"Open it," Ian said again, more firmly.

Bianca shook her head.

Ian caught her face in his hand and gently turned it toward him. When he spoke, his voice was softer. "Please, Bianca. Open it."

It was not his words but the look in his eyes, the hungry look of a gambler risking everything on one slim chance, that finally made her acquiesce. Still petulant, she brought the box toward her and lifted the hinged lid.

What she saw inside rendered her at once remorseful and breathless. "They are beautiful! They are perfect," she said drawing her father's precious scissors, now fixed, from their green velvet casing. "Oh, Ian, how can ever I thank you?"

The adoring expression on her face when she turned it toward him was all the thanks he wanted, or almost. He cleared his throat, met Bianca's eyes, cleared his throat again, and opened his mouth. There was still one little question nagging at him.

"Would you like some soup?" was what he was sure came out of his mouth.

"You are irresistibly attractive," was how he was sure Bianca responded.

"It is pumpkin soup." Ian went on as if she had not spoken.

"My heart beats faster every time you touch me." Bianca went on as if he had not spoken.

"It is best while it is hot." Ian was nonchalant.

"You are everything I've ever dreamt of." Bianca was nonchalant.

"There is just a touch of cinnamon." Ian shifted so she could not see his face or the unaccountable moisture gathering at the corners of his eyes.

"I think you are the most wonderful man alive." Bianca moved closer to him.

"You might try it with some almonds." He handed her a small bowl.

"Ian Foscari, I love you." She raised his hand to her lips.

This time there was no mistaking. She had said it. She loved him. The almonds fell to the floor with a clatter, but neither of the diners heard it, Bianca because her heart was beating too fast, Ian because his ears were still ringing with her words. He crushed his lips to hers, wanting to lift the magic sentiment from them and impress it on his soul. He could not remember ever feeling better in his life.

The table was suddenly an unbearable impediment to their comfortable movement, as were Ian's tight leggings. Scoffing at the voice in his head that suggested he might soon want food, Ian took the gold carafe in one hand and two goblets in the other and motioned Bianca toward a door at the back of the alcove.

The smell of jasmine faded as they entered the room, which was filled instead with a musky scent that perfectly complemented its decor. Depicted on each wall of the octagonal room were couples engaged in what appeared to be extremely pleasurable acts in a variety of positions. Bianca was momentarily tempted to pause and study them, particularly one that featured a large feather headdress, but Ian's fingers on her shoulder filled her with a more immediate yearning. He led her toward the central attraction of the room, a massive square bed. The cover was silver silk, edged in gold braid with immense gold tassels at each corner. Sterling silver sconces hung from the bedposts, emitting both light and the fragrant smoke of an exotic incense. Every aspect of the room exuded sensuality and seduction.

Bianca was still absorbing the atmosphere of the magical space when she felt Ian's hands fasten something around her neck.

"If I say I bought them more for me than for you, will you wear them? As a favor?" Ian had never been so uneasy about giving a woman a fortune in sapphires before.

Bianca's hand went to her neck, and she looked around for a mirror. Realizing what she was seeking, Ian pointed up to the ceiling above them. It was covered in one great mirror, designed so that the inhabitants of the bed could easily compare their activities with those painted on the walls around them. As she looked at the sapphires interspersed with diamonds that banded her neck, Bianca was too preoccupied with wondering if the Foscari palace had more mirrors than any other building in Venice to berate Ian about giving her jewels. How could she, since he said he had bought them for himself? she reasoned logically. It was certainly easier than admitting, to him or to herself, that she was moved by his present and rather liked the feeling of the cool stones against her flesh.

"As a favor, I will wear them," she answered nobly. "But only if I am permitted to ask a favor in return."

"Certainly. Anything." Ian, having weathered that dangerous storm, was feeling magnanimous.

"Undress." It sounded more like a command than a favor, but Ian was undaunted.

Bianca seated herself on the bed to watch. Under her unwavering gaze, he slowly unhooked the diamond clasps on his jacket and shrugged out of it. Her eyes were locked with his as he undid the fastenings on his silk shirt and let it fall to the ground. When he reached for the lacings on his hose, he could feel her eyes follow his hands to where the cords were knotted over his straining shaft.

Under her intense gaze his throat grew dry and he found himself strangely nervous. He worked slowly, his fingers trembling with excitement. He could not remember ever feeling this entranced, this vulnerable, this sublime. The laces slid gradually from their holes, each one taking longer than the last, until he was sure her breathing had quickened to match his. Then he turned, displaying first his beautifully muscled back to her and then his impossibly graspable rear as he stepped out of his hose.

A thousand fantasies flashed through Bianca's mind at that moment, a thousand ways she would like to bite, lick, kiss, hold, push, knead, and caress Ian's body, but none of them superseded her earlier fantasy. She rose from the bed and ordered Ian to lie down on it.

She admired the rise and fall of his behind as he turned, the enchanting movement of his hips as he approached, the straining of his shaft as it preceded him, the flexing of his thighs and of his calves as he climbed onto the bed. He extended his body to its full length, lying on his side with his head raised on one elbow, a look of intense desire on his face. He found his breathing grew difficult as Bianca reached for the carafe of sparkling wine and filled her mouth with it. His temptation to reach out and wipe the splashes from her lips was quenched when she leaned over him and took his straining organ in her mouth.

Bubbles floated by his shaft, cold liquid encased it, her tongue skimmed over it, her tender warm lips caressed it, and Ian forgot to breathe altogether. When she swallowed, sucking him into her deeper, her cheeks pulling in to make the passage tighter, Ian's breathing resumed but only because he began to moan. Encouraged, she encircled his shaft with the fingers of one hand, moving it with her mouth, up and down its length, her thumb running ceaselessly over the organ from its base to its tip. Ian opened his eyes long enough to watch Bianca in the mirror above and wonder how she had known what he would never have guessed, that feeling her mouth on him would be even more arousing if she was clothed.

As he was reaching down to stroke her head, she began to flick the underside of his shaft with her tongue, still using her fingers to stroke the other side. A voice was shouting out with pleasure, and Ian realized it was his only when he saw his mouth open in the mirror above. All at once he could hold out no longer. He arched his back, pressing against her lips, and released himself into her waiting mouth, shuddering repeatedly as she relentlessly drank him dry.

Bianca was well pleased with her experiment. Still clothed, she wriggled her way up his body and into the crook of his outstretched arm.

"We must never do that again," Ian said breathlessly when he had gathered her to his chest.

Worried she had mistaken cries of pain for cries of pleasure, Bianca regarded him wide-eyed, looking rather than asking the question.

"I have only your best interests at heart when I say that," Ian resumed seriously, still panting. "If you entirely exhaust my vital powers, I shall be in no shape to attend to your needs."

He smiled when he finished speaking, and Bianca could have told him that with a smile like his he barely needed to lay a finger on her to attend to her needs, but decided not to give in too easily.

"That is terribly thoughtful of you, my lord," she said finally. "But you need not worry. Right now what I need most is food."

"*Mmmm.*" Ian nodded thoughtfully. "*Ahhhhhh,*" he said slowly. "I see," he admitted finally, and then abruptly said, "No."

"No?" Bianca raised her eyebrows.

"No." Ian shook his head positively.

"No what?" Her eyebrows were still raised.

"No food. No food until you have taken off your lovely gown. You might soil it." Having said that, he reached for the silken ribbons that tied it together in the back and began unlacing them.

"Your solicitude for my wardrobe is touching, my lord." Bianca spoke over her shoulder as he continued to rid her of her dress but left the sapphires in place.

"Someone needs to think about it," Ian said, his beleaguered tone indicating the full weight of the responsibility he had assumed.

"*Mmmmm,*" Bianca was now saying as Ian ran his fingers lightly down her naked back. "*Ahhhhhhhhh,*" she added when he cupped her behind in his big hands, and then, "No!" as he pushed her off the bed.

"You said you needed food," Ian explained, producing two silver silk robes from an armoire Bianca had not noticed before. "Perhaps if you are good, we can attend to both your needs at once."

Incited by this prospect, Bianca eagerly donned the robe and followed Ian into the other chamber. The table had been cleared of their earlier leavings and completely reset, this time with a dark red damask cloth. Just moments after their return three servants entered, each of them carrying a lidded platter, followed by a fourth with a silver flask. Ian declined their offer to serve, and they quickly left.

This time the wine was a bold Tuscan Chianti to accompany the thick beefsteaks prepared Florentine style. Though neither romantic nor terribly refined, it was Ian's favorite dish, and he had asked his cook to prepare it because he felt a strange compulsion to introduce Bianca to all the things he liked best. As Ian sipped his wine and watched her, she not only spoke her approval of the dish but demonstrated it, using a piece of the fresh baked bread to soak up the last of the meat's juices from her plate. When she had captured every remaining morsel, she looked up at him and grinned. Ian, who had never considered it possible that someone could grin while wearing sapphires, could not keep himself from grinning back.

"I have had enough food," she announced, savoring the flavor of the Chianti on her tongue. "Is it time to satisfy my other needs?"

Ian nodded thoughtfully. "I was just asking myself the same question. Let us go and see if the room is ready."

Rather than responding to Bianca's look of puzzlement, he led her back into the salacious bed chamber. From the threshold she noted that the silver cover had been pulled off the bed and the linen sheets turned down, but only upon stepping into the room did she see the large platter holding a block of ice carved into a bowl which contained multicolored balls. She had long since given up wondering how the servants knew what to bring where, but she was curious about the identity and purpose of the colored balls.

"Flavored ices," Ian told her unasked, holding out a little gob of the pink one. "Try it," he coaxed when she looked skeptical.

Bianca's eyes closed and her head tilted back as the flavor of raspberries filled her mouth. Before she could reopen her eyes, Ian had removed the spoon and brought it back to her lips, this time with peach. He had her recline on the bed, then repeated the exercise with all of the remaining flavors. After each one she announced positively, "I like that one the best."

Filling her mouth with a large serving of her most recent favorite, blood orange, Ian abandoned the spoon and used his hands to remove both their dressing gowns, letting his fingers gingerly caress her body. When she demanded "lemon," he gave them both big spoonfuls, then bent his head to suck in her nipple.

The contrast between the cold ice and his warm mouth ignited Bianca's desire into a sharp, white heat. She rubbed her pelvis against Ian's thigh, with the idea of subtly reminding him of her needs. It seemed to work, for he drew away for a moment and when he returned, he began moving down her body, trailing a stream of icy cold liquid.

But instead of following her unspoken directions and taking her sensitive nub into his mouth instantly, he took his time, licking up the stream he had left behind, then letting the ice drip slowly, maddeningly slowly, between her legs. As it melted it began to drip more quickly, and Bianca soon felt herself responding to the cold drops, each one making her more aroused.

Ian bit the scoop of the ice he had taken, almond flavor, in half. He slipped one half in his mouth, then began gently rubbing Bianca's most sensitive place with his lips. He darted his tongue out, extending its cold surface over the tense little nub, moving it from one side to the other as Bianca twisted and pushed herself toward him. Finally he slipped his mouth over her tender bud and sucked her into him, using his tongue now to push her against the cold little orb of ice.

The contrast between hot and cold that she had felt on her nipples was nothing compared to the way it felt between her legs. Bianca was wild with pleasure, unable to push herself into Ian deep enough, to feel the hard, cold ice and his wet, warm, yielding mouth enough. It was melting quickly, filling his mouth with pockets of hot and cold liquid that deliciously surrounded Bianca's body. She gasped as, instead of sliding the other half of his ball of ice in his mouth, he slid it instead against the opening of her tight little passageway, letting it melt in the collected heat of her arousal. He opened his mouth wider to take that part in too, holding his tongue flat against her and massaging her nub with his teeth. Then he began running his tongue up her whole length, from the bottom of her opening to the tip of her nub and back down again, flicking the delicate bud a little harder each time he reached it.

She remembered the mirror in the ceiling, and she tilted her head to look. Wide-eyed, she saw his head moving up and down as he pressed his whole mouth against her, then she watched as, mouth as wide as it would go, he sucked her into him. She saw herself arch up and throw her legs over his shoulders to pull him closer, saw him slide his hands under her, first holding her bottom, then slipping his fingers into where his mouth was. She watched as he took his mouth away and pressed her hot, waiting lips open with one hand, using all five fingers of the other to stroke the tender nub that proudly stood out from them. He began grinding it between his thumb and forefinger, and then, when he saw she was close to a climax, covered it once again with his mouth. His fingers pushed her into his tongue, pressing and kneading her against its abrasive surface, until, nipping at her with his teeth, he sent her over the edge. She bucked against him once, twice, thrice, then collapsed with a wild moan, her thighs still straddling his shoulders.

Disentangling himself from her legs minutes later, Ian moved up her body until he was lying beside her, admiring the way the sapphires sat against her collarbone.

"Was that all right?" he asked disingenuously.

Bianca opened one eye. "It was likable."

"More likable than I am?" Ian sounded worried.

Bianca opened the other eye. "About the same."

Suddenly Ian sat up. "Did you mean what you said before?"

"Before?" Bianca looked confused, then amused as comprehension dawned. "About the soup you mean?" When Ian nodded, she pulled him back down and pressed her body against his.

He was not sure if he had gotten an answer to his question, but with her body pushed close to his like that it suddenly seemed unimportant. Bringing her to her climax had made him thoroughly aroused, a condition only exacerbated when she twisted his ankles between hers and wrapped her arms around him. His already hard shaft was being tickled by her soft patch of curls as she moved her hips in small circles.

"Shall we make love again, Ian?" she asked in the voice of one whose sensual hunger was anything but slaked.

"If you insist," Ian answered gallantly, pushing his organ between her thighs and into her.

It had begun like their lovemaking always began, but there was something different about it, and they could both feel it. Neither of them even noticed the mirror on the ceiling, too intent were they on looking into each other's faces. Ian studied Bianca as he lay over her, peering into the depths of her fascinating eyes, searching for a clue to help him understand the miracle of her caring about him. Bianca looked back up at him, trying to convince him he would be safe with her, to penetrate his last defenses. They gave themselves to one another without reservation, without apprehension, without limit, and without question.

Both Ian and Bianca would soon look back on the moment and wonder how they could have been such fools.

Chapter Twenty-Two

The young man drew his finger down his bare chest. "I could cut here, then pull the skin back and take out her heart."

The woman smiled her half smile, humoring him, for she still needed his obedience.

"There is always flogging," the young man continued, his thoughts making him hot. "It would be much more exciting to watch her writhe in chains."

The woman shook her head and pursed her lips. "Can't you come up with anything more original? Or does your near relation to her preclude your affections for me and cloud your judgment?"

It was a dangerous challenge. "It is only your pleasure I was concerned with. I did not have originality in mind, only what would entertain you most," he defended himself.

She ran her hooded gaze over him, decided he had told the truth, and began to gently stroke his chest. "In that case, I have an idea. Bring her here, to me. I will take care of her."

"Will you tell me what you intend?" The thought of the girl as his mistress's captive was as wildly arousing as anything he had thought of that day.

The woman spoke in a matter-of-fact tone, as if discussing one of her business transactions. "Of course, I shall want some time with her alone, to find out why she has gone to such great lengths to hurt me. And then you will have a turn. After that, I have not decided. Perhaps the treatment you gave that Enzo creature," the woman said, her hands moving lower on the young man's anatomy. "But there are always the giants."

"The giants?" the young man queried, but only halfheartedly, so preoccupied was he with the movement of the woman's hands on his body.

"Oh, yes," she said, matching her tone to the moans emanating from his lips. "She must be terrified. She must know how it feels to be abused and taken advantage of. She must get what she deserves. But that is only part of it." Her hands were still on the young mans' body, but she was speaking more to herself than to him. "There must be marks, and scars, many of them. The real triumph will be that bastard's face when he sees the body, sees it and knows that justice has been done." She smiled and let the young man climb atop her as she reached the climax of her vendetta. "It will be even better than I had planned. He will be broken, destroyed, completely undone by his utter failure to protect her."

The couple lay spent, breathless, he with the exertions of his body, she with the breathtaking beauty of her plan. When the woman had recovered enough to speak, she pulled the young man close to her and gave him his orders. "Bring her to me tomorrow. You know where to find her. Bring her and we shall enjoy ourselves."

Chapter Twenty-Three

Crispin was too preoccupied to think before he walked into Ian's room that morning, and too embarrassed afterward. He knew that his brother was exercising the privileges that betrothal gave him over the delectable Bianca, but he had not expected to find the two of them entwined quite so closely in one another's arms. They were asleep when he burst in, but when he stubbed his shin on the divan and muttered an obscenity, they awoke.

Crispin looked contrite. "*Mi scusa,* Ian, if I had known you were, *um,* accompanied, I never would have barged in this way."

"Don't worry," Bianca answered with a gaping yawn. "I was just leaving. Indeed, if you would turn your back for just a moment, I will be off."

Ian, barely awake enough to follow the conversation, was trying to summon up the words to protest, but Bianca had hopped out of bed, slid into the silk robe she had worn the night before, planted a tender kiss on his forehead, and scurried out of the room before he had even managed to open his mouth. She wanted nothing to interfere with the revelation she was sure Crispin was about to make.

"Kindly explain why you have spoiled a perfectly nice morning of dalliance," was Ian's warm welcome to his brother. Then he studied him more closely. "You look like you haven't slept. What did you do last night?"

Crispin regarded him with amusement. He could not remember the last time anyone had taken the slightest interest in his comings and goings, not to mention his nocturnal amusements. "I assure you, I am well out of short pants and need no supervision from you. Interesting though they may be, I did not come to tell you about my night's adventures. I came to show you this." He flourished a piece of cream-colored stationery. "This was brought up to me this morning, as I was changing."

It took Ian only a few seconds to absorb the content, for the message was admirably brief and to the point. "Isabella Bellocchio told me how tightly you are bound to her. Should the details fall into the wrong hands, your life could become very disagreeable. To avoid such unpleasantness, come masked to the small reception room at Ca'Dona this evening as the clock strikes five."

"Lovely." Ian looked placidly at his brother. "You are being blackmailed. How much do you suppose they will want to keep from publishing your engagement?"

"I have already given you my word of honor on that." Crispin moved to the divan and sat. "I am not now, nor was I ever, engaged to Isabella Bellocchio."

"Can you offer another interpretation of this note?" Ian held the paper up to the light to see if it bore any identifying marks.

Crispin crossed his legs and leaned back. "I don't have any idea. That is why I brought it to you. You seem to have taken some interest in her recently and I thought you might know something."

"Have you ever told Isabella anything that could be used to blackmail you?"

"*I* do not disclose business secrets to women, if that is what you are asking." Crispin's pointed reference to an indiscreet act in Ian's past, the source of Mora's financial success, should have sliced through his brother, but its effect was disappointing.

Ian went on as if Crispin had not said anything inflammatory. "Let me tell you how it looks to me. By your own admission, there is nothing that Isabella Bellocchio could blackmail you with. Therefore, it would seem that the threat is empty and you have nothing to fear."

Crispin was rising to his feet, visibly relieved, when Ian resumed speaking. "On the other hand, just because there is no real information does not mean that someone has not manufactured something incriminating. We both know well that gossip need not be true to be dangerous."

"Oh, *capisco!*" The divan creaked as Crispin plopped back onto it, the full weight of Ian's words finally hitting him. "What you are saying is that with that rumor out about Isabella's engagement to a patrician, none of us are safe—at least none of us who are blond. It would be easy to stigmatize my name just by asserting that I am Isabella's fiancé, especially because I would have no definitive way to refute it until she comes back. I shudder to imagine the effect that the slightest hint of such an association would have on our credit."

Ian looked surprised. "Why just yesterday someone was suggesting it might be beneficial."

Crispin, disliking the feel of having his own words thrown back at him, glared from his perch on the divan. "I doubt whether Queen Elizabeth or even the lord chamberlain will still receive me after news reaches them of my engagement to a courtesan. We may as well prepare to cut our trade relations with England."

"L.N. might be able to do something. Or Miles." Ian was trying to be encouraging. "And there is always the black market. We could become renegades."

Crispin's glare turned to a look of confusion. Was this Ian, his brother, joking with him about the possible destruction of the Arboretti? Maybe the blackmail attempt had shunted him into madness. Or maybe it was that woman. He would have liked to probe for clues, but at that moment Giorgio knocked and was told to enter.

"The oversized man is back," Giorgio reported to Ian, not sure how much his master wanted Crispin to know about his personal activities. "He insists on seeing you. He says it's urgent."

"Did you bring him up to the library?"

Giorgio nodded. "With difficulty."

Ian grinned at the joke, remembered that he did not grin, and turned it to a grimace. Crispin, who was still concerned about his state of mind, took the operation as another sign of his brother's plunge into madness.

"Are you sure you are feeling well enough to dress?" Crispin asked with an unusual level of brotherly concern.

"Of course." Ian peered quizzically at his brother. Maybe the blackmail attempt had shunted him into madness? Clearly Crispin could not be trusted to attend the meeting at Ca'Dona that night. "Besides, I'll have to be wearing clothes if I am to attend that soiree tonight." Ian was giving orders to Giorgio to find his mask and great cape when Crispin interrupted.

"I could not ask you to do that. I will go."

"No, you most positively will not." Ian spoke emphatically in his old tone, calling upon the full force of his cold, intimidating exterior. "Being less closely involved, it will be easier for me to remain objective. Plus, as nominal head of the Arboretti, I feel it is my responsibility to stave off any threat to the company. I will go in your place, and I will brook no argument."

Crispin ignored the last part. "What if your presence instead of mine is unacceptable to them? What if they take that as a sign of disobedience?"

Ian held out the paper to his brother. "It specifies that you arrive masked. I hope you will not take it as an insult to your superior comeliness when I point out that in a mask and cape no one would be able to distinguish me from you."

It was true that in a mask the brothers would look identical and equally true that Ian, with his sangfroid, was much better suited to attend a touchy meeting than the more volatile Crispin. And yet, Crispin could not rid himself of the feeling that he should assume responsibility for the situation. He racked his brain for another excuse.

"What if they are dangerous?" he supplied lamely.

"Are you implying that my swordsmanship leaves something to be desired?" Ian's chilly tone gave no hint of his amusement at Crispin's pathetic attempt to dissuade him.

Crispin leapt to defend himself. "No, no of course not. It's only that I don't feel quite right—"

"You don't look quite right either. Why don't you go take a nap?" Ian rose from his bed and headed for the screened-off corner of his room to relieve himself.

That was a dismissal if Crispin had ever received one. He paused for a moment, considering a retort, decided against it, changed his mind, changed it back, admitted to himself that he was relieved to be excused from attending the delicate meeting, and finally turned his thoughts to other matters, like wondering how his near-sister-in-law was planning to spend her afternoon. Bidding adieu to Giorgio but ignoring his unmannerly brother, Crispin took his leave.

Observing the brothers together, Giorgio felt he now had something else to thank Bianca for. Not only had she apparently kept silent on the topic of his ministrations to Marina, but it seemed that she had somehow brought back the old Ian, the Ian who was wry rather than bitter, and a pleasure to deal with rather than a curse.

Valdo Valdone would have been surprised to hear Giorgio's assessment that Ian was a changed man. He would not have described him as a curse perhaps, but the words "wry" and "pleasure" were certainly not those that sprang instantly to mind as he examined the meticulously dressed, impassably formal, and completely imperturbable Conte d'Aosto later that morning. If Ian was shocked to see the twin of Crispin's invitation, or if his curiosity was piqued about the intentions of the sender, he did not show it. Indeed, his reaction to the note Valdo held out to him with large sweating fingers was entirely disappointing. Valdo had hoped for at least surprise, if not spitting outrage or desk-beating contempt, but the cool d'Aosto just sat and nodded.

"Have you any idea where it came from?" Ian asked, handing the piece of cream stationery back to the large man as if it were just a normal note.

"You know, from whoever is holding my precious Isa!" Valdo refused to take the paper back, the look on his face showing clearly that he did not trust it to maintain its present shape and not transform itself into a grotesque and poisonous adder at any moment.

Ian let the paper fall and went on as if Valdo had not said anything, as he had not, or at least not anything helpful. "It does prove one thing. Even if my talk with her the other night had not persuaded me, we can now be completely sure your wife is not holding Isabella." Ian looked up, saw that Valdo was baffled, and explained himself slowly. "Certainly your wife would not threaten to disclose information to herself that she was already in possession of."

"My wife." Valdo repeated the word as if he had never heard it before and was sampling its flavor on his tongue. "My wife."

Ian watched, fascinated, as Valdo used the sleeve of his overtight velvet jacket to remove the little beads of sweat that had collected on his forehead, an operation that required the large man to shift dangerously about in his chair. Ian was on the point of offering his own sleeve rather than watch his furniture be destroyed, when Valdo regained his powers of speech.

"I promised my wife I would take her this evening at five to Piazza San Marco, you know, to see the Moors ring in the hour. But how can I if I have to go to this Ca'Dona place? What excuse can I make? She'll see through anything. " The expression of acute misery on his face changed suddenly to one Ian learned momentarily signaled joy. "But here's an idea! Why don't you take her? I know it is much to ask, but if you offered to escort her surely she could not refuse, and I am sure it would make my absence much easier for her. You could even tell her you wanted to be with her alone."

Ian had to think hard to come up with a prospect less appealing than having to spend time alone with Lucretia Valdone and when he finally did think of something—a flight through the air in the talons of a bloodthirsty eagle who would drop his body into a craggy mountain pass to stun him and then eat his vital organs while he was still partially alive—he was not really convinced it would be worse than being her escort. There had to be a better way.

"You flatter me by suggesting your wife would condescend to my company, but I am sure I would prove an unsatisfactory substitute for you." The fine example of Ian's wry wit was lost on Valdo, whose broad face again clouded with misery.

"What can I do? What can I tell her?"

Ian was ready with his generous offer, but he tempered his voice to avoid sounding overeager. "Why don't I go to the meeting at Ca'Dona in your stead?"

"You would do that for me, d'Aosto?" The man's eyes looked as if they might fill up with tears of appreciation.

"Certainly. It will be the most efficient way to find out who is holding Isabella," Ian responded brusquely, hoping to scare the man out of his gratitude.

Valdo sat staring at Ian with an expression bordering on worship, then abruptly stood and made a deep bow. He stayed that way for so long that it looked as though he might be unable to right himself, but finally, with only a minimum of huffing, he managed it.

Unwilling to allow anything to impede his perfect delivery, Valdo waited until his breathing had returned to normal to address Ian. When the time was right, he pulled himself up to his full height and boomed, "May the only thing harder than your heart be your word." He paused for effect, then rushed ahead in a slightly less boisterous voice. "What do you think of that? I composed it just for you, and I've been dying to use it. I am putting together a book of phrases for every occasion, phrases I make up myself. That way no one will ever be at a loss for just the right thing to say."

Ian, gripping the side of his desk for support against the massively unpleasant sounds emanating from the being before him, spoke quietly. "An extraordinary idea. I am sure you are just the man for the job."

Valdo was smiling ear to ear when the door of the library finally closed on his large back, as was Ian at the prospect of a brief span of uninterrupted silence. But within a few minutes his solitude was again disturbed when Bianca knocked and entered.

She had decided to see him on the spur of the moment, after catching sight of the unmistakable form of Valdo Valdone leaving the house. She had sent a note to Valdo, who was not actually one of her suspects, in order to insure that Ian would find out about the gathering she was planning even if Crispin failed to mention it. If she had correctly guessed his reason for calling on Ian, everything was going just as she had hoped it would. Exultant at the continued success of her stratagem, she felt brave enough to take a risk. Ian's permission to leave the house was not crucial to her plan, but it would certainly make its execution easier. Indeed, she found that the prospect of alighting from her balcony had lost much of its appeal in the hours since the ball.

"I am sorry to bother you, Ian," she paused and faced him across his desk, "but I wanted to ask your permission for something."

The sapphires were still clasped around her neck, an attractive adornment to the gold silk gown embroidered with little blue flowers she was wearing. Ian was so busy admiring her and deciding whether to pull her onto his lap that at first he did not clearly hear what she had said.

"My permission?" he asked incredulously when it became clear that she was moving her lips for a purpose, not simply to remind him how kissable they were. "For what? Are you planning to launch a flotilla or storm a castle? Anything short of that and I know as well as you do that you would go ahead on your own initiative."

Bianca smiled her most winning smile and leaned farther across the desk. "Come, Ian, I am not that bad. I would never wage war on any sovereign nation. I know my limitations."

Ian grunted.

"For example. I came today to ask if I might go to my house, the house I shared with my brother before I had to move in with Aunt Anatra, to get another work dress and gather my few remaining belongings. Is that so outlandish?" It was partially true, she reassured herself.

Ian grunted again. "No."

"No?" Bianca stopped breathing. She should never have asked.

"No, it is not outlandish. You may go. But take someone with you."

Her breathing resumed. "Will a gondolier do or shall I hire some off-duty members of the Palace guard?"

"Out!" Ian ordered, not wholeheartedly. "I have work to do."

Bianca complied, but only after circling around the desk to plant a deep kiss on his lips. Ian spent the next half hour at war with himself, one part arguing that he would be more productive later if he went and dragged her into bed, another suggesting that he should skip the bed and bring her back to the library, a third pointing out the commodiousness of the dining room, a fourth wondering if the gardenia section of the plant rooms was empty. But it was the fifth, which reasoned logically that he would have time later to experiment with all of those if he concentrated on his work now, that eventually won the day. That and the perplexing question of the double invitation to Ca'Dona.

It was not unthinkable that a blackmailer would try to gull more than one person, but it seemed unwise to allow his various targets to meet or know of each other's existence, which was exactly what would happen if they were all present at the meeting that night. A desperate man might be convinced to cough up gold, but a group of desperate men could fight back as a body, and probably would. Unwittingly he had walked into a situation that promised to be not only volatile but even explosive.

"Good work," he spoke aloud to the empty room, all thoughts of Bianca's delicious curves quickly receding. He had not touched a weapon since Christian's death, had not even planned an experiment with gunpowder, too insecure in his abilities and too afraid of the memories it might ignite. All of his weapons, like all of his feelings, had been locked tightly away in a small room that he had sworn he would never revisit. Now, it seemed, he had no choice.

"So Ian spoke the truth," Crispin was saying to Bianca, the only other occupant at the luncheon table. "You do think me hideously malproportioned and cumbersomely dull." He put up his hand to stop her protest. "Don't try to make it better by complimenting me on my lustrous hair or slim ankles. I would just see right through that."

"What about your imperial nose or your striking jawline?" She hoped her voice sounded playful.

Crispin shook his head. "It's no good. There can be no other reason why you refuse to spend your afternoon with me."

Bianca felt pleased and trapped at once. Crispin's willingness to put himself at her disposal suggested that it was Ian who would accept the invitation issued on the cream-colored stationery, which was exactly what Bianca had hoped. But Crispin's unwillingness to forgo her company was a less than facile complication. Under any other circumstances the opportunity to pass time with Crispin would have been a treat, just not that day. It was out of the question. She was having trouble concentrating enough to eat, let alone enough to make conversation with someone for hours. Not to mention the obvious objection of her need to get to Ca'Dona in advance of her invited guests.

"It is not you, my lord, but me." Bianca hoped flattery might weaken his dogged persistence. "I fear I am feeling completely witless today and should find it impossible to pay you the attention you deserve."

Crispin was determined and undaunted. "Nonsense! I shall require no witticisms from you. I will even undertake to do all the talking."

"I also have a bit of a headache." In a few more moments it would not actually be a lie.

Crispin lowered his voice to a whisper. "In that case I won't speak a word. We can relish each other's company in ideal silence, like poets."

Bianca was desperate. "There are some errands I must attend to which promise to bore even me."

"*Miracoli!* I have some of those myself. We can be bored together."

Crispin smiled broadly at her, and she knew she was doomed. Just when everything seemed to be going so well, she found herself against an immobile impediment. She wondered how she had failed to notice earlier the rocklike qualities that he shared with Ian.

It soon became clear that in addition to being stubborn, he also heard otherworldly voices, voices that gave Bianca's consent completely without her knowledge. That was the only explanation she could contrive when she watched him push his chair from the table and heard him say, "Good, then it is all settled. Let us leave at half past three, less than an hour from now. We could leave earlier, but I will want to make myself presentable if I am to be seen in public with you."

He was gone before she could file a pointless protest. Alone in the dining room, Bianca surveyed her options. She could sneak out of the house as she had originally planned, but with Crispin expecting her in less than an hour, her absence would quickly be spotted and it would be difficult to evade pursuit without an adequate advance start. She could concoct some way to detain Crispin at the house, but short of putting something disabling in his meal, an opportunity she was sorry she had missed, she could think of nothing viable. Only one course of action remained to her, to somehow escape from him while they were out together. She hated having to entrust the success of her carefully laid plan to fate, but she could see no other way.

At half past three, a spruce Crispin handed a dejected Bianca into his gondola. Even in her downcast state, Bianca had to admit that it was a particularly nice gondola, the cabin complete with lit candles and small crystal bud vases filled with flowers. Once they were off and he had assured himself that Bianca was well settled among the embroidered cushions, Crispin announced their itinerary.

"I need to make a brief stop at a friend's house to deliver something, and then I thought we could pay a visit to your charming cousin Analinda."

Bianca nodded, hoping she looked more agreeable than she felt. "I am sure she will be beside herself with joy to receive you. But would you mind if first we stopped at my former house in San Polo? I would like to get there before dusk, you know, so we won't have to waste time lighting candles." It was a weak excuse, particularly because the dark low-hanging rain clouds that had blanketed the city for days permitted little if any light through at all. Luckily, Crispin was not feeling inquisitive.

"If it would put your mind at rest, why don't we go there now?" It made no difference to him, his delivery would be eagerly received no matter when it arrived.

"I should feel terrible if I were to inconvenience you too much." Bianca tried to sound as if the most wonderful idea in the world had just occurred to her. "Why don't you leave me at my house while you do your errand, then return for me on the way to Analinda's?"

Crispin leaned forward earnestly. "That will not do at all! Where you are concerned, there is no such thing as an inconvenience. Besides, as you can see, we have already arrived."

Bianca peered through the glass of the cabin and saw that they were indeed nearing the water gate of her old house. After a week in Palazzo Foscari, it looked decidedly small and dingy to her as they pulled abreast of it. The gondolier tethered the boat and Crispin and Bianca alighted.

Although it had only been empty for the few weeks since her brother's last departure, the house had a decided air of abandonment. Their footsteps echoed on the stone floors as they ascended from the ground level to the main floor above.

"Make yourself as comfortable as you can, my lord." Bianca was removing dust covers from the furniture and opening the drapes while she spoke, trying to keep her back to Crispin so he could not see the color rising in her cheeks. "I must gather a few things from my old room, but I will return shortly."

As she turned to go, Crispin was thinking that this was the perfect situation for a libertine to take advantage of a lady. Then he got distracted by the sight of a strange plant in the corner of the room. He pulled it out for closer inspection and discovered that it was not actually strange, just dying. All it needed, he diagnosed, was a few days under Luca's watchful eyes and a strong dose of his newest fertilizer. He was so pleased at the discovery and the possibility of testing out his newest concoction that he did not hear the creaking of the back stairs, or the squeak of the rusty kitchen hinges as Bianca stealthily exited the house.

She pulled her dark cloak closely about her, more to hide the expensive gown and jewels she was wearing than to keep off the unceasing rain. Her plan had been to change into less noticeable attire at her house, but she had not had time, Crispin's presence making instant flight a necessity. As she wound her way on foot through the back streets of San Polo, she kept her eyes down and prayed no one would recognize her, turning around frequently to see if she was being followed.

Her heart was pounding as she entered the crowded streets around the Rialto Bridge. It was the financial heart of the city, attracting merchants of every stripe from every country known to man. She saw men in turbans speaking Arabic, others in long robes speaking Spanish, Frenchmen with their small hats and smaller mustaches, Englishmen notable for their padded shoulders, monks begging alms, even a Turkish holy man. What she did not see, what one never saw there, was anyone else like her, an unescorted noble-woman on foot. Though the crowds thickened, she found herself garnering more and more unwelcome attention.

She climbed up the bridge, ignoring the inviting wares of the gold-smith's shops that lined it, and instead scanned the streets she had just walked down for signs of pursuit. She saw nothing. Then, just as she was turning back, a flurry of motion below her caught her eye and the unmistakable blond head of Crispin came bobbing into view above the sea of turbans and berets. At the same moment that she spotted him, he spotted her and began frantically pushing his way through the crowds toward her. He had no idea why Bianca had run away from him, but he knew he would get no thanks from anyone if anything happened to her. Not to mention if she disappeared completely.

Bianca's heart was racing as she flew down the stairs on the opposite side of the bridge, ignoring the taunts and pushing by the arms that opened to receive her. A glance over her shoulder showed her that Crispin was gaining on her, and she wondered if Ian had put him up to the task of following her that day. Whatever his reasons, he had the advantages of both size and breeches, and he was using them. Bianca was only a few steps ahead of him when she reached the bottom of the bridge, almost close enough for him to grab.

Without stopping, she reached under her cloak for the little purse she was wearing at her waist, and unhooked it from her dress. She opened it and brought it over her head, shaking it out behind her. The unexpected windfall of gold and silver coins brought people running from all sides of the square to form a large, immobile, and greedy crowd right in front of Crispin. He tried pushing his way through but found his way blocked by a fruit seller who had no intention of sharing his cache of coins with anyone. When he was finally able to get through the crowd, Bianca had vanished.

The undesirables lounging along the Sottoportego della Bissa, the most dangerous street in Venice, denied having seen a woman dressed in black pass by, even when Crispin offered them gold coins from his purse. If the lady wanted to get away from him so badly that she spilled all that gold, who were they to interfere? Bianca had turned down the Calle del Paradiso, crossed Campo Santa Maria Formosa, and was in sight of the front door of Ca'Dona before Crispin found anyone who would even admit to having seen the woman in black.

It was not a servant but Tullia herself who opened the door to admit the panting, frantic Bianca. The courtesan seated her friend on one of the kitchen benches while Daphne ladled a goblet of water for her, then another after Bianca had gulped the first down. With fairly steady hands, Bianca unhooked her soaking black cloak and let it fall onto the bench.

Tullia let out a low whistle of admiration. "Were they after those sapphires? That necklace would buy any of my clients a lifetime pass to my bed."

Bianca touched the stones at her neck, having forgotten they were there. "No. At least, I don't think so. It was Crispin, Crispin Foscari who was chasing me. Ian's brother."

"But why—?" Tullia let the question hang, remembering what she had learned the previous day. "*Bellissima*, I find that I owe you an apology. Last week when you were here I had no idea that you were betrothed to Ian. When I found out, I felt just dreadful. You do know, though, that nothing happened? He was," Tullia paused, searching for the right word for the count's odd behavior that day, "unwilling...but very charming. Completely uncharacteristic, actually. At any rate, I am terribly sorry."

Bianca waved aside the apology, surprise and, strangely, delight filling her mind. "You have nothing to feel sorry about. In fact, in some ways I have much to thank you for." She smiled to herself as she remembered the night of their reenactment. "But that will come later. It is after four o'clock, is it not?"

Tullia nodded and Bianca stood. "Do you think you could send someone out to see if Crispin is still pursuing me? Perhaps even to send him in the wrong direction. If he realizes how close he is to your house, he might figure out where I have hidden."

Tullia complied immediately, giving one of her manservants a detailed description of Crispin and precise instructions about what to say. That accomplished, the two women went up one flight of stairs to the small reception room.

"I had Daphne draw all the shades and bring in just one candelabrum." Tullia pointed at the candles burning on the table. "Are you sure that will provide enough light to see their faces by?"

"Easy visibility is exactly what I want to avoid, at least until the end." Bianca spoke quickly, her excitement resurging. "In addition to not wanting to slander the innocent, I would not want anyone to be able to recognize me."

Tullia gestured gracefully with one hand. "Of course. Daphne and I stayed up half the night trying to imagine why you asked me for a mask and robe, but now it seems clear. I fear the robe will be a bit long on you, *bella.* Would you like to borrow a pair of *zoccoli* as well for added height?"

The thought of herself in the impossibly high sandals that the courtesans wore brought an unexpected smile to Bianca's lips. "I think it would undermine my credibility if I were to teeter and fall over in the middle of my threatening speech, don't you?"

"On the contrary." Tullia put a persuasive hand on her friend's arm and steered her from the room. "The added height will make you more intimidating, as well as harder to distinguish."

Bianca allowed herself to be led into an adjacent room where she found robe, mask, and *zoccoli* laid out for her. By the time she was disguised and had made at least one successful pass around the room in the high shoes, thanks to Daphne's careful instructions, the clock was ringing five. Tullia and her maid sat with Bianca to distract her as she waited for her invitees to arrive but, being almost as anxious as she was, were of little assistance. When a manservant finally appeared to tell her that the room was full, Bianca's heart was pounding hard enough to be heard on the other side of Venice. She took a deep breath, kissed Tullia and Daphne on the cheeks, rose, and made a faultless entrance into the small reception room.

Her eyes quickly took in the five men standing silently before her. "I demand to know—" one of them began, but she cut him off.

"There should be six of you. If one of you is missing I shall have to request that you all unmask so I can determine who it is."

A voice came from the corner. "That will not be necessary. I am here at the request of two of your invitees."

Bianca was glad the mask covered the flush that Ian's unmistakable voice brought to her cheeks. It had worked. He had come. Her nervousness gave way to excitement as she felt success within her grasp. All that was left was to reveal the murderer in his presence.

Bianca bowed her head minutely to indicate she had heard him. It was that gesture that convinced him of her identity. When she entered the room, he had felt there was something familiar about her, but he had ascribed it merely to chance or to the fact that he had been a regular visitor at Tullia's house for long enough to know most of the girls who worked for her. And yet he was not quite sat-isfied with his logic. There was something about her that reminded him of Bianca. That was foolish, he had told himself, Bianca would have no reason to stage an absurd charade, and plus she was consid-erably shorter than the girl in front of him. He was sure it wasn't her. Then, with that minute bow, he became sure that it was.

He was trying to decide whether to storm up to her, to storm out, or fume in place when she resumed speaking. "Very well, then we may proceed. You all received identical messages threatening to disclose your relationship with Isabella Bellocchio if you did not come."

"Then you admit you have nothing on us? That this is some kind of hoax?" one of the men asked in a nasal whine.

Bianca shook her head. "This is no hoax. I admit that I have nothing on all of you. But before this meeting is over, I will have shown that one of you is a murderer, a thief, and a traitor."

All five men reacted noisily when she spoke her last word, one of them appearing on the point of collapse. He swooned forward, hitting the table in the middle of the room and sending the cande-labrum flying to the floor. The candles flickered out as they fell, plunging the room into total darkness. Bianca had leaned down to retrieve one of them when she saw a flash and felt a horrible surge of pain in her right shoulder. Reflexively she reached up and felt a warm trickle that could only be her blood. Clutching her shoulder, she had just maneuvered herself back onto her feet when she saw a second flash of light. She held her breath, waiting for the pain to come again, but it did not. Instead, she felt rough hands on her body. Before she could fight or even figure out what was happen-ing, she was being grabbed firmly by the waist, swung over some-one's shoulder, and carried from Tullia's house. Her only consolation as she slipped from consciousness was that she would no longer be in pain when she was dead.

Chapter Twenty-Four

It was not death, at least not immediately, that waited for her on her return to consciousness. Her first sensation was pain, then hunger, then profound disorientation. The room was pitch black and the bed was unfamiliar. Turning her head to the right, she saw a narrow band of light coming from under a door and heard indistinct voices. Turning her head to the left she cried out sharply, the full force of the pain hitting her.

She heard footsteps approaching from the direction of the door on her right and saw the room grow brighter, but she was afraid to either turn her head or open her eyes, not because of the pain but because she feared what she might see. She had told Nilo to be careful, that one of the men would be dangerous, but she had scarcely predicted how dangerous. Kidnapping her, she feared, was just the beginning of his plan. Fearful of what else he might have in store for her, she said a silent, fervent prayer.

"Bianca, can you hear me?" For a moment after she heard the voice, Bianca lay immobile in the now broken darkness, blinking back tears of joy. Then she turned, slowly, and nodded at Francesco.

"No, don't try to sit up." Roberto pushed her back down. "You should keep still for a while. The bullet just grazed your shoulder, but you lost quite a large quantity of blood."

"Where am I?" were the first words Bianca could find.

"You are in our spare room. We wanted you near us so we could monitor you," Francesco explained, too quickly.

"But my apartment is just across the ballroom," Bianca's mind was beginning to function again.

"Yes, so it is." Francesco looked imploringly at Roberto.

There was a long silence before he spoke. "Ian thought you should be in a room without quite so many doors and windows."

If Bianca had had enough blood in her body, she would have blushed. "Is Ian hurt?"

Francesco shook his head. "No. Apparently you were the only target there today."

There was a knock on the open door, and they all turned to see Crispin enter the room.

"I just wanted to tell you that next time you don't like the fabric of my waistcoat, you have merely to tell me. No need to go dashing around the city throwing your money about." He smiled brightly as he spoke.

Bianca extended her hand to him, and he took it in both of his. "It wasn't the waistcoat, really, it was the way it went with your jacket." She looked up at him. "Can you really forgive me for what I did today?"

He nodded, not releasing her hand. "I have to admit you had me baffled, but Ian explained it all to me and I think I understand."

"Really? Because I must say that I do not." No one had heard Ian enter, but his words cooled the atmosphere in the room to somewhere near that of the frozen north. "I was hoping you could explain it to me. I am sure we will have a good laugh."

The thin line of his lips, lips that promised never to laugh again, belied his statement. Bianca raked her eyes across his face, search-ing. The man she had so recently seen, the man she had fallen in love with, the one to whom she had striven to prove her innocence, was gone. She shuddered when she looked into his eyes, the color of slate in the dead of winter.

"My intention, my lord," it was no struggle for Bianca to

address him formally, "was to scare the murderer into revealing himself."

"Murderer?" Crispin asked, surprised.

Ian ignored his brother. "What a delightful idea. And did it not occur to you that this revelation might come at the expense of someone else's life? Your own, for example?"

"Murderer?" Crispin tried again, with equal success

"I must admit," Bianca said only to Ian, "that it did not. I see now that I was mistaken."

"*Mistaken?*" Ian boomed at her in a tone worthy of Valdo Valdone. "You call almost losing your life a mistake?"

"Did I have a choice?" Bianca shot back at him. "Did I have any other way to prove my innocence to you? You told me that you would believe I was a murderess until and unless I brought you a more likely candidate. You left me no alternative."

Crispin, completely baffled, swiveled his head from Bianca to Ian. "Murderess? Her?"

Ian ignored him once again, his lips even thinner. "You dare to blame me for what happened there today?"

"It is nothing compared to what you have blamed me for." Bianca's face was white, not from blood loss but from rage. "I suppose you have already figured out some way to use this as additional evidence of my guilt. No doubt I even arranged to be shot."

"I put nothing past you, Signorina Salva." Ian turned and stalked out of the room.

He made directly for his library, desperately in need of a drink and solitude. He was furious with her for her idiotic scheming, furious at himself for making it necessary. With his first deep gulp of grappa he admitted that he was confused down to the bottom of his being, racked with a hundred unanswered and unanswerable questions. The one most prominent in his mind was also the most painful: if he had told her earlier that he knew she was innocent, could he have prevented her from endangering her life? The second glass of grappa brought with it a thought almost as bitter as the liquor itself, that her life might not really have been in danger.

Could this have been just another part of a wildly elaborate plot to falsely convince him of her innocence? Could she indeed be a murderer? He had long since ceased to believe it possible, but he could no longer remember why. The pieces all still pointed to her. She had, after all, suggested the possibility herself. By the fourth serving of grappa, Ian could not recall what it was that convinced him of her innocence, and he decided to decide that she was guilty. Only his heart refused to concur. He directed a twisted grimace at himself for being taken in by her coy smiles, her feigned expressions, her passionate sighs, her words of love. The grappa bottle was emptied with the last thought, and Ian sat unthinking, staring into space. He was still sitting there when the guard came with the news.

Bianca Salva, unmarried *gentildonna*, had been anonymously denounced for the murder of the courtesan Isabella Bellocchio. The said Signorina Salva was requested to appear in the chambers of the civil judges at the stroke of nine the next morning, Thursday, to hear the evidence against her and make her defense, if she could think of one. Only her relatives and her betrothed husband would be admitted to submit pleas on her behalf. These were capital charges, the guard needlessly specified, bringing with them a mandatory sentence of death.

Isabella Bellocchio went from being a social-climbing whore to being a pitiable victim of female jealousy, literally overnight. By the time the clock at San Marco was striking nine the next morning, the second-floor hallway in front of the chambers of the *Civile* judges was packed with people, despite the shin-high puddles that had to be traversed to get there. The Doge's Palace, which housed all the organs of the government that kept Venice prosperous and safe, was built at the lowest point of the city. This made it prone to flooding even during mild winters, and the unflagging rainfall the city had experienced that winter had turned the ground floor first into a puddle, then into a lake. That did nothing to slow the influx of spectators, however. No hardship was too great to suffer, no body of water too deep to cross, for the privilege of watching a young, beautiful, rich, headstrong patrician get what she had coming to her.

The denunciation had been read to Bianca in bed, and a guard had been posted in the room with her to make sure she did not escape during the night. He also seemed bent on ensuring that she did not sleep, for he spent the entire time humming a tune to himself that sounded strangely like a funeral march. In spite of having spent a less than salubrious night, the Bianca that faced Bianca in the mirror early that morning looked better than either of them would have expected.

She dressed with care, wincing in pain each time her shoulder moved. Her appearance that day was of paramount importance, she knew, because her fate lay exclusively in the opinions of the three judges appointed to hear her case. More important than any evidence for or against her was their perception of her. A nod, a wink, a smile, or a frown that looked like the nod, wink, smile, or frown of a murderess would be enough to doom her.

Not that it made much difference anyway. Upon hearing the accusation of murder she had ceased to care what happened to her. There was only one person who knew enough to make a persuasive denunciation, and only his opinion mattered to her. If Ian thought her guilty enough to denounce, then her future held nothing for her. Innocence, like guilt, would mean a life without him and that did not seem like much of a life at all.

When she announced to Roberto and Francesco that she would not even attempt a defense, they were frantic. They struggled to persuade her to change her mind and would even have argued with her, but she merely answered their questions with the silence she planned to maintain before the judges. Though she refused to yield to their persuasions, she did agree to wear whatever they selected for her. Seeing that her wardrobe would have to bear the full weight of her defense, Roberto and Francesco had stayed up well into the night arguing about what she should wear. The gown they finally selected for her was of somber burgundy silk with cream trim that matched the two large pearls pinning back the sleeves. It was the epitome of elegance and refinement, perfect for a day spent in courtly visiting. Or a day spent in court.

The way the gown complimented her skin tone was one of the two main topics of conversation when Bianca arrived, under guard, at the Doge's Palace. The other was the large contingent of courtesans and prostitutes who were standing slightly apart from the rest of the spectators. Everyone else held their breath as Bianca passed by them, secretly expecting the women to rip her limb from limb for killing one of their number. What actually happened was more extraordinary, and never seen in those halls before or since. The women of the demimonde did indeed reach out to touch her, but with affection rather than malice. One woman, richly dressed in a tapestry gown that was rumored to cost seven hundred ducats, stepped forward and kissed her on both cheeks.

"Our prayers are with you, *bellissima*." Tullia's voice was hoarse with emotion. "We know you did not do this horrible deed. We will do anything we can for you."

All the setbacks, all the hardships, all the physical injuries Bianca had suffered did not affect her as much as this simple gesture of solidarity from the women who seemingly had the most cause to hate her. The looks of sympathy and support on the faces of Tullia and Daphne and the others who crowded around them made her ashamed of her earlier decision. How could she have thought that life without Ian was life not worth living? How could she allow a man to determine the value of her existence? Particularly a man who, contrary to all appearances, insisted on thinking the worst of her. She would not be destroyed by the fact that he did not love her and refused to understand her. She would not give up that easily.

The eyes she turned on Tullia were misty. "Thank you. You have no idea what this means to me. Someday, if I am able to leave here, I hope I can tell you." She would have liked to say more, but there was no opportunity. The guards on either side of her were urging her forward. The judges were ready to enter the chamber. It was time for her trial to begin.

The immense chairs for the three judges were already in place along the back wall of the chamber under the window when she entered. Bianca turned her head from left to right, taking in the dark, dismal room. Carved mahogany benches lined the side wall, all of them occupied by people whose faces were familiar to her. The only other woman in the courtroom was Aunt Anatra, flanked by her son, Angelo, on one side, and her husband, Guiellmo, on the other. Anatra was glaring at her, horrified by the notoriety that was accruing every half minute to the Grifalconi family name. Angelo, looking overwrought and a bit green, appeared to be animated by the same strong emotions as his mother. And so deeply did they effect Guiellmo, the scion of the family, that he had dozed off.

Next to her kinsmen were the Arboretti, accompanied by Francesco and Roberto. All of them but Ian. They nodded amicably when she looked in their direction; Miles even attempted a smile. But no quantity of goodwill could compensate for Ian's glaring absence. It was simply more evidence, if any were needed, that he was behind the denunciation. Her new sense of purpose had all but ebbed from her when the door to the chamber burst open and Ian stalked in. Ignoring Francesco's and Roberto's inquiring looks, he settled himself alongside the other Arboretti and sat scowling straight ahead, his brow wrinkled and his eyes squinting, as if he were deeply pained by a blistering headache.

As indeed he was. While making free with the bottle of grappa had seemed like a good idea the previous night, and using the bottle of amaretto as a chaser an even better one, the cool light of morning found him feeling less than his best. And if that were not enough, he had just endured two horrendous hours closeted with the Senate, the only body capable of lifting the death sentence hanging over Bianca. He had hurtled the full force of the Foscari name at them on Bianca's behalf, to no avail. They had listened to his reasoned arguments about how she could not possibly be guilty, nodded sympathetically as he explained that even if she were guilty it was wildly disrespectful to try the betrothed of one of the oldest patrician families in Venice for murder, even sighed in agreement as he listed the many services he and his ancestors had rendered to the Republic that would make it an act of propriety—not mercy—to release the prisoner who was as good as a Foscari herself, but they had refused to drop the charges. He could not face Bianca, could not bear to look at her and let her read his failure in his face. He had tried to the best of his ability, had used the full weight of his title and political position, had even offered to take Bianca out of Venice and become a voluntary exile with her, and now all he could do was sit on this uncomfortable bench and watch as the one woman he had thought he might one day possibly find a way to begin to love was found guilty of murder.

His headache was not helped any by the guards who suddenly pulled themselves to attention and pounded the floor with staffs. Still scowling, he lifted his body from his seat along with the others in the room for the entrance of the judges. Until they entered the room, no one knew who they would be, an antique custom designed to eliminate judicial bribery. It did not, however, preclude someone making a liberal offer to all the likely candidates, as someone had that very morning. Walking into the chamber, at least one of the judges was busier trying to decide whether to spend his twelve hundred ducats on a new gondola or a new mistress, than trying to gauge Bianca's guilt or innocence.

The judges passed before the spectators and seated themselves in their mammoth chairs. The crowd outside was making loud noises of protest as the porter struggled to shut the massive door on them. If they were not to be admitted, they argued, couldn't he at least leave the door open so they could hear. He looked imploringly toward the judges, who often agreed to the measure, but they gave a unanimous "No." They knew from experience that murder trials were apt to stir the passions of the masses, and this was no ordinary murder trial. When the door closed with difficulty, an ominous hush fell over the chamber.

Bianca stood alone in its middle, the light of the window hitting her squarely in the face, and did not flinch. Her earlier resolution returned and she determined to fight. She would not give Ian, who seemed unable to even meet her eyes, the pleasure of getting rid of her so easily. One of the judges, a tall thin man Bianca recognized as Alvise da Ponte, rose. The only difference between him and a corpse, Bianca thought as he opened the proceedings, was that corpses' beards could not grow. Neither his outward aspect nor his hollow, ghostlike voice did anything to improve the atmosphere of dark foreboding that permeated the chamber. When he had wheezed the customary opening prayer for wise judgment, he turned his long, death-mask face to Bianca.

"Signorina, as you know, the court does not act on anonymous denunciations unless they are accompanied by compelling proof. The accusations against you are weighty and well documented. You are denounced for the murder of Isabella Bellocchio, courtesan in this city. If you do not admit to the crime, you will be confronted with the proof we have and be given an opportunity to make a defense. The process will likely be time consuming and pointless; the proofs against you are manifold. I therefore advise you to admit your crime now. Doing so will save all of us much trouble, and God will be clement in his mercy. Will you?"

Roberto and Francesco stopped breathing.

Bianca looked right at him and spoke in a voice that did not falter. "I did not murder Isabella Bellocchio."

Ser Alvise sighed with disappointment. He had hoped to spend a few days at his house in the mountains, out of the rain, but now it looked as though he would be stuck in Venice. "Very well. The accusation claims the following: on the afternoon of eleven November of this year you took the life of Isabella Bellocchio, courtesan, in her own bed. It says that having pressed your advances unsuccessfully upon Signorina Bellocchio for a long time, you were finally seized by a fit of jealousy and driven to stab her in the heart. Still not satisfied, you sequestered the body and spent days dismembering it and, what is worse, drawing it."

Ian suddenly rose from his seat and loudly muttered, "*Ha-ha!*"

Ser Alvise turned his spectral face toward the disturbance. "I shall have to ask you to keep your seat, d'Aosto, or leave the courtroom. Another outburst like that and you will be escorted away."

Ian, who had already reseated himself, was too preoccupied brooding over his lap to make any sort of response.

Even before he had interrupted the proceedings with signs of obvious delight, Bianca was fuming at Ian. Denouncing her for murder was nasty enough, but it was needlessly cruel to talk about her anatomical work and precious drawings as if they were signs of perversion and derangement. She turned to glare at him, the fiercest, meanest glare she could muster up, but her line of sight was interrupted by a guard holding something before her.

"Your fierce scowl suggests that you recognize the paper, signorina." It was not a question, which was just as well, for Bianca could scarcely have explained that she had intended the scowl for her betrothed.

"Yes, I do, Your Excellency. It is Petrarch's third sonnet."

Archimede Seguso, the second judge, regarded her through his slitlike eyes. "We are not here to see displays of your learning, signorina. Do you recognize the hand in which the poem is written?"

Bianca nodded slowly, with dawning comprehension. "Yes. It is mine."

"How many such love sonnets did you send Isabella Bellocchio?" That time it was more of a demand than a question.

"None."

Ser Archimede opened his eyes as wide as they would go, about the width of a cat's whisker. "Kindly explain how this love sonnet written in your hand came to be found in Isabella Belloccio's lodgings."

"I wrote it there." Bianca was calm. Even someone with eyes as small as Ser Archimede's should be able to see she was telling the truth. "Isabella was illiterate, and I was teaching her to write. She asked me to leave her a love sonnet that she could practice copying over in her own hand."

She had miscalculated her audience. The eyes again became slits. "I advise you, signorina, not to overtax our credulity. For how long were you in love with Isabella Bellocchio?"

"I was never in love with Isabella Bellocchio." Bianca shifted, trying to keep her wet feet from getting numb.

"Of course. Perhaps your type does not call it love. When did you begin making advances to her?"

"I never made any advances to her." It was hopeless. The numbness was moving up her legs.

"Signorina Salva, consider your position. We have ample proof that your interests do not run toward men."

"Indeed." All the warmth in her body seemed to be leaving, taking with it her self-control. "I hope you will produce it. I am sure I shall find it diverting."

The third judge lifted a large magnifying glass to one eye. Cornelio Grimani was known for his inscrutable statements and his ineffable ability to catch criminals. Many people ascribed the latter entirely to his magnifying glass, which was supposed to possess the power of revealing people's thoughts and penetrating their souls.

More spirited men than Bianca had felt their strength ebb under the scrutiny of his glass, but she did not even flinch. She was too busy trying to figure out what Ian had intended by including this in his denunciation. For while it was just slightly probable that despite his interest in science, he thought her anatomical drawings were perverse, it was completely inconceivable that he thought she did not like men. She could think of no purpose that such a lie would serve, nor could she believe that Ian would be purposely deceitful in his denunciation. Could he really have understood her that badly, even after all they had shared?

"You may be right," Ser Cornelio said at the conclusion of his examination of her, jolting Bianca back to attention. "I believe it will indeed divert you," he added after a pause, then gestured for the guards to bring the witnesses in.

To Bianca's utter surprise and later horror, Giulio Cresci entered the room. He looked around, bowed slightly in the direction of the spectators, then faced the judges.

"Signore Cresci, please repeat what you told us earlier," Ser Alvise commanded, and although she was paying close attention, Bianca was not sure his lips actually moved.

Cresci made a face designed to suggest deep thought, but which looked more like acute constipation from where Bianca stood. After he had held the expression for a moment, he whined loudly enough to be heard on the other side of the door. "I think I started off saying, 'Everyone says that Bianca Salva is as cold as they come.'"

"Yes, you did." Ser Cornelio made a face. "What we would like to hear is not what you have heard, but what you personally experienced."

Cresci's eyes darted furtively to Bianca. It had been easier to tell the story when there were only men around. Or maybe just when she was not around to challenge him. "It was Monday night, at her betrothal ball. I went to give her my congratulations on her marriage, perhaps help her with a few pointers, and you will never believe what she did. She stood up, looked at me as if I were a vile rodent with beady little eyes and greasy hair, and marched away."

Bianca was torn between trying to make him repeat the exact comment that had made her march away and commending him for his admirable self-description.

"What conclusion did you draw from this, Signore Cresci," Ser Alvise probed.

"Why the obvious one." Cresci shifted to give the spectators a view of his heavily padded legs, a posture designed to underscore Bianca's obvious lack of appreciation for male beauty. "I concluded that she hated men."

"Wouldn't the more obvious conclusion be that she hated you?" Ser Cornelio asked seriously.

For a moment it looked as if Cresci was going to challenge the judge to a duel, but since dueling was illegal in Venice and Cornelio Grimani had celebrated his seventy-fifth birthday several years earlier, Cresci decided against it. The old man was known to be a little loose in the head, he reminded himself. It must have been a joke.

"That is funny, it really is. But as I told you, there are many more than me who have gotten the same treatment at the hands of Signorina Salva. And you heard that fellow about the clothes."

Bianca cocked her head to one side and looked at the judges. It was Ser Archimede who spoke. "A servant belonging to the Foscari palace has testified that you gave him a rather large sum of money in exchange for his clothes. Would you like to see him?"

"No, it is true." Bianca saw no reason to conceal it, and there was no reason to prolong the ordeal. The numbness was beginning to creep into her stomach, and soon her blood would be frozen in her veins. "But what can that possibly have to do with the murder of Isabella Bellocchio?"

"The assumption is that women who like to fill men's clothing, also like to fill men's places in other ways. For example, in the bedroom." Ser Cornelio's tone suggested the theory had been developed by someone with considerably less judgment than himself.

"By Santa Teresa's collarbone, that makes no sense!" The stupidity of the idea reheated Bianca's blood. "For one thing, if I hated men, why would I want to act or dress like them? For another, there are plenty of good reasons a woman might want to wear men's clothes besides impersonating men."

"Perhaps you will enlighten us." Ser Cornelio had his magnifying glass out again. "I can think of several reasons, but none of them are good. What was your *good* reason for wanting men's clothes."

Bianca realized she had made a mistake. If she explained why she had procured the clothes, to break into Isabella's house and snoop for evidence, her guilt was as good as confirmed. But she was convinced that if she lied, Ser Cornelio would see through it in an instant.

"They allow greater freedom of motion," she answered in compromise, then hurried on with a question of her own. "Why would proving that I dislike men, which I deny, mark me as a murderess?"

It was Ser Alvise who answered. "It does not mark you as a murderess, but it certainly increases the likelihood that you were in love with Isabella Bellocchio."

Bianca was puzzled. "You seem to be concluding that I was in love with Isabella Bellocchio simply because I am not in love with Giulio Cresci. Is that correct?"

The comparison between the shapely, sylphlike courtesan and the spindly legged, self-described rodent was patently ludicrous. Anyone in their right mind would have preferred even a dead Isabella to a live Giulio.

"We have concluded nothing. We are merely acting on the information provided in the denunciation," Ser Archimede interjected swiftly. "Can you deny that you had a conversation with Signore Cresci that ended as he has described?"

All at once, Bianca saw how she had been betrayed. Ian had led her on, taught her to trust him, only so that he could use what she told him against her. Like a bloodthirsty tiger, he had leapt at the tiniest scrap, even her brief conversation with Giulio Cresci. He had spared nothing in his exertions to have her condemned for murder, refusing to believe in her innocence despite all of her efforts. His hate for her obviously ran so deep that he would stop at nothing to prove her guilty.

Not even faking a robbery.

Without even thinking, she asked in a low voice, "At the beginning, you mentioned some drawings. Do you have them?"

"I don't see what bearing this has on the question of your affection for Isabella Bellocchio." Ser Alvise adjusted the cuff of his robe, the equivalent for him of a massive fit of the fidgets.

"Nor do I, Your Excellency. I was just wondering if you have them." She had not realized that she was holding her breath for the answer.

"No. Or, I should say, not here. But we have seen them. They were submitted with the denunciation and we do have them. We decided they were too, *ah,* detailed for this setting."

It was the answer she both feared and anticipated. Bianca stepped backward, suddenly unsteady on her feet as the full scope of Ian's perfidy struck her. He himself must have arranged to have her drawings stolen, wanting to have them in safe custody when he decided to submit the denunciation. With growing anger, she remembered the way he had berated her that night, accusing her of having an accomplice who stole her papers and ransacked her tools for her, when all along it had been him. He had known she was telling the truth when she denied his accusations because he had been behind the theft himself, but he had persisted anyway. He had purposely framed her for murder, had purposely betrayed her.

Suddenly everything was so clear. It was he who had an accomplice, *he* who was protecting someone. Someone about whom he cared more than anything else. Someone whose regard he valued so highly that he would do anything to secure it. Someone like Morgana da Gigio.

Ian had plundered Bianca's body, had toyed with her, had lied to her, all to protect the woman he really loved and had always loved. Bianca cursed her lack of self-control as despair for the love she could never inspire in him tried to overtake the deep and horrible feeling of betrayal that had settled in the pit of her stomach. She would not allow herself to keep on loving him. She would not mourn for the fact that she could not occupy his heart. She would hate him for deceiving her, for repeatedly beguiling her, for purposely making a fool of her.

Color rose in her cheeks as she imagined first the immense effort it must have cost Ian to pretend that he enjoyed making love to her, and then the hours he must have spent regaling Mora with tales of Bianca's naïveté, her pathetic attempts to win his heart, or at least his concern. What made it worse was that he had gone to such lengths to trick her, even fabricating that nightmarish tale about Sicilian bandits and cowardice and being left by Mora. Her anger rose with her color. He had gone too far. She would not allow herself to be used as a scapegoat. She would no longer play the fool. She would not allow him to sit placidly by as she was condemned to death for a crime his lover committed.

"I am disheartened that you found my drawings too distasteful for public viewing," Bianca responded finally to Ser Alvise, her voice steely. "I had intended to publish them. Before they were stolen, that is."

"Stolen?" Bianca was pleased to see that she had forced Ser Archimede's eyes open, this time two whisker-widths.

"Yes, from my laboratory at Palazzo Foscari."

"Stolen?" Ser Archimede repeated. "By whom?"

She had taken the risk that he would begin asking about the body in the drawings, but he had not. Instead, he had asked the perfect question. "Obviously, whoever was planning to frame me for the murder of Isabella Bellocchio. Either the murderer alone, or *her* accomplice."

"You assert that someone is deliberately blaming you for a murder they committed?" For the first time in ten years Ser Alvise's face exhibited signs of life.

"Yes." Bianca stood perfectly still and stared forward, scarcely controlling her urge to look over at Ian to study the effect of her disclosure upon him.

Ser Archimede's eyes returned to slits while he studied Bianca, trying to decide if she was in earnest or playing a dangerous game. He came forward in his chair to address her. "If that is truly the case, how do you explain all the evidence which points specifically to you, Signorina Salva?"

She would have liked to ask exactly what evidence he was referring to, if only to make his eyes pop open again, but there was too much at stake. "I have already provided explanations for all of it. It is hardly difficult to manufacture evidence, or even to plant it."

"Plant!" Ser Cornelio exclaimed so loudly that even Ser Alvise jumped in his seat. Bianca was suddenly worried that she had antagonized the acute man, but he was paying no attention to her and was instead gesturing emphatically at the guards. "Plant, plant, plant," he declared. Only moments later, as if by magic, Luca entered carrying the vicious plant with the two red flowers.

Ian leapt from his seat in the courtroom and flew to confront Luca. "Why didn't he tell me? What did they—" Ian's badgering of the witness was brought to a hasty conclusion by the two guards who clamped themselves firmly to his sides.

"You have been warned," the spectral Ser Alvise reminded him. "However, in view of your position we are willing to give you one more chance if you promise to cease these disruptions."

"Don't bother." Ian shrugged off the guards. "I am leaving anyway. There is nothing for me to learn here." Blind with rage, he moved to the door unescorted and unimpeded.

"When you leave, you will not be granted readmittance," Ser Archimede advised his back, but Ian just waved the notice away and closed the door behind him.

The crowd on the other side of the door, who had been subsisting on mere scraps of words, could scarcely believe their bonanza when the betrothed of the murderess coolly exited the courtroom. Yet even if his reputation had not rendered him unassailable, the expression on his face was enough to make the horde part for him without asking a single question, or even speaking a single word. Only Tullia was brave enough to approach him as he strode by her, but unhearing, he continued in stone-cold silence through the hallway and down the stairs to the landing where his gondola awaited him.

Bianca's eyes had grown wide, first at the puzzling presence of one of Ian's staff, then at the even more puzzling behavior of Ian himself. She wished she could chastise herself aloud. What a fool she had been! Rather than compelling him to admit what happened, her allusion to the part he had played in framing her had instead forced him into retreat. He had realized that she would soon be pointing a finger at him and had seized the first opportunity to leave the courtroom. Instead of getting him exactly where she wanted him, she had frightened him off, with devastating effect. Nothing he could have done or said could have worked better to convince the judges of Bianca's guilt than his early departure from her trial. It was only in her mind that his hasty leave-taking proved beyond a shadow of a doubt that he was involved in the crime.

She had been a complete idiot, Bianca told herself, first for trusting Ian, then for provoking him. Her independent spirit, her rational mind, her extensive book learning, had all gotten her nowhere. Or rather, they had earned her a few nights in a cell and a death sentence. Ian's early departure made reading out the verdict almost unnecessary.

The sadness that washed over her then, standing in the middle of the soggy courtroom, was so powerful that she thought she might drown in it. Then she sneezed.

Luca had set the plant down on a table as far from her as possible, but its effect on her seemed to be unstoppable. She sneezed again as Ser Archimede addressed her.

"Do you recognize this plant, Signorina Salva?"

Bianca sneezed, started to speak, sneezed again, and settled for nodding.

Ser Archimede lifted something from the pot and held it up. It was a long, thin dagger, exactly the right size and shape to have been used on Isabella.

"Can you explain how this dagger, probably the murder weapon, came to be hidden in the soil of this plant?"

Bianca was momentarily baffled. "No," she sneezed, "I have never," she sneezed again, "seen that dagger before."

"You did not put it in the soil of the plant?" Ser Archimede asked incredulously.

"No. I can scarcely," she sneezed twice, "get near that plant without," she sneezed, "breaking into a rash."

"I hardly see how that precludes your concealing a dagger in it." Ser Archimede turned to Luca. "Please repeat what you told us earlier."

Luca cleared his throat, glanced nervously at Crispin, made a short study of the wall behind Bianca's head, and finally addressed the judges. "It was Sunday, the day before that big ball, when I find Signorina Salva there wandering around the glass rooms, all sneaky and curious. She asks me about my boy—that is, about Crispin Foscari—and I tell her he's not there, but still she lingers on, damn—that is, eat my hose if she don't, and then she goes tearing up between the flowers, swishing them with her women's things, and stops right in front of this one and starts asking questions about it. Now I see the way the plant and she get on, so I know that the plant has got no good feelings for her, and I won't tell her a word. But it got me to wondering, and then last night you all come and ask for the plant and what do you find but a dagger, and that's a mighty good reason for a plant to wish harm on a woman, eat my hose if it isn't."

"That will not be necessary." Ser Cornelio had observed the entirety of Luca's speech through his glass. "Could Signorina Salva have had an opportunity to put the dagger in the plant?"

Luca snorted and looked at the judge, scandalized. "You speaking about a woman and asking if she had opportunity? Opportunity is a woman's best friend."

The answer was inscrutable enough to make even Ser Cornelio proud, so he decided not to pursue it. He felt he had heard or, at any rate, seen enough, and the other judges, by this time hungry and cold, concurred. When Ser Alvise turned, as was the custom, to ask if any of the Grifalconi contingent wanted to say anything on their kinswoman's behalf, he received two hard glares and a snore. Since Ian and Bianca were not yet officially married and under the law only kin were allowed to make a plea, none of the Arboretti were consulted. Only Ian, as her legal betrothed, would have been eligible to speak in support of her, and he had made his position more than apparent. The lack of support from any of Bianca's past or future kin was almost exceptional in the experience of all three judges. Their silences spoke more eloquently than any condemnation they might have made.

Bianca spent the twenty minutes during the judges' absence standing stick straight in the middle of the room. The only sounds that could be heard were the rain on the windowpanes, the shuffling of the crowd outside, and the regular snoring of Guiellmo Grifalconi. The numbness was back, not just in Bianca's body but in her mind as well. She had tried to puzzle out the new piece of information, to guess whether the murder weapon had been hidden in the plant while it was at Isabella's or if it had been placed there by Ian later, but she could not follow her own train of thought, and it did not seem terribly important anyway. When the judges read the verdict, she neither cried out nor faltered.

"We find you guilty of the murder of Isabella Bellocchio, as denounced," Ser Cornelio read out quietly, much to the dismay of those outside the door. "You will be put to death at the hands of the state within two days."

Bianca's eyes swept across the faces of the judges, then over the grim countenances of the spectators. She let her gaze linger only momentarily on her aunt and her cousin, who were regarding her as if she had suddenly grown a large, green boil where her face used to be. But as her eyes reached the Arboretti, first Crispin, then Tristan, Miles, and Sebastian, each gave her a nod or a wink of complicity, and Francesco and Roberto raised their clasped hands to her in a gesture of prayer and support. They would stick by her, they seemed to be saying, they who had so little reason. Alas, it was too late.

Before she had time to adequately acknowledge their kind gestures, the two guards were back, each gripping one of her arms. She made an awkward bow to the Arboretti, then allowed herself to be led out a side door. From there she was taken down three flights, into the partially flooded basement cells for the condemned. As the guard slid the heavy iron lock into place on the outside of her dank cell, the clock in Piazza San Marco began to strike twelve. The time to prove her innocence was over. Her one-hundred and sixty-eight hours had indeed run out.

Chapter Twenty-Five

Ian arranged and rearranged his body two hundred times that hour. First he sat in the chair, rigid, feet in front of him. Then he tried crossing one leg, resting his elbow on his knee, leaning his head on his palm. That completed, he went through the same motions on his other side, this time using his fist instead of his palm. He ran through the whole routine on two chairs and a stool. Finally he got up and started to pace the length of the good-sized room. But none of these exercises set his mind at rest. For that he would need a conjurer, because Giorgio seemed to have disappeared.

When his servant failed to appear five minutes after being summoned, Ian had thought he must be busy with lunch. Ten minutes later Ian decided he had gone out to do an errand. Fifteen minutes after that Ian became concerned that he had been injured in some unguessable way that no one knew about. That was the excuse he used for bursting into Giorgio's room uninvited. With mixed feelings Ian saw that Giorgio was not, in fact, lying injured on the floor. Indeed, he was no where to be seen.

That was when Ian began his acrobatics. He told himself he was just passing the time until Giorgio came back, but he was actually trying to keep himself from thinking. Because if he started thinking, he would be forced to admit that Giorgio was not coming back, that his absence was a more explicit admission of what he had done than any words could be. The only reason he did not want to think about that, Ian assured himself, was because finding a trustworthy manservant was so hard. It had nothing to do with what it meant about Bianca's guilt. No, absolutely nothing to do with that at all.

At the beginning of the trial Ian had not been paying much attention to the narration, knowing its details intimately, but by the end the haze around his brain had begun to lift and his curiosity was piqued. If the drawings were to be used as evidence against Bianca, then whoever had stolen them must not have been her accomplice. If he was not her accomplice, how did he come to know that the body was in the laboratory? Or, for that matter, that Isabella had been stabbed in the heart? To the best of his knowledge, only three people—himself, Giorgio, and Bianca—had seen the body. He had not filed the denunciation, and although he would not put it past Bianca to accuse herself in some ill-guided scheme, he knew she'd had no opportunity to do so. That left only two mutually exclusive options: either Giorgio had denounced her or someone else was the murderer.

When Luca, as a member of his household staff, was called into the courtroom, Ian's suspicion that Giorgio was behind the denunciation had turned into a certainty. Or an almost certainty. If Giorgio had submitted the denunciation, then by Ian's own logic there was no other murderer trying to frame Bianca, and she had to be guilty. Ian was filled with a rage and a despair that clouded his vision, rage at having Bianca ripped from him, despair for what might have—should have—been between them. Fueled by these strong emotions, his need to know, to verify his suspicion, had grown so overwhelming that he had left the courtroom without even thinking about how such an action would appear to the judges. To say nothing of how it would look to Bianca.

Ian was so well embarked on his course of not thinking that he did not pause to ask himself why Giorgio would have left all his belongings behind if he had actually fled. He did wonder why Giorgio had decided to denounce Bianca without telling him, and devised the answer that he had done it as a personal sacrifice to save a master too blinded by the charms of a woman. When Ian found himself heavyhearted, he knew it was not because of the loss of Bianca and all the strangely ebullient moments she had brought to his life, but only because he was so touched by Giorgio's selfless gesture. He would have to find him and bring him back. Servants like him should be rewarded and encouraged, not let go. Strangely, Ian did not feel any better when, after reaching this momentous decision, he rose from Giorgio's chair and left the room. The heavyheartedness even dogged him up the flight and a half to his library, and was still there as he seated himself in his chair. He was about to send for some grappa, which suddenly seemed a good idea again, when a servant appeared to announce an unnamed visitor.

Ian examined his pocket watch. Twenty minutes after twelve o'clock. It was improbable that the verdict had been announced yet, he decided, so it was improbable that his visitor was coming to congratulate him on his narrow escape from Bianca. That meant that the visitor had to be someone with some other business, and though Ian could not really remember what other business he was involved in, he decided it would be safe to see the caller.

"Show him in," he ordered, then hesitated for a moment, trying to make a decision. "And bring some grappa," he added finally, sitting back to wait.

When Angelo appeared on the threshold of the library, Ian was filled with two conflicting emotions at once: anger with himself for having miscalculated the length of the trial, and appreciation for his good judgment in having the grappa brought. Too busy pouring himself a dose of the vile-tasting liquor, he did not stand as Bianca's cousin entered and crossed to him.

Angelo accepted the proffered glass of grappa and sat on the proffered chair. Then it was his turn to do the proffering. He wasted no time with inanities, moving directly to the point of his visit.

"I've come to offer you our regrets for involving you in such sordid business." Angelo crossed his legs and sipped at the liquor, looking more at ease than remorseful.

Ian, suddenly less in the mood for grappa, set his glass down. "I do not see that you have anything to apologize for. The betrothal was of my own doing."

"You may be right, d'Aosto," Angelo said and bowed his head in agreement, "but if I had acted as I should have," he paused and sighed, looking remorseful, "well, none of this notoriety would have accrued to your name."

"You need not concern yourself with my notoriety." Ian pushed his grappa glass away, toward the far end of his desk. "Nor with my decisions. I assure you there was nothing you could have done to change my mind about the betrothal."

Angelo shifted in his chair, his face pained. "I hope never again to be in this position, d'Aosto, but I must tell you that you are mistaken. You see, Bianca and I were betrothed to one another over a year ago. Having seen so much of each other growing up, you know, it was only natural. Anyway, one day a few weeks ago we had a little fight in bed, nothing unusual, but the next thing I hear she has gone and publicly betrothed herself to you."

Most of the words coming from Angelo's mouth were a surprise to Ian, who had never heard Bianca speak about her cousin with anything like affection, but only one word made him feel short of breath. "Bed?" he blurted out before he could stop himself.

The smile on Angelo's face was perhaps the most remorseful smile ever smiled by any man. "Of course, we consecrated our betrothal the same day the papers were signed. That was the only reason she agreed to it, actually, her insatiable desire. She even made me promise that once we were betrothed, she could have as many men as she wanted. At first I balked, but her appetite being what it is... Well, it's no shame to tell you that I couldn't keep her satisfied and pay adequate attention to my business affairs. I'm sure you've had the same experience."

Ian made a mental note to find out what business Angelo was in and crush it. And maybe every bone in Angelo's body as well. The sight of the smiling, relaxed, self-assured, handsome Angelo sitting across from him was suddenly more than Ian could take. "My experience with Bianca or any woman is none of your business." Ian could barely grind the words out through his clamped jaws. "You are going now. You will understand if I don't wish you a good day."

Angelo saw Ian's jaw tighten as he spoke, saw his host's face darken, but he did not rise from his chair. Instead, Angelo congratulated himself. He had made the great man wince.

Enjoying the game, he decided to push a little harder. "I don't think anything could be more sensual than that delicious little clover shaped birthmark just above Bianca's right thigh."

Ian's reaction was a disappointment. Nothing changed on his face, but he dragged his grappa glass toward him again and, gripping it tightly, drank its contents down in one gulp. He was wishing he had his hands around Angelo's throat instead. "If you were so attached to your cousin, why didn't you protest when you heard about our betrothal?"

"With the kind of power you wield?" Angelo asked rhetorically, then shrugged. "Besides, I guess I was growing a bit tired of her. Not only did her demands leave me no time for my mistress, but she did not seem able to conceive."

With even his unasked question about the absence of progeny answered, Ian found that he had less than nothing to say to Angelo and could not bear to have him in his library for another moment. He would have to be sent away, out of Palazzo Foscari, maybe even out of Venice. The city was definitely too small for the two of them to coexist in. This decided, Ian rose, indicating that the interview was entirely over, but Angelo remained stubbornly seated, his embassy still not completed.

"As I said, I feel responsible for this whole mess, but I have an idea of how to make it up to you."

Ian, who now knew that even Europe would be too small to accommodate both of them peaceably, unwillingly resettled himself in his chair. Angelo's bones should be crushed and made into paste, he elaborated on his earlier scheme. And fed to donkeys.

"Since Bianca is going to be put to death—oh, you did know the news, didn't you?—well, since she is going to be put to death, her fortune will go to my sister, Analinda, as a dowry. If you would condescend to take her in place of Bianca, I am sure the arrangements can be made quickly. We can even move her in here, just like you did Bianca, should you so desire it."

If Angelo had gotten lost in the darkest reaches of the bowels of a constipated whale who dwelled in the most distant of the seven seas, Ian would not have thought him far enough away. Although he would have missed the pleasure of murdering the man himself. He was about to ask if Angelo could recommend his sister's skills in bed as highly as he had spoken of his cousin's, but found that his jaws were too tightly clenched to speak. He was saved the effort of unclenching them to order his visitor out by the timely arrival of his uncles and the other Arboretti.

They had stopped at the house Tristan and Sebastian shared to confer about how to approach Ian. Crispin was for strangling, Miles argued heatedly for swords, Tristan immediately thought of Ian's rock-hurling machine, and Sebastian recommended that a little device involving gunpowder might be nice. Even Francesco joined in, suggesting something about itch-inducing salves that no one else understood. Only by pointing out that killing Ian would drastically hinder their efforts to save Bianca did Roberto finally convince the rest of them to try speech before weapons. Miles checked to make sure his dagger was sharp, just in case.

Their belligerence was not lost on Angelo, who rose as soon as they entered, and took his leave.

"Make sure he goes," Ian ordered a servingman, then turned to face his relatives. "I take it, from your expressions, that you have heard the news."

It had been agreed that Roberto would do the talking, but Crispin got in ahead of him. "We did not need to hear it. We were there. We witnessed it."

"It must have been moving." Ian sipped his grappa. "Did she fall on her knees and plead to her saints?"

Crispin's customary playfulness had been transformed into icy sarcasm. "No, she cried your name three times and begged for your everlasting mercy."

Ian raised one eyebrow. "She outdid herself, then. Calling on me for mercy, though." He shook his head. "Certainly that was misguided. She should have been calling on the Deity."

"Oh, I don't know. Since you walk around acting so godlike, toying with the lives and affections of mere mortals like Bianca Salva, it's not surprising that she got the two of you confused."

"Come, Crispin." Francesco put his hand on his nephew's arm, only to have it shrugged off.

"It is time that someone tells him what a selfish bastard he is."

Ian interrupted him, unconcerned. "I already know all about that. You may save your breath."

"No. No, you do not." Crispin was shaking his head violently. "You think I mean the kind of selfishness Mora accused you of, whatever that was, but you are wrong. I mean the kind of selfishness that shuts out the people who love you and makes it impossible for them to be close to you, the kind of selfishness that keeps dangerous, painful secrets which hurt other people. I mean the kind of selfishness that compels you to walk out on the only woman who has ever really loved you, and whom, I suspect, you would love if you were capable of it. And the kind of selfishness that forces your brother, day after day, to stand helplessly by as you destroy yourself. That is what I mean."

Nobody moved.

Then Ian brought his glass to his lips and drained it. "Anything else?"

Crispin collapsed into a chair facing his brother, his head in his hands.

"It was a moving speech, really, but I find I don't understand it. You seem to think that Bianca loved me, and that by not sticking with her, I am destroying myself. Avoiding marriage to a lying, betraying murderess is a way of destroying myself? That, I am afraid, I simply cannot understand. Nor do I see that there is any evidence for your saying that Bianca loved me. Indeed, her cousin was just here making it explicit that she did not."

Crispin still had his head in his hands, but he appeared to be listening. The other Arboretti shifted behind him as Ian went on. "He claims not only that he was betrothed to her long before I was, but that they had consummated the betrothal many times."

"It would not be the first time a man had lied about making a conquest of a woman, Ian." Miles stepped to Bianca's defense.

"Perhaps," Ian went on, his tone never varying, "but he had proof. He could describe the most intimate details of her body, down to the birthmark above her right thi—" Ian stopped because he had been hit in the stomach with a boulder. Or at least that was how it felt. The idea came to him so suddenly that he was literally thrown back in his chair. He racked his memory, rushing back over the conversation with Angelo just to be sure. There was no mistake, Angelo had said the birthmark was over her right thigh. But it wasn't. Anyone who had ever had his lips on it, who had allowed his hands to skim across her silky soft flesh, could not have forgotten that it was over her left thigh. Her right thigh was totally different, silky and soft in a completely separate way. The mistake was unforgivable, Ian's inner voice declared indignantly. But not, it cautioned with unusual carefulness, impossible. It was just as likely that Angelo's tastes were not refined enough to tell the difference. As evidence that Bianca had never actually lain with Angelo, that she had not been deceitful to Ian, had not enchanted him with false innocence and falser words of love or betrayed him in the deepest possible way, as evidence of that sort, the voice ruefully admitted, it was sorely lacking.

The boulder settled on his stomach, and Ian sat forward again, suddenly drained of energy. He reached for the grappa bottle but Francesco moved it out of his grasp, giving him such a threatening look that Ian did not dare stretch toward it. Then he sighed and his eyes moved to Crispin.

"You accuse me of keeping secrets, painful secrets, and you claim that they hurt others. I can only suppose you mean secrets about

Bianca. Very well, I will spill them all, and you can draw your own conclusions." Crispin wanted to protest that there were older, harder secrets that he was keeping, but Ian was speaking as if in an impenetrable daze.

"I betrothed myself to Bianca Salva because I thought she was a murderess." With that as prelude, Ian knew that he would have all their eyes upon him. "Having received an urgent summons to the house of Isabella Bellocchio, I went, entered, and ascended to the woman's apartments. There I found Bianca standing over the stabbed body of Isabella, brandishing," he paused while he fished in the drawer of his desk for a moment and brought out the garish dagger, "this. As you can see, it has the Foscari arms on it. Like anyone confronted with a woman, a corpse, and a weapon, I assumed that she had murdered Isabella, and I accused her. She, like the stubborn, muleheaded female that she is, denied it."

His eyes moved to where Francesco and Roberto were standing together. "You had been pressuring me to marry, arguing that comfortable companionship would help quiet the demons that tormented me and other such nonsense. Looking at that woman, covered with blood, I saw the opportunity to teach both her and you a lesson. Betrothing myself to her publicly and irrevocably was completely without risk, I concluded, because she would soon be put to death as a murderer, and sharing a house with her would undoubtedly stop your lectures about the necessity of taking a wife."

Ian's eyes left his uncles and moved across the faces of his cousins. When he spoke his voice was tight. He had to bite the words to get them out. "Because she needed something to do while she waited to be condemned to death, I allowed her to undertake a sham investigation into the murder of Isabella Bellocchio. I gave her until midday today," he stopped and consulted his watch, "a little over an hour ago, to produce the real murderer. If I am not mistaken, it was almost exactly that hour when her sentence was read. It would appear, therefore, that she behaved quite punctually."

Francesco was horrified by what he heard. "You mean to say, you were just using her to get at us for caring about you? You hurt her this way because you were upset with us? Dear God, I cannot bear the thought of it." Roberto gripped him by the arm, to support him, and was going to pull up a chair, but Francesco balked. "I don't want to hear any more. Please let us leave." Roberto acquiesced, pausing only to glare fiercely at Ian before moving to the threshold of the room.

There was silence until the door closed behind the two men. "That is foul," Miles declared then with emotion before Ian could speak, if he had been planning to. "I suppose you figured that since she was a murderer, she had no right to little things like honesty or, worse yet, happiness."

Ian's only response was to reach for the now unguarded grappa decanter. He was pleased to see that they were finally coming to understand what a monster he was.

"What evidence do you really have that she committed the murder?" Tristan challenged.

"More than I have that she did not." Ian's renewed assault on the grappa bottle had been successful, and he now sat back in his chair sipping at his glass, not offering any to his visitors.

Sebastian moved a chair up next to Crispin and sat down, wanting to be at hand in case Crispin's appetite for strangling was suddenly awakened. "You were still there today when she mentioned some drawings. What were they? Were they really stolen?"

Ian studied the bottom of his glass. "Yes, they were really stolen." He sighed, and looked up at his cousin. "I had Giorgio move Isabella's body into one of the vacant rooms on the top floor and told Bianca she could dissect it or do whatever perverse thing she pleased with it. Apparently, her tastes ran toward drawing. She cut the girl open and drew her organs and her bones and things. The pictures were still in the laboratory after the body was removed, and the night the prowler broke in, he took them."

"If the court had the drawings, then what Bianca said is correct, that whoever stole them must have denounced her. Or are you saying she organized the whole thing herself?" Tristan was incredulous.

Ian pushed back his chair and stood. He had told them everything but he could not listen to any more rational arguments, nor did he need to hear his secret doubts articulated by others.

"Unless, afraid that she might produce proof of her innocence and you would have to marry her and be happy, you denounced her yourself." Crispin stood and was meeting Ian's gaze, the slate gray in his eyes exactly matching that in his brother's. "Yes, I am sure that is what happened. She threatened to become inconvenient to you and you got rid of her. *Bastard!*"

At last. At last it had happened. At last even Crispin had given up on him. Ian had often wondered what had taken his brother so long. A strange sense of calm suffused his body. Without bothering to either confirm or deny the accusation, Ian moved past him to the door, shutting it quietly behind him.

Returning five hours later, Giorgio was informed by every member of the household staff that Ian was desperately seeking him. If he waited, he knew he would lose his nerve, so Giorgio went in search of Ian as soon as he heard, without even changing his wet boots. After checking in all the likely places, he finally found his master in his laboratory. Ian was sitting on a stool, strangely placed before a mirror, intensely scrutinizing nothing. When Giorgio entered, he did not turn around, but made a sign of greeting in the mirror and beckoned him over.

"I am glad you have returned." Ian spoke to Giorgio's reflection in a voice so completely without emotion that even "glad" sounded like an overstatement.

"Of course. I should never have left like that, for such a long time, without leaving word," Giorgio conceded.

Ian continued to speak into the mirror. "No, you shouldn't have, but I understand why you did. It makes perfect sense."

"It does?" Giorgio scanned the reflection of his master's face, looking for a hint of sarcasm or irony—or even emotion—but found none.

"Yes. Completely. You did the right thing."

"I did?" Giorgio was too perplexed to question Ian's intonation. "You really mean that? I thought you would be furious with me."

"How could I be? There are times when a man becomes bewitched by a woman..." Ian waved a hand in the air as his voice trailed off.

"There are? I mean, yes, there are. But I did not think you would understand so easily." Giorgio looked closely at the mirror, as if he suspected it might be distorting the conversation or at least Ian's mind.

"I must admit that at first I did not. I was actually very angry. But then I thought about it and I saw how correctly you acted. And how selflessly."

Giorgio was not sure that he had acted completely without self-interest, but who was he to quarrel with his master. "Thank you."

"You know, you took a grave risk." Ian pointed a finger at him in the mirror. "I might have been furious with you. You could have lost your place here. I considered letting you go."

"I know, but it was a risk I had to take. The way I saw it, there was nothing else I could do. The situation called for desperate measures. You seemed to be getting more comfortable with the idea of marriage, and it looked to me like in time you would become accustomed to and even happy about having her around."

Ian glared at himself and his weakness, so clearly evident to everyone but him. "I am a fool, Giorgio. I am lucky I have you. Sometimes I think you know me better than I know myself."

"Only where women are concerned," Giorgio stated without hesitation.

Ian sighed deeply and admitted his servant was right. But he did not think he himself was entirely blameworthy. "I am sure you will agree that she is a very remarkable woman," Ian stated rather than asked.

The pleasure Giorgio felt hearing his master describe her that way far outweighed his surprise. "I concur completely. 'Remarkable' is exactly the right word for her—if I may take the liberty of saying so."

"Of course you may. After all, you were the one who got her in the end." Ian turned from the mirror and reached for a half-empty bottle of grappa sitting on one of the worktables. "I think that deserves a drink." He filled the one glass, took a sip, then held it out to Giorgio to do likewise.

Giorgio had been so overwhelmed by Ian's easy acceptance of his action that he had not bothered to wonder how, when he had purposely told no one, his master had come to know about it. As the liquor burned down his throat, it finally occurred to Giorgio that this might be the right time to inquire.

"May I ask how you found out?" He set the glass down, still half full.

Ian raised it to his lips and drank down the remaining contents in one swallow. "That was easy. I just guessed. It seemed so obvious once I stopped to think it through."

"Then she did not tell you?" Giorgio took a sip from the replenished glass.

"She?" Ian scowled at his servant.

"Your betrothed, Signorina Salva." Giorgio was holding the glass out to Ian, who looked, suddenly, desperately in need of a drink.

Ian wondered if perhaps one or both of them had not already imbibed too much grappa. "Bianca? Tell me? How would she know?"

"I think she suspected." Giorgio grinned slightly as he remembered the scene Bianca had burst in on. "She saw us together once, and I think it must have been fairly obvious."

"She knew that you denounced her?" Ian was incredulous.

"Denounced her? Why would I denounce Signorina Salva?" Giorgio reached for the grappa bottle and held it up. "How much of this stuff have you drunk?"

"Not enough, apparently." Ian scowled for a moment, reached out for the bottle, withdrew his hand, scowled some more, then looked at Giorgio. "Then you did not denounce Bianca?"

"No, why would I denounce her? I think she is innocent."

"Will you swear to it?" Ian's voice was suddenly deadly serious.

"S'blood, my lord, you have my word." Giorgio put his hand over his heart. "I swear that I did not denounce Signorina Salva."

Instead of lessening, Ian's scowl only deepened. "Then what the devil were we just talking about?"

Giorgio took care to move the grappa bottle out of Ian's reach, newly apprehensive about his master's reaction to his announcement. "My getting married."

"Married?"

"Married."

"Married?"

Giorgio made a quick inspection of Ian's head to ensure his ears were still in place. "Yes, M-A-R-R-I-E-D. Married. To Marina, Signorina Salva's maid. When Signorina Salva was denounced, I was worried that you would make Marina leave, so I took her out this afternoon and asked her to marry me."

Ian's reaction was not at all what Giorgio had expected. "That is all? You are getting married? That is all we were talking about?"

Giorgio was almost hurt by Ian's casual attitude to this major change in his servant's life. "That is all *I* was talking about," he said indignantly. "I wouldn't hazard a guess as to what was going through *your* head."

Ian was shaking the just mentioned body part slowly. "Nor would I, Giorgio, nor would I. The right thigh indeed! I think I lost my wits for a time. But they are back now, and we haven't a second to lose. We must devise a way to rescue Bianca from the Doge's prison."

Giorgio regarded his master with keen skepticism. "Oh, certainly. This is fine evidence of your wits coming back. You know that prison is famous, or rather infamous, for being impossible to escape from. It's said to be the most impregnable prison in Christendom."

"Then we'll just have to be devious, won't we?" There was a gleam in Ian's eye that made Giorgio shudder.

Indeed, his skepticism turned to alarm when, before his very eyes, Ian's face assumed the aspect of a man who whistles and chuckles and explodes hunting lodges. "What a fine idea, my lord." Giorgio assessed the situation and saw that he would need reinforcements. "Why don't we include the rest of the Arboretti in our scheme? Certainly we could use their help too."

Ian's frightening zealousness did not waver, but it became slightly subdued. "You are probably right. Tristan's skills with locks will be indispensable. I suppose it is inescapable that we shall have to share the glory with them."

"Glory?" Giorgio echoed. "The glory of being banned from Venice when the Senate hears that we have helped a criminal break out of prison?"

"Come on, Giorgio. Don't be so inflexible. People might mistake you for a block of stone." Ian pushed past his sorely abused servant and out the door.

"Mistake *me* for a block of stone?" Giorgio asked the empty room, before turning to follow his master. He wouldn't want to miss out on his own share of the glory.

Chapter Twenty-Six

In the large meeting room below the library, Tristan was glaring at the jeweled dagger, glad that his family arms had not been so aesthetically abused.

"Are you thinking about adding it to your collection?" Crispin asked, observing his extensive study of the object. "If you offer me a fair price for it, I'll undertake negotiations with Ian."

"Tristan, I suggest you consider Crispin's offer," Sebastian counseled. "I think it would look perfect displayed just under your Michelangelo."

Tristan pushed the dagger aside. "Thank you both for your consideration of my collection, but I am not planning to extend it from contemporary painting to other, *um*, objects. Besides, this eyesore is the only clue we have to guide us."

"That and the fact that Ian was summoned to the scene," Sebastian interjected. "Obviously someone wanted him to find the body or, rather, wanted to find him with the body and this self-identifying dagger. Someone who took the time to replace the actual murder weapon with this toy solely to direct suspicion at Ian. So the question we need to answer is who would want to frame Ian for murder?"

"We would have a much shorter list if we asked instead who *wouldn't* want to frame Ian for a murder." They all knew Crispin was only half joking. "I for one have considered it plenty of times."

Miles, who had been deep in thought the whole time, pushed a stray lock of hair off his forehead and spoke up. "Perhaps we are going about this all wrong. As Crispin pointed out, Ian would win no popularity contest, so we could spend days examining all the possible people who bear him a grudge."

Sebastian interrupted him. "Are you suggesting that the decision to frame him for the crime might have been made merely out of spite rather than to satisfy some personal craving for revenge."

"Yes, exactly," Miles resumed. "Which means that we might be better off devoting our energies to the question of why anyone would want to kill Isabella Bellocchio. You two knew her best." He turned to Tristan and Crispin. "Do you have any ideas?"

Crispin shook his head. Tristan looked pensive for a moment, then spoke. "The only thing that comes to mind is the rumor Bianca told us about. Remember? That Isabella was going to marry a nobleman?"

"If what Ian told Crispin is correct, Bianca made that rumor up just to scare all those men into meeting her at Tullia's," Sebastian objected.

"No." Crispin, fired by his memory, rose in his seat. "No, that can't be. A few days before Bianca told us about it, Ian called me into the library to ask me in front of her if I was planning to marry Isabella Bellocchio. That means that they both believed the rumor, at least enough to badger me with it. You should have seen them." He shook his head, recalling the less than amicable atmosphere in the room. "Anyway, I think we can be fairly confident that she did not make it up."

Miles spoke to Tristan. "Are you suggesting that Isabella's fiancé killed her? Why would someone who loved her enough to risk being ostracized by his class decide to kill her?"

"Maybe he was mentally unsteady. Look at Ian," Tristan offered in his standard wry tone. "One moment he's draping Bianca with the family jewels, the next moment he is denouncing her for murder."

"So what we are looking for," Sebastian summarized, "is some-one who resembles Ian—"

Tristan pointed to the dagger. "—But dislikes him in an ugly way."

"That's it!" Miles hit the table with his palm. "The dagger. If we find out who commissioned the dagger, I bet we will find out who the murderer is."

Tristan pointed to the clock behind his cousin, the clock Miles himself had made. "Unless all your work with timepieces has taught you some way to stop the hours from passing, I think that method is too slow. It is now almost five o'clock. If we are to get any evi-dence we'll need to have it by this time tomorrow and there are probably five hundred goldsmiths in Venice alone. Not to mention those in Mestre, Firenze, Pisa, Milano, Napoli—" He gestured the infinitude of places with his hand.

"Well, then, what do you propose? What can we do?" Miles asked, slumping back into his chair.

"I should say that's obvious." Ian's voice from the doorway star-tled all of them, but not as much as the look on his face when he entered the room. "We must break into the prison and free her."

"'Obvious,'" Sebastian repeated tentatively after Ian, his blue eyes showing confusion. "I am not sure I am familiar with that use of the word."

"Don't put on any of your linguistic airs," Ian said with surpris-ing good nature. "You know damn well what I mean. Crispin and Miles will create a diversion while Tristan undoes the locks and you and I disable the guards. The way I see it, we'll be in and out in less than half an hour."

"Have you ever visited the cells in the basement of the Doge's Palace?" Tristan, who had passed some time in one years back, regarded Ian skeptically and spoke slowly, as to one who is not mentally sound.

"No, but you know your way around them, don't you?"

Tristan looked imploringly at Giorgio, who returned his look with a shrug, but Tristan was saved by Crispin from the agony of explaining that the prisons are a maze of unassailable locked doors.

"Wouldn't it be easier to free Bianca by merely withdrawing your denunciation?" Crispin's voice was cold, but color was rising in his cheeks. "Or are you too proud to do that, too stubborn to admit you made a mistake?"

Ian shook his head at his brother piteously. "Come on, Crispin. I did not denounce Bianca. What kind of a monster do you think I am?"

Crispin's mouth opened to answer the question, but Sebastian shot his cousin a look that cautioned silence and spoke in his stead. "Even if you did not denounce Bianca, you still think she is guilty."

"Thought," Ian corrected him. "I thought so until a few moments ago. But I am past that now."

"How do we know you won't be past thinking she is innocent in a few minutes?" Miles challenged.

"There is no question of her innocence. I have proof of it."

"Proof?" the others asked in unison.

Ian nodded. "Not enough to produce before a court, but enough to satisfy me. That is why we must break her out of prison. There is really no time to lose."

It was Giorgio's turn to look imploringly at Tristan. Tristan sighed, turned to Ian, and said simply, "That is out of the question."

For a moment Ian just blinked at him. Then he moved to a chair and sat. "It really is impossible? You aren't just saying that to get back at me?"

"Whatever my present feelings toward you may be," Tristan eyed him, "my primary concern is to save the life of an innocent and much abused woman. If I thought there were any chance that we could break her out of the basement cells, I would already have tried."

"Then we will have to use our heads to have the denunciation withdrawn." Ian grimaced. "And if my deductions are correct, the only way to do that is to find the murderer."

Heavy silence fell over the room until Miles decided to pursue his earlier theory. "Have you any idea who commissioned that dagger?"

Ian nodded. "Yes, Giorgio found the man who made it. But it won't help at all. It was ordered by Bianca's brother."

Miles sank back into his chair, his theory crushed to bits. "No! That could not be any worse."

"I can't really see it, but is it possible that Giovanni Salva is the murderer?" Giorgio looked around the table at the cousins.

Sebastian and Tristan slowly shook their heads. Giovanni Salva was too preening and conceited to be a favorite with any of them, but they couldn't see him as a murderer.

"I guess you can never tell just by looking at someone whether they are a murderer." Tristan conceded after a long silence. "Take Bianca, for example—"

A growl from the end of the table interrupted Tristan. He would have gone on over Ian's bestial protest, but he could not compete with the excited voice that followed it. "It wasn't Giovanni. It could not have been." Ian stood and began to pace the room. "Whoever killed Isabella also killed Enzo, her manservant." He continued despite the questioning looks of his cousins. "And Giovanni certainly could not have done that, because he was not in Venice when it happened. I had that confirmed by our agent in Trieste."

In any other circumstances they would have showered him with questions and probed his conclusion about Giovanni's innocence, but they hadn't time. When Miles spoke, his voice was heavy with despair, his poetic soul stung to the core by his impotence to help a lady in distress. "Then we are back where we started, with the entire blond patriciate as our suspects, limited only by the dual requirement that the person be a friend of Giovanni Salva's and an enemy of Ian's."

The others nodded grimly, each calculating how much that reduced the pool. "That brings it from about three hundred to only a hundred men," Crispin began, trying to sound relieved, "since Giovanni Salva has so few friends." The unspoken but understood fact that all those men could have harbored grudges against the Conte d'Aosto was completely lost on the pacing Ian.

He continued walking back and forth across the room, every now and then emitting a sigh or a snort, and occasionally a grunt. None of them could be sure if he was listening to their conversation, until suddenly he stopped short, declared, "We are idiots," pulled another chair up to the table, and sat.

"There are nowhere near a hundred possibilities," he announced grimly, disgusted with himself for not seeing it earlier. "In fact, there are only four."

"Who?" Miles demanded, asking the question for all of them.

"That's the difficulty. I've no idea." All eyes were on Ian as he continued. "Bianca invited six men to her friendly gathering at Tullia's house and declared that one of them was the murderer. That alone would mean nothing if one of them had not shot at her, because only a cornered man would take the risk of shooting her in such a public manner. God alone knows how, but in some way she managed to shorten the list to those names. Two of them, Crispin and Valdo Valdone, we can ignore not only because I doubt if either of them would murder but also because they were not there to do the shooting. Although I did not get to ask her about it, I am fairly sure that she only included them to guarantee that I would be present, or at least interested in the proceedings. That leaves only four others."

"Four others who were masked," Crispin said grimly.

"Do you have any idea who they were?" Miles spoke to Ian, who just shook his head.

"What about Tullia? The gathering was held at her house." Sebastian's hopeful suggestion perked them all up.

"She might know," Ian allowed, "but she certainly would not tell me. My lack of partisanship for Bianca seems to have earned me a whole new string of enemies."

"Oh, good," Crispin said in a voice that had nothing good in it. "Let's hope no more than half of them have homicidal instincts."

"One of the rest of us could call on her." Sebastian spoke over Crispin. "We may not be clients of hers, but if the concern she showed for Bianca today before the trial is any indication, I am sure she would be willing to do all she could to help her."

Giorgio, who had been leaning against a wall in the back, cleared his throat. "There might be a faster way, though I doubt it will be easier. Bianca trusted Marina's nephew, Nilo, with most of her correspondence. Perhaps she had him—"

"Yes!" The memory of Tuesday night seized Ian in a flash. "You are absolutely correct, Giorgio, she must have had Nilo make the deliveries. I'm sure he will remember the names. Bring him at once."

Giorgio was shaking his head. "I will try but I can't promise anything. I think you might need to add him to your list of enemies. He is convinced that you betrayed Bianca."

"Damn it, this is no time to humor a young boy's fantasy, Giorgio. Use your influence over him. You're going to be his uncle, after all."

"Uncle?" Crispin repeated, and Giorgio blushed furiously.

"Yes, Giorgio has decided to yoke himself to that woman with the baby named Cosimo," Ian explained.

"I think his name is Caesar," Crispin hazarded, but Ian, too busy glaring at Giorgio to make him gone, did not hear.

When Giorgio had left, Sebastian spoke. "I agree that it is a fine thing to have reduced our pool of suspects, but realistically we are no better off than before. We still don't know who the murderer is, or even what drove him to murder."

Ian frowned for a moment, then let out a groan. "We do know the motive, at least I do. Bianca figured it out days ago, but at the time I discredited it. She guessed that Isabella had overheard some compromising information and was using it to blackmail someone into marrying her. I told her she was drawing conclusions from coincidences," Ian admitted, grimacing at himself as he remembered his haughty tone, "but now it seems she was right."

"What kind of information did Bianca say she had?" Miles queried.

"She did not know precisely. She just guessed that Isabella had been listening in on some clandestine meetings which Enzo told us were being regularly held at her house."

Tristan was shaking his head. "I can't see Isabella sneaking around, listening at key holes. That was not her style."

"No, indeed, it was much more devilish than that," Ian explained quickly. "There is a listening tube in her room that goes directly into the room below where the meetings were held. It is fashioned so that you can see as well as hear. Through that she would not have missed a single word or facial expression."

"That still doesn't tell us anything about what she heard," Miles said.

"No, but perhaps with the names we—" Sebastian was cut off by the sounds of a scuffle outside the door. Rising to investigate, the Arboretti were confronted with a sight that at any other time would have been comedic. Giorgio had his arms extended, pulling with all his manly might on Nilo, who had planted himself like a hundred-year cypress tree in the middle of the floor and refused to budge. As the Arboretti emerged from the room, he could be heard reiterating his strong objections to moving.

"I heard how he did not even wait to hear her sentence read and did not even look at her. I heard how he laughed in the middle of her speech and then left because he had a headache. And how he met in secret with the Senate today to make sure they would convict my mistress and then paid the judges twelve hundred ducats to find her guilty just in case that didn't work. I will not talk to him. He is a traitor. I hate him, and I don't care who knows." His eyes flashed defiantly over the Arboretti as he spoke this last sentence.

Miles turned to glare at Ian. "Is that true? Did you pay twelve hundred ducats to have them find her guilty?"

"No, only five hundred. The other seven hundred must have come from someone else," Ian responded dryly.

"S'blood, Ian, this is no time to joke." Crispin was insistent. "Did you bribe the judges?"

"No!" Ian was equally emphatic. "I may be a monster, and I may even have left in the middle of the trial, but I certainly did not bribe any judges."

"And the Senate?" Sebastian regarded Ian narrowly.

"No, damn it, I was trying to convince them to *release* her not condemn her."

"Even though you thought she was guilty?" Miles looked suspicious.

"I didn't really. I...I couldn't. But all of this is immaterial because guilty or innocent she will be dead if we don't soon take some action."

Giorgio had released his grip on Nilo, whose sad eyes had grown large as the cousins exchanged words. When they stopped talking he stepped forward and addressed Ian.

"You swear you did not bribe the judges?" He was so solemn and melancholy-looking that Ian almost wanted to laugh.

Instead, he responded with equal solemnity. "I swear. And I did not laugh in the middle of her speech."

"You did grunt," Crispin put in, "be honest."

Ian rolled his eyes at his brother. "It didn't have anything to do with what Bianca was saying. That was when I realized that Giorgio had denounced her." Nilo had turned to Giorgio and looked ready to spit fire at him, so Ian rushed on. "He had not, of course, I simply thought he had. I tried to ask Luca when he was called to testify, but you all saw how successful that was, so I left the trial to find out another way. And that was how I discovered Bianca was innocent." Ian turned to face Nilo directly. "Now I need your help to prove it."

The Arboretti stood motionless as Nilo studied Ian intensely. Ian could of course order the information out of him, but then there would be no guarantee of its accuracy.

"What can I do?" the boy asked finally, as if accepting a difficult military commission for the state.

There was a collective sigh of relief as the Arboretti returned to their meeting room, accompanied by both Giorgio and Nilo. Ian invited Nilo to take a chair next to his, then spoke to him.

"We need to know the names on the invitations you distributed last Tuesday night. I already know two of them, Valdo Valdone and my brother, Crispin, but we must know the other four."

"I can't tell you, because there were no names," Nilo answered simply, then added, "They were addressed by initials only."

"Then tell us those," Ian said impatiently, then caught himself. "They will serve just as well."

Nilo paused for a moment, then rattled off the four other sets of initials and addresses that had been printed on the cream-colored packages while Miles set them down on paper. When Ian thanked him and told him he could go, he was reluctant to leave but was finally persuaded by Crispin, who promised to alert him instantly if he could be of any further assistance.

Alone again, the Arboretti and Giorgio studied the list that Miles had made. It took only a few moments to identify the men to whom the initials belonged, and then they found themselves again at an impasse.

"We could go as a group and confront each of them. That way we would be less likely to get shot at," Tristan suggested, only half in jest.

"Yes, and equally unlikely to screw a confession out of any of them. At least not on the first try, and we don't have time for seconds." Ian pushed the list away from him toward the middle of the table. "We just don't have enough information to threaten them with exposure."

Sebastian thought for a moment. "That may not be true. We have everything that Bianca had, maybe even more, and she posed a big enough threat to them to make her worthy of shooting. We must be overlooking something, something crucial."

"I've just been going over everything in my head," Crispin said from the end of the table, "and I can't think of anything. We know the motive, we know who commissioned the jeweled dagger, we—"

Miles hit the table with his hand, unusually animated. "How many of the men Bianca invited to her gathering were also at the ball on Monday night?"

"All of them," Ian answered with interest. "Why?"

Miles pushed his hair back and shook his head with resignation. "If they were all there then it doesn't matter. I was hoping to eliminate at least one of them on the theory that the dagger, the real dagger used for the murder, was put in that plant during the ball. But if they were all here, it doesn't do any good one way or the other."

"Besides," Crispin added, "we have no evidence that the dagger used to commit the murder was not already in the plant when it arrived."

Crispin's words sent Ian into a daze. No one spoke as he stared, unseeing, into the room before him. He was no longer with them but had instead returned to the scene of the crime. He drew his mind back to the room, calling up the details he had absorbed in his quick view of it. What came back to him was not the visual image, but rather the sound.

He had not fully returned to the meeting room when he finally spoke in a slow voice. "That plant was there at Isabella's. I can't picture it, but it had to be. I distinctly remember Bianca sneezing the whole time I was speaking with her."

"If the plant was there, then it is more than likely that the dagger was put in it right after the murder to hide it, so that the jeweled dagger could be found on the corpse and taken for the murder weapon. That would explain how the denouncer knew not only where the dagger was but also where the plant was. Whoever sent the plant must himself be the murderer." Miles's excitement was soon dulled by Crispin.

"I don't know who sent the plant," Crispin explained miserably. "It just arrived the day before the party, wrapped in plain paper, no card, nothing. I thought it might be from one of our ships just returned from the East, but I asked around, and no one seems ever to have seen it."

"What about some other ship from the East? There are ships arriving from Constantinople every day," Miles pointed out.

"Like the ship Saliym came on," Sebastian said quietly. "The ship that was to receive the shipment of gunpowder."

"Twelve hundred tons of gunpowder," Tristan put in slowly, with dawning awareness. "Twelve hundred tons of gunpowder and twelve hundred ducats paid as a bribe. That is quite a coincidence."

"What are the chances," Crispin asked, "that the conferences

Isabella overheard were in fact the negotiations about this shipment of gunpowder? That the plant was given by the Turks as a 'good faith' at the conclusion of those negotiations?"

"Very, very high," Ian said, too disgusted with himself for not seeing it earlier to sound excited. "Indeed, that is exactly what Bianca must have concluded." The Arboretti's eyes were glued to him as he explained. "She opened the meeting by announcing that one of the gathered guests was 'a murderer, a thief, and a traitor.' She must have understood the significance of the plant, the fact that it linked the meetings at Isabella's to the Turkish gunpowder deal. At the time I thought she was just being overzealous, but now it's so clear. It was that last designation, traitor, that almost got her killed. I'm sure of it."

"Then we have found our man." Tristan tried to keep his voice level when he spoke, telling himself not to get excited, that this could easily be another dead end. The others looked up at him, wondering if this was another joke, but he shook his head and continued. "Sebastian, do you have that list we drew up of the likely participants in the ammunitions deal?"

Sebastian nodded slowly. He produced a sheet of paper from within his tunic, studied it for a moment, then set it in the middle of the table next to the other list with a grim smile. The others, including Giorgio, crowded around the two lists, but only for a few moments. When they drew back, their faces wore a smile akin to Sebastian's. There was only one name that appeared on both Bianca's list of possible suspects and their list of possible traitors. There could be no question about it. They had found their murderer.

Chapter Twenty-Seven

As darkness raced the water to see which could creep up the walls of her unlit cell more quickly, Bianca sat staring into space atop the wood-plank bed at the center of the room, a semi-dry island amid the rising tide around her. What had been only a finger-deep puddle when she entered the cell, was now more than ankle deep, and the level was still climbing.

Even more than wet, Bianca felt cold. It was not an ordinary cold that had gripped her and left her trembling amid the rising water, but a deep, saturating cold that came from inside her. She was utterly alone, utterly without hope. And utterly without self-respect. She had allowed herself to be taken in by Ian, even to fall in love with him! She had played right into his hands, blind to the truths so clearly arrayed before her eyes. Why had she been so eager to believe in his innocence at the scene of the murder, so quick to accept his pat explanations, so willing to overlook the detestation he made obvious from their earliest encounters? She forced herself to vividly recall the night he made her undress under his gaze, to remember the way he had repudiated her, pushing her from him with loathing as if she were a monstrous, stinking beast. Which was what she felt like, some disgusting creature who begged men to embrace her despite their obvious abhorrence.

She wondered at the effort it must have taken him to conceal his disgust when he lay next to her, the exertion it must have cost him to pretend to enjoy their coupling, to call out in just the right way, to lick and kiss and caress her body to climax. Beneath the stiff fabric of her bodice, her nipples tightened as she remembered his lingering touches, the feel of his soft hair brushing against her thighs, the sensation of his shaft pushing into her, the way he shuddered as he attained his release. Was that, too, faked? Was even that part of his plan to deceive her?

Her blood warmed slightly with that thought. Yes, she had been a fool, but she was not completely at fault. He had striven to earn her regard, had lied, cajoled, and compelled her to believe him, even telling that horrible tale about watching his best friend die before his eyes. He had made her feel for him, pity him. And love him.

She remembered how pleased he had looked when she told him what she felt for him, and now saw through his joyful expression to the triumph it must have concealed. *The bastard!* she thought to herself, suddenly filled with contempt. What right had he to toy with her life? Why had he chosen her as his victim? Why did she have to die for someone else's crime? Especially if that someone was Ian?

She did not, she realized with a flash. She did not and she would not. She may have been duped and betrayed by Ian momentarily, but that moment was over. She would see that justice was served, even if it meant accusing the man she loved of a crime. The man she *once* loved, she corrected herself.

She was so fired with her new purpose that she rose from the bed and began to pace her cell, as heedless of the water that now filled it to mid-calf level as of the obstacles—among them her having been condemned for the very crime she wished to pin on him, and therefore not appearing as the most credible of witnesses—in the way of her denunciation of Ian. He would pay for what he did to her, she assured herself. He would not be allowed to get away with it.

Only when she walked smack into the wall of her cell did the severe limitations on her abilities occur to her.

"*Owwww*," a voice said, which, although she neither recognized it nor was aware that she had spoken, she knew had to be hers. After all, she was the only one in the cell.

Wasn't she? She turned her head cautiously from side to side, peering intently into the darkness for signs of life, and had just concluded that she was indeed completely alone when the voice came again.

"*Owwww*," it whined, and Bianca leapt away from the wall. This time she was sure she had not spoken. A cold chill ran down her spine, undoubtedly the result, she hurried to persuade herself, of standing in calf-deep cold water, and having nothing to do with the potential presence of a phantom. She was not scared, her mind assured her, nor was she going mad. It was perfectly common and safe to speak with the souls of the dead. Even the souls of dead murderers lingering around the cells of their condemnation, no doubt waiting to extract morbid justice on the bodies of their successors. Perfectly safe.

She cleared her throat and approached the wall, wondering what the proper salutation for the phantom of a dead murderer might be, when her musings were interrupted.

"Don't be a-coming back here to go a-bashing into the wall. Ain't no one going to come down here with the water like that, and I'm a-liable to die of the shock. I'm delicate, I am." He pronounced it "deleeecat."

Bianca froze where she stood, her heart pounding wildly. The voice was definitely coming from somewhere in front of her, but all she could see was empty darkness and the wall of her cell. Curiosity about what type of infernal monster the Deli-cat might be momentarily overtook her desire for revenge, and taking a deep breath, she turned slowly to face the voice.

"I am sorry, I did not realize that there was anyone nearby." She spoke politely into the darkness. "Where exactly are you?"

"If you'd a-move your eyes to where you've been moving your legs, you'd see me straight enough. I'm over here, where I always am."

Of course, Bianca reminded herself, Deli-cats, like all phantasms, must hover in dark corners. She squinted toward the left corner of the cell, from which the voice seemed to emanate, and thought she could just see the outline of the head of a small man, hovering body-less slightly below her eye level. She drew back, not sure whether she was actually prepared for her first encounter with a phantom. As she did so, the phantasm smiled widely at her and a disembodied hand appeared next to the face, beckoning her over.

"Why are you a-hesitating like that? What kind of a murderer are you, without even the wits to come and greet old Cecco?"

"I'm not a murderer," Bianca insisted, "but I know who is. I must reach...someone." She stopped abruptly, realizing that she did not even know whom to turn to. Her family had completely abandoned her, and even if the Arboretti did not think she was guilty, she could hardly count on them to denounce Ian.

Cecco's head tilted to one side, observing her. "If you're not a murderess, what are you doing down here, aye? That's a trickier rid-dle than the old sphinx's, it is."

"Someone made it look like I committed a murder, but I didn't." Tullia's promise of help suddenly flashed through Bianca's mind. "Please, you must help me get word to my friend so I can be freed."

Cecco shook his head. "You amateurs are all alike. Up and com-mit a perfectly nice murder and then you won't even take the credit for it. Bah! In my day a murderer was a murderer and that's all there was to it. I'd happily take the credit for all the murders I caused, happily, I say. This generation got no spunk in them."

"I tell you, I am no murderer!" Exasperated, Bianca approached the floating head. "I must get in touch with my friend to tell her what I know. Do you have any special powers? Can you help me?"

"Ha!" The little face looked savage, and Bianca drew back. "You want my help, do you? You, a woman? Once I had freedom and a partner but I lost them both, and do you know why? On account of a woman!" He paused to study Bianca. "Of course, you look noth-ing like her, that witch. Compared to her, you're just a stick with legs, you are. But still, you are a woman."

Bianca was too busy wondering if all Deli-cats lacked manners or if she had just been lucky enough to get a cell haunted by a particularly misogynist one to take offense at his unflattering appraisal of her appearance. "If I am nothing like her, then maybe you could help me?"

"*Ha!*" Cecco frowned at her. "I was the best, the very best there was. If there was a fellow you needed taken care of, I was the one you got. D'you hear that? A *fellow*. I was a professional and would only deal with other professionals, that meant other men. But then that woman sent for me. She went all womanly on me, a-cooing and a-flattering, all about my beautiful eyes and my adorable little ears." He sneered into the darkness, disgusted with himself. "Well, I would trade them adorable ones for a pair that didn't work so well because they went traitorous on me, they did, letting her persuade me to do what she asked and where did it get me?"

Bianca, unsure whether she was supposed to speak and unwilling to antagonize the Deli-cat any more than she already had, only shrugged slightly.

"Nowhere! And now I have to go a-limping about in corners, waiting until night falls. Me, old Cecco, that once was the best of them all!" He scowled indignantly.

"Did she kill you herself?" Bianca asked, curious in spite of her more pressing needs.

"She would have if she had a-known. She wanted to. But I fooled her and disappeared. Now she can never find me."

Emboldened by the Deli-cat's semirational replies, Bianca decided to probe his powers. "Can you move around? Why don't you haunt her instead of staying here?"

"What, am I supposed to go a-sneaking about her bedchamber saying, 'boo'?" Cecco squinted at her.

Bianca shrugged. "Why not?"

"I never want to lay eyes on the witch again. Besides, I don't know about you, but I ain't got the pro-pensity to walk through masonry."

"But you are doing it now," Bianca pointed out reasonably.

"I am, am I?" Cecco laughed. "You think I am some sort of spook hovering through the wall? Ain't you never seen a window before?"

Startled by his laughter, Bianca waded closer to the head. As she neared, she saw that yet again she had proven herself a dim-witted fool. This was no phantom, no ghost, but rather a man with his head sticking out of a good-sized square opening in the wall. "Aren't you a Deli-cat?" she demanded finally.

"Delicate?" Cecco repeated quizzically. "I already told you I was. I got a very delicate constitution. Your ears aren't any too good are they, mistress?"

"You're just a prisoner like me, then?" Despair colored each of Bianca's words. A ghost might have been able to assist her, using his ghostly powers to fly through walls and deliver messages, she had reasoned, but a fellow being was perfectly powerless.

"I ain't nothing like you!" Cecco's lips curled as if he had just consumed an entire tree of lemons. "For one thing, I've got them adorable ears. For another, you're a woman. An' if that ain't enough for you, I ain't a prisoner."

"If you are not a prisoner, what are you doing in a prison cell?" Bianca countered.

"Isn't that what I was just explaining to you? Them ears of yours could use a good cleaning they could. I just live here."

"You live in prison, but you are not a prisoner?" Bianca was clearly incredulous.

"An' tell me, where would you live if you were a-hiding from a witch? Can you think of a better place?" Cecco demanded.

"You are hiding? You live here voluntarily to avoid being seen by someone? Who? Why? What could compel you to live here?" Bianca gestured to the sodden cell, now filled with water up to her knees.

There was silence while Cecco eyed her scrupulously. "I don't expect you could keep a secret, being a woman and all, but what with them ears of yours and since you'll be drowned dead before tomorrow, I just might tell you."

Bianca, trying to understand what he meant about drowning, made a move to interrupt him and tell him not to bother, but he put up a hand to silence her. "I'll tell you, to pass the time friendly-like, but you can't be interrupting with women's questions." Cecco shuddered, as if women's questions were some sort of extra painful version of the inquisitor's rack. "But I don't fancy standing up all this time." He reached his hands through the hole. "Take these and I will pull you across."

Bianca hesitated for a moment. If the Deli-cat was not in fact a prisoner, perhaps he could help her get a message to Tullia. But she would first have to overcome his antipathy for women. Realizing that the only way to accomplish that was to put her own needs aside for a moment and act agreeably toward him, she took the proffered hands and let herself be pulled through the hole, falling headfirst into the water. When she stopped spluttering and coughing, she opened her eyes and took in her surroundings. She was in a cell equivalent in dimension to hers and equally filled with water, but there the similarities ended. It was lit with a glass oil lamp hanging from a stand over an ancient brocade divan, which was elevated above the rising level of the water. The wooden bed had been made taller and covered with a cloth, atop which she could see an assortment of food and plates. One whole wall was covered with shelves containing everything from broken pieces of pottery to animal tusks and a crude rendering of the Virgin Mother. Another was hung with a faded tapestry depicting a knight bathing in a stream, looking especially lifelike as the real water flooded the banks of the depicted river.

She turned to the left and let out a shriek. All the stories she had ever heard about jokes played by the malicious souls of the dead came back to her instantly as she saw the disembodied head next to her. It was bobbing up and down with a ghoulish smile on its face, until her screaming began.

"Why you got to a-screaming?" it demanded, spitting water out of its mouth. "Ain't I told you startling jolts aren't good for mine constitution?"

"Don't hurt me. Please, I beg you, just let me go!" As Bianca spoke, she pressed her body against the wall behind her.

"Hurt you? An' I'm the one with the sore ears, that I am." The head bobbed toward the furniture, muttering. "Hurt you! *Ha!*"

Under Bianca's fearful gaze the head drew abreast of the divan. First one, then a second little arm emerged from the water, followed by a torso and two small legs. Five years earlier, the man's curly ponytail, heavily padded shoulders, puffed leggings, and pointed shoes would have been the height of fashion. Or rather, Bianca corrected herself, the low of fashion, for there was nothing high about him. In fact, he was a dwarf.

When Cecco had pulled himself completely onto the dry safety of the divan, he turned to face his guest.

"Now do you want to hear the answers to all them questions or not?" he demanded fiercely. Bianca nodded, too stupefied to speak, and waded silently toward a stool that hovered above the level of the water. Once she was seated, Cecco cleared his throat and began his narration.

"I was the finest in my line of work, that I was, until that witch came and got me."

"Exactly what type of work was that?" Bianca interrupted as politely as possible.

Cecco glared at her. "What kind of work? Ain't you never heard of Cecco the Assassin? Finest paid killer in the land? Don't tell me you've never heard of me. *Bah!* You're just kidding."

Bianca, quickly deciding that it was better to go along with anything a potentially ghoulish dwarf Deli-cat said, managed a sheepish smile of agreement.

"No more of those questions, you understand?" Cecco asked ferociously. "I get all muddled up when I get interrupted. As I was a-saying, I was at the top of my profession, even had me an underling name of Carlo. The witch called me and offered me a job, simple as pie, it seemed. One of her admirers was boring her or some such women's problem, and she needed to get rid of him. 'Not entertaining enough,' that's what she said, and a woman like that is in constant need of entertainment.

"I felt a little sorry for the man and asked her if killing him might not be a bit much, but she said it was the only way. An' then she offered me that pile of gold, enough gold to buy me-self one of them New World islands, if I were the island-buying kind, and said she would send along her new lover to make sure nothing went wrong. I was still unsure, but Carlo, he only needed to see gold a league away an' he was ready to risk life an' limb. Between him persuading and her going on about my adorable ears," Cecco shrugged to himself, "there was really nothing for it. I took the job."

"That does sound bad," Bianca commiserated. "Indeed, I have had a bit of bad luck myself. I wonder if—"

"There you go again, butting in with them questions. You ain't heard even the smallest bit of it yet." Cecco put his hands on his hips and frowned intently at his uncooperative audience of one. "I don't see why you're in such a rush, mistress, it ain't as though you'll be leaving here anytime soon. Not especially if the water keeps a-coming as it is. No, you'll have plenty of time to drown your sorrows here, I promise you that." The dwarf let out a little laugh at his clever pun that did not inspire reciprocal mirth in Bianca's breast.

"Do you mean the water will keep filling the cell until I cannot breathe?" Bianca's eyes were wide.

Cecco nodded. "An' what else could I mean? I heard the guards talking about it this noon. Never happened before in the history of the prisons, but with all this rain it's a-fitting to happen now."

"If the prison is going to flood, why hasn't someone come to move us?" Bianca challenged him.

"What for? If'n you drown, you'll be saving the state all that money for an execution. Bloody expensive them things are, what with the ropes and the knives being sharpened and all. It ain't as easy to kill a body as you might think, especially if you are innocent like you say you are, and haven't had any firsthand experience with it. Them executioners are a lazy lot, basically. They're just as happy to let nature work its way with you and by tomorrow when the tide goes out, their job will be done for them."

"Why aren't we trying to escape?" Bianca moved forward on her stool. "I must get word to my friends! Why are we just sitting here doing nothing?"

"*Bah!*" Cecco looked at her disdainfully. "Doing nothing? I'm a-trying to tell the story of my life to a woman. Look at the thanks I get."

"How can you just sit there and wait to die?" Bianca was incredulous.

"I ain't said nothing about my dying, have I? I swear, if'n you weren't going to be dead by the end of the night, I'd have them ears of yours examined. I'm not a prisoner like you." Cecco pointed a finger at her. "I am free to go anytime I want."

"You know a way out of here? You can escape?" Bianca was desperate. "Please, please, I beg you, let us go at once. I will reward you handsomely, I promise."

Cecco's sneer might have been lethal on the face of a larger man. "An' I ain't never heard them kinds of words before. 'I will reward you handsomely,' that's what that witch-woman said before she ruined my life. Next thing you know, you'll be agog over my adorable ears. That's what really fixed it for me. She mentioned my ears and I before I knew it, I was on that boat to Sicily, cutlass in hand, to take care of her man." Cecco grabbed a dagger from his waistband and flourished it in the air for emphasis.

Bianca's desperation was tempered by surprise. Did all men set their made-up tales of woe in Sicily, she wondered to herself, her face assuming a quizzical aspect. Taking her new expression as a sign of interest, Cecco continued, using the dagger to punctuate his narrative. "Took two days to gather men together and another three days just to find the prey, wandering about as he was, and then we had to wait until they got out into the open countryside. An' don't think it was easy to find them out on them hot plains, not for one with my delicate constitution. Carlo and me and our three hired hands, we a-searched high and low before we find them, an' then they don't act as they ought to. There they was, like they was supposed to be, the two of them traveling together, the witch's old lover that she wanted to get rid of, and her new one. But she had promised me that the one she wanted alive would stay behind and make the one she wanted dead ride out alone during the daytime, with only a few native guards who would go a-running off when we approached, but it ain't happened like that at all.

"Night had just come, and at first I think to myself, Cecco them eyes of yours are going, because not only do I see two of them coming a pounding toward me, but two of them looking for all the world like twins. 'Carlo,' I says, 'how many of them men on horseback you see there?' and faithful Carlo tells me, 'Two, master, two looking just the same.' So now we are in a pickle because we're only supposed to kill one of them, only agreed to kill one man, an' I always stick to my word, an' besides, the witch wanted one of them alive, so we've got to choose which one. I tell Carlo that since it was his big idea to get into this mess, he'd better do the choosing, so he takes one of our hired men and I take the other two. Carlo goes riding up to the one he's chosen and gets ready to do his business, and I go riding up to the other one to keep him from a-interfering, but damn me if he didn't start lashing out like a fury. For a moment I think to myself, maybe Carlo got the wrong one because this one before me sure ain't very entertaining at all, but I look over an' see that it's too late, Carlo'd already gone an' done his business," Cecco drew the dagger across his throat in demonstration, "an' there's my prey heading over his way. Without so much as a by-your-leave, my man goes over and is about to slice Carlo's head clear off. But I can't have that, can't have him killing good partners, so I get him from behind and knock him off his horse, an' that's the last of him." The hilt of the dagger came down on Cecco's palm with a loud thud.

Bianca's interest in the story had grown from casual to acute during Cecco's relation, and by the end she was so absorbed that she did not notice that the water now came up to the level of her stool. The parallels between the dwarf's tale and the story Ian had told her that night in bed were staggering. If what Cecco was saying was true, then Ian's story might not have been made up. Everything, from the ill-fated journey to Mora's leaving, could have really happened. Perhaps Ian had not betrayed her. Perhaps he had not actually framed her deliberately for the murder. And perhaps he was not still in love with Mora.

But she would not be duped again if she could help it. The whole thing could be a coincidence. There were, after all, probably many bandits on the plains of Sicily, she surmised. She had to know more before she could be sure. Too much was riding on the veracity of the tale to take it without further questioning. "What happened then?" she asked with a degree of interest that did Cecco's heart proud.

"Seein' as the witch wanted one of them alive, we patched up the living one as good as we can, dragged him to Messina, an' left him for someone to find. He kept wakin' up and yellin' stuff, so we hit him on the head a few times," *thud-thud-thud* went the dagger, "but other than that we wanted to keep him in good condition for the witch." Cecco's face grew mournful. "Meantime, Carlo's not looking any too good and by the time we got back to Venice, he's a-gone and died on me. He was a great one, that Carlo, an' I ain't been the same since he left me." He paused and sniffled a little, using his frayed velvet cuff to wipe a tear from his eye. "But it was just as well, anyway, 'cause it comes out that we gone an' killed the wrong one, and the witch, she ain't willing to stop at anything but our heads for revenge. That was two years ago an' I'm still afraid to peek my head out of this cell when the sun is a-shining out there. Either that witch-woman will send some of her hell minions to get me, or the other one, the one I was supposed to kill, will recognize me and do me in himself." To amplify the piteousness of his tale, Cecco took the dagger and aimed it at his heart.

The light glinting off the raised hilt of the dagger where four rubies had been gaudily set caught Bianca's eye and illumined her mind. "Santa Graziella's tongue," she gasped, "what a fool I have been!" The jeweled dagger was the key to the entire mystery of Isabella's death. She wasted several minutes berating herself in the name of various saints for not thinking of it sooner, then reminded herself that the oversight was excusable since the jeweled dagger had not been mentioned during her trial and she had been convinced of Ian's guilt. Even so, she was less than pleased with her powers of reason because it suddenly seemed so clear. Whoever had made use of the jeweled dagger to frame Ian had been on good enough terms with her brother to trust Giovanni to procure the ugly item for him. While Giovanni was undoubtedly acquainted with all the men she had invited to Tullia's, there was one man whose name stood out prominently. This particular man was not just a close friend of her brother's, but indeed closer than a friend, for he was his cousin. And hers.

Bianca's mind was racing. Not only did Cecco's story confirm Ian's, but she now felt confident that Ian had not been involved in the plot to frame her. She saw that he had not betrayed her, and had, in fact, been betrayed himself. There could be only one woman, Mora, with the kind of resources and determination that Cecco had described. Even if Ian did still love Mora, surely the dwarf's tale would show him the error of his ways, for there was no doubt that she was Cecco's witch.

It took the full force of her reason to cool the emotions that reignited in Bianca's heart and to dampen the flames of passion that began to blaze anew. Even if Ian had not framed her, her reason reminded her, he had refused to believe in her innocence. He had persisted stubbornly, like a mule or some even less dignified and cleanly creature of nature, to believe that she was guilty. What clearer proof could she ask for that he felt nothing for her, and never would.

An image of Ian rushed into her mind, and she had to choke back a sob. Even sporting mule's ears, he was her ideal of male beauty, her ideal man. Or might have been, her reason corrected, if only he could have loved her back. For a moment, her emotions conquered her intellect, and her heart raced with the thought that her innocence proven, there would be nothing to stop their marriage. Except, her reason put in, her good sense.

To live with him, knowing that he did not love her, would be worse than not to live with him at all. She loved him too much, she admitted to herself, to condemn him to a life with a woman he could not feel for. At first it would probably be fine, but as the years went by, she knew he would come to resent and finally to despise her. Although it was going to be hard, it would be better to let him marry a woman he could love than force him to carry out a betrothal that would only make him hate her later. The thought of Ian's despising her made her shudder and firmed her resolve.

She would not see him, would make no call on his affections, expect nothing of him. She would disappear from Venice and free him from their betrothal, letting him live the life he wanted to lead, with the companion of his choosing. But she had to be sure he knew of her innocence. She could not bear the thought that he would go through his life thinking that she had betrayed him and lied to him. She knew what it had done to her to harbor those emotions in her breast for even a short time, and she was determined to spare him that. She would not be another Mora.

There was no time to lose, she saw with alarm. The water was rising faster, seeping up through the floors with unstoppable energy. She had to get out of there and convey a message to Ian, to make him know about her and about Mora. . . .

Bianca spoke quickly, a plan taking shape in her mind. "If I promise to have you absolved of this crime and to restore you to your, *ah*, illustrious profession," she addressed the dwarf, "will you help me?"

"After all I said, you still offering me them women's promises?" Cecco made a face.

Damn Mora and her poison, Bianca thought to herself, struggling to stay calm. "You must believe me. I am telling the truth. I know the man you were supposed to kill, and I know the woman who gave you the commission. The man, Ian Foscari, is tall, handsome, with light hair and blue eyes. The woman," Bianca stopped and shuddered, whether from relief or jealousy or the cold water now creeping up to her midsection was unclear, "is dark and very very beautiful. Her name is Morgana da Gigio."

Cecco eyed her. "What if it is? What does that matter to me?"

"I can help you. I can intercede on your behalf. If Ian Foscari hears this tale, in the right way, he will praise you not attack you, I promise you that. And I can tell you just how to present it to him for the best effect."

Cecco grunted incredulously. "I try to kill him and knock him in the head with this here dagger and you say he's a-going to thank me? You're one of the strange ones, aren't you? No thanks. I seen how that man fights and I want no part of putting myself in his way."

Bianca pushed her concerns to a corner of her mind and summoned all of her powers of reason to her aid. "Surely, it must be distasteful to a man of your abilities and tastes to be stuck down here all the time? And if you didn't mind it before, what are you going to do now when the entire room is filled with water and all your possessions are ruined. Certainly you won't be able to come back here for weeks, maybe even months. Where will you go? What will you do?"

She paused to let her words sink into Cecco's mind, like the water that had been inexorably seeping into her gown. For several moments the two of them, the drenched dwarf and the bedraggled Bianca, stared at each other, their eyes locked in a battle of wills. Finally Cecco spoke.

"I bet you can't even swim, can you?" When Bianca did not contradict him, Cecco shook his head. "I ain't risking my life again for a lady, especially one as can't even swim. No thank you. Promises. Bah."

"You won't take me with you? You won't help me escape?" Bianca could no longer keep the desperation out of her voice.

"An' how can I, even if I was liable to—which I ain't, make no mistake—how can I if you don't got the good sense to know how to swim. Plus you're too big. Them sewers can't barely hold me."

"You swim out through the sewers? Couldn't you just lead me to them and then go on your own? Couldn't you just point me in the right direction?"

Cecco made a new face. "That would be plenty joyful, to come back here in a few weeks an' find your corpse a-stinking up my front door."

"Please, please, you must help me. I must get out of here. I am not a murderess. I don't want to die."

"Why didn't you tell that to the judges when you had the chance?" Cecco's tone softened a bit, as he pulled himself to the edge of the divan. "Look, mistress, I believe you ain't a murderess, you ain't got the stuff for it, but I still can't take you with me. Maybe, if you'll put in a good word for me with that Foscari devil, maybe I'll carry a message to your friends."

As he spoke he rose to the edge of the platform on which the divan was perched and made preparations for his departure. Bianca saw that this was her last chance, indeed her only chance. She could and would try to follow him, but the goddess of fortune seemed predisposed against her. At least she could see that Ian knew the truth about what had happened in Sicily and the truth about her innocence. It could be her gift to him, she thought dramatically, still harboring a secret hope to inspire some strong emotion in his breast. Even more secretly she imagined an emotion strong enough to compel him to rescue her from prison. She would have plenty of hours for these idiotic fantasies, she told herself, while she was waiting to drown. The time called for action, for the sooner that Cecco left and she followed him, the better her chances of survival.

With a deep sigh, she realized she had no choice but to place her fate in the hands of the recalcitrant dwarf. It was probably for the best that she be left there to drown, she assured herself, because otherwise she would not be strong enough to keep from seeing Ian. "I would be most grateful if you would go to Palazzo Foscari," she instructed the waiting Cecco, "and tell Ian Foscari everything you have told me. Tell him how we met and that I sent you. Then tell him I am innocent, that Angelo, my cousin, is the murderer I was seeking." She paused, considering the impropriety of her next words and deciding that since she would soon be dead, it did not matter much anyway. "And tell him that I love him."

Cecco grimaced. "I should have known a woman would go a-putting them womanly sentiments in it. I'll say what I say, an' then we'll see how good them promises of yours are." With that, he leapt into the water and swam over to the far corner of his cell, dived down, and disappeared.

"Signore! Signore Cecco!" Bianca called, slipping from her stool into the water which now came just below her breasts, and moving toward the spot where she had last seen his head. She moved her feet and hands over the walls and floor around her but felt nothing. He had disappeared completely, leaving her alone with the eerie sound of water seeping ever faster through the cracks in the prison walls.

Chapter Twenty-Eight

The young man watched with a hint of arousal as the woman extended her arm across his lap to reach for another sugared grape. Seeing that he was growing bored with the interminable wait, she took no pains to conceal the milky breast that slipped out of the low-cut bodice on her deep burgundy gown. Instead, she pulled herself up next to her companion and ran the grape over her exposed nipple, covering it in sugar. Her hand behind his head, she pushed his mouth over the enticing sweet, moaning gently as he sucked the sugar off.

"That is only the beginning of the reward for your fine work, *angelo mio*," she said huskily when their eyes met again. "You shall have everything you have ever wanted."

"Right now, all I want is to feel your hands caressing my cock." The young man spoke insistently, newly confident.

She rolled her head back and laughed, a slow, deep ripple that made the veins on her creamy throat tremble deliciously, then turned the half smile on him. "I see we are already learning to command. But that—"

There was a knock at the door, and two men dressed in her brother's colors entered the room, interrupting her. The woman immediately recognized them as her brother's personal guards, Jenö and Roric, gifts from the pope himself. They were a pair of fair giants, with the light golden hair and piercing blue eyes of people from the northern countries. They were so tall that they had to bend their heads to avoid hitting them on the lintel, and their broad shoulders barely cleared the doorway. In answer to the woman's gesture, they approached the couple on the divan, each making a deep bow.

"Well?" The woman sat forward, her eyes alight with expectation.

"Your brother sends his regards and asks us to report that all has been prepared exactly according to your wishes, madonna." The elder of the two spoke with the slight accent of his country.

A new fire came into the woman's eyes. It was the news she had been waiting for, the news that her victory was at hand. She had only to wait for her triumph.

"The boat is prepared and awaiting your embarkation," the fair giant went on after a pause. "Your brother will join you within three days. In his place he offers you our company, to provide any assistance or service you may desire."

The woman let her eyes linger over the two immense, muscular bodies before her and smiled appreciatively at her brother's choice of messengers. She was pleased to see he prized her at her worth, sending the guards he adored most to protect and care for her on the journey like the treasure she was.

"You will do nicely," she said finally, turning back to her companion. The young man had risen and was moving toward a passageway that led directly to the canal and their waiting boat, but he halted abruptly when she called to him. "Soon, my angel, soon we shall go, but not yet."

"This delay is stupid," the young man whined, his hand lingering on his codpiece. "We would be so much safer and more comfortable in the gondola."

Inexplicably, she had grown fond of the young man, and therefore tried to keep the displeasure out of her voice. "My dearest would not begrudge me my crowning moment of triumph, would he?" she coaxed him, using her hand to move him toward her. As she was cooing at him, the sounds of commotion outside the door filtered into the room. The woman stopped talking and listened with concentration for a moment, then smiled widely.

"At last. This promises to be very diverting." The young man had just resettled himself alongside her on the divan when the outer door burst open, admitting her Moorish servant, turban askew and very harried, being carried in by two tall men. The servant was trying to speak, blustering something about daggers and orders from the Senate, but the woman silenced him with a nod. When he had departed, so distraught that he forgot to shut the door behind him, she focused her attention on her two unexpected but not unwelcome guests, favoring them each with a devastating smile.

"I can't tell you how delighted I am to see you, Ian," she said in a voice filled with genuine satisfaction. "Although I am not surprised, I had planned it this way. However, the hour was growing so late that I feared I would have to make do with secondhand reports of your suffering. It will be much better to witness your demise *in proprio persona*. How nice of you to oblige by calling upon me so opportunely."

"I fear I shall have to disappoint you, Morgana, for I have no intention of dying just yet, nor have I come to see you." Ian spoke with deep disdain. "I console myself with the fact that you have grown to expect such unbecoming behavior from me."

"He used to call me 'Mora'," the woman said not to him but to the assembled company at large, "and hang dotingly on every word I said. Though he was clumsy and ill-mannered, I kept him on out of pity. But now look at him. Invading my house, gracelessly challenging my authority." She shook her head with reproof and addressed Ian specifically. "Yet again you fail to understand. You have indeed come to call on me. And you will indeed meet your end soon. In one way, however, you are correct. You shall not die right away, for I have decided to destroy you before I kill you. What I have planned for you is much more hideous than mere death. And completely unstoppable."

"The prospect is thrilling, and I would love to hear more," Ian, followed by Crispin, moved toward the young man, "but we have actually come to arrest your new favorite for the murder of Isabella Bellocchio."

"No," Mora shook her head, "that won't do at all. Another of the little fictions you devise to console yourself for your incompetence, Ian. Your arresting him would be most inconvenient. You see, Angelo and I were just leaving for a journey to Zante." As she spoke, she made a slight gesture to Jenö and Roric, who stood on either side of the divan. "I hear the climate there is much better than this dreary rain, which I find does nothing for my disposition."

Ian looked serious. "I would hate to interfere with the improvement of your disposition. By all means, leave at once. It is only Angelo Grifalconi that we want. You are free to go."

Ian made a move to take Angelo's arm, but was stopped by a supernatural force that held him immobile. His first irrational thought was that Morgana was indeed in league with the devil and had cast some sort of infernal spell on him, but he soon realized that it was no more than one of the giants gripping his arms from behind. Mustering up all his energy, Ian jammed his elbow backward into Jenö's abdomen and received nothing but a grunt and a sore elbow for his pains. The man was made of some sort of metal, he decided with alarm. Turning his head, he saw that the other giant had seized Crispin's right arm in a similarly disabling fashion, but had allowed his left arm to hang free. Ian said a silent prayer of thanks to whatever deity had made his brother left-handed.

It was the only advantage they had, and he would have to use it to its utmost. Clearly brute force was not on the side of the Arboretti. They would have to rely upon their wits to free themselves, let alone to take Angelo prisoner. And they would have to do it fast, before Morgana decided it would be diverting to listen as their necks were snapped in two.

"Call off your little toys and let me have Angelo." Ian's voice was commanding. "I really do not have time for these games."

Mora regarded him with unfeigned merriment, both sides of her mouth curved into a smile. "I'd forgotten how diverting you could be, Ian. Describing Jenö and Roric as 'little.' Indeed!" She laughed to herself softly. "You must know how it pains me to deny you anything, after what we have been to one another, but Angelo is going nowhere with you."

Crispin had been studying his brother with astonishment. What could he possibly be thinking? No one knew better than Ian how cunning Mora was, yet he was acting as if he were negotiating with a child. At the moment in his life when he needed to be the most subtle and coy, Ian was coming out with direct orders and proclamations. Maybe the tension had gone to his nerves, Crispin thought with panic. His panic deepened as he watched Ian's head and left arm jerk slightly. Was his brother going to have some sort of nervous fit, right there, with so many lives hanging in the balance? Acting on instinct, Crispin was about to reach his free arm toward Ian to steady him when, all at once, he understood.

"Morgana, I am surprised at you." Ian worked to keep the relief out of his voice when he saw that Crispin had gotten his signal, focusing instead on holding Mora's attention. "What has Grifalconi got that a thousand other men, and at least a hundred dogs, could not offer in equal measure?"

"You are jealous!" Mora closed her eyes to savor the prospect, just long enough to keep her from seeing the slight motion of Crispin's left hand. "At least you have finally come to know my value, to appreciate what I might have been to you if you had been brave enough."

"You really know how to drive a point home, doesn't she, Crispin?" Ian asked, willing his brother to look at him. As their eyes met, Crispin winked and then jammed the dagger he had quietly freed from the waist of his doublet deep into Roric's left thigh. Roric emitted a groan so loud that it startled everyone, including Jenö, whose grip loosened for split second. That was all it took for Ian to wriggle away, freeing his long sword from its sheath at his side. He moved directly toward the divan, sword drawn and aimed at Angelo's heart.

"If you come any closer, I am afraid your brother will have to die," Mora said in a conversational voice, as if passing a polite remark at a party.

Ian stopped where he stood, a hand's width from where Angelo sat languidly on the divan, and turned to look at his brother. Roric had pinned Crispin's arms behind him and had pressed a dagger to his neck. While Ian watched, Roric demonstrated the dagger was not just for show by pricking Crispin's throat ever so slightly, just enough to draw a steady stream of blood.

And then everything blurred. As Ian watched, the luxurious hall became the plains of Sicily, Crispin's face became Christian's, the blood dripping down his cloak Christian's blood. The nightmare was becoming real again, he was in it, but this time he would not let Christian die. This time, he would charge the assassin himself. This time he would drive his sword straight into him. Still in his dreamlike haze, Ian pulled his sword up before him and moved directly toward Roric and Crispin. Crispin watched Ian first with surprise and then horror as he drew closer, his eyes unseeing, completely devoid of emotion or personality. Roric's dagger dug deeper into Crispin's neck with every step Ian took toward him.

"Ian!" Crispin called to his brother, desperate to penetrate his horrible daze and pull him back into the present. "Ian!" he gasped again, Roric's knife piercing deeper into his throat.

Ian neither stopped nor slowed. He kept coming, moving closer with clocklike precision, his expression glacial, his intent clear. Crispin, seeing that his death was on the horizon, had just begged the Deity to be merciful with his soul, when Ian halted.

He was almost close enough to drive his sword into Christian's assassin when a curtain lifted from his mind, and he found himself standing before Crispin and Roric. Ian looked quizzically at his sword, extended in front of him and ready for battle, then at his brother. Crispin, cloak covered with blood, was regarding him with terror and dread. Even with the haze lifting, it took Ian a moment to realize where he was, and another to grasp what was happening.

Ian's arm dropped to his side. The full horror of what had almost occurred washed over him in a disabling wave.

"Ian," Crispin mouthed plaintively, relief warring with worry as he watched the dead look in his brother's eyes replaced with a deep despair. "Musn't...give up.... Remember...Bianca."

As Crispin spoke, a clock somewhere in the house struck nine times, breaking through Ian's lethargy. Sicily and the horrors it held for him receded, allowing his reason to return and with it his determination. He may have failed Christian, but he would not fail Bianca. Or Crispin. Damn it, he would not again stand idly and watch as another of the people dear to him got his throat cut. He was being given a second chance, and he was going to take it.

Ian's mind whirled, examining—and then discarding—every possible course of action. He knew Mora well enough to know that she was in earnest, and that she would not hesitate to kill Crispin if Ian took another step toward her favorite. He knew equally that surrendering his sword probably would not keep her from having Roric kill Crispin, just for the pleasure of it. And if she had Crispin killed, there was no question but that she would kill him too.

When he heard Mora shift on the divan behind him, Ian's spine stiffened, preparing himself for her taunts. But instead of mocking, her voice came even and unhurried, as if he had not fallen into a strange stupor, indeed as if nothing at all had happened since she issued her ultimatum.

"I find it excites me to have drawn swords in the house," Mora said with a playful shudder that brought a smile to Angelo's lips. "If you care at all for your brother, I suggest you resheath yours. Now."

In a flash, Ian realized that she and Angelo, still seated behind him, could not have known of his murderous daze or seen what had just happened. That was what gave him the idea.

It was a dangerous plan, but from where he stood, it was the best he could think of. Praying he still knew her well enough to gauge her responses, he took a deep breath and turned to Mora again, working to keep his face a stony mask. "You should know better than to use such threats on me, Mora. You know that since you left me I have been incapable of feeling anything for anyone."

"It is all your own fault, you know. I tried to teach you how to love, how to sacrifice yourself for others, but you were too selfish. You understood only when it was too late, after you had lost me." Mora sighed deeply with the memory of her wasted effort. "And yet, I could never help feeling that even once you had ceased to care about others, even then, you harbored a certain fondness for your brother."

Ian's heart was beating fast. "No, your destruction of my emotions was complete. I care no more for Crispin than I do for that whore I was betrothed to or some stranger I might meet on a deserted street." Ian's tone became confidential. "In fact, I find him tiresome. You can hardly imagine what a trial it has been to put up with him these two years."

Mora eyed her former lover intently. Even after the transformation her leaving him had wrought, he could not possibly be as completely heartless as he was pretending to be. It was impossible that he felt nothing for his kind and loyal brother. He had to be bluffing. But he was a fool if he thought she would not call him on it.

She spread her hands wide. "If that is the case, why are you hesitating? Why not let Roric kill him?"

"I would rather have the pleasure myself," was Ian's cool reply.

"Really?" Mora was momentarily caught off guard. She sat forward on the divan. "How would you do it?"

Ian's eyes gleamed with an unholy excitement that sent a shiver down Mora's spine. "I've just been considering it. Nothing crass like a simple stab in the heart. That would be too quick, unsatisfying." Ian shook his head. "No, I was thinking of something slow and personal. I would begin, for example, by cutting through his right arm. It would be painful but not fatal, so he could have the thrill of watching while I did the rest. Then I would take this dagger," Ian took the small knife from his waistband and held it up, "and use it to cut open his stomach and carve out his bowels. After that, I'd have to see." Ian casually slipped the dagger back into his waistband, leaving the hilt clearly exposed and ready. "I could do it right here, although with the mess it is bound to make, it might be better to do it outside."

Mora smiled slowly. Did he really think she would be that easy to deceive, that all he would have to do is persuade her to move Crispin's execution onto her boat landing outside so he could escape? It was amusing, but also a tad insulting. She had hoped he thought better of her. And she certainly would not let him get away with it. "No, I shouldn't like to stand outside in the rain, and I wouldn't want to miss anything. By all means, proceed here. The servants will attend to the mess."

Much to Mora's dismay, Ian looked neither surprised nor crestfallen but rather pleased. He bowed deeply to her, then turned his back to the divan and approached his brother.

"Did you hear what I described, *fratello mio?*" he asked Crispin in his chilliest voice.

Roric was still holding Crispin's arms behind his back, but on a command from Mora he had moved the knife away from the man's neck. Crispin merely nodded, watching his brother for some sign that this was a joke, some hint that he was not actually planning to execute him in the grisly manner he had just described. Look though he might, Ian's face remained an impenetrably stony mask.

But not his eyes. They held Crispin's locked in a powerful unflinching gaze, even as Ian lifted his sword to sever his brother's right arm. Crispin held his breath and waited stoically for the pain to follow the blow, steeling himself for it.

It didn't come. All he felt was something warm and wet spilling onto the back of his neck. He was momentarily fascinated by the fact that he felt no pain from his wound, until he realized that it was not his blood he felt but Roric's. Ian had brought his blade down on Roric's shoulder, catching him unawares and causing the giant to loosen his grip on Crispin's left arm, which was now free to take the dagger Ian had carefully placed within his reach moments earlier. Crispin took a deep breath and grabbed it.

He was overwhelmed with relief but even more with joy. "You don't hate me?" he whispered breathlessly to his older brother, sounding like an insecure schoolboy rather than a man of twenty-nine. Ian made a mental note to spend some time, soon, describing how he had aged ten years in ten seconds when he saw Roric's knife at Crispin's throat, but for the time being he simply rolled his eyes at his brother. They had no time to lose, because, though Ian's back was blocking her view, it was only a matter of seconds before Mora discovered what had happened.

"You take Angelo, and I—" were the only words Ian got out before Roric's bellow of pain made the situation clear to the observers on the divan. Crispin wriggled free of the bloody giant's body just before it collapsed to the ground, and was soon heading directly for Angelo. Ian had moved around Roric toward Jenö who, taken off guard, was too surprised to block Ian's deep thrust at his abdomen. He doubled over with a groan, and Ian used the hilt of his sword to knock him on the head. Jenö teetered once, twice, then fell over sideways, completely unconscious.

Ian looked up in time to see Crispin seize Angelo at dagger point. Mora's favorite was unarmed and put up little resistance as Crispin prodded him toward the outer door. Ian followed them, pausing only long enough to make sure Roric was truly unconscious and would not unexpectedly rise up behind them. As Ian neared the door, he heard his former mistress clapping behind him, undoubtedly her mocking tribute to his fine performance, which was fine with him, since he had won the day.

It was only when Crispin threw open the door to leave that Ian saw how wrong he was. There, blocking the way, were five giants, each one as large as Jenö, and all in armor.

"You did not really think I would let Angelo go that easily, did you?" Mora called from the couch. "I find I am rather enamored of him. He appreciates the honor of my affections. I am grateful for the diverting show you put on for me, it went exactly as I had planned, but now I am anxious to be on my way."

Ian and Crispin were not only outnumbered, they were outweighed. They had no choice but to surrender their prisoner and their weapons to the new giants. Angelo strode casually back to the divan as if he had expected exactly this outcome, and resettled himself in the open arms of his mistress.

"Tie them up along the wall so they cannot escape," she ordered the leader of the new giants. "But don't hurt them. I want them to be able to hear me when I speak."

"Since you are obviously planning to kill us," Ian addressed Mora almost with impatience as one of the new guards attached the irons to his hands, "why don't you just go ahead with it instead of boring us first?"

"Haven't you been listening? But of course not, the great Ian Foscari is too preoccupied with his own thoughts, too selfish to pay attention to other people's needs." Mora addressed him in the tone of a strict mother. "If I had simply wanted to kill you, I would have done it hours ago, years ago even, instead of delaying my journey. No, I have many other tortures in store for you before you die. Merely putting you to death is not part of my plan."

"I wish it were," Ian said frankly, knowing he had nothing to lose. "Anything would be better than having to listen to your deranged chatter. Every moment you delay your departure increases your danger."

Mora spoke sincerely, as if putting his fears to rest. "Your concern for my welfare moves me, but a slight delay will be well worth my while, I assure you."

While she was speaking, the giant had hung Ian and Crispin above the ground, their manacled hands suspended by a chain from one of the iron rings in the wall usually used to hold torches. The position might have been less comfortable, Ian reasoned, though he could not actually imagine how as the sharp pains moved from his shoulders to his wrists. Maybe if the torches had also been in place, heating the metal links of the chains and dripping hot wax on his head... He had been in the middle of thinking of other potential tortures, trying to drown out Mora's demented words, when something caught his ear.

She had returned her attention to Angelo, whom she was now addressing conspiratorially. "Shall we explain what we have prepared for your cousin? Don't you think it will make the wait so much more exciting for them, to hear the clock ticking and think about her?" Her eyes were hooded as she ran her tongue over her lips on the word "exciting." Angelo could only nod with expectation.

"What have you done to Bianca?" Ian demanded, suddenly unaware that he had arms, let alone arms that were being stretched like pieces of wet felt.

Mora drew two fingers along the sweep of Angelo's shoulders. "It is not what I have done. It is what you have done. Or will do, to be more precise. You see, in exactly two and a half hours, when the clock in Piazza San Marco strikes twelve, the east wing of the Doge's Palace will explode, and it will be your fault. You know the wing I mean, the one where Veronese has just been retouching paintings, the one where the notaries live, the one which contains—"

"The prisons!" Crispin interrupted her. "*Dio mio*, she will kill Bianca!"

Mora nodded and turned her gaze toward where he was suspended next to Ian. "Yes, exactly. Why were you always so much quicker to catch on than your brother?" She focused again on Ian. "But actually that is just the beginning. Shortly thereafter you, Ian, and the rest of your dear Arboretti will be denounced as traitors. Your arms negotiations with the Turks, culminating in a plot to blow up the Doge's Palace, will be revealed." She paused here, shaking her head back and forth with a short sigh. "But in your normal bumbling way, you will have missed and blown up only one corner, leaving plenty of barrels of your trademark gunpowder with the Arboretti name painted on them lying about. Your reputation, like your little slut, will go up in smoke. Should you try to get there to stop it, despite your bonds, your presence at the explosion will only confirm your guilt. As will a secret denunciation to be submitted tomorrow. The whole plan will go like clockwork. Clock-work indeed!" She smiled a half smile at Angelo as if they shared a private joke. Then she took a deep breath and resumed, her air distraught. "My only sadness is that I won't be able to see what delightful tortures the Senate dreams up for traitors of your rank and station."

Ian shuddered. It was a brilliant plan. Absent or present, his guilt would be manifest. And Bianca would be dead. "You seem to have this very well thought out," Ian said through clenched teeth.

"You of all people should know how thorough I am." Her thick black eyelashes raked him up and down. "It is a perfect plan, isn't it?"

The question had been directed at Ian, but it was Crispin who spoke first, his voice tight with impatience. How could Ian sit or, rather, hang there making small talk with a maniacal murderess when all their lives hung in the balance? "Why are you doing this?" Crispin demanded brusquely. "Why are you punishing Bianca? What has she done to you? What have any of us done?"

Mora regarded him, wide-eyed with disbelief. "You dare to ask me that? What have you done?" Her hands left Angelo's body and fluttered angrily toward the brothers, her gaze pinning Ian. "I gave up everything I had for him, lost everything I valued most. Tell him, Ian, how I waited upon you. Tell him how I fulfilled your every wish, attended to your every need."

"That is not exactly how I recollect our arrangement," Ian began dryly but was cut off.

"Listen to his selfishness and ingratitude. After all I endured from you! I sacrificed everything for you, my own happiness, the best years of my youth, even my one true love, and what did I get in return? Nothing."

"By my calculations," Ian computed, "you actually received about a million gold ducats, not to mention business tips worth twice that, as well as the house you live in now, your two custom gondolas, a dozen or more gowns, the string of rubies you are wearing, the matching earrings—"

Morgana sneered at his accounting, then made a wide arc with her hand. "What is all of that without true love? After years of deluding myself that you would grow to be a better man, a man capable of the love I deserved, I saw our relationship had to end. I tried to break things off amicably, but you would not let me."

"That is strange, I thought it was I who tried to break things off because I did not love you."

"You always were good at spinning little tales to bolster yourself, weren't you, Ian?" Morgana interrupted him, then continued speaking before he had time to respond. "You pretended it was you who wanted to end the affair, but anyone could see the truth. Selfish and heedless of others, you were blind to what was going on around you, blind to my love for another and his deep, pure passion for me. I begged for release you refused. Finally, I could no longer live in the prison of your affections. And yet, being kindhearted, I could not bear the thought of causing you pain. I wanted to spare you the agony of discovering, too late, how much you needed me, and the anguish of seeing me happy with someone else."

"I assure you, you need not have concerned yourself," Ian interjected, but Mora was too entranced by her narrative to take any notice.

"And then I saw the way, the way to free you from the dangerous passion you had for me. As my parting gift to you, I sent someone to Sicily to make sure you would never come back to Venice and have to see me in the arms of another."

"What do you mean? Are you saying you sent someone to *assassinate* me?"

"Such an ugly word for my act of kindness. I was only trying to spare you, so I could lead my life without always having to worry about you and the misery I was inflicting on you. I went out of my way and spent piles of money to hire the most noted man in the profession, because I wanted to see that it was done properly. But even when I had only your welfare at heart, you could not let me have my way unfettered. Instead of you, they killed *him*, my beloved Christian, while you remained on the sidelines unharmed. Ungrateful of my kindness, you practically helped my paid assassins to butcher the man I loved."

Ian's face, already registering shock at her narrative, showed complete disbelief at the mention of Christian's name. "Christian?" he spluttered.

"Yes, Christian. He and I were in love, true love. Something you could never understand."

It took a moment for the pieces to slip into place. "Then you *planned* that? You were responsible for our attack…" Through the stinging of the chains that were boring into his wrists, he suddenly saw it all so clearly. For the first time everything that had happened in Sicily—the reluctance of the bandits to hurt him, his waking up unscathed in Messina—everything made sense. What did not make sense were the wounds he had allowed Mora to inflict upon him, wounds for which he had punished those around him.

He had known that Mora was selfish, had suspected that she was amoral, but he had failed to see how completely ruthless she could be. For her the poles of right and wrong were defined by what pleased and displeased her, what met with her wishes and what opposed them. Ian was staggered by how destructive this single-minded ruthlessness could be, and by how effectively he had allowed it to destroy his life and his happiness. But not any longer, he promised himself. Assuming he got out of there alive.

When Mora's voice penetrated his thoughts, it had a new tone. No longer the wronged innocent, she now spoke as the victorious conqueress harvesting the fruits of her labors. "You ruined all my plans two years ago, Ian Foscari, but you shall not do it again. You have tried repeatedly to destroy my life, and now, finally, I will destroy yours. It would have been simpler if that inconvenient whore of yours had not picked up the dagger that I'd had her brother commission in order to frame you for murder," she paused considering, "but I find I like this outcome even better. It is more dramatic, and much more exciting. And I have had the passing pleasure of watching you suffer, to make up for all the suffering you caused me." She turned to the two guards who had shackled and suspended the brothers. "Are the locks sturdy? Did you see to it that they won't escape?" The giants each went over to inspect their captives, one of them enduring a halfhearted kick in the groin from Crispin without even twitching, and confirmed that the brothers were in no danger of liberating themselves.

"You three," Mora motioned to the smaller of the five giant guards, "take Jenö and Roric back to my brother's house and stay with them. I will take you two to help the oarsmen row through the storm," she turned to Angelo, her hand now pressing hard against his codpiece, "and you, my little angel, to entertain me all the way to Zante."

The brothers were still trapped, suspended from the wall of the room with no possible means of escape in sight, when the clock struck ten.

Chapter Twenty-Nine

The voice was too filled with emotion to be Ian's and too high to be Crispin's, but its message was unmistakable.

"Help!" Tristan, Miles, and Sebastian heard through the door of the library. "Help! Help! Someone come quickly!"

Nilo's race up the stairs ended at Tristan's chest, which he smacked into hard enough to knock the air out of both of them. He stepped back, blinked twice, and then yelled, "Help!" again at the top of his lungs.

"We will, we will, but you'll have to tell us how." Miles kneeled before the boy. "*Shhh,* it is all right."

"No, it's not all right!" The boy spoke loudly, sending droplets of rain flying from his hair as he vehemently shook his head. "No, no, no! She is going to explode Signorina Salva, and the others are tied up, and there are giants and—"

"Why don't we move in here." Tristan put a soothing hand on Nilo's shoulder and propelled him toward the library and into a chair. "Sit down and take a deep breath and start at the beginning."

"There's no time for sitting, don't you see?" Nilo moved his huge eyes from one face to the next. "We must go there now, before the clock strikes twelve."

"Go where? To do what?" Sebastian asked.

Realizing that there was nothing for it but to explain, Nilo took a deep breath, concentrated for a moment, then began. "Master Ian and Master Crispin went to that woman's house, the woman who came late to the party, the one everybody says is a witch."

"Morgana da Gigio?" Tristan put in skeptically.

"Yes, her." Nilo nodded. "They went there because that man, Signore Angelo, was there, and they tried to take him, but then the giants came and grabbed them from behind, and then—"

"Giants?" It was Miles's turn to sound incredulous.

"They looked like giants. Anyway, there was a fight, and I couldn't see what was happening, but then the lady, Signora da Gigio, ordered that they be chained up, and then she told them what she had done to my mistress." He paused to take a breath, his melancholy eyes looking even more miserable than usual, and his chin quivering. "She said that when the clock in the piazza strikes twelve, the prison is going to explode and everyone will think you did it and you will all be traitors and there is nothing you can do to stop it. But you must stop it, you must! You have to! You can't let my mistress die!"

Sebastian scowled at the boy. "Did Ian and Crispin take you with them?"

Nilo bit his lip. "No. I followed them, without them knowing it. I hid in the gondola, then I followed them up. I was afraid..." He hesitated, trying to pick the best way to say it. He tried again, "I didn't think," then blurted out, "After what he did today at the trial, I did not trust His Lordship to save my mistress. I thought maybe he was trying to hurt her, and I wanted to be sure. So I followed him." Color rose in his cheeks and he began to speak faster. "I was wrong about that, but anyway, it was a good thing I was there because now you can save her. You must go at once!"

Giorgio, who had heard Nilo's shouts from Marina's room below stairs, came bounding into the library demanding, "What's wrong? What is going on?"

"Nilo has just given us some disturbing news," Sebastian told Giorgio, then returned his keen blue eyes to the boy. "You say that Ian and Crispin are tied up?"

"Chained up, yes, but that is not the important part." Nilo, caught between despair and frustration, was gesturing wildly with his hands. "The important part is that you have to save Signorina Salva!"

"We will do our best," Tristan said in a soothing and even voice, "but we need to know more. I have heard your mistress talk about your incredible memory. Do you think you could remember everything Morgana said."

Giorgio had moved behind the boy and put an avuncular hand on his shoulder. "Just try your best, Nilo. Whatever you can remember."

Nilo creased his forehead and squinted his eyes, as he had seen adults do when trying to remember something, then recited Morgana's entire description, word for word.

He had never had such an attentive audience before, and he was almost sorry that the retelling had to end, until he remembered there was work to be done.

"It sounds like she's loaded that wing of the palace with our gunpowder," Sebastian concluded. "But she must have left someone there to ignite it. If we can just find where they are standing and—"

"Not necessarily," Miles broke in, brushing the hair from his forehead, his tone excited. "Let me see if I have this right." He turned to Nilo. "She said, 'The whole plan will go like clockwork,' and then repeated, 'Clock-work indeed!'?"

The boy's expression was puzzled. "She did," he conceded, "but that was just a joke. The important part is where she said that—"

Miles cut him off as well. "I think it was more than that. I have heard of people attaching fuses to clocks, so that when the clock strikes a certain time the fuse gets lit and causes an explosion. The fuse is almost impossible to detect, and it's foolproof because no one need be in the vicinity to ignite it. I believe it's more common in the Ottoman Empire than here." He looked over at Sebastian, who nodded slowly. "I suspect that using her Ottoman connections, Mora has somehow connected a fuse to the clock in San Marco and rigged it so it will light when the clock strikes twelve."

"Then all we have to do is disconnect it!" Tristan declared with enthusiasm.

"*Magari!* If only it were that simple!" Miles threw up his hands. "Connecting a fuse to a clock and also to a container of explosives the hundred-lengths distance to the east wing of the Palace is a very sophisticated undertaking. It requires a mechanism as complicated as a clock, and far more precise. Disconnecting the whole thing would take even the man who constructed it hours. It might take me days. Not to mention that one wrong move could ignite the fuse and explode the whole thing early."

"Fantastic." Sebastian's tone was sharper than he meant it to be, and he softened it slightly as he went on. "What you are saying, then, is that it is completely impossible to disconnect it. But you can do it, can't you?"

Miles was the only one of the Arboretti to underestimate his skills. He paused, his face a study of concentration, then sighed. "I can try. I've never actually seen a mechanism like this. I have only read about it in letters and travel accounts. But I would be willing to try it."

Knowing Miles's talents, Sebastian knew that meant the situation was not completely hopeless—only *almost* completely hopeless. "You and I will go to San Marco—"

"No, I will go alone," Miles interjected, his voice deep and serious. "It is very dangerous. Practically like putting yourself at the center of an explosion. If I make a single mistake, the explosion will happen instantaneously. I don't want to be responsible for risking anyone's life but my own."

Sebastian's tone was equally serious. "It's my decision to go, and I have made it, so technically I am risking my own life. Don't bother trying to talk me out of it. You can't expect to perform miracles on your own all the time." He went on, his tone slightly lighter. "Besides, why should you get to have all the excitement?"

"I bet he's still vying for Bianca's hand." Tristan's dry observation brought a blush to Miles's fair skin. "Undoubtedly saving her life while Ian is chained up in a dungeon will make a fine impression on her. But what about me? What am I to do? If I sit here quietly while you two become heroes, I'll never be able to woo another woman in all of Christendom. "

Sebastian ignored Tristan and spoke instead to Nilo. "You take Tristan to where you left Ian and Crispin. If anyone can free them, he can. He used to be a thief."

Nilo moved to Tristan's side and regarded him with wide-eyed admiration.

"Thanks for the recommendation," Tristan said with an amused snort, already moving toward the door with Nilo at his heels. "We'll meet you in San Marco within the hour." He said that optimistically, but his voice had lost all hint amusement when he spoke his final words crossing the threshold. "That is, if there's anything left of it."

"How did you come up with that part about stabbing me in the bowels?" Crispin asked Ian over his shoulder. "That was the part that really made me shudder."

"I think it was something about the way my stomach felt when I saw that man on the point of killing you," Ian admitted with unusual candor.

The brothers hung there in silence for a moment; then Crispin spoke again. "I did not realize that Mora was so...insane."

"Neither did I. When we were together, I thought she was capricious. *Ha!*" Ian grunted at himself. "Of course, I also thought Bianca was a murderess."

There was a moment of silence, broken by the fierce pounding of the rain against the windows, then Crispin asked, "Do you think we will be able to hear the explosion from here?"

Ian exhaled deeply. "I would rather not think about that. I am enjoying concentrating on the pain in my wrists."

"You can still feel your wrists?" Crispin asked incredulously. "I am numb almost to my knees."

"Count yourself lucky," Ian muttered back, gritting his teeth against the pain.

"I wonder if I will ever feel anything aga—"

"*Shhhhh!*" Ian cut him off. "Listen."

From somewhere deep in the house Crispin could hear the baying of dogs. It started faintly but got louder as more and more animals joined in. Then, suddenly, it stopped.

"How many men do you know of who have that effect on animals?" Ian whispered over his shoulder.

"Only one, the prince of thieves. But how would Tristan have found us?" Crispin countered with his own question.

"I haven't got the energy to guess. Let's just hope we are right."

The brothers lapsed into silence again, straining their ears in the darkness. At first they heard nothing except the omnipresent falling hard rain, but then came a creak, barely audible, then a scuffle, then another creak. Silence fell again for a moment, followed by the distinctive sound of rusty hinges opening.

They heard Nilo's and Tristan's soft footsteps before they saw their rescuers. The two figures were nearly in front of them before they could make out their outline in the dark.

"Ian! Crispin! Can you hear me?" Tristan asked in a hurried whisper as he approached the two dangling bodies. "Are you conscious?"

"Only of the pain in our arms," Ian replied, also whispering.

"Not me, I can't feel my arms," Crispin added helpfully.

"*Grazie a Dio!*" Tristan exhaled sharply. "I was afraid I would be too late."

"If it's anywhere near eleven o'clock, you might be," Ian answered grimly. "We must get to Piazza San Marco before the clock—"

"—strikes twelve," Tristan interrupted. "I know, I know. Miles and Sebastian are already on their way there. Miles thinks he knows a good way to disconnect the fuse, or else to blow us all up. But first we need to get you down from there. I can't see from here. What have they got holding you, Ian?"

"Manacles, like those from the slave galleys, and chains about that thick. The locks are new. They look like those Gianferuccio made for the prisons, the ones with the triangular keys and the two prongs."

"I am pleased to see you still remember your lessons," Tristan said, smiling to himself as he dug in the dark through the satchel he was carrying. When Ian had approached him years earlier and asked to be tutored in the fine art of lock picking, Tristan had initially thought he was being mocked for his seedy past life. But he soon found out that he had misjudged his quirky older cousin, that Ian was genuinely interested in what he called the "mysteries of thieving."

"I won't recall them for much longer if all my vital fluids keep moving from my head to my feet," Ian replied in an anguished whisper.

"That will be the least of your problems if those damn dogs roused the household. I'm working as fast as I can. *Aha!*" Tristan took the ring of keys he had just found and set the satchel aside. "Nilo, is there a chair or stool or something I can stand on at hand?"

"You brought the boy along to help you?" Ian sounded surprised. "What good will he be? Beware Giorgio if he finds out you've brought him here."

"Giorgio knows he is with me. But I wouldn't be here and Sebastian and Miles would not be in San Marco if it weren't for Nilo. He overheard everything Mora said and ran back to Palazzo Foscari to get help." Tristan had climbed atop the stool that Nilo had dragged over and was fiddling expertly with the large lock that yoked the brothers together on the ring. "*Ah.* I think I have almost got it. Be ready to fall," he warned the brothers, and the lock sprang open.

Ian and Crispin hit the floor with thuds and one scarcely concealed yelp of pain. "There's no time to get the manacles off right now, we can get them in the boat." Tristan climbed off the stool. "Can you walk, or better yet, run?" he asked hurriedly, replacing his tools in his satchel.

Ian nodded and allowed Nilo to help him up as Tristan did the same for Crispin. "Come on. This way," Nilo said, tugging Ian's cape hopefully in the direction of the door. He pulled so hard that he soon had the entire thing in his hand, empty of its occupant who was still standing motionless where Nilo had left him. Without telling Ian, someone had replaced his legs with immobile hot pincers that dug painfully into his body each time he tried to move one.

"You go ahead," he whispered to Nilo. "I will catch up in a moment."

"I'll do that too," Crispin whispered, wincing with the pain of standing.

Nothing Tristan or Nilo could have said would have convinced the brothers to move, but the sound of footsteps approaching the outside door was more than enough incentive. They leapt rather than walked to the small door with the rusty hinges that had admitted their saviors earlier, and had just closed it when the outer door burst open.

The six guards who entered the room and found it empty knew they would receive worse than dismissal from their demanding mistress if they let the two captives get out of the building. "Bar the doors! Close off the stairs! Let out the dogs!" the head household guard shouted, and the orders were executed almost before they were given.

At the foot of the stairs leading to the kennel, Tristan halted, and the others fell into line behind him. He motioned them to be silent, then opened the door a finger's width and peered around. The dogs were barking ferociously at two bewildered-looking Moorish servingmen who had been given the task of letting them out. Putting on his most authoritative air, Tristan pushed open the door and emerged from the staircase, pulling Ian and Crispin behind him by their chained hands.

"It's all right, men," Tristan told the two servants, "I have the captives." He held up the chains that were still binding Ian's and Crispin's hands so the servingmen could see them. "Go upstairs and tell the head of the household guard that everything is under control. I will see to the dogs and bring these two traitors," he spit at his cousins with contempt, "as soon as I have finished."

The relief on the faces of the two servingmen was unmistakable. "Yes, sir." They bowed to him. "We will go immediately." Tristan inclined his head slightly to acknowledge their bows, then moved toward the dogs, emitting a low whistle that quieted them immediately. As the servingmen scurried off, Nilo emerged from behind the door of the passageway. The admiration on his face as he approached Tristan made even Ian envious.

"That was fantastic, Master Tristan," he said breathlessly.

"Did you have to spit at me?" Crispin demanded.

Tristan waved aside his cousin's demand. "It's just an old trick," he told Nilo dismissively. "But it won't be worth anything if we don't get out of here quickly. Lead on!"

Nilo nimbly moved ahead, following the path he had found earlier that night. They wound past the kitchens then down and to the left. Finally, after what felt like fifty hours to Ian and Crispin but was really no more than three minutes, they ended up in the narrow *calle* that ran the length of the house. Never had Ian and Crispin been so happy to find themselves standing, underdressed, in the midst of a raging storm.

"It's just a few more steps to the gondola." Tristan spoke to the brothers over his shoulders. "We're home free."

No sooner were the words out of his mouth than the shouting started. "There they are!" someone called behind the escaping Arboretti. "Follow them!"

Tristan spun around to see three large guards emerge from a different side door of the house and take after them. Nilo had run ahead and was long gone, but Ian and Crispin were too weak to move quickly. Tristan watched with horror as the guards gained on and finally overtook the brothers, who seemed to be moving hardly at all.

But his horror turned to amusement when he saw that Ian and Crispin had only been feigning incapacity. On the count of three, they each raised their manacled hands and brought them down on the heads of two of the guards. The third guard, witnessing the treatment of his peers, turned on his heel and sped away faster than he had come.

If it hadn't been for the possibility that he was summoning reinforcements, Tristan would have burst into laughter right there.
Instead, he and the two brothers made haste around the corner of
the palace, to where Nilo was already waiting in the gondola.

"San Marco, as fast as you can," Tristan shouted, leaping after
Ian and Crispin into the boat. "I think I just heard the clock strike
eleven."

The wind blew torrents of water into their faces as Miles and Sebastian ran from their boat to the clock tower. There was no doubt that
someone had been there. The lock on the door had been broken, leaving it to flap around in the gale force wind, banging against the structure in time with the rhythmic ringing of the hour. Miles mounted
the stairs, three at a time, and stood panting before the huge clock
mechanism as it struck for the eleventh time and fell quiet.

His eyes took a moment to adjust to the darkness, but as soon as
they did, he saw it. The apparatus was almost as complex as the
clock mechanism itself, with four wheels and several weights. Miles
walked around the narrow platform put in place to enable artisans
to fix or clean the clock, and maneuvered himself for a better view.
Sebastian stayed where he was, not sure he wanted to be any nearer
to such a sinister-looking device.

"*Madonna!*" Miles whistled through his teeth in admiration.
"This is a fine piece of work." As his admiration grew, so did his
despair, for he hadn't the vaguest clue how to begin dismantling
such a device. He tentatively reached out a hand to touch it, then
drew it back, as if the little device had hissed at him.

"Does it bite?" Sebastian asked, not entirely joking. With all
those gears and pulleys it certainly looked like some infernal
automaton.

"It's too early to say." Miles's voice was not playful. "Did you
remember the leather pouch?"

Sebastian edged over to Miles, extending the pouch of tools in
his hand. Miles opened it, looked from it to the device, then carefully selected a long, thin metal implement with a flat end.

"Can you see?" Sebastian asked as Miles moved with his tool toward the device.

"No," was the encouraging reply.

"I hope you know what you are doing," Sebastian added after a brief pause.

"I don't," Miles said calmly, then reached down with his tool and began prying at one side of the device. Sebastian could not see what Miles was doing, but he heard the scraping of metal.

Suddenly, there was a loud snap, and the clock tower filled with a blazing white light. Sebastian hurled himself against the wall, shading his eyes and face from being scorched. As quickly as it had come, it left, leaving behind the acrid smell of exploded gunpowder and a massive quantity of smoke.

"What happened?" Sebastian demanded into the darkness. Getting no answer, he struggled to get to his feet, coughing out the thick, grim-tasting smoke. "Miles? *Miles?*" he shouted with growing alarm.

The only response he got was the echo of his words off the stone walls of the chamber. "Miles!" he tried again. *Miles-Miles-Miles,* the walls whispered back.

The silence was almost worse than the unsettling echoes. Sebastian had just cupped his hands over his mouth when he heard a cough, then another.

"Here…I'm down…here," a voice said with difficulty from below the floor. Squinting into the smoky darkness in the direction of the voice, Sebastian was finally able to make out the top of Miles's head, hovering somewhere under the platform on which Sebastian was standing.

It took a moment to register. Miles was dangling by his finger-tips from the narrow platform, hanging in space at least seven body-lengths from the ground.

"Sebastian…" the voice said plaintively, "my grip…slipping."

Before he had finished speaking, Sebastian had leaned over, grabbed his wrists, and pulled him up. He allowed Miles a minute to cough, then began the questions.

"What happened? How did you get down there? Was that it? Is the Palace exploded?"

Miles shook his head, using his cuff to wipe the soot off his face. "I am not completely sure, but I think that was only a protective measure. The real fuse has to be much more potent than that one, but it was enough to do its job."

"Which was?" Sebastian demanded.

"To discourage anyone from tampering with the apparatus. I'm telling you, whoever constructed this is a genius. I can't do anything to it without risking another explosion like that, or possibly worse."

The two men regarded each other in silence as the full import of Miles's words sank in. "Are you saying," Sebastian clarified, "that there is nothing at all you can do? That we are just going to sit here while the Doge's Palace explodes?"

When Miles didn't respond but continued staring unhelpfully into space, Sebastian decided to needle him. "Are you just going to let Bianca die like that?"

"It is hardly my problem, she is not my betrothed," Miles said with a petulant indifference that Sebastian saw through immediately.

"Of course," Sebastian agreed. "All I meant is that she is practically one of us. And you would not just stand about idly while one of our lives was on the line."

"Who said I was standing idly by?" Miles demanded fiercely.

"I thought when you said that there was nothing you could do that meant—"

"Nothing I could do with that machine," Miles corrected him, pushing his hair off his forehead and leaving a sooty streak in its place. "There is still one more solution to try."

"Which is?" Sebastian asked, not allowing himself to feel excited.

"We could stop the clock, and keep it from chiming twelve," Miles explained simply.

Sebastian regarded his cousin with alarm. Had he lost his mind? "But you know that this clock was designed to run perpetually, and that they say if it stops the entire Venetian Empire will fall into ruins."

Miles shrugged.

"What does that mean?" Sebastian demanded with exasperation.

Miles shrugged again, then seeing that Sebastian was on the point of throttling him, opened his mouth. "I think it is the only chance we have. If we are lucky, the entire Venetian Empire is snug in their beds and no one will notice that the clock has stopped. That is, if it is stoppable."

"Couldn't we just go position ourselves near the bells and stop them from moving when it becomes time to ring the hour?" Sebastian offered.

"Obviously you've never seen them up close. Each of the bells is large enough to crush a man with its clapper. Besides, that would only solve the problem temporarily. As soon as we moved away, the clock would strike twelve and the fuse would ignite. What we need to do is stop the clock entirely. At least until tomorrow, when the gunpowder can be traced and that thing," he said, gesturing at the device with a mixture of ire and awe, "can be removed."

"All right. I agree that is the best way left. Go ahead. Stop it." Sebastian spoke with the stoic determination of a man who has just been told he has to have his arm removed.

"Just like that?" Miles asked with disbelief. "You yourself pointed out that the clock is designed to run perpetually. Do you expect me to stop it by snapping my fingers? I am flattered by your assessment of my abilities, but I must confess, I haven't the faintest idea of how to halt it."

Sebastian was still gazing at him with his blue eyes wide open when the wheels began to spin and a loud bell struck above him. It was half-past eleven.

The gondoliers fought staunchly against the relentless storm. Not only had their cargo been augmented by the two large forms of Crispin and Ian, not made any lighter by the irons they were sporting, but the wind had picked up. The Grand Canal more strongly resembled a tempestuous sea than the peaceful main artery of the city as the boatmen struggled toward San Marco.

Even in the best of weather, Ian recalled from the protected enclosure of the cabin, the trip from Mora's palace to the main square took almost half an hour, but this day it was interminable. If only his arms, newly freed by Tristan's magic from the restrictive iron jewelry Mora had so thoughtfully provided, didn't ache quite so much, and if only his legs did not throb, he would get out and face the storm himself. Instead, he had to be content with sitting and muttering impatiently.

They were nearing the *bacino* in front of San Marco when they heard the first gong of the clock.

"Was that...?" Crispin started to ask, but let the question hang in the air when he saw the grim expression on Ian's face. The pulses of the three men and the boy in the gondola began to race.

They had just passed the point of Dorsoduro and come into sight of the Doge's Palace when the second gong came.

"Tell them to hurry," Nilo pleaded to everyone and no one in particular.

As the boatmen struggled to turn the gondola in toward the boat landing, the third gong arrived.

"Does this mean that Miles...?" Tristan ventured without a hint of playfulness, but left off and lapsed into silence.

The clock rang four.

Ian's throat was dry and his heart was pounding. Everywhere he had previously felt pain, he now felt expectation.

He had just decided to jump in and swim for shore when the boat pulled up alongside a mooring. One of the gondoliers threw out a rope to secure it to the post. It caught by the slimmest possible margin, and he moved to tighten it.

Just then, the fifth gong resounded across the square.

The wind whipped up from the outer lagoon, and the gondola bucked against the posts. With a snap, the mooring rope broke in two, sending the gondola spinning back into the basin.

The sixth gong sounded.

Ian could wait no longer. Ignoring the protests of Crispin and Tristan, he climbed out of the cabin of the boat and leapt into the churning water.

When he brought his head up for air, he heard the seventh gong.

The water was freezing. He had to fight against the downward pull of the current, which was doing its best to drag him to the bottom of the basin. Breathing hard, he forced first one arm, then the other, to pull him through the freezing water, and propel him toward the shore.

The clock struck for the eighth time.

He hauled himself up, panting and sopping wet, onto the marble boat landing in front of the ducal palace. Without even turning to check the progress of the boat, he stood and lumbered toward the clock tower.

The ninth gong struck.

He was only vaguely aware that he was probably moving toward his death. His only coherent thought was that he had to stop the clock from ringing, and it did not matter if he had to use his entire body to do it. He had to stop the clock and then save Bianca. He would not be happy until he had her in his arms again. Heedless of the rain and the chilling wind, he ran ahead toward his goal.

He heard the tenth gong as he finally reached the clock.

From behind him came the sound of voices, but Ian neither paused nor turned to look toward them. He found the door open, still banging in the wind, and ascended the stairs.

The eleventh gong was so loud that it seemed to come from within his head. He was momentarily so stunned by the noise and the reverberations that he did not immediately perceive Miles and Sebastian hanging perilously from two of the large gears of the clock.

"Stop this thing!" he ordered them fiercely. "You must stop it! Stop it!"

Stop-it-stop-it-stop-it. His words reverberated around the stone room. *Stop-it-stop-it-stop*.

When the reverberations stopped, there was silence. Miles held his breath. Sebastian said a Turkish prayer he thought he had forgotten. Ian clenched his jaw.

The silence continued. And continued.

"I think," Miles began, his voice low and unsteady, "I think we stopped it."

Sebastian made a sound that was something between laughter and weeping as Ian helped him step across to the narrow platform. Miles had also been restored to safety when Tristan bounded through the door.

"You did it!" he announced triumphantly, moving aside so Crispin and Nilo could crowd in. "The Palace is still there!"

"I can't quite believe it," Miles said, his voice still shaky. "I can't believe it's over."

"It's not over," Ian corrected him. "Not yet. We still have to get Bianca. I am not leaving here tonight without her."

"Come on, Ian," Crispin moved toward his brother. "She is safe for the night. Tomorrow we'll go to the judges, and—"

"No! I will not leave her. I will not leave her anywhere that Mora can get to her. God alone knows what that witch had planned for her if this failed. With or without you, I am going to get her."

"Me too!" Nilo joined in. "I won't leave without her either."

The other Arboretti exchanged pained looks.

"What are we waiting for, then?" Tristan asked, attempting to affect a jaunty tone. "Let's go break her out of prison."

"Just what I suggested in the first place," Ian pointed out perversely as he led the way out of the clock and across the piazza toward the entrance to the Doge's Palace. The sentinel on duty that night poked his head out of the guard shack, where Ian could see a small fire blazing.

"Halt!" he shouted to the bedraggled pack as they rushed up. "State your business."

Ian was momentarily surprised when Tristan pushed him aside and began addressing the guard quickly and firmly, like one accustomed to giving orders and being obeyed. "Sergeant, we just heard bandits entering the clock tower. How many of you are on duty here tonight?"

"Four," the sentinel responded promptly, pleased to have been mistaken for a solider of higher rank.

"You must take them all and pursue these bandits. They are in the tower now. Go at once."

Tristan had no sooner spoken than the sentinel called together his peers and told them what had happened. He hurried the others on, then returned to address Tristan. "You all stay right here and wait for us to return."

"Of course," Tristan answered solemnly. "Might we use your fire?"

The sentinel considered for a moment, then nodded and ran off to follow his fellows across the piazza. The Arboretti ducked into the guard shack just long enough to ensure that the sentinels could no longer see them, then made haste toward the wing containing the prisons.

There was another guard posted there, this one larger, older, and smarter-looking than the first. Ian eyed at Tristan, who shrugged and shook his head. "This one is all yours," Tristan offered helpfully, and stepped back to join Crispin, Miles, Sebastian, and Nilo.

Ian marched right up to the guard and announced himself. "I am Ian Foscari. I must see one of the prisoners. Right now."

The guard, who was busily excavating his dinner from one of his rotting teeth, slowly raised his eyes. He gave Ian an appraising look from his sopping leggings and boots to his grimly determined jaw. "Can't," he said finally.

"I am afraid I do not understand. I cannot see the prisons?" Ian asked in a voice that suggested the guard might be speaking an Outer Mongolian dialect.

The guard, who had found a particularly enticing nugget in his tooth, nodded.

"Why not?" Ian demanded with feeling.

"Closed."

"Well, open them!"

"Can't," the guard said laconically, crossing his arms on his chest.

"I think Tristan's approach worked better," Crispin said from behind his brother.

"What do you propose?" Ian turned toward Crispin, his eyes blazing.

"We could try a variation of the method we used on Mora's giants," Crispin offered. "They seemed to respond well to that."

While they were speaking, all six of them moved closer to the guard. He stood stock-still, arms crossed over his chest, feigning nonchalance, but his eyes began to shift nervously.

"If you gentlemen are planning to harm me, I ought to warn you that there is an entire stable of guards in that warming house over there." He pointed a nervous finger toward the now empty guard shack.

"I doubt it," Tristan said coolly, not halting his approach. The guard found himself surrounded by a half-circle of very tall men and one small boy. He was about to protest, this time more loudly, when Sebastian brought the side of his hand down against the back of the man's head, knocking him completely unconscious in one blow.

"Very neat!" Miles said with admiration. "You'll have to teach me how to do that some time."

"Just after you teach me how to stop unstoppable clocks," Sebastian shot back as Tristan rifled through the unconscious guard's pockets. In a moment he stood up holding two keys and handed them to Ian.

"Those should do it. Why don't you and Crispin go get her, while the rest of us stay up here to make sure those guards aren't too bored."

Ian and Crispin made straight for the staircase behind the guard's stool and went down. There were intermittent torches lighting their descent, but the darkness was still almost impenetrable. When they had taken no more than twenty steps, they heard and then saw the water lapping against the side of the staircase.

Undaunted, they continued their descent, wading deeper and deeper into the cold water.

"This place is flooded," Crispin stated needlessly to Ian's back. "I am not sure," he continued, seeing that Ian had not halted, "that we can go much farther."

"*Um*, Ian—" Crispin ventured again.

"The gate must be just down here," Ian shouted back with manic optimism as he rounded a corner. The water was now up to his collarbone, exactly the point the top of Bianca's head came to on his chest, he remembered. The recollection brought a lump to his throat, which got larger with each further step down he took.

Two more steps brought the water to his ears. A third had it almost over his head. It was not until he was completely submerged that he reached the iron entrance door to the prison. Crispin was right. It was completely flooded, filled with water from the floor to the ceiling.

His mind suddenly became very calm and very rational. There was no way anyone could be alive down there, it told him. All that effort to get the keys from the guard had been a waste, he thought calmly. It was too bad, it reported, but Bianca was most assuredly dead.

Chapter Thirty

Ian turned around and ascended the stairs. Crispin was waiting for him halfway up, at the landing before the turn, his heart beating with dread.

"Well?" he asked as his brother neared, not sure he wanted to hear the answer.

"Bianca did not know how to swim," Ian said calmly as he brushed by Crispin and continued his ascent. "I believe she is dead."

Crispin watched with shocked horror as his brother proceeded on like an ultraefficient machine. Had he really heard him correctly? Did he really say that Bianca was dead?

"Ian!" he shouted, following up the stairs. "Ian! What did you just say?"

Ian paused at the top of the stairs and waited for Crispin to catch up to him. "I said that Bianca did not know how to swim and is most assuredly dead."

Ian ignored Nilo's small cry and the questions of the other Arboretti, proceeding instead with frightening coldness toward the reviving guard. He pulled the man up by the collar of his cape and shook him until his eyes opened and he began making noises.

"What happened to the prisoners who were in the basement cells?" he demanded.

The guard looked confusedly up at the soaking wet man gripping him by the neck, then remembered what had happened.

"I'll see that you are charged with molesting the duke's guards, I will," he spluttered. "I'll see you tried and hung! You'll regret this, you—"

Ian interrupted the man's babbling, his voice even and hard as the blade of a dagger. "What happened to the prisoners in the basement cells?"

"Nothing," the guard responded, looking quizzically at the man above him. "They're down there just as they ought to be, ain't they? Hey, Signore Gianni, or whatever you said your name was, d' you think you could let loose on my neck a little?"

Ian ignored him. "They were not moved? No one evacuated them?"

"An' why would we do that?" the guard asked, suddenly surly.

"The cells are flooded. The water is almost up the staircase. No one could be alive down there."

"Look, Signore Gianni, those prisoners were going to die soon anyway. Let's put it that the water has just saved the executioner a trip from his bed. Let's put it that way, shall we?"

"Are you saying," Ian asked, tightening his hold on the man's cloak and lifting him from the ground, "that the prisoners were just left to die in the flood?"

"This isn't so funny anymore, Signore Gianni."

"My name is not Gianni. Answer my question."

"You put it about right." The blood was draining quickly from the guard's face. "They were just left there. If they died or not, that's up to them and the Deity, ain't it?"

Ian let go of the man's cloak and let him fall to the ground. He turned, marched past his cousins and Nilo, and out into the piazza.

Pulling his soaking wet cape around him, Ian made for the boat landing where the gondoliers had finally managed to tie up the gondola. Roused by his approach, the boatmen were already in position by the time he reached the gondola and gave them the order for home. They had just pulled away from the dock when Crispin arrived and, with a running leap, jumped on.

"Are you all right?" he asked his brother lamely when he entered the cabin, panting from the exertion of catching up with him. As soon as the question was out of his mouth, he was sorry he had asked.

Ian pressed his lips together tightly and answered, in a voice that lacked even a semblance of emotion, "Of course. I am always fine."

Crispin shuddered. Ian's tone was dead enough, but his expression was even worse. Crispin would have given anything to see the slightest flicker of animation in his slate gray eyes.

"You can't pretend she didn't matter to you," he began, hoping to at least antagonize Ian.

"I have said nothing like that." Ian's expression did not change, his tone did not waver.

"I think you were in love with her," Crispin continued boldly, willing to try anything to coax an emotion out of his brother.

"I think you are right," Ian replied in a voice that made it seem doubtful he even possessed a heart.

Crispin's jaw hung open, stunned by his brother's admission. "You mean, you admit it? You agree?"

Ian's brows went up but his tone did not change. "Why shouldn't I? You are right."

"But, just like that? You sit there like some sort of talking statue coolly admitting that the woman you loved is dead?"

"I am sorry if my behavior is displeasing to you."

"It's not that it's displeasing," Crispin fumbled to explain. "It's just that it's, well, incredible."

"*Ah,*" Ian replied, hoping that the single syllable conveyed enough understanding to make the conversation be over. He suddenly felt weary, very, very weary, as if his entire body were twice as heavy as normal. The wind had died down and the storm had reverted to a light rain that made a soothing noise against the cabin of the gondola. Perhaps if he just closed his eyes for a moment, just let himself slide into the sleep that beckoned so welcomingly.

Suddenly, the day became sunny and warm. Ian alighted from the gondola, not as expected, at his boat landing, but instead in the grassy park of a friend's summer villa. At first he heard only the rustle of the leaves and saw no one, but soon the sounds of a pastoral melody wafted to him on the summer breeze. He followed it and found himself in a shady clearing, with a stream running on one side and soft, grassy benches all around. In the center, on a velvet blanket, lay Bianca. She had no clothes on but was completely covered with flowers, like some sort of woodland nymph come to life. As he admired her, she smiled at him and called his name.

"Come, Ian, come here," she said warmly, extending one of her slim, graceful arms toward him.

"But you are dead," he blurted, without realizing what he was saying.

She laughed and shook her head, the light of the sun catching magically on her fiery mane. "No, no. Not me. Come, Ian. I am here."

Ian's body filled with warmth when he understood what she was saying. She was not dead at all, she had been waiting for him in this idyllic spot the whole time. He smiled and started toward her, his heart filled with happiness.

"Come on, Ian," she said again, her voice somehow deeper, more urgent, and less pleasant.

"Come on." Crispin was shaking him harder. "We are here. We're home."

Ian awoke with a start. He turned his head about confusedly and blinked. "I was...dreaming?" he asked his brother, still dazed.

"I guess so." Crispin looked concerned. "You were only asleep for a few minutes. The gondoliers made good time."

"I was dreaming," Ian repeated, this time to himself. "It was only a dream."

With horror he discovered that all the emotions he thought he had left at the foot of the prison stairs had only been in hiding. Without warning, they welled up within him, spilling throughout his body and leaving him with a feeling of despair more acute than anything he had ever experienced. He needed to be alone. Immediately.

"I will be in the library if anyone needs me," he told Crispin in a voice that wavered, then added, "Please see to it that they do not."

Crispin watched his brother's back disappear up the stairs, unsure whether to be relieved that his emotions seemed to have returned or terrified of what he might do to himself. Deciding that he was himself too exhausted and upset to make such a decision, he took a different set of stairs toward the kitchen, in search of some warm water and a much needed drink.

Ian had chosen the library because it was his favorite room, but as he neared the door he shied away from it. Memories of the time he had passed with Bianca there washed over him, first the delightful hours they had spent arguing and at each other's throats, and then the even more delightful hours they had spent in each other's arms. He remembered walking into the library that first night they made love and seeing her stretched out before the fire, her supple body golden in the light of the flames, her nipples taut, her back arched in pleasure as she gracefully stroked herself.

He closed his eyes when he opened the door and crossed the threshold, savoring the image of her there again. When he opened them, he nearly jumped out of his skin. The room was exactly as it had been that night, shadowy and dark but for the fire blazing in the hearth, and there was indeed a figure stretched out on the rug before it. But it was not Bianca, not even close. For one thing it was too small. For another, it was a rather grotesquely dressed man.

As Ian approached, it turned around and squinted at him. "You that lazy servant finally come to bring me some grappa?" the small man demanded.

"No, I am the servant's master." Ian's voice was contemptuous. "Who might you be?"

The small man hurried to his feet and bowed deeply. "Beggin' your pardon, but the way you're dressed you don't look much like a lord, Your Lordship."

Ian was in no mood for either criticism or company. "I accept your apology, but you still have not answered my question. Who are you?" *And when are you leaving?* he added to himself in an undertone.

The last comment was interrupted by a knock at the door, followed by the entrance of one of Ian's servingmen with the grappa decanter and a glass.

"Bring another for His Lordship, won't you?" Cecco ordered, and the man left hurriedly without even looking at his master. "That one's good enough," Cecco said, gesturing to where the servant had just been standing, "but slow on his feet. I've been a-waiting these twenty minutes for that grappa. I wouldn't tolerate it if I was you."

If Ian had not been immersed in deep despair and self-pity, he would have found the little tyrant's remarks by turns amusing and annoying. As it was, he just wanted to know his name so he could kick him out in a personal manner.

"I am sorry that my staff does not meet your approval, Your Highness," Ian said, crossing to a chair and sitting with his head in his hands.

"'Highness,' that's funny, it is," Cecco said with a smile, seating himself opposite Ian and taking a gulp of grappa that would have flattened a larger man. "You're a funny one. My name's Cecco, Cecco the Nano. The woman was right, we'll get along fine."

Ian raised his head. "What woman?"

The servingman reappeared, bearing a second glass and handed it to Ian. Cecco waited until it had been filled and motioned to Ian to take a sip before continuing.

"It looks like you could use a drink. That murderess who ain't a murderess woman. Bianca. She ain't told me her other name. But she told me you and she were a-fixing to get married and I should come an' see you and tell you a story I told her, an' also something else." Cecco paused to drink back the rest of his glass and wipe his lips daintily with his sleeve.

Ian's bloodshot eyes widened, and he moved forward on his chair. "Bianca? You saw Bianca? Where?"

"Where do you think? In those damn wet cells at the duke's house. Where else would I have met a lady o' that quality?" Cecco's appreciation for Bianca had gone up markedly when he saw the style in which her friends lived, and he saw no reason not to pour on the flattery.

"You saw her in prison? When?" Ian was hovering on the edge of his seat, his despondency momentarily lifted.

"Oh, must have been a good five hours ago, I reckon. If them clocks of yours are right."

Ian slid into his chair, settling back into his misery. Five hours ago was an eternity. "Was she still alive?"

"Must have been, mustn't she, if she told me to come a-calling to tell you my story."

Ian was confused. On her deathbed Bianca had sent a dwarf to entertain him with fairy tales? "What kind of story?"

Cecco gulped down more grappa and held out his glass for a refill. "She told me that you would be grateful to me when you heard it. I just want you to know that from the outset, in case you forget it in the middle and get some murderous idea into your head. Do you promise to let me finish the story?"

Ian nodded dejectedly, not thrilled by the prospect of company. He just wanted to be alone, to let his grief wash over him.

"An' not do any badgering with questions?" Cecco went on.

As if he had the energy for questions. Or even for listening. Ian nodded again.

"All right, then. It's a story of what happened two years ago. In Sicily. Outside Messina." Cecco waited a moment, decided he had as much of Ian's attention as he was likely to get, and went on. "I'm to tell you as how a witch-woman an' her lover hired me an' my partner to ambush you in Sicily and kill you. Now I had nothing against you, personally see, but that witch-woman, she went on and on about my adorable ears an' there was nothing for it but to take the job." Cecco studied Ian, who appeared to be only half listening. "Your ears aren't any too bad either if you'd a-use 'em," he observed, then went on. "Problem is, we made a mistake an' we killed the wrong one. But it wasn't really our fault, see, because there was only supposed to be one of you in the first place. "

Cecco stopped talking because he had lost his audience. A far-away look came into Ian's eyes as he digested the half-heard words being spoken by the dwarf. So deeply was he consumed by misery, that it took him almost a minute to realize what Cecco was telling him. Mora and Christian together had hired an assassin to kill him. His best friend and his mistress. What kind of fool was he that he had never seen it, never even suspected it?

But even that horrible revelation could not hold his interest. His mind kept drifting to Bianca, to the blissful years they should have passed together, to the family they should have had, to the abysmal emptiness his life would be without her. The pain of his loss was so profound that he doubled over in his chair, his hands pressing hard against his skull, his lips squeezed shut to hold in his anguished cries. She was gone. She would never come back. He had lost her forever, lost the only person with whom he had ever known true happiness. For the first time in years, more than two years, he allowed first one, then a dozen slow tears to trickle down his face.

He had completely forgotten that there was anyone else in the room when, a quarter of an hour later, Cecco cleared his throat. "That's not the end of the story. Then we dragged you to Mes—"

"I know how it ends," Ian interrupted, not removing his head from his hands. "I know what happened afterward."

"Know it all, do you?" Cecco rose in his seat and made a fist at Ian, who turned his head slightly to regard him. "Did you know the blow you dealt killed my partner? Best damn friend a man ever had?" Cecco asked savagely.

"No," Ian spoke into his lap, quietly.

Cecco brought his fist down. "Ha!" he said. "Never thought about that, did you? Did you know I had to hide, spend these two years locked in by my own choice, afraid to show my head in the streets of Venice?"

Ian raised his red-rimmed eyes to study the dwarf. As he shook his head in negation, it occurred to Ian that he and Cecco had a lot in common. They had both lost their best friends on the plains of Sicily. They had both spent the past two years locked away, afraid of Mora, afraid of what might happen to them if they showed their true face in public. And now they had both been given their lives back, freed from Mora's curse, by Bianca's final gesture.

Ian gulped back the lump that had been in his throat since he saw the flooded prison. The small man seated before him, glaring at him and drinking his grappa, suddenly became, as Bianca's final legacy to him, very dear. He did not bother to keep his voice steady or to keep the misery out of his expression when he addressed Cecco. "I am sorry. I had no idea."

Ian's apology caught Cecco off guard. The glare left his face as quickly as it had come. "An' if that ain't the most unexpected thing ever. Thank you. You are some kind of man. But you don't look so good. D'you want to hear the rest of your lady's message now, or—"

"Yes," Ian said with a wretched urgency that was painful to hear.

Cecco cleared his throat to ensure proper delivery. "She said to tell you it wasn't her as done the murder but some Anzelo or Angelo fellow, a cousin of hers. An'," Cecco made a face, but decided he owed it to the girl in exchange for the apology Ian had tendered, "she said to say she loved you."

Still, Ian thought to himself. After all that. She still loved me. The realization sent a shudder up his body, sharpening the edge of his misery.

Cecco saw the dark mood descending on his companion with surprise. Surely the news that his betrothed wasn't a murderess should be received gleefully. "I don't know if you caught that first part. I was saying as how she said to tell you about her being innocent—"

"I know." Ian cut him off grimly. "I already knew she was innocent. I knew it all along. But it hardly matters now that I have lost her."

"You're a fine one for giving up, then, ain't you? I put her on that boat not more than two hours ago an' I don't reckon they up and a-weighed anchor yet, not on a night like this."

"What do you mean?" Ian asked, his heart suddenly starting to beat again.

"I see I was wrong about your ears. You people can't understand a little plain language to save your lives, can you?" Cecco shook his head. "What I mean is that I put her on a boat not more than two hours ago and I don't think it's a-left yet." He spoke the last words loud and slow, hoping that would overcome the gentleman's hardness of hearing.

"How? She's alive?"

"That wasn't no corpse I went back and dragged through the sewer with me, I tell you that. Of course, I can't say for positive she's still alive, sometimes death is mighty sudden you know, but two hours ago, when I put her on that boat—"

"Why? Where to?" Ian spoke as he rose from his seat. "Why did she want to get on a boat?"

"Some nonsense about an unwanted betrothal, and trying to get out of the way or something. Believe me, she wasn't in much better shape than you are."

"She was running away from a betrothal?" Ian said more to himself than to Cecco. Bianca was running away and leaving him. But why?

It hit Ian like a thunderbolt. She must think he hated her after how he had treated her. Not only had he refused to believe in her innocence, as far as she knew, but he had gotten up and marched out in the middle of her murder trial without even so much as a look in her direction. He had behaved like the most despicable, unpleasant monster in all Italy. He could not blame her for wanting to get away from him. He would have to make it up to her, explain it to her. Certainly he could not allow her to go.

Cecco cowered low in his seat as Ian leaned over him. "Where was the boat going?" he demanded with a degree of animation that Cecco thought had to be unhealthy for at least one of them.

"I don't know," the dwarf answered plainly. "She didn't tell me." Ian, like a man possessed, was heading for the door. "But I am sure you'll have no trouble finding it," Cecco said helpfully to his broad back. "There can't be more than a hundred galleons moored out in the lagoon tonight."

Chapter Thirty-One

The water lashed against the prow of Ian's boat as he and Giorgio took over for the weary gondoliers and rowed up to the millionth, or perhaps the fourteenth, merchant marine ship.

"*Bianca!*" Ian started bellowing, in what was, by this point, a familiar pattern to Giorgio. "Bianca! Are you there? Bianca!"

Giorgio wondered if he should tell his master that since the wind and rain made it almost impossible for him, only three arm-lengths away, to hear Ian's shouts it was highly improbable that anyone on a ship would hear them, but he decided against it, reasoning that anything that would alleviate the strange madness that had gripped his master was to be encouraged. They were pulling along the side of the large vessel when a head poked out of one of the lower portholes.

"What d' you want?" an old sailor with a tanned face and a stark white beard demanded, not friendly. "We're getting ready to lift anchor, and we ain't got room for more passengers."

"Do you have a woman on board?" Ian asked with such desperation that the sailor let out a whoop of amusement.

He flashed Ian a toothless conspiratorial grin. "You come all the way out here for a woman? You loony or something? There's dozens, hundreds of 'em right back there in Venice. 'The Paradise of Prostitutes,' that's what they call the city, and not for nothing. I can give you the address of such a one that knows a thing or two about feathers—"

"No." Ian was shaking his head and struggling to get a word in. "I am looking for a particular woman. My, *ah*, my sister. She's small, with a beautiful oval face, silky light brown hair, and eyes that glitter like molten gold when she is excited."

"Don't sound like you're talking about your sister to me," the sailor said with raised eyebrows, "but it ain't none of my business. 'Specially seeing as how we ain't got any merchandise of that quality aboard, I'm sure. What?" the sailor demanded of someone behind him. He turned back to Ian, said, "Don't leave yet, you hear," and disappeared into the interior of the vessel.

"We'd better move on," Giorgio cautioned Ian after they had waited two minutes that felt more like two years in the freezing cold wind. "All of these boats will be making off as soon as the tide comes all the way in. That gives us less than an hour, and we still have about forty to see. I'm sure if you just leave your name, that nice sailor will send along the address of the feather woman."

Ian struggled to decide whether to punch Giorgio or ignore him. He had just opted for punching, hoping it would relieve some of his tension, when the head popped back out of the window.

"Supposin' that someone knew something about your, *ah*, sister," the sailor rolled his eyes backward and motioned slightly with his head. "Why would you be looking for her, *eh?*"

"I've made a terrible mistake," Ian confessed loudly to the man, "and I want to make it up to her. I must see her and speak to her."

The man nodded, disappeared into the hole for a moment, then reemerged. "What do you want to say to her?"

"I will tell her when I see her!" Ian was exasperated. "Don't play games with me, man. I must find her, even if it means sailing all the way to China. Is she there or isn't she?"

The sailor gestured upward with his chin. Following his suggestion, Ian trained his gaze on the deck of the ship. There, among the two dozen sailors readying the vessel for departure, was Bianca. As she stood against the railing, her eyes alight, her hair being whipped about her by the wind, she looked like an ancient maritime goddess come to do battle with a mortal enemy.

Bianca was kicking herself. She had known she should not allow herself to see Ian, should stay as far from him as possible, but she could not help it. On first hearing him shout her name she had tried, but she did not have the power. Her traitorous heart had leapt up, racing with joy, thrilled by the sound of his voice. He had come after her. He had come to find her.

Or, her cool head told her, to drag her back to prison and punish her. To tell her to her face how he hated her. How sorry he was she had not died in her flooded cell. Her heart was beating so loudly with excitement and dread as she stood on the deck of the boat that she was sure it could be heard all the way back in Piazza San Marco. She struggled to keep her face expressionless, her voice noncommittal.

"You found me," she stated intelligently to Ian, below.

Ian did not know what he had been hoping for, but the emotionless welcome he had just received turned his insides to ice. He had rowed all the way out there, purposely putting himself in the way of a blustery storm for the second time that night, risking pneumonia and worse, to tell her how his life would be nothing without her, how he needed her, and all he got was a frosty 'You found me.' His heart, now frozen, shattered into a thousand bits.

"I certainly did!" His tone pierced her like glittering shards of ice. "Did you really think you could simply up and leave, just like that? Need I remind you that you are a fugitive from justice and technically under my care?"

Bianca's heart seemed to drop through the deck and into the lagoon below. So that was indeed why he had come. He had come not out of love but only to win himself the prestige of having found a fugitive. His tone, his expression, told her clearly that he felt nothing for her but disgust. She bowed her head, hoping he was too far away to see the tears welling up in her eyes. "I had forgotten. How careless of me."

Hearing her voice, so cold, so uncharacteristically devoid of emotion, confirmed Ian's worst fears. She had fled because she did not want to marry him. She enjoyed him physically, but there it ended. The prospect of spending her life with him was distasteful to her, even hateful. But she had said...

The words came out before he knew he was speaking, his voice no longer a voice of ice but a voice of pain. "Why won't you marry me? You said you loved me."

Bianca blinked at him for a second, wondering if it were just an accident of the wind or if she had heard correctly. Then, compelled by some supernatural force, she revealed the deepest, most private secret of her soul. "Because you don't love me."

"But of course I do!" Ian said with puzzlement. *I have always loved you.* "It is so obvious."

"Obvious!" Bianca echoed. "Walking out of my murder trial before it is even over? Obvious?"

"I was practically thrown out. Besides, I had to...I had to check on something." The excuse sounded lame even to Ian's ears.

Bianca felt as if someone else had taken over her body and she was only being allowed to watch from the highest mast of the ship. Here was the man she loved, saying that he loved her back, but instead of throwing herself over the side and into his arms, she was arguing with him. "If you really do love me, why haven't you ever said it?"

"Haven't I?" Ian avoided meeting her eyes. "I've meant to."

Bianca shook her head. "That won't do. It's not good enough. You have to say it. Now." Bianca gestured at the preparations for departure going on all around her. "In a few days I will be out of Venice and likely out of Italy and then you will never have another chance."

Ian stood and admired her, stunned once again by her beauty. Without realizing what he was doing, he raised his hands to her in a gesture of supplication. "Don't go," he begged rather than ordered. "Please, Bianca, don't go."

She wavered for a moment, still a proud goddess, then asked in a voice filled with anguish that could only be human, "Why? Why should I stay? I am giving you your freedom, Ian. I am canceling our betrothal. Don't you understand? This is what you wanted all along. You never wanted to marry me, remember? You said it yourself. Now you are free to marry whomever you wish, whomever you truly love. If you married me without loving me, you would grow to hate and despise me. This is how it should be, how it must be—" Bianca had been so determined to say her piece that she had plowed ahead, heedless that Ian had long before responded to her first question.

"Because I love you," he had said while she rambled on.

"What?" Bianca asked, startled, when she realized she had missed something.

"If you didn't talk so much you would have heard it," Ian scolded wryly, his heart beating so fast he could hardly keep up with it. "Now it's too late."

Maddening, she thought to herself, he was absolutely maddening. And sinfully handsome. "I would be much obliged, Ian," she asked politely, "if you would tell me what you said."

"I said that I love you, Bianca Salva," he shouted up to her in a voice filled with joy and triumph. The work on the deck of the boat ceased as the sailors gathered along the railing to see better. "I said that is why you should stay. Because I love you."

Bianca resisted the urge to fling herself into his arms. Before she took the potentially life-threatening plunge from the side of the boat, she wanted to be sure there was no mistake. "Do you think... Could you say that again?"

Ian cupped his hands around his mouth and addressed her. "I love you, Bianca. I think I have loved you from the first moment I laid eyes on you. I love every devilish, murderous, obstinate, difficult, argumentative, brilliant, succulent, glorious bit of you. I love you with every muscle in my body, every breath in my lungs, every thought in my head. I love you and I want you with me forever."

For centuries afterward, Venetians talked about that wonderful night at the end of 1585 when their great clock stopped and a goddess flew like a crane from the deck of a galleon into the waiting arms of her lover.

Epilogue

The March sun streamed in through the half-open drapes of the bedroom, dappling the couple lying on the bed with its rays.

Ian, sitting up and leafing through a book, nudged at the small lump lying beside him. "Come on, Bianca. You don't want to be late for your own wedding."

"*Hmfph,*" was the lump's reply.

"Bianca. Don't make this any harder for me than it already is." Ian's voice lacked even the faintest emotion as he continued to flip through the volume.

"*Mlmfeh,*" said the lump. It moved to resettle itself in the crook of Ian's arm.

He tried a new tactic, though still studying to sound preoccupied. "Roberto and Francesco will never speak to either of us again if you let the dress they had made go to waste. Not to mention Nilo. He's probably pacing up and down the aisle already."

"*Sphhhhln,*" the lump began, then decided to give in. "All right," Bianca said lazily. "If you are so eager to have me married off, I'll get up and out of your hair."

"Excellent," Ian said with the air of a man who does not know what he is saying.

Bianca scowled at him and then at the book he was holding or rather, which was holding his attention from her. She moved around behind it and scowled at the cover, hoping for some clue to its identity, but all she saw was FOSCARI stamped in large gold letters on the spine. Ian was sitting distractedly reading a family history? That certainly had to be stopped. She moved and popped up over the top of the book to face him.

"Hello. I am going now. Leaving. To be married. This is your last chance to take me before I become an honest woman. Forever after I will be someone's wife."

"*Mmmm,*" Ian said, not moving his eyes from the page he was studying.

That did it. If he was already heedless of her propositions before their wedding, she shuddered to think what he would be like afterward. A vision of their life together—side by side, in bed, never talking, with Ian reading some big tome or another and her struggling to revive his interest—stretched before her like the road to Dante's inferno.

"Ian, since you seem to be more fascinated by the author of that book than you are by me, perhaps you should marry him."

"Her," Ian corrected. "The book is by a woman."

Bianca, spurred on by a mixture of jealousy and interest, pulled herself up next to Ian to get a better look.

"See," Ian said, flipping to the title page and allowing her to study it.

"*De Corporis Feminae Fabrica,*" she read aloud, her eyes wide. "Why, it's a book of the female anatomy. Someone did it before I could." Bianca sounded momentarily sad, but then her tone brightened again when she added, "At least it is by a woman. What is her name?"

Ian was having trouble holding the book, not to mention his voice, steady. "You may know her." He paused, as if searching the title page for the name, then read out clearly, "The Most Reverend and Illustrious, Bianca Salva Foscari, Contessa d'Aosto."

Bianca looked at the name for a moment, confused. She repeated it to herself silently, then let out a cry. "Oh! Oh, my! That is...Ian, you have...Oh! That is me! This is my book!"

Ian's smile stretched from ear to ear. Her reaction to his surprise was even better than he had expected. "Do you like it? Is it all right?"

"I...Oh, Ian...I really...I'm speechless." Bianca threw her arms around his neck, pulling him close as tears quivered in her eyes. "This is the kindest, most generous thing anyone has ever done for me. Santa Agata's finger, to have my book published!"

"Breast," Ian corrected her.

Bianca pulled away slightly to look at him. "What?"

"Breast. Santa Agata's breast. I learned that from your manuscript." Ian was beaming at her like a schoolboy proud of his erudition. "Besides, my act was not completely selfless. The idea of rendering you speechless was rather appealing."

Bianca's smile turned to a smirk. She returned her attention to the volume, flipping lovingly through the pages. "How did you get my manuscript back from the judges? I thought they were going to keep it until they caught Mora and Angelo and they could hold a proper trial."

"I have connections," Ian said mysteriously. "Besides, the evidence against those two is plentiful enough to convict them without your drawings. If they are smart, they will stay well out of the Venetian Empire for a good long time."

Bianca moved her eyes from her precious book to the scars still visible on Ian's wrists. "They had better. I am well tempted to try my next anatomical experiments on them."

Ian raised one eyebrow suggestively. "I'd rather you tried them on me."

"Really?" Bianca's smile was fiendish. "Fancy having your heart cut out?"

Ian grimaced. "Maybe nothing quite that severe, to begin with."

Bianca nodded knowingly. "Actually, there is one theory I've been meaning to explore. I hear that complimenting a man on his adorable ears is the best way to his heart."

Ian groaned. "Have you been taking lessons on seduction from Cecco again?"

"I think you are jealous," Bianca declared positively with a playful grin. "You'd be amazed at some of the tips he's given me."

"Like what?" Ian was not sure he wanted to know what his diminutive new steward and his devilish fiancée spent so much time together talking about.

"Come here." Bianca beckoned. Ian moved closer to her, carefully setting the volume on the floor. She pulled his head down to hers and began whispering something in his ear.

With dismay Ian felt his member growing hard, bucking against the sheet for attention. "I hope this isn't what you are thinking of trying on Angelo," he managed to get out with difficulty.

Bianca laughed, her breath tickling his ear. She moved her hand to his thigh and then up it, tickling him gently, without stopping her suggestive whispering. Ian groaned, willing her to stop talking or start caressing his beleaguered organ, but she did neither. He was on the point of begging for either mercy or extreme unction when she pulled away slightly.

Bianca studied her fiancé with an appraising eye. "You're performing very well as a subject," she complimented him. "Better than I would have expected. I'll have to use you in all my projects. I hope your wife won't mind."

"My wife?" Ian countered. "What about your husband? What if he objects to your experiments?"

Bianca shook her head. "There's no chance of that. I am sure he will understand that, as a published scientist, it is my duty to devote myself entirely to the pursuit of knowledge." As she spoke, she undertook a new experiment involving the tips of all ten fingers and the gardenia-scented oil she kept next to the bed. "Wouldn't you agree, my lord?"

Ian, selfless crusader in the quest for scientific advancement, managed only to groan his approval.